KETTLE
of
TEARS

ROBERT BOYCE

Fulton Books, Inc.
Meadville, PA

Published by Fulton Books 2021

ISBN 978-1-64952-618-2 (paperback)
ISBN 978-1-63710-868-0 (hardcover)
ISBN 978-1-64952-619-9 (digital)

Printed in the United States of America

To all the men and women who believe in the intangible truth that our commonality is far greater than our differences and employ it as a beacon for their journey through life.

Be not deceived; God is not mocked: for whatsoever a man soweth, that shall he also reap.

—Galatians 6:7

CONTENTS

PART THREE
ALL SCORES SETTLED

List of Illustrations

Cover Art and Illustrations by James Mann
Map by Robert Boyce

ACKNOWLEDGMENTS

I have so many people to thank for helping me get this book to market. Some had small parts and others large, but all contributed to making the *Kettle of Tears* a reality.

I started writing *Kettle of Tears* in 1987 while living in Manhattan on Thompson Street. My brother Neil, who stills lives in New York City, was visiting one evening, and we started talking about our favorite Louis L'Amour characters, the Sacketts. When I told him I was thinking of writing a Western and my hero would be named Tallhelm, he said, "Tallhelm eleven days out of the nation and every day a hard ride." That was all he said, but that night after he left, I wrote out ten pages on a legal pad, and *Kettle of Tears* was born.

My ex-girlfriend Sammi Gavich was a word processor at the time, and we had shared custody of our dog. I would have him for two weeks, and she would have him for two weeks. At the exchange, I would give her ten handwritten pages, and she would give me back three typewritten pages. This process went on for three years, at which point I had about half of the manuscript written.

Then I stopped writing. About twenty-seven year later, in 2017, I picked up the unfinished work and told myself I was going to finish this. At that point, I had a computer, and with the help of Pages and Google searches, I was able to finish the work.

My wife, Amy, who is a voracious reader, was my first editor and critic. Every time I finished a chapter, she would clue me in on what was working and what wasn't. Her encouragement kept my level of enthusiasm up right to the end.

Then the editing started.

My good friend and published author Paul Leeper was the first one to read the whole manuscript. He provided me with any number of corrections to the punctuation and spelling while also giving me encouraging feedback on the work as a whole.

Another friend, Steve Adams, read the book and, with a yellow highlighter, made more corrections to grammar and some content. He also was very encouraging as to the general overall worth of the plot and prose.

This scenario was played out several times with various friends and family. As a first-time author, I was keen on getting as much feedback as possible—what people thought of the story as a whole, what they liked, and what they found confusing or unclear. Each person helped me arrive at a more polished work, and I would like to acknowledge them here: my late brother, Captain Brian F. Boyce USN, ret.; Mike and Dianne Allen; Mark Polon; Ricky Meekes; and Richard Shapero.

The two people most responsible for making *Kettle of Tears* the finished work it is are my brother Barry Boyce, founding editor of *Mindful* magazine, and his good friend professional editor John Sell. Their editorial expertise helped me arrive at a work that allowed the plot to flow from one scene to the next. My brother Barry, especially, was able to help me trim and cull out unnecessary and redundant words and paragraphs. His suggestions on how to smooth out the overall work gave *Kettle of Tears* that extra something that only a pro could provide.

Also, many thanks to my old friend James Mann at www.jamesmannartfarm.com for his wonderful cover art and interior illustrations. I've enjoyed Jim's art going way back to the midsixties. I couldn't have been happier when he agreed to do the artwork. He was very patient with me during the whole process.

Last but surely not least is my father, Donald Boyce Jr. My father, as well as being an accomplished business executive, was an excellent writer and sometime poet who instilled in us an appreciation for the English language that lives on in me and in all my siblings.

I would also like to thank Suzanne McQuane, literary development agent at Fulton Books, also Karlee Dies and the editorial staff at Fulton Books for all their help and hard work in getting my work published and to market.

Part One

HELP ON THE WAY

1

A HARD RIDE

Tallhelm was seven days out of Wyoming and every day a hard ride. Light from the just risen moon filtered through the pines as he let the dun and mule set their own pace on a stretch of the trail that had finally flattened out. Normally, he wouldn't ride quite this hard or quite this long, but word had come that one of his kin, his cousin, was stove up and had no way of getting out before heavy winter set in. The year was well on, and the weather was liable to change any day. Farther back the trail, the leaf trees had a dark look to them, a look that told you a stiff wind could blow them bare. A cloud passing the moon darkened the trail briefly as a cold wind found its way down the neck of Tallhelm's coat. He turned up his collar, lowered the brim on his hat, and looked ahead to see the clearing that lay beyond the evergreens at the upper edge of the tree line.

The tree line marked a big milestone as far as this trip was concerned. Here he was within striking distance of where he was headed. From here on, he'd be checking his back trail a little more, paying more attention to the lay of the land. Tallhelm didn't know what awaited him, but if he had to make a stand somewhere, he preferred to know the terrain as best he could.

Pushing the dun up a small bank, he made the clearing, happy to be free of the gloom of the now-dark trail through the thick pines. This rocky slash across the mountain was maybe a mile wide and allowed an unobstructed view of the surrounding country that stilled Tallhelm with its grandeur. As the wind whipped the edges of his trail coat, he moved slowly across the clearing. Turning to check his back trail, he thought the trees had more the look of a solid wall than what he knew to be there. Here he took a moment to wonder aloud why a man wouldn't stay his whole life in a spot like this. The sky brilliant with the biggest, brightest stars a man could stand to look at. Some so close, it seemed an hour's ride would bring you near enough to grab ahold.

The heavens were always an interest for him, seeing as how he had spent most of his life beneath them, day or night. He knew the constellations and most of their stars. Anyone crossing the plains would look to Polaris as he made his way over such a wide and unmarked expanse, very much like a mariner. Many of the first explorers and pioneers were nautical men, men who knew the sextant and mapmaking. Tallhelm's great-grandfather was such a man, but that's a story for another time. Stars or not, he couldn't stop. He had to drive on. One of his kin was in trouble, and he had gotten the word. This wasn't to say a Tallhelm couldn't stand and make his own fight. Or had to call for help if the odds got a little dicey. No, here it was a case where someone had opened the ball with a bushwhacker's bullet, and he was just on his way to set things square—whatever that took.

Nathan Tallhelm, by nature, wasn't a violent man, but he had learned that when you're in amongst a lot of folks, fights sooner or later break out. That's why he preferred to stay shut of most people to begin with. Not to say he was a man without friends. Time was, in his younger days, he even rode with a bunch when he was hired to clean up some trouble down in Arizona up in the Mogollon. Now, though, more and more he made his way as a solitary rider, settling more for the company of his horse than that of most men. This troubled him some, wondering if ever he'd have a spread of his own, a wife, some young'uns.

With these thoughts on his mind, he turned his attention back to the job at hand. Stopping, he surveyed the land, a deep granite-lined canyon stretched off to the south. Some miles in the distance, the sides of the canyon came together to form a bottleneck. Looking beyond that opening, a longer and, if possible, deeper canyon could be seen, its hard granite sides glistening in the light of the now fully risen moon. Each of these canyons held a high mountain lake, the cold blue water spilling over from the upper canyon to the lower. Indians for a millennium had called these "Our Laughing God Lakes."

These lakes were fed by a myriad of small creeks that flowed down from the far north. ending their journey south in an array of waterfalls, shrouding the northern wall of the canyon in a curtain of falling water. The lakes were also fed by an untold number of underwater springs. During the alpine thaw, these hidden springs made the lakes chum like water boiling in a kettle. The beauty of all of this unfortunately changed for the Indians here when, several generations ago, the Spanish arrived. Eventually the Indians abandoned their lodges hereabouts and now called these lakes the Kettle of Tears. The grim history of the area, nevertheless, could not lessen its beauty as Tallhelm surveyed the majesty of the scene.

As twilight gave way to night, Tallhelm could see the Crow's Nest, its lights sparkling like fireflies across the dark expanse of the canyon. As the crow flies, the distance was less than twenty miles. For Nathan Tallhelm, however, the route he'd have to take meant at least a day's ride, maybe more. Still, it was some comfort to finally see his destination.

Reining the dun back from the canyon rim, he made for a stand of tall pines on the other side of this open slash. Soon he would be at the Crow's Nest and meet the man who ran it, a close friend of his cousin, the legendary figure Jonathan Keith. Tallhelm, of course, had heard of Keith but had never met him. Not one given to idle speculation, Tallhelm, rather, honed his thoughts to a smoldering resolve, sharpened his wits, and prepared for what might lay ahead. For now, the best thing he could do to that end was get some grub and a good night's sleep.

Ducking a limb, he brought his horse and mule up inside a vaulted room of evergreen limbs. As he dismounted, Tallhelm's boots scuffed into a thick cushion of needles spread below the pines. Clearing a bare spot, he set to making a small fire. Here, the chance of unwanted eyes seeing the flames would be slight, and the little bit of smoke would be lost by the time it made its way through the upper branches of the several trees under which he made camp.

Leading the animals away from the firelight, he hitched them to the lower limbs just within reach overhead. After checking the quickly unburdened animals for any sore spots possibly caused by the packs carried over such a long and arduous trail, he gave both a thorough rubdown, as well as water and oats. He carried this grain to give them good feed, well deserved considering the last four days had been a steady uphill climb.

The care he showed toward his horse and mule were routine and came easily to him. Tending to the mounts first was the rule for men like him—men who relied on their horses for much of their survival. Tallhelm was such a man, more at home on a high mountain bluff than any bunkhouse. His horse allowed him this freedom, sharing his quiet thoughts, enduring his singing, discovering vistas together, vistas like the one just passed.

He never questioned this way of life. Sure, his folks had wanted him to stay closer to home. But from early on, any feather floating by found its way under his collar, moving him right out the door and down the road. That road had now led him here. He didn't know what awaited him at the Crow's Nest. The little he did know pointed to something bad. Just how bad, he reckoned he'd find out soon enough.

Tossing off the last drops of coffee, he settled down on the bedroll laid over some freshly cut pine, checked his .44, and passed into an uncommonly deep sleep.

The slight breeze that found its way inside stirred the gray ash off the slowly dying coals, brightening the camp for an instant. The light that caught the easy expression on Tallhelm's weathered face betrayed little of the man that lay beneath. A short dark growth of two weeks covered his keystone-shaped jaw, stopping just below his eyes. Long days facing the wind had drawn his cheeks closer to his thick eyebrows, narrowing his eyes and settling a slight grin on his otherwise solemn countenance. He found a lot of humor in life. He also saw a fair bit of tragedy. He stopped short of letting the tragedy amuse him.

As he dreamt, he rode a flying horse to a congress of Indians watching a murky gray pool until they turned to him as one. They all spoke. He heard nothing. His horse turned into a high-back chair. He slept.

It was just before dawn when Tallhelm woke, yet he was angry with himself for sleeping straight through the night. Before retiring, he had pulled deadfall in around the gaps in the pine trees. This might have given him a moment's warning in case some beast came after his food or an Indian had a mind to come after him. Deadfall or not, he knew he couldn't be sleeping this hard. He allowed that the long ride and the high mountain air would do that. The sleep had done him good though. As he pulled on his boots, he felt the readiness in his body. The coil returned to his limbs, slightly numbed from the long days and nights of riding. His mind was clear and steady as well. The thought that tonight might find him at the Crow's Nest sharpened his wits.

Rising to his full height of better than six feet, Tallhelm mechanically drew and checked his sidearm. His thumb registered the presence of each cartridge firmly pressed into the six chambers of the giant revolver.

Sliding the pistol into his side holster, he reached down for the brace of .38s still flanking the broad depression in his smooth leather bedroll. Breaking each pistol, he checked the dual barrels. Satisfied, he slid the exquisite brass and bloodwood-handled firearms snugly into the fleece lining of his faded canvas coat.

Poising himself for a moment, Tallhelm crossed his arms; instantly, the weapons reappeared in his outstretched hands. Keeping a bead on an imagined foe, Tallhelm relaxed his grip on the handles. The weight of the brass barrels spun the guns forward. In one motion, they twirled, the dark red handles snapping back into Tallhelm's palms. He repeated this action several times till the guns became as one with his hands and arms. Recrossing his arms, he deposited each gun into its resting place. The dull brass butts of the pistols, long devoid of their woven leather fobs, kept vigil just below the inner armpits of Tallhelm's coat.

Hunkering down to retrieve the coffee pot, he crudely remarked to his horse that "these weren't the only pair of .38s I've slept with." But with a wry laugh to himself, he added, "But for the life of me, I can't remember just when." His horse, seemingly understanding every word, shook his head and snorted twice.

Placing some small sticks on the fire, he dug the coffee pot back down into the coals, its dented black sides giving little hint of the blue speckled finish that lay beneath.

Having checked his mounts, Tallhelm went outside his pine enclosure to look at the valley that had been such a presence in his dreams of the past night. Climbing onto a large boulder, he looked south. He watched for several minutes as the winds from the west dumped silky clouds into the canyon, eventually shrouding the rim beneath a blanket of silvery gray. The moon was out of view by now, but looking to where it had gone, Tallhelm could see the outline of the faraway blue mountains, their peaks snow-covered year-round. He never tired of looking at those mountains, solemn and majestic. Today, however, they were the harbingers of bad weather. The temperature had dropped overnight, and the air was moist enough to make him think of snow.

Turning his collar up against the imagined snow, he climbed down from the boulder. First light from the east was slowly chasing away the night. If the weather was turning the way he thought, he had better be prepared. Parting the limbs with an outstretched arm and ducking slightly, Tallhelm re-entered the sheltered world of his pine enclosure. This movement stirred the coals to flame. The giant shadow of the coffee pot danced off the tree trunks momentarily, then vanished as the fire returned to a blue velvet glow that whispered to and fro across the top of the red coals.

He gave the horse and mule their morning ration of oats and each a few horse apples he carried along as a little something extra. Feeding the apples to the dun, he gently spoke to the animals, exclaiming how they were "the best old beasts he ever knew." To the dun he said, "If this velvet diamond on your face were any blacker, I'd have to say you were sire to the whole breed." Being careful not to make the big mule jealous, he added, "And you, you're a breed all your own." Tallhelm hoped the sarcasm had gone by the mule. Two apples and nearly a finger later, he didn't care.

Working in near darkness, Tallhelm took a full inventory of his food and ammunition. Aside from his food, the animal feed, and a bow and two quivers of arrows, the rest of the mule's load was ammo and a spare rifle, a long-barreled Sharps his uncle had lent him. He had brought as much food and ammunition as he could carry, but not knowing what kind of fight he might face, couldn't say if it was near enough.

He saddled the horse and cinched the packs to the mule. The food was holding good, and he had seen enough animal sign to know fresh game was about. If the trail around the rim didn't push him back above the tree line, he should be amongst game all day.

Running his fingers back through the waves of his chestnut hair, he set his hat, tipping the coffee-colored brim down slightly, and led the dun and mule out into the first gray light of dawn. Automatically, he checked his back trail, then paused to take in the trail ahead: it was just as Peepsight Guyer had described.

On his left was the upper valley, the Bottleneck Falls, and the lower valley. On his right and far to the north, tall snow-covered mountains rose up, one next to the other like fingers of a giant hand, all pointing south. Mountains that send all the water they gather south and eventually over the edge of the rim. Water, which at one time or another had cut away everything in its path on its journey south. Now what remains is a ten-mile expanse riven with creeks, washed-out gullies, and arroyos. Arroyos that could run like rivers in the blink of an eye. The few large trees that survive the spring floods could be seen commanding the high ground; otherwise, the trail that lay before him snaked its way west through shoulder-high shrubs and waist-high thickets.

Looking due west to the other side of this high diluvian delta, the dark green outline of a pine forest—his destination. From what was described to him by the old trapper who brought the news of his cousin, once in that wood, "just head south and that will lead onto what everyone calls the 'cut,' and the cut leads right to the Crow's Nest."

Spurring his horse down a steep embankment, Tallhelm began to make his way across the delta. Looking south, he could see that the valley was still enveloped in white. He knew the rim to be several hundred yards off, and as he was riding parallel with it, he figured to be safe but shuddered to think of misjudging the trail in heavy fog, or when it was covered in clouds, as was now the case. The rim had a near vertical drop of a quarter mile to the valley floor. He remembered part of his dream from the night before. He was riding a flying horse. As great as his dun was, Tallhelm was sure he couldn't fly.

Turning his mind back to the task at hand, he wondered if the snow would hold off till midday. The air had snow in it all right; it just hadn't started falling yet. As he followed the sketchiest of trails, around thickets and through shallow creeks, he decided to be on the lookout for game. If it were possible, he would just as soon show up at Keith's with some fresh game. He never liked to arrive empty-handed if he could help it. He didn't know what the situation was there, but the longer he made his grub last, the better. His staples were holding, but last night he finished the last of his dried fish and the paper-wrapped tomatoes his aunt had given him eight days ago.

Tallhelm thought back to the events of the summer that had led him here. Events that again brought the specter of death within arm's reach. He knew the feeling well enough. Ready to kill or be killed, being on that razor's edge. When it came to situations where there was a chance of dying, being ready to kill is the only way you stand half a chance of living.

2

BAD NEWS

Nathan Tallhelm's life wasn't always like this. Fact was, by nature, he was fairly easygoing. He had spent this spring the way he spent most of his time after the winter thaw, keeping his scalp while scouting the Rockies for a place to call his own. He had a picture in his head of a high meadow with a cabin pushing its eaves out of the pines, game in the mountains behind, fish in the swift creek running close by. He had found just such a place this year. A place that had an unbroken view for nearly a hundred miles. A view that showed one small valley woven into another as far as the eye could see.

Tallhelm spent a month clearing brush and cutting timbers. But as happy as he was to further his dream, each morning found him less focused and given over to daydreaming. If he couldn't concentrate, he couldn't work. He knew what was missing—someone to share this with. Leaving his efforts behind, he spent the next month following the trails his horse preferred, as much as his own. This meandering eventually led him down to the foothills. He began entertaining the notion of heading south and west to California when he stopped by his uncle's place, a decent spread in the foothills just east of the divide.

Bill Darcy's land fronted the Snake River and was once the site of a long-gone French settlement. A place whose existence would be all but forgotten except for the yearly testament of several rows of daffodils. The neatly planted flowerbeds bloom eager and yellow each spring, only to find themselves overlooking bare ground, sentinels to the long-deserted remains of a once hopeful community. Like so many quiet mourners looking across an unmarked grave, the faithful perennials eventually wilt, returning all to anonymity for another year. In time, even the flowers will forget. Such was nature's cycle in these hard climes.

Bill Darcy's job as a surveyor had moved him west as the country moved west. Eventually, when he found this spot, he went back east, gathered up his wife and three boys, and planted his flag here. This decision came with a price. That price was the death of his twin boys at the hands of the Shoshone. The Darcys had fought with the local Indians only twice. The first skirmish was fought to a draw. Several years later, there was another attack. This time the Darcys' twin boys and five Indians were killed. Following this, an uneasy truce existed between the two sides. Eventually that truce turned into mutual respect. Then after a number of years and shared crises, friendship.

Several years had passed since then, and that friendship had held. One reason Tallhelm enjoyed visiting his uncle was the respite from the near constant vigilance necessary while traveling the territory.

His uncle easily pressed him to stay on and help with some work before winter. Tallhelm didn't mind this. Once he had stayed almost a year helping the Darcys re-dig their well. This time Darcy needed help rounding up some half-wild mustangs that had bolted their high log corral, led off by a devil of a horse his uncle called Fuego, Spanish for fire, after the horse's bright red mane.

Returning to the ranch one crisp afternoon with three mustangs in tow, Nate and his uncle spotted two men in a canoe tying up to the small dock. They watched as two trappers climbed out and made their way across the open field that fronted the house.

The old trappers were near exhaustion and barely making the porch where they related their tale so excitedly that they nearly caused Mrs. Darcy to faint. Tallhelm and his uncle looked to one another, thinking that the trappers had exhausted themselves to the point of delirium.

"Easy, men. Calm down here. Let's get you two something to drink," Bill Darcy said in his calmest voice. "Nate, go inside and get some water and a bottle of whiskey."

Nate quickly returned to the porch with a pitcher of water and a bottle. Both trappers reached for the whiskey at once. The shorter and, from the looks of it, older of the two won the tug of war. But quickly, and without taking a drink, handed the bottle to his companion. He also didn't take a drink and pushed it back to the other. Exasperated, Bill Darcy grabbed the bottle, took a drink, and handed the bottle to Nate, who also took a swallow. Finally, the trappers figured they had better get while there was still something to get, took the bottle from Nate, and passed it back and forth between themselves till it was half empty.

Bill Darcy had known these old trappers for some time. Darcy's place was one of the few spots along this river where you could still trade some pelts for food and maybe some silver. These trappers had done that many times over many years.

The whiskey seemed to have the desired effect because now, as they related their story, it was all too apparent that it had been painfully real.

Peepsight Guyer, the older of the men, spoke first. "It's your boy, Bill. Trader's come to no good. It's been little more than a week now that Carl and me was in Cornertown unburdening ourselves of the few pelts we was lucky enough to trap when a woman, fancy that, comes into Pop Nelson's place. She gives Nelson a bloodstained shirt pocket and says she needs his help."

Carl Bowersox, the other trapper, picked up the narrative and went on to explain how Trader had once joked to his good friend Nelson that "he wouldn't give him the shirt off his back, but maybe a breast pocket."

Here old Peepsight broke in, "Well, this told Nelson that for sure this was from Trader, and this gal must be his woman."

"What about Trader, Peep? What did she say about Trader?" pressed Mrs. Darcy, barely able to contain herself.

"Said he's alive but stove up something bad. That most likely he had some broken ribs, a broken collarbone, and one of his legs broken."

Hearing this, Mrs. Darcy fainted into her husband's arms. Looking up from the floor where he was reviving his wife, Mr. Darcy queried, "Just how bad is he, Peep?"

With heartfelt sorrow in his voice, well aware of how painful this news must be for the Darcys, Peep went on. "She said that he had lost some blood but was patched up enough that that wasn't a problem. And the leg had been set, but with the broken ribs and collarbone, he was in too much pain to move. Now, Bill, we both know Trader's got the bark on, but if he couldn't make it down to Cornertown and his woman could, you know it's got to be a little worse than she's letting on."

"How'd he get hurt?" asked Tallhelm evenly.

"All she would say when we asked her that same question was that it was no accident," said Peepsight Guyer.

"Yeah, no accident," added Carl Bowersox.

"No, you don't get hurt like that missing a stirrup," chimed in Peep.

Hearing this, Nate Tallhelm's eyes drew themselves into narrow slits focused on some as-yet-unknown foe.

"The woman, what was her name, Carl?" the bent and whiskered old man asked in a low aside to his partner.

"Her name is Veronica," Mrs. Darcy offered, having regained her head but barely containing her anguish as the tale unfolded.

"Yeah, that's it. Her name was Veronica," added Carl.

"Veronica. Is that Veronica Darcy?" asked the surprisingly proper Peepsight Guyer.

"Yes, Peep. For God's sake, Veronica is Trader's wife. Please go on," pressed Mr. Darcy.

Punctuating his narrative with a slow drink of whiskey, the one-eyed trapper continued, "He's holed up in a shallow bear cave, least-wise he was. From what she described, Carl and I put it somewhere just below Thorn's Peak."

"Thorn's Peak!" blurted Bill Darcy. "What the hell were they doing all the way over there?"

"She's a strong woman, Bill. I'd say stronger than most. Trader told her to go to Cornertown, and that's what she did. All in all, she was pretty close-lipped, but her main message was that when we got to your place, you should go to the Crow's Nest. Keith would know what to do." Peepsight Guyer, figuring the narrative was finished, settled back into the leather armchair and finished off the last of the whiskey.

With a slight look of disapproval toward his partner, Carl continued the account. "That night, Nelson cooked a meal, of which Peep and I partook. Then we cleared out his spare room and fixed the lady up real nice for the night. No sooner did she hit that bed than she was sleeping. I tended her horse while Peep and Nelson put together all the provisions her horse could carry. Nelson only has the one horse for himself. Otherwise, he would have packed that as well.

"Anyhow, the next day, we outfitted her with what we could and saw her off. We offered to go back with her, but she wouldn't have any of it. She was cresting the bend in the river trail when Peep and me shoved off, making for your place. That was, what, eight, nine days ago?" Pleased with his account of the events, Carl looked to his partner for recognition. Peepsight Guyer indicated his agreement with several nods.

It was plain to Bill Darcy and Tallhelm that Nate was the one to make the trek up to Keith's and the Crow's Nest. With the help of the trappers, who knew the mountains as well as any white man, the men sketched out the best route to Keith's. The route would take Nate through Teton Pass, up toward Missoula, through the Lolo, and on over to the Crow's Nest. Satisfied with the plan, he directed the men to rest up as his wife prepared a well-deserved home-cooked meal. Darcy and Nate had no sooner left the living room than the two old trappers were fast asleep. Knowing these two, Bill Darcy had no doubt that they hadn't tarried none bringing the news about his son.

Having partially recovered from the initial shock, Mrs. Darcy set to making a meal for Peep and Carl and put together the provisions Nate would need for the trip up to the Crow's Nest.

Ruth Darcy knew just what to pack and what not to. No reason overloading a packhorse with anything that wasn't absolutely necessary. She had always been the one to pack the food and gear for her husband's surveying trips. And once Trader was old enough to hold a survey rod steady, she packed his gear as well. Outfitting the men in her family, she had become very keen as to what might mean the difference between survival and death.

As she retrieved one item after another from the pantry and placed it on a side table, her mind raced with unbridled conjecture as to her son's fate. Bill Darcy, seeing the tortured fear in his wife's eyes, took her in his arms, held her tight, and comforted her as best he could.

"Don't worry, Ruthie. Our boy will be all right. This is bad news, but it could be worse. We'll get through this, just like we've always done. He survived that damn war, and he'll survive this. Trader is as tough as they come. We'll get our boy home. Hell, he wrote us about his new bride, and I can't think that when we get to meet her that she would be a widow, dammit."

An obviously frustrated Bill Darcy had maybe said too much because Ruth Darcy almost burst into tears. But she bravely told her husband, "You're right. He's strong. He'll make it. He'll be okay."

Trader had fought in the Civil War in the Union cavalry. He was wounded twice and recovered. However, when he returned from the war five years ago, his soul had never quite recovered. Upon hearing of his marriage to Veronica, they had hoped this would release his tortured mind. Now that hope was far in the background. Seeing their boy alive would be more than enough to fulfill their wishes.

Bill Darcy was no less apprehensive than his wife. It was late September, and winter was still a ways off. However, where Trader was holed up and where the Crow's Nest was located, a heavy snow could come anytime. The weather was only one of his concerns. The Indians up that way, though abiding by a treaty for the time being, might just break that treaty, and who knows what then. Also, Indian or white, whoever was behind the attack on Trader in the first place would surely be wanting to finish the job.

Bill Darcy was reluctant to wake the sleeping trappers, but the food was ready, and Nate wanted to get a little more information from the men before he struck out at first light.

"Mrs. Darcy, you sure can cook up some good vittles. Can't she, Carl?"

"She sure can. But compared to your cooking, most anything would be good," said Carl.

Peepsight and Carl's attempt at small talk did little to lighten the mood that hung over the dinner table. But Nate got some of his questions answered about the route he was to take up to the Crow's Nest.

After supper, Nate went about getting his horse and mule ready for the long trip. He carefully checked each hoof, shoe, and nail. They were going to be covering a lot of ground, and it wasn't likely they'd be finding a blacksmith anywhere along the way. The shoes were a bit worn, but they would have to do. He next gave each a double ration of oats and barley. Trail grass along the way might be enough to graze on, but they would have to do that when they stopped at night. Lord knows there would be precious little time to stop during the day.

Another concern for Nate, and maybe one of life and death, was how well he could handle his six-shooter. He hadn't had any real call to draw a firearm in some time. He knew he was fast, but speed was only one part of the equation. Focus and resolve were as important as speed. Nate reached up and took down a worn gun belt and holstered revolver from off a high peg. Once he cinched on the belt and tied the bottom of the holster to his leg, he again felt that sense of purpose that tying on a gun always gave him.

When out riding on his uncle's spread, he had his rifle and a saddle-holstered dragoon. Those guns were used for game and the occasional rattlesnake. This revolver was reserved for two-legged snakes. The gun belt and holster were well worn, but the gun wasn't. The pistol was a brand-new Smith and Wesson with a single-action trigger and .44 caliber cartridges. A gift from his uncle for helping him round up the mustangs.

Drawing himself to full height, he checked the feel of the gun in its holster. He slowly drew out the pistol, held it at eye level, and spun the cylinder. Satisfied, he placed it back in the holster. In an instant, the gun was in and out of its cradle a half dozen times, appearing and disappearing in what was, to the human eye, a single blur of blue metal.

Feeling confident that his gun hand hadn't lost its memory, he went about checking his rifle and supply of shells. He had no way of reckoning just how much ammunition would be enough. But he was sure Bill Darcy would see to it that he had more than enough. When lead starts flying, nobody wants to worry about rationing their bullets.

Nate thought to get some shuteye now that he felt prepared for his journey. First light was some hours away, and a little sleep would put him in good stead for the morrow.

In predawn lamplight, Ruth Darcy prepared breakfast for the men. For Nate, she made extra portions of everything. While he finished his breakfast, Bill and the two trappers packed his mule and saddled his horse.

After a few last-minute tips, Peepsight and Carl stood in the silvery light of dawn and watched as Bill and Ruth Darcy tried to think if there was anything they had forgotten to tell Nate.

"Nate, this saddlebag here has the same kind of rig I gave you and plenty of shells. When you get to Trader, give it to him so he can deal his own justice," Bill Darcy instructed as he lashed the hickory-ribbed saddlebags over the horse's rump.

"I'm sure, when I see him, he'll know what to do. Aunt Ruth, don't you worry about Trader. You just plan on what you're gonna cook for him and that wife of his when he gets back."

With that, Tallhelm clucked a few times and reined his horse onto the trail north.

That was eight days ago.

3

DEADLY ENCOUNTER

Since breaking camp, Tallhelm had kept an even pace through the morning. The trail he followed roughly paralleled the northern rim, at times bringing him within a few hundred feet of the edge, other times forcing him well away from it. Though the trail zigzagged, it always worked its way west. It was during one of these swings away from the rim, where the trail crossed a small creek, that Tallhelm spotted a half dozen elk. He was downstream and downwind from the elk as they grazed on the short grasses lining either side of the creek. The overcast sky was clearing as the sun was just now beginning to burn off the morning mist. The elk were unaware of Tallhelm as he ground-hitched his mount and quietly retrieved his bow and a quiver of arrows.

With bow drawn, he crept closer, closer still, close enough to get a decent shot. With a single well-placed arrow, Tallhelm dropped a midsized buck. When it came to hunting game, he always preferred a bow and arrow to a rifle. For one thing, he didn't want to alert anyone to his presence if he could help it. And on top of that, it was just more respectful to the elk. The Sharps he carried could crease a blue jay's crown at five hundred yards, parting his feathers right or left, depending on the fashion of the day. It hardly seemed fair, shooting an animal who didn't have a chance of knowing you were even in the wood.

No, Tallhelm reserved his firearms for that other kind of animal, the kind that can shoot back.

Normally, he would have packed the elk down to a camp, salted and jerked what he could, and staked the hide. Couldn't do that here. He trail-dressed the elk, wrapped what cuts of meat he could carry in the elk hide, and lashed it tightly to his horse.

Forgoing any kind of noonday meal, he pressed on. Looking back on the scene, he watched as several timber wolves emerged from the underbrush and slowly converged on the elk carcass.

The trail he was on as he headed west had no chance of avoiding the myriad streams that worked their way south. Some small, others wide, and a few almost too deep to ford. Tallhelm, not wanting to put more distance between himself and the Crow's Nest but having no choice, reluctantly headed north in an attempt to cross these streams where they weren't as deep or wide.

Nature had surely fashioned this land with broad and dynamic strokes. The headwaters that fed these streams and drained the mountain sides far up north were but mere remnants of the great rivers that flowed here over the millennia. He marveled to think of how some of these valleys and gorges were formed in a matter of hours. Great river washes blasted into the earth when frozen walls of huge glacial lakes gave way, releasing unimaginable walls of water in a mere matter of minutes. Whole valleys washed clean, treated with the indifference a river shows a mud spit during the spring thaw. Vast tracts becoming scalloped and waved like the contours of a magistrate's wig. When Nate contemplated the immensity of such a wall of water, the prospect of a little snow seemed laughable by comparison. Finally, Tallhelm was clear of the last of the streams. From here, he had fairly open ground to the edge of the pine forest. Finding an opening through the thorny underbrush which grew thick at the edges of the wood, he spurred his horse up the steep embankment. Here a dim game trail led him through the thicket and into the forest proper.

Tallhelm found himself inside a pine forest whose tree trunks were as big around as small houses. Here, with little sunlight to speak of, underbrush was sparse, leaving the forest floor a wide-open expanse. Overhead, the lowest branches of the towering pines, as high up as a cathedral ceiling, were all but lost in the haze of the wood. He was awed by the sight of these trees, their trunks rising up from the forest floor, straight and true like huge wooden columns. Trees that seemingly sought some ancestral zenith known only to them. The old trappers, Guyer and Bowersox, had told him about this wood, but what they described could never do justice to the humbling beauty of what his eyes beheld.

His horse and mule, happy to be clear of the rock-strewn creek beds and uneven trail, set a brisk pace. In short time, the trio was at a near gallop as they worked their way south. Sometimes Nate had to rein his horse around the few patches of mountain laurel that grew in the low spots of the forest floor.

Tallhelm smiled to himself when he saw the dried laurel leaves curled and brown. He remembered how as kids, they used to stuff these with dry pine needles, trim off the uneven ends, and fashion the stuffed leaves into what looked like store-bought cigars. He had to laugh. They sure looked great, but you damn near choked to death if you tried to smoke them.

As much as the pine needle carpet was a relief for the mounts, Tallhelm was hoping to cut a regular trail before the daylight gave out. Under the canopy of towering pines, little sunlight was finding its way in. What did shone through as white shafts of light, occasionally spotlighting him as he rode through these beams of sunshine.

Here he was looking to find the trail that Peep and Carl called the cut. The one that would take him down to the Crow's Nest.

In the morning, the sun had been reduced to a milky white spot in a gray sky. By afternoon, the sun had fought through the haze and remained shining all day. But the snow clouds were not to be held at bay much longer. Here in these woods, nightfall came early and quick. Under the sheltering pines, it'd be easy enough to strike a camp, but Tallhelm had hoped to make the Crow's Nest before nightfall.

In due course and with light fading, Tallhelm rode out of the forest and picked up the trail the trappers had mapped out. Now he was on the cut, which paralleled the western rim and would lead him down to the Nest.

Here the trail followed a ledge that had been cut out of the mountainside over countless years of rain and erosion. The high gravel bank on his right was interlaced with exposed tree roots from the forest above. On the left of this wide shelf of a trail, the ground dropped away, which on a clear day would have allowed Tallhelm a view over the upper valley and onto the Bottleneck Falls, and beyond that the eastern wall of the lower valley—an unbroken view of better than seventy miles. Now, though, he couldn't see much farther than the tops of the trees that clung to the cliff face.

The first flakes of snow fell big and moist on his shoulders and downturned hat, first a few, then many. As long as this shoulder provided an opening in the trees for what little late afternoon light there was, he could press on. *One more camp before the Crow's Nest*, he thought. Several times he had to lead the horse and mule around fallen trees. Sometimes, the toppled trees formed bridges from the upper bank to the treetops on his left. Here, Tallhelm stayed tight to the bank and walked underneath. Some fallen trees nearly blocked the trail, having caught all the deadfall that would wash down the notch during heavy thunderstorms. With little work, any one of these tangled dams could provide a decent lean-to and camp.

Soon the full weight of the storm settled onto the area. Within an hour, Tallhelm was leaving deep tracks in the unblemished carpet of white. Half mesmerized by the swirling snow, Nate rode on. The silence and tranquility of the moment accented the solitude that was so much a part of his life.

That silence was abruptly broken when he heard what he thought was game crashing through the forest above the bank on his right.

He looked up in time to see an Indian in full flight leap across the trail some forty yards in front of him. The brave had sprung from the high bank in a desperate leap for the upper branches of the pines on his left. An instant later, a spear followed the flight of the Indian, pinning him to a tree with a throw through his deerskin shirt. The two spears that followed exploded in midflight. A moment later, the muffled report of Tallhelm's .44 could be heard through the heavy snow.

With his weapon drawn, Tallhelm kept his pace. Three mounted Indians silently watched as he brought himself between them and the tree-bound brave. Each was held by Tallhelm's gaze till the closest and fiercest of the trio sprang from his horse, unsheathed a knife, and leaped the high bank. Tallhelm's .44 rang out again. The bullet tore the knife out of the brave's hand an instant before he hit Tallhelm full force. The Indian, as ferocious as a bobcat, wrestled Tallhelm from his horse.

The two men grappled, rolling and tumbling in a death match the likes of which Tallhelm had never been in before. Unaware of and unable to stop themselves, the pair went careening off the trail and down the steep embankment.

Tallhelm caught ahold of a thin sapling and regained his balance a moment before the Indian. Holding to the sapling, he sent his boot crashing into the jaw of the brave, who had gained his footing farther down the bank. Climbing back up to the shoulder, Tallhelm found his fallen pistol and caught up to his horse, but too late to catch the mule, as it bolted down the trail.

The two remaining Indians watched with seeming indifference from the upper bank as the tree-bound brave, whom Tallhelm was later to learn was named Diving Hawk, freed himself of the spear which had missed his flesh by inches. Scrambling down from the tree, the brave made the even ground of the notch and was ready to meet his pursuer as the near-raging Indian made level ground.

Tallhelm was anxious to catch up with the mule, but with the outcome of this fight still in question, he had no choice but to stay. Tallhelm could see his boot had put a nasty gash in the side of the Indian's face. It didn't, however, affect his ability to fight.

Grabbing one of the broken spears, the Indian wiped away the blood that ran from the gash and lunged at the shorter Indian, who parried the thrust with the spear that had pinned him to the tree. Ripping off his torn shirt and holding both ends of the spear, he challenged his pursuer to grab hold. He did. Now instantly the two were rolling over and over as both tried to wrest the weapon free. Planting his feet for an instant, the now bare-chested Indian, the one Tallhelm had helped, dropped to his side. At which point, he twirled the spear and dropped the taller Indian with a scissor kick. Wrenching the spear free, he continued to twirl it and smashed the shaft of the spear into the side of the Indian's face, breaking it in two. The sound of the snapping hickory rang like a gunshot.

The force of the blow sent the brave reeling, but somehow he regained his footing and lunged headlong at the poised brave. The charging Indian, beside himself with rage, had lost his head, his temper, his strength. He made one blind charge, which was sidestepped. Whirling about, he charged again. This time, rather than step to the side, the brave crouched and planted the remaining half of the broken spear deep into the charging Indian's chest.

The dying brave staggered, vainly trying to remove the splintered shaft from his chest. He lurched forward, falling face first to the ground, driving the head of the spear through his chest and out the back of his broad deerskin shirt.

Rising up, the victorious brave silently looked at Tallhelm then at the two statue-like braves who remained motionless as they watched from the bank above. Nearly exhausted, the victor managed to climb the bank and reclaim his horse. In one motion, he swung up onto the horse and turned to face the other two. He spoke several words and made a sign that Tallhelm knew to mean the matter was resolved—finished. Hearing this, the two turned and disappeared into the forest with the dead Indian's horse in tow.

The victorious Indian brought his horse to where the bank wasn't as steep and gingerly guided it down onto the trail and came face-to-face with Tallhelm. With a few clipped hand gestures, he indicated his appreciation of Tallhelm's ability to shoot his pistol so quick and so true. Tallhelm answered with a single nod and reined his horse down the trail, catching up to the mule, who had stopped a few hundred yards down the trail. Dismounting, he quickly checked the lashing on the packs. Satisfied, he led the horse and mule around the mass of deadfall that had caused the mule to stop. Hitching the animals to a large root that looped out of the bank, he drew and reloaded his revolver. He hardly remembered drawing his .44 and splintering the spears. Something inside him didn't like what he was seeing. That something reacted.

Tallhelm was unsure exactly what to expect from the two Indians who rode off, but he was pretty confident the one he had helped presented no threat. This was proven out when the brave walked up moments later and, without exchanging a word, set to making camp.

A large pine that had fallen onto the trail from the bank above caught everything that washed down the notch. The Indian, with very little effort, hacked away the branches hanging down from the slanting tree. The remaining cavity provided more than enough room to shelter the men from the elements. Tallhelm, making ready use of the deadfall he cleared away from under the makeshift lean-to, built a fire. Soon its glow replaced the ghostly grayness of the snowy twilight.

Nate undid his saddle and packs and put them under the lean-to, in the dry. He then tended to the animals. Rocky trails and swift running creeks could make for a tough day. He gave each a double ration of feed and some horse apples. Noticing the brave noticing the horse apples, Tallhelm tossed him two as well. The horse and mule would not be under the shelter, but being in the firelight would warm their spirits if not their flanks.

Tallhelm motioned to the Indian that his horse was welcome to some of the feed. The brave nodded and, with his moccasin, cleared the snow away from in front his horse and poured out a small pile of grain from the cloth bag.

Now that the animals were fed, Tallhelm realized just how hungry he was. Also, he was sure the Indian would be doubly hungry, having been pursued like he was for who knows how long. Tallhelm fetched out some trail bread and an extra shirt and handed both to the Indian. Next, he set the bundle of elk meat in the snow and untied it. Moving aside some still flaming sticks, he placed four large chunks of meat on the bed of red coals.

The Indian quickly motioned, in an almost comical manner, that when the other two smell this food, they will be wanting to come in out of the dark. Tallhelm made a gesture that told the Indian that it was okay with him if they did. With that, the brave rose from the ground, walked out and around, and shouted back up the trail.

Tallhelm came from under the lean-to into the darkness in time to see the two Indians emerge from the night. As they got closer to the light, Tallhelm could see the body of the dead Indian draped over one of the horses. Combined with the flickering firelight and the snow, the scene bore more the look of an apparition than anything real.

The Indian Nate helped seemed to bear no ill will toward the other two. Ironic, considering that but a short while ago, they had hurled their spears with every intent of killing him. He could tell they were from the same tribe by the red and black tattoos that circled their arms from the wrist to the elbow. Whatever the trouble was, Tallhelm wasn't interested in finding out. He usually stayed shut of people's personal business; however, for better or worse, he had bought into whatever drama had led these Indians to pursue their tribal brother.

Snarling Wolf, who Tallhelm learned was the name of the dead Indian, was lain against the bank on the north side of the lean-to, far away from the horses and the firelight. Perhaps they did this so as not to spook the horses or maybe to add an element of closure to the recent deadly encounter. Either way, Nate appreciated the fact that his horse and mule would be spared the company of the dead Indian.

With a bit of effort, the four men found room under the lean-to and arrayed themselves around the fire. They sat silently as the elk meat seared. After several long minutes and as if on cue, the three drew their knives, and each speared one of the elk steaks. A moment later, Tallhelm did the same. What trail bread he had left, he divvied up amongst the four of them. The men nodded their appreciation to Tallhelm for the obviously welcome repast. Noticing with what dispatch they made of the steaks, he gestured to the elk hide, which had more meat wrapped inside. The Indians waved off the offer, quickly noting among themselves the generosity of this white man.

Nate watched absently as some melted snow worked its way through the pine and fell drop by drop onto the red coals, which hissed angrily, seemingly in protest at being disturbed.

Curiosity was an urge that Tallhelm treated with caution and rarely indulged. Whatever the dispute between this brave and the dead Indian, he was willing to remain ignorant of. The Indian he had helped, however, had other ideas. Staring into the fire as he poked the coals with a bare stick, the Indian began an unbroken account of the whole affair.

4

THE YEAR OF THE
HORSEMEN

The Indian spoke in a Nez Perce tongue that Tallhelm had learned from a Nez Perce trader that used to frequent the Paiute village he had lived in. Between that and hand gestures, Nate was able to follow the narrative.

"For eleven moons, no game has come to our valley. The wind whispered to all the animals to leave our mountain. Even the fish in the streams, seeing the animals leaving the woods, follow the beaver away from our lands. We know not why. Braves return from hunting, carry only persimmons on their horses instead of fresh game. The women in our tribe are good women. Seeing the empty-handed hunters, they keep their eyes downcast, not wanting to embarrass their men when their faces go so quickly from hope to fear.

"The old and infirm, not wanting to burden the tribe, leave their lodges at night seeking the depth of the forest to rejoin their spirit brothers. The loss of the old ones was of no help with the hunger in my village.

"I resolved me, Diving Hawk, not to return to the village till I have fresh meat to feed the women and babies. I roamed far from our lodge, far enough to find where the animals had gone. There I killed three deer and four turkeys. I walked for three days, leading my horse. The village had food enough for more than a week, but soon hunger returned.

"The elders told me to lead a hunting party to where the animals had gone, four suns from our lodges. Here we were successful. Enough game was brought back to the village. The babies no longer cried.

"Snarling Wolf accused me of stealing the game from the spirits of the rim people. Snarling Wolf was an enemy of mine from the day his woman put her moccasins in front of my lodge more than twenty winters past."

Tallhelm knew that in the ways of the Indian, this amounted to a divorce and a marriage proposal.

"When I did not take the moccasins into my house, he hated me even more. His woman, shamed within our village, was forced to leave the tribe, living now in the lodge of one of our enemies, a constant source of shame to the proud Snarling Wolf.

"A council was called. The game that I killed was within two days' ride of the Kettle of Tears. This is forbidden by all the people of all the tribes."

Tallhelm gave a sidelong glance to the hide of "forbidden" elk meat sitting in the snow.

"The council elders let their full bellies decide the worth of the Snarling Wolf's accusation and found no guilt.

"Snarling Wolf would not abide by the council ruling. He says he can find game that will not anger the spirits. But after three days of yet another barren hunt, he excites my friends with talk of me bringing a curse to our village. So after a night of drinking berry juice, at dawn they laid a club to my head, took my horse, and set me on foot. Snarling Wolf had become like a bear blinded in battle who chases sounds in his head rather than what he sees."

Diving Hawk paused to show Tallhelm a large knot on the side of his head from Snarling Wolf's blow.

"They chased me all day yesterday, and in the night I put many miles between myself and them. The chase forced me farther from our valley. In the late morning today, they crossed my tracks left unwillingly in the snow."

This told Tallhelm that the snow had started to the northwest, the direction from which the brave had come.

"Where the bosom of the mountains meet, they began chasing me again until I pretended I was an eagle and flew across your trail. Never since I draw a breath did I venture this close to the Kettle of Tears.

"Not since the Year of the Horsemen do my people hunt here. The game here is reserved for the spirits of the old ones, who roam the mountains and valleys here about. We believe that if their spirits die, we would lose the light from our lodge fires. A fire that has no light burns before it is seen. Such a fire would leave our lodges in chaos, scattering our people, leaving the sun watcher alone when he comes down from his tower, our houses empty when they should be full with the laughter of fat mothers and shouts from happy babies.

"Before the horsemen came, these mountains were known as Laughing God Mountain. Many other places our peoples warred with one another, but here at the Laughing God Lakes, there was always peace. We respected the Tribe of the Rim. Tribes traveled freely, taking only the game they needed as they moved through the high range that flanks the rim and upper and lower valleys, the broad delta above, this very ledge. Here also, the great medicine men of our tribe would come and live, watching the sun etch the granite walls lining the valley.

"All of this changed when the horsemen with their fire sticks and lust for gold took all joy from my people.

"These men who came, some who prized gold more than their very own teeth, slaughtered the rim people. They plundered the gold that Stone Eyes was guarding for the Great Spirit, leaving only when they could plunder no more. They took all that their horses and their squat slaves could carry. Two summers later, they returned. The warriors of our tribes were ready.

"The horsemen, on their return, seeing no sign of our people in two moons of travel, think they have killed or scared off all the braves. They were like a man who catches five fish and seeing no more in the water thinks he has caught all the fish in the creek. But as the soldiers slept and dreamt of gold, our warriors attacked. Every soldier was captured or killed, some choosing to jump from the rim rather than become our prisoner.

"For four days and nights, the men were tortured, tortured for defiling Laughing God Lakes, tortured for killing the rim people and turning these lakes into what we now call the Kettle of Tears. For four days, the agony of these men made sounds no man should hear. When each man had lost his sense of pain, his eyelids were sliced off, and the skinless wretch was marched wide-eyed in front of his comrades to the edge of the rim and cast off. The body-strewn rocks created a river of red to match the roaring water that splashed off the rocks below the Bottleneck Falls. After many moons, the rain washed away the bloodstains of the soldiers. But no rains could wash away our pain or our sorrow. Our people say on rainy nights, the screams of horsemen cry out from the high bluff. The cave of Stone Eyes was sealed forever, lost behind the prickly bush that grows over the steep walls of the valley.

"The horsemen came one more time. Three winters later, they came looking for their brothers. These ones are more wary. Our warriors scattered these soldiers with the help of our buffalo brothers. The battle lasted two days, and when the war hoops fell quiet, every brave now rode a horse, and their spears were draped with many scalps.

"After the great battle, many winters passed and no white man came to the Kettle of Tears. None of our people came either. The old ones, the ancient people of the rim, were gone. The game was left forever to the spirits of the old ones. Now though, the spirits also need the game from the valleys and mountains of our village. The animal sign left in the forest say the deer and fox, wolf and elk come now to the Kettle of Tears. Our people are hungry. If we are to live, we must follow the game. To do so is to break the ancient law of our people. The way is not clear. The trail is dim for my people.

"At our lodge fires, we talk of the time before. The time when the Kettle of Tears was our Laughing God Lakes. For the time of ten generations, no one comes to this place. Then the man who builds his house on the place we call the beaver tail comes. The man you call Keith."

Tallhelm had heard smatterings of this legend. He knew there were some whispers out of the fog of history that the Spanish had gotten this far north. But until right now, he was never sure that the lore was myth or indeed fact.

The brave went silent. He gazed into the coals, aimlessly rearranging the embers with a dry, bark-less stick, the small black knots along its length signaling a slight change in direction of the crooked branch.

The brave fell asleep. The stick caught fire, burning up its length till the round rock border was reached. Here the stick split in two, the unburnt half falling to the ground. Tallhelm picked the remnant off the ground and tossed it in the fire. Settling his chin on his chest, he slept. The snow continued to fall.

Meanwhile, ten miles to the south at the Crow's Nest, Johnathan Keith peered out the window at the snow falling into the upper valley.

5

THE CROW'S NEST

Jonathan Keith watched as large flakes landed on the glass, melted, and ran down the pane. This first snowfall brought him heightened concern for his young friend and his wife, Veronica, and the two men he sent out to find them. Trader Darcy was more like a son to Keith, who had become estranged from his own son, who lived a continent and an ocean away.

Trader and his wife had left the Crow's Nest sometime in early August, and Keith figured he should have gotten a signal from them by now. Keith was the only person other than Trader's wife who knew what kind of quest Trader was on. He had prayed that this day would never come, but most times the arc of history pays little attention to prayers. Keith dared not bring himself to utter the word. A word whispered like a piece of deadly gossip, spoken in the lowest of tones so as not to reach unwanted ears. The word was *gold*.

The legend of an ancient cave of gold was known to Jonathan Keith. He had heard enough about it over the years to suspect that there was more than a grain of truth to it. However, not until Trader Darcy confided in him that he had a map that might have pinpointed its location did he give it much thought.

Myths and legends are ofttimes the touchstones of dreamers who prefer the unknown to the known. The willingness to escape into a world tethered to the vague hope that deliverance awaits those who become privy to some "real" truth was of no interest to Jonathan

Keith. His world was anchored in hard facts, known truths. But this map of Trader's had cast all that aside. Life as he knew it was about to change. Now his world was set to erupt. A fuse had been lit, and whether or not it could be extinguished remained to be seen.

Keith had kept Trader's secret to himself, not even telling his right-hand man, Sunny. But an uneasiness had taken over his thoughts, and the time had come for some action. He had become increasingly concerned that Trader had run into some trouble. Before he and Veronica set off, they agreed that Trader would signal back to the Nest from Initiation Bluff, if he had any luck locating this so-called "cave of gold." The bluff, although thirty miles south, was still visible from the deck of the Crow's Nest. He had supplied him with a mirror to use to send the signal, but no signal had come.

Keith's concern was further heightened by the recent arrival of Walt Tallhelm, Trader's cousin. Walt Tallhelm had been to the Nest several times in the past but told Keith that for some unknown reason, he felt compelled to stop what he was doing and make his way here. One look at Walt Tallhelm and you knew this was not a man given over to idle urges or fanciful whimsy. He told Keith he felt he had little choice but to show up.

Hearing that his cousin had recently been at the Nest and had more or less gone missing resonated with his inner concerns. The Tallhelms were a close family—maybe not geographically but in every other way. If the Tallhelm boys heard one thing from their father, and heard it many times, it was "you boys stick together." As kids, they found this strange. Why wouldn't they stick together? They were family. However, over the years, and more than a few times, they've come across siblings who were sworn enemies. In hindsight, their fathers' admonishments were anything but idle words.

It was five days ago that Keith decided that some action needed to be taken and had summoned Sunny and the others to his quarters.

"Sunny, go get Sarusha, Lucien, and Tallhelm. I've got something we need to talk about."

Sunny, a former seaman, was a broad wedge of muscle. His boyish blond hair belied his fifty plus years. His body seemed to ignore the aging process. He was a man who at fifty was just reaching his physical prime. His deliberate movements gave hint to the brute strength he could summon in the blink of an eye.

Sarusha was a half-French and half-Nez Perce habitué of the Nest. He had been Jonathan Keith's guide years ago when he first explored the Northwest.

Keith had met Lucien, a former Negro slave, in Martinique, where he bought him his freedom and hired him as a freeman to be his shipboard cook. They have been together ever since.

"What's up, Captain?" asked Sunny.

"You'll know soon enough. Just get those others."

With that, Sunny retreated through the thick oak door, returning ten minutes later with Sarusha, Lucien, and Walt Tallhelm in tow.

Walt Tallhelm stood almost a head taller than the other three. Wide and rawboned, he could probably equal Sunny in brute strength. Sporting a week's growth of a dark black beard that grew to just below his bearlike brown eyes, the man was a bigger, rougher casting than his younger brother, Nathan. A Dragoon Colt sat loosely in a gun belt cinched waist high. A quilted brown leather vest hung open, exposing four gleaming tomahawks ribbing the inside of the garment like the whale bones of a corset. Not one to go unprepared, Tallhelm also sported a large Bowie knife nestled snugly in its sheath and tucked sideways under his gun belt. All in all, a very imposing figure.

"There's whiskey over on that table. You men help yourselves. I don't know how not to be dramatic about this, but I got a feeling, Walt, that your cousin Trader has come to no good.

"Maybe it's just something in my bones, or maybe I'm just getting on and am fretting like an old woman, but I know something's up. What I'm gonna say can't leave this room, or we'll have hell to pay. You men know me. You, Walt, not as well these three, but they'll tell you, I'm not given to empty pronouncements. So trust me when I say not a word. Not one word can leave this room." With that, Keith walked over to the door, opened it, looked out, and shut it tight.

"This summer, Trader and Veronica showed me a map. It turns out one of her far-removed ancestors was able to steal a horse and flee the Spanish. What was passed down through the generations, along with the story, was a very ornate Spanish saddle and a leather saddlebag. While admiring both, your cousin chanced to notice markings burnt into the underside of the saddlebag. Long story short, he took gray ash and dusted the markings, and the rough outline of a map became clearer. Enough definition remained that he was able to make out the words *sal lago,* salt lake, and north of that, the distinct contours of the hourglass shape of the Kettle of Tears. Whoever made the map must have known something about surveying because Trader recognized several faint indicators of distance and bearing. He showed me the saddlebag, and unfortunately for me, what Trader had suspected looked to be true. Of course, the Kettle of Tears runs for what, forty, fifty miles? But one of the markings clearly showed an *X* not too far south of the falls. Maybe he could find it, maybe not, but whichever way it went, he should have got word to me by now.

"Sarusha, I want you and Tallhelm here to head south and see what you can find. Lucien, you have Evie pack them enough grub for a couple of weeks. Sunny, how many men are in the Nest right now?" Jonathan Keith spoke with the command that comes easy to a former sea captain.

"Well, there's the regular crew. That's five, and then four more," answered Sunny.

"I thought there were more downstairs than that," queried Keith.

"There were, but Tice, Dagget, and those two Johnson brothers took off this morning, supposedly on their way to Missoula to find some women." This answer from Sunny elicited grunts and guffaws from Lucien and Sarusha. Not because of the women part but because Tice and Dagget were two of the singularly most unlikable individuals one would have the unfortunate experience of ever meeting.

"Till this thing gets figured out, keep an eye on those four that are still here. Those two that showed up yesterday, who were they?" asked Keith.

"Severman and Dean," answered Sunny.

"Oh yeah, Severman and Dean. I imagine they wore out their welcome at the Settlement Bar. I don't trust those two as far as I can spit. What are they doing here anyway?"

"They said one of their horses went lame and they needed a place to light till it healed. I really think they just had nowhere to go, 'cause I didn't see much wrong with either of their horses."

"As soon as they can travel, send them on their way. I've seen it before, and I imagine you fellas have as well. Where gold is involved, you can usually count on some blood being shed. Let's hope that's not the case here. That's it for now, men. And remember, not a word.

"Walt, looks like I press-ganged you into this search. I expect that's okay?"

"Don't you worry, Cap. Trader and me was brought up in the same house till he was all but growed. Can't get much closer than that. I'll do whatever you need, Cap. I'll be right glad to get this caution off my mind. Don't abide by worrying and fretting. You can count on this, sir. If Trader's come to no good, God help the man what did it. I know ways to make a man remember the day he was born." Walt Tallhelm, as he finished this statement, reached down, filled his whiskey glass, downed it in one swallow, and followed Sunny and Sarusha out of the room.

Keith didn't quite know what that meant—"make a man remember the day he was born"—but it sounded ominous as hell. He thought to himself that he was glad Walt Tallhelm was an ally rather than an enemy. As the men left the room, Keith walked over to a large globe and gently spun it. The amber and cocoa-brown orb spun effortlessly. Keith placed a finger on it, slowing its motion. When the globe stopped, the first two fingers of his right hand were gently pressed over England.

England was where his estranged wife, son, and daughter lived. Although not one to nurture regrets, he had to admit to himself that at times, he wondered what life would have been like had he plotted a different course.

Born in 1801 in New Bedford, Massachusetts, Jonathan Keith was the oldest son in a prominent shipbuilding family. By the age of eighteen, he was well on his way to becoming a master shipwright. By the age of twenty, he was one. The young Jonathan excelled at all the various skills needed to build a proper ship. From choosing the right trees to be milled to hoisting the banner that waved atop the finished vessel, he guided the construction with the grace and conviction of a maestro conducting a grand opera. Soon his yard was building lighter and faster ships than his competition, and they could hold more cargo. Shipping companies were lining up at his family's shipyard to get on a waiting list to purchase the next vessel to come down the slipway.

Jonathan's talents weren't limited to shipbuilding. While frequenting the rough-and-tumble dockside bars of New Bedford, he found that he had a natural talent as a brawler. Already well-respected by the professional community, Keith also earned—with his fists— the hard-won respect of the seamen who sailed in and out of port.

When it came to shipbuilding, what held sway over the arc of Keith's efforts were two things: invention and perfection. After a decade in the yard and at the drafting table, Keith wanted to feel one of his creations under his feet, in action, firsthand. Also, as financially successful as he and his family were in the shipbuilding business, he saw the real money to be made was in the shipping of goods and mail packets.

With little effort, he was able to cajole the legendary sea captain Patrick Moran to come out of his recent retirement and take the helm of his newest vessel. Pap Moran, as he was known, had probably forgotten more about sailing than most deepwater skippers thought they knew. As it turned out, he was praying for a chance to get back to sea, given his quarrelsome wife's incessant demands and her apparent desire to elevate any small transgression on his part into a capital offense.

Pap also owed Keith a favor, really more than a favor. Years before, Keith had thrown Moran a lifeline. The captain had been unable to find work owing to an unfortunate series of nautical disasters, none of which could be blamed on Moran. But considering the amount of money lost, someone had to take the blame. Pap Moran was the one. Jonathan Keith heard tell of this and convinced a client of his who had just taken possession of a commissioned vessel to hire Moran. The old Captain was never again without a ship to helm.

So when Keith asked him to come out of retirement, Moran was more than happy to help out his young friend any way he could.

The vessel, which incorporated the latest features perfected over the years, was a thing of beauty. Its slick design and extra canvas made the ship he christened the *Celine* faster than any ship of the day, be it navy, privateer, or pirate.

Under the expert tutelage of Pap Moran, Keith soon became an accomplished mariner. With a policy of trading in the rarer commodities, the *Celine* plied the known and unknown trade routes. Profits were sometimes phenomenal, sometime not, but sufficient enough to allow for the construction of a second then a third ship. In time, Keith and Company became the carrier of repute.

Trade between one port and another is by nature often tinged with intrigue. None of this was lost on Jonathan Keith. He found out quickly that there were written laws, and then there were unwritten laws. His reputation and stature in the maritime community brought him into the confidence of men of wealth and power. While in foreign ports and capitals, his ear and opinion were often sought. Due to the relative speed of the *Celine* compared to other ships and overland routes, he was ofttimes privy to information well in advance of others. For some, that information had a value far greater than any tonnage of goods carried in the hold.

Keith, keen to maintain his independence, was always vigilant in keeping his personal sense of integrity intact. Not an easy task, considering the turbulence of the political theaters in which he found himself. But as tumultuous as a situation may be, a fair witness who remains above the fray can always find firm footing. People of import saw this in Jonathan Keith.

Being known and trusted from the far-flung ports of the China Sea to the dockside bars of New Bedford, unfortunately, came at a price. The price he paid was the loss of the love of his wife, son, and daughter. Too long absent, he was more a stranger than husband and father. And although financially secure, wealthy even, Rebecca Keith had yearned for too many years to again have the young shipwright she married sitting across from her at evening dinner. So over the years, she was forced to fashion her life to her liking, based on what she and her children wanted and needed.

For many reasons and no reason, her widow-like countenance was seemingly more apparent while her husband was back in port as not. One evening, while commenting on that very phenomenon and with little more than a suggestion that she and the children should maybe take a trip abroad as a way of dispelling her gloom, his wife released upon him an invective-filled diatribe that lasted well into the night.

The cloth had been rent. Within days, she had teamsters load the entire contents of their home—down to the brass tacks that held the ornate tapestries that hung throughout the house—onto a ship, sailing to England, never to return.

Following this event, Keith lost himself in his business. He bought valuable properties in his familiar ports of call. He hammered out ironclad arrangements with the oldest and most trusted banks of Europe and the Far East to oversee these investments. He managed to double and redouble his wealth. He became a very rich man.

In time, though, he grew restless. He became weary of the world and all it had to offer. The world he had grown to know had become small. His wealth and the luxury it afforded him was not enough to shield him from what he saw about him—a world that retched itself forward, substituting one form of human degradation for another. Jonathan Keith had seen enough of this world, a world adrift, forged in greed, fueled by fear, anchored in nothing.

When he headed out west, he had an idea where he was going. Years before, while still sharing the helm with Pap Moran, they took the *Celine* around Cape Horn and up the west coast. Captain Moran thought his young protege` should have his mettle tested "rounding the cape" before he could fully relinquish the helm. Keith more than proved up to the task. Making port in Seattle, Keith became intrigued by the description of the lands that lay inland up the Columbia River. But his curiosity would have to wait.

So years later, he returned to the Great Northwest after leaving his business interests in the capable hands of others. That long-ago curiosity was finally to be satisfied. Keith had, in all his travels, seen any number of lofty citadels and cliff-bound monasteries, high on a seaside bluff or perched on some rocky crag. They all spoke one thing to him, and that was "I'm unassailable."

Keith knew what he was looking for. Whether he would be able to find it was another matter. He enlisted the services of the French Indian guide Sarusha and spent two years navigating the Columbia and the Snake, end to end, and traversing the divide from the Canadian border to the Great Salt Lake. Sarusha knew the kind of place Keith was searching for, and being half Nez, was familiar with the Kettle of Tears. But given his native beliefs, he was reluctant to tell Keith of its existence. However, after seeing a kinship in the timbre of the man, he brought Keith to the Kettle of Tears and the rocky half-forested outcrop the Indians called Yixa Walwas, the beaver tail.

Keith had the wherewithal to hire the tradesmen and transport the materials it would take to realize his design for the edifice, which one of his workers dubbed the Crow's Nest. The name stuck, as it was every bit what a crow's nest on a ship is—the highest perch.

It took several years, but Keith built his citadel, and for the last twenty-some years had aged along with its rough-hewn timbers. He had fully expected to watch his own sunset from the deck of his mountain-bound ship. Now, though, because of Trader Darcy's chance encounter with an old Spanish saddlebag, all that was about change.

Keith tried not to put himself in situations where his peace of mind was held hostage by events not in his control. This situation with Trader was just that. He hoped Sarusha and Walt Tallhelm would return soon and return with good news.

As he turned away from the dark mirrorlike windowpane, he felt a pang of sadness for his estranged wife, realizing firsthand the gnawing pain of the endless months of waiting she must have endured.

6

THE STAMPEDE

Nate Tallhelm woke several times during the cold snowy night. He was awake to see the last bit of snow fall across the front of the warm lean-to. Sometime toward morning, he pushed the unburnt ends of the logs into the dying coal and yanked some of the tangled branches out of the wall of the lean-to and onto the fire.

The dawn had broken on a day as clear and bright as any you could imagine. A day so crisp you felt that if you snapped your fingers, you would get a spark. Only a heavy snow can cleanse the air that way, and it was a heavy snow. With keen anticipation, Tallhelm pulled on his boots, knowing that today would find him at the Crow's Nest.

Tallhelm's usual breakfast consisted of black coffee and a hunk of trail bread. However, this morning he felt a need to fortify himself with something more substantial. He made as much porridge as his cast-iron trail pot would hold, ate half of it, and offered the rest to Diving Hawk. When Diving Hawk finished the oatmeal, Tallhelm made another pot and gave it to the other two braves.

The Indians seemed in no great hurry to leave the warmth and comfort of the lean-to. Tallhelm had learned from his time spent living with the Paiute that in large part, Indians took a more leisurely approach to life than white men.

Nate, however, was ready to hit the trail. He filled his coffee cup for a second time and went about breaking camp. This stirred the Indian trio into action. As Tallhelm lashed the packs onto the mule, he motioned to Diving Hawk that he was welcome to the remaining elk meat. With enthusiastic gestures from the other two, Diving Hawk accepted the offer and set to tying the elk meat wrapped in the hide to one of the horses. As the three gathered their things, Tallhelm overheard an exchange that he translated as the one brave asking Diving Hark, "What was the name of the man who shoots once? So if we hear his name mentioned at our lodge fires, we can say we know this man."

Diving Hawk realized that not only didn't he know this man's name but that, in fact, he hadn't heard him utter one word last night or this morning. Mildly embarrassed for not knowing Tallhelm's name, he admonished the Indian by answering, "The name of the man who shoots once should not be bandied about among those not worthy of knowing it."

This amused Tallhelm, and in passable Nez told the Indians, "My name is Tallhelm, Nathan Tallhelm, blood brother to the Paiute of the Lower Snake River."

Diving Hawk turned to the other two, who had heard everything Tallhelm said and repeated, "This is Tarlton, the man who shoots once, blood brother to the Paiute of the Lower Snake River."

In unison, the braves repeated, "Tarlton, the man who shoots once."

Nate corrected Diving Hawk and the others. "My name is Tallhelm."

"We are proud to know you, Tarlton. You are welcome at our lodge fires," said the one brave.

Tallhelm didn't know what to think. Maybe they couldn't pronounce *Tallhelm*. In any event, he asked by what names they were known so he could tell his blood brothers he knew these men.

"I am Kiwkiwlass Tpish." (Drum Face.)

"I am Amash Achash." (Owl Eyes.)

Tallhelm could see why Drum Face had been given that name. His face, save for his nose, was nearly as flat as a pane of glass.

With these introductions out of the way, Nate went about saddling his horse as Drum Face walked back up the trail and tied Snarling Wolf's body to his horse.

Diving Hawk thought, *This man Tarlton has strong medicine. His eyes are those of a brother. Last night, he listened to our history with his heart as much as his ears. In my lifetime, our plight has gone from whispered concerns to raging fears. At his end, Snarling Wolf had become sick in his head, stung by jealousy and enraged by hunger.*

What happened to the times when we sat around our lodge fires with our happy women and young ones? What of the winters spent fixing weapons, treating hides, trapping beaver? Now they seem like they never were. Spring brings the arrival of only more of the white man's wagons clanging over the game trails. One year has nothing in common with the next. The fear in the eyes of our women is a pain greater than any I have known.

This Tarlton, maybe he would know how to read the sign of the Great Spirit. The way is so bleak when the mountain and valley sparkle so bright. He shared these thoughts with Tallhelm and listened intently as Tallhelm began to offer his advice.

"The Great Spirit is a compassionate Father. He would not want His children to suffer the pain of hunger when He has filled His forests with so many of their animal brothers. Go tell your council elders that you have eaten meat taken from the broad delta above the Kettle of Tears and the light still shines in the fire of our camp." Tallhelm pointed to the burning fire and with a sweeping gesture continued, "The Great Spirit would welcome the return of the tribes that have abandoned the Kettle of Tears and would be pleased that again it may be known as Laughing God Mountain."

Diving Hawk said nothing and slowly took in all that he could see. He so wanted to believe what Tarlton had said, but the beliefs of his people were so ingrained that he really didn't know what to think.

Nate had no idea if the Indians would take his advice, but he felt that what he had said was more than valid. In any event, it was time to get moving. He kicked some snow on the fire till it hissed itself out and mounted up. He knew the dun was ready to travel, having spent an uneasy night. The horse never got used to the strong smell of Indians. This didn't bother Tallhelm, for he had grown accustomed to it. The scent didn't burn the eyes like he had experienced with some of the men whose path he had crossed. Rather, the constant exposure to woodsmoke and animal hides gave the Indians a strong scent of musk.

Diving Hawk, as the natural leader, led the way. The men rode single file. Nate, leading the mule, took up the rear. Several times the absence of trees on the left provided an unobstructed view of the upper valley, the Bottleneck Falls, and the blue haze of mist rising off the lower lake far in the distance. The Indians took turns breaking a path through the deep gleaming snow. Keeping closer to the bank where the snow wasn't as deep, for several miles the men rode in silence, each lost in their own thoughts.

Tallhelm thought back to the time when he was within a day's ride of Keith's. He would have made his way there to meet this man his cousin had spoken so well of, but it was one of the few times when his time wasn't his own. An Austrian noble had hired him to lead a party of two landscape artists and three hunters deep into the Rockies.

Nate never understood hunting as sport, and these Austrians had elevated their pursuit of trophy heads to a level of pure absurdity. The artists had heard of Thorn's Peak and wanted to capture its splendor on canvas. He had led them there in late spring. Some even-handed trading with the tribe that camped in the shadow of its lofty peaks insured a safe stay for the brief summer months.

Tallhelm winced and turned his head as he was caught by a deeper memory. There had been several women in the party. One, the full-grown daughter of one of the artist, had a come-hither way about her. One summer night, he couldn't tell which was sweeter, the honey on the biscuit or the sound of her voice. Nate had only been a curiosity to her as it turned out.

He had reckoned with some wily foes in his time, but none could hold a candle to this gal. He cursed himself for being a fool. Even now, it embarrassed him to think he entertained the thought of traveling abroad to see her famous Alps.

Tallhelm was shaken out of his spiraling thoughts by Diving Hawk, who had slowed his pace and come alongside.

"Look there." Diving Hawk pointed to woodsmoke far in the distance.

Tallhelm saw the smoke and had an urge to quicken his pace, but checked that impulse. The cut was a gradual downhill trail that leveled out not far from the switchback that led down to the Crow's Nest. He should be there soon enough.

The pair rode in silence, watching the rising smoke in the distance, when Diving Hawk told Tallhelm, "Soon the trail we share will fork. I will speak your words to the elders. They will decide. I have lost a tribal brother but gained a friend." With that, Diving Hawk passed Drum Face and Owl Eyes and regained the lead position. No sooner had he done that than Tallhelm heard a rumble break the silence of the still morn. Turning, he looked back up the trail to see the steaming faces of several bighorn sheep as they led a rumbling herd numbering in the hundreds. The Indians heard the sound as well and, as if of a single mind, began to gallop three abreast. Drum Face, unable to hold tight to the reins of the horse carrying Snarling Wolf, lost his grip. He watched helplessly as the horse careened over the edge and into the abyss. Desperate to avoid the same fate, the three made for a pile of deadfall some hundred yards down trail.

Tallhelm never felt more appreciation for his horse and mule as they valiantly gave everything they had to stay ahead of the surging herd. As Tallhelm passed where Snarling Wolf's horse went over the edge, he saw its upturned legs as the braying beast disappeared out of sight. One by one the Indians leapt their horses over the pile of deadfall and pulled them tight to the bank. Tallhelm could do the same, but that would leave the mule as good as dead. Sizing up the situation, Diving Hawk signaled to Tallhelm and in the blink of an eye grabbed the reins of the mule as Tallhelm flew by. Tallhelm let go the reins, and Diving Hawk, holding tight, yanked the mule to a stop, causing the pair to crash into the bank but safely away from the surging bighorns. Tallhelm kept a hair's breadth ahead of the thundering herd. Each hoofbeat his horse took seemed like an eternity.

The bighorns had come on them in a matter of minutes. Caught in the higher range by the early snow, the sheep, alarmed, were making their way to lower climes, their normal wintering spot.

Nate could feel the dun reaching a deep second wind as the proud horse started to gain on the herd. Soon, the trail began to level out and open onto the flat expanse at the foot of the cut. This allowed Tallhelm to rein the dun hard to the right as the ocean of bighorns went flying by. Several minutes later, Diving Hawk and the other two rode up to join him and handed the reins of the mule back to Tallhelm. The men looked at one another and, wearing expressions of bewilderment and relief, burst into laughter.

Words could not describe the kinship Nate felt toward these three whom he had known for less than a day. Reaching into a slit in the side of his saddle, Tallhelm drew out a double-edged fighting knife and handed it to Diving Hawk. "Thank you for saving my mule."

Diving Hawk, happy to return the favor, reached down to his knee-length moccasins and drew out a foot-long knife. The handle was deer antler with the face of a bear carved into the top. The blade was a fashioned piece of obsidian, its sides rough and irregular, the cutting edges sharp as a razor blade.

"Tarlton, this knife belonged to our great warrior chief, Standing Eagle. In the time of many drums, this knife sliced the hide of the antelope as fine as the skin of an onion. Take this knife and know your face at our lodge fires is a welcome one."

The knife was an exquisite piece of work. The yellow handle had marbleized over the years, showing hundreds of hairline fissures. Tallhelm thought the carved bear face looked like his older brother, Walt.

Diving Hawk pointed out the all-but-obvious trail down to the Crow's Nest, the smell of its woodsmoke redolent in the late morning air.

"If I were you three, I'd catch up to those bighorns and add a few of them to that hide of elk meat," suggested Nate as he thumped his chest with a clenched fist, nodded to the trio, and happily made his way toward the switchback leading to the Crow's Nest. Pausing, he looked toward the west and watched as the Indians, in causal pursuit of the bighorns, disappeared into the distance.

7

THE ARRIVAL

The trail down to the Nest started out wide, but with each hairpin turn got narrower and narrower, bringing the edge closer with each step. Nate was starting to wonder just how thin this trail would get till it reached the flat and what appeared to be a stone gatehouse. In any event, he was already leading his horse and mule single file.

Stopping to check the packs on the mule, Tallhelm took a moment to take in the view the switchback provided. The Crow's Nest, with several of its chimneys sending ribbons of gray smoke into the blue sky, was a welcome sight. Tallhelm couldn't really tell the size of the edifice or just how far he was from it, perched as it was atop its rocky crag. Its background, the open expanse of the upper valley, robbed the eye of perspective.

Looking up and beyond the Crow's Nest, he was able to catch his first full glimpse of the upper falls, twenty miles to the north, the roar of the thundering water too distant to be heard. The silver ribbon, a half-mile wide, fell uninterrupted for a thousand feet. The basin at the foot of the falls formed a wide lake that constantly overflowed its banks. The surplus water regathered itself into a river that flowed south through the deep valley till it dropped off the Bottleneck Falls. Peering through the palisades on either side of the falls, Tallhelm could see the early afternoon sun reflecting off the eastern face of its flat granite walls.

The last switchback led onto a flat stretch wide enough for four riders abreast but not much more, with a two-hundred-foot drop straight down on either side. Thankfully, Nate soon came to the gatehouse. The stone building ran the full width of the trail, its sides flush with the sheer rock face. Two log-and-plank doors centered in the wall were dwarfed by a high stone facade, above the doors a pair of windows.

Tallhelm saw a knotted rope hanging to the right side of the doors. Assuming it was attached to a bell, he reached for the rope. Just then, the window opened, and an ashen-faced old man looked down at him. "Pull the rope," he said and abruptly closed the window. The man's face was visible for only an instant, but Tallhelm was sure he wouldn't be forgetting it too soon. A dark blue scarf, knotted at the neck and drawn up over the head, framed a chalk-white face and watery gray eyes. It seemed more like a mask come alive than a face.

Tallhelm pulled the rope. A loud bell pealed once, and its sound repeated countless times as the echo cascaded down the valley. As Nate waited, he looked up to the Crow's Nest and could see a man with a spyglass looking back at him. A bell from up the Crow's Nest rang twice. Before the echoes had time to subside, the large doors were swinging open.

Nate led his horse and mule into an arched passageway. He followed the light from the whale-oil lamps as the hallway curved to the left and led to another set of doors that were just swinging open as Tallhelm approached.

From the top of the switchback, this gatehouse looked to be little more than a facade with a small rampart. Now seeing its real size, he wondered to himself how much he might have misjudged the size of the Crow's Nest. How Keith built in a place where most people would wager nothing could ever be built astounded Nate.

But build he did.

As Tallhelm led his horse and mule up the ramp, he craned his neck to look to the top of the building. Tallhelm could see the nautical inspiration in the design. Each of three ascending level terraced back all the way to the top, which offered a commanding view.

Nate was again met by a pair of heavy oak doors, but this time someone pulled one of them back and welcomed him inside.

"My name is Sunny. Can I ask you straight out what brings you all the way up here?" Sunny's voice had more a note of curiosity than confrontation.

"My name's Nathan Tallhelm, and I have a message for Jonathan Keith," announced Nate, relieved that he'd be able to do what he had promised his aunt and uncle he would. Where things went from here, who could say, but in any event, Keith would get Veronica's message.

At first, Sunny was uncharacteristically silent, struck by the import of this man's arrival.

"Nathan Tallhelm, I'm Sunny Martin. Glad to meet you. Damn, another Tallhelm. You know, or maybe you don't, but your brother was just here last week and expected back. We don't know just when."

"My brother...you mean my brother Walt?" asked Nate, trying to check the excitement in his voice.

"Yup, Walt Tallhelm. Boy, I tell ya, he's one to ride the river with! When's the last time you saw him?" asked Sunny.

"Hell, I reckon twenty years. We didn't know if he was dead or alive for the longest time. How is he?"

"Oh, he's good. We got to know him some years back, but he still puts a caution into me and the Captain. But enough of that. Let's get you upstairs."

Tallhelm was just getting accustomed to the dim light of the cavernous stable when a voice out of the dark said, "I'll take your horse, mister. Curry and feed fifty cents."

"Is that a day or a week?" asked Nate as he handed the reins to the thin Black groom.

"Fifty cents for the horse and fifty cents for the mule. We go day by day," announced the first groom's older brother, who emerged out of the darkness along with a pair of scruffy terriers and took the reins of the mule from his brother, adding, "Iffen you don't have money, our pa will talk barter."

"Nathan, this is Ernest and Everett Samms, and these two"—pointing to the terriers—"well, that's Star and Maggie. We don't get much work out of them but keep 'em around just the same. Boys, this is Nathan Tallhelm, Walt's kin." Sunny, knowing he'd get a rise out of the boys, put emphasis on the name *Tallhelm.*

Sunny had scarce time to get it out but that the boys were looking at each other and shaking their heads. "You and him friends?" asked Everett.

"Sure we're friends. He's my brother!" answered Nate.

"You wouldn't wanna be his enemy, that be for sure," added Ernest.

Tallhelm slid his rifle and his uncle's Sharps out of their scabbards and grabbed his two sets of saddlebags as the dun was led away.

He was a bit surprised by how easily the mule took to being led by the wiry colored groom.

"There's some oats and barley left in that poke. Give that to them too!" Tallhelm shouted down to the boys as he followed Sunny up the long staircase that ran up the eastern wall of the room.

Reaching the landing halfway up, Sunny turned to Nate and said, "Here, Nate, let me take those saddlebags. You look like you could use some dinner. I'll have Evie fix you something. Matter of fact, the kitchen is where we'll probably find the Captain." Sunny, once halfway up the second flight of stairs, turned back to Nate and, in a whisper, added, "The boss been powerful worried about your cousin."

To this comment, Nate just nodded and would leave any utterances for Keith's ears first.

Sunny led Nate around the railing next to the staircase and back toward the front. Here Nate looked out a window that provided a view down into the upper valley and across to the eastern wall of the rim. He thought back to the other night when he was on the other side looking back across the valley, watching the lights of the Crow's Nest come alive. Now here he was.

Sunny made his way to a doorway that was flanked by a pair of matching brass lanterns. Tallhelm, hesitating a moment, reached up and gently pushed one of the hanging brass octagons. The soft light shining through the beveled glass set the shadows in the hall moving. As the lamplight settled, Sunny pushed open the door. Tallhelm, out of habit, checked the feel of his large revolver, loose and easy in its holster.

The large wood-paneled room was dimly lit with the amber light of two long ceiling lamps. To the left on the southern end of the room, a row of glass doors opened out to a deck. Out on this deck, two men were shoveling snow and tossing it over the waist-high railing. Across the room, along the western wall, were a series of booths, each booth illuminated by a parchment-shaded sconce, each shade painted with an exquisite scene from a foreign city, a port, mountain vista, or verdant river valley. The booths were unoccupied save for one, where two men sat facing one another in silence.

Tallhelm followed Sunny past a long mahogany bar, which sported a row of ladder-backed stools; peach-tinted mirrors; a standing supply of brown goods, the labels on the whiskey bottles attesting to their far-flung origins, and shelves with cut crystal glassware. This room rivaled anything Tallhelm had ever seen back East.

"Right through here, Nate," directed Sunny as he led him through the dining room adjacent to the bar, through a pantry, and finally into a room off the side of the kitchen. Evidently, this was where Jonathan Keith spent most of his time.

"Is this the fella that rang Ghosty's bell?" asked Keith as he got up from behind a table and stood to face Tallhelm.

"Captain, this is Nathan Tallhelm, and he's got a message for you," announced Sunny.

"Nate Tallhelm, I've heard about you, and it was all good. What's this message you have for me, and who's it from?" said Keith.

"It's from Trader, but really from Veron—" Nate didn't get to finish his sentence but that Keith put his hand up quickly, bidding Nate to be silent.

"Sunny, close that pantry door," directed Keith as he walked over to a side door to the kitchen and shut it.

"Now start at the beginning. Oh, sorry, do you want something to drink?" asked Keith, anxious to hear what Nate had to say but trying to maintain some level of proper hospitality.

"I wouldn't turn one down, if you men will join me," answered Nate.

Sunny was out the door and back before Nate could clear his throat, not that Sunny was pining for a drink. He just didn't want to miss any of the story.

"Lucien, Lucien, could you come here?" shouted Keith through the closed kitchen door. "Lucien should hear this too. No sense trying to answer all his questions later."

By the time Sunny had poured four glasses of whiskey, Lucien Samms appeared out from the kitchen.

"Lucien, I'd like you to meet Nathan Tallhelm, Walt's brother and Trader's cousin," announced Keith.

"Glad to meet you, son. I can see that Tallhelm in your face. Boy, he's better looking than his brother, that's for sure," joked Lucien Samms, father to Everett and Ernest.

Keith sat back into his green leather chair and set his drink on one of its wide wooden armrests. The terriers, who seemed as intent on hearing what Nate had to say as everyone else, took up positions on either side of Jonathan Keith's chair. "I can't tell you how concerned we are about Trader. I'm not a religious man, but I must say I believe the hand of providence is at play here. First your brother shows up and now you. You started to say you got a message from Veronica," Jonathan Keith asked as excitedly as he allowed himself to get.

Tallhelm started his narrative from the very beginning with the arrival of Peepsight Guyer and Carl Bowersox at Bill and Ruth Darcy's place and ended it with his watching Diving Hawk, Drum Face, and Owl Eyes riding after the bighorns.

The three men sat silent the whole time, trying to make sense of everything Nate was saying. They spoke among themselves almost as if Nate weren't in the room, speculating on one thing or another. Eventually, Keith, thinking out loud, said, "I bet this has something to do with Chance Parker and that one he was with, that Herzog."

"This is a hell of a note. Did Peep say why he or Bowersox didn't go back with Veronica and help doctor Trader?" The exasperation was clear in Keith's voice and on his face. Jonathan Keith wasn't one to let things get to him. His even temper had allowed him to navigate through or around any number of dire situations. But he was a younger man then. He wondered, for the first time in his life, if he was losing a step.

"Bill Darcy asked Peepsight and Bowersox that same question. Seems like the only person Trader was willing to trust was you. When Guyer offered to go back with her, she said no. Trader told her not to come back with anyone," answered Nate.

"Hell, she may never have even gotten back to him. That's bad country she was traveling through," reasoned Keith.

"I could leave here tomorrow. If he's somewhere below the Thorn, I could find him," offered Nate. This suggestion came more in response to Nate's frustration than any body of reason. There was very little chance of Tallhelm picking up their trail before the snow, now absolutely none.

What Keith and party now knew was that Veronica and Trader were alive. Leastwise they were three weeks ago. And they thought they were holed up somewhere not far from Thorn's Peak. Aside from that, the men were still left with more questions than answers.

Keith had decided not to inform Nate of Trader's saddlebag map until it was absolutely necessary. He didn't want that circle of knowledge to grow any bigger than need be.

"Men, we're gonna have to tread water for a while till Sarusha and Walt get back. They've been gone five days now. I can't imagine them being gone much longer. Hell, of course, whoever did Trader dirt could've got Sarusha and Walt too. Frankly, I kinda doubt that. Sarusha could skin the spots off a leopard without it even taking notice. And your brother, who knows what he's capable of. In any event, Nate, you make yourself to home. Sunny will see you get settled.

"Lucien, have your boys put Nate's gear in number six, and have 'em light the stove. And if you could ask Evie to fix Nate here some grub. He looks like he could use it," directed Keith.

"Nate, you can eat out in the dining room or at the bar, wherever you like," added Sunny.

"I'll eat at the bar if it's all the same." As he reached for his saddlebags, Sunny waved him off.

"They'll be safe here. Nobody gets back here," assured Sunny.

Just the same, Nate took his rifle and his uncle's Sharps out to the bar and took a seat at the end. He laid the rifles against the side wall, just within arm's reach. Nate didn't quite know how he felt. He'd been so focused on getting to the Crow's Nest that he suspended the regular tempo of his thoughts. Once here, he was hoping to get some questions answered and some fears assuaged, but now he found himself caught in a waiting game. Limbo was a place Tallhelm preferred not to be.

The aroma of the steaming bowl of ham and bean soup Evie Samms placed in front of him chased away all thought. Nate hadn't eaten a thing since that bowl of oatmeal in the morning, a morning that seemed like three days ago. The long hard days of riding had burnt up any spare weight Ruth Darcy's home cooking had put on him. It was true. A little hunger will make a man keen, but the news about Trader had made Nate about keen enough to reach down the throat of a bobcat and yank it inside out. Thinking back over the last ten days, he'd hardly had time to strike a camp, let alone cook.

"Hi there. I'm Evie Samms."

"Nathan Tallhelm's the name. I met your boys earlier. Seem like they know what they're doing."

"They're good boys. They sure get a kick out of your brother," Evie Samms said this as she sliced a large loaf of bread into four pieces. "Would you like some water? That soup can get right salty." Evie Samms was a light-skinned native of Antigua. The beauty she had in her youth still showed, but her graceful calmness was what Nate took most note of.

"Yes, thank you. Some water would do just fine," answered Nate, wondering to himself just how they got their water up here.

"You look beat. How far you had to come to get here?" asked Evie, who had a good working knowledge of the mountains and river valleys hereabouts.

"Well, let's see. As the crow flies about four hundred miles, but overland I couldn't say. I left from down on the Snake, in Wyoming, through Teton Pass, then up the Bitterroot, to the Lolo, then over to here. I reckon eight or nine days," said Nate.

"I think by now the boys should have your gear squared away. If you're still hungry later, you can always come down and get more. Not much going here. There's a poker game at night. Just the old boys sitting around lying to each other and trading nickels," Evie said as she cleared away the empty soup bowl and the one piece of bread Nate hadn't eaten.

As he took his trail coat off the back of the barstool, he reached into his trouser pocket and brought out a five-dollar gold piece and placed it on the bar.

Seeing this, Evie began shaking her head. "Lucien said Mister Jonathan gave instructions. Anything you need, you get. No charge. Thank you, but no need for that."

"Well, that gold piece been wanting to get out of that pocket for so long. I don't have the heart to put it back in," countered Tallhelm.

With a wink, Evie said, "I'll give it to my boys. They thank you."

Tallhelm was just ready to retrieve his saddlebags from the back-room when he heard the gatehouse bell. It made him instantly think, *I hope it's Walt and that Indian, Sarusha.* Nate quickly made his way through one of the glass doors and onto the deck. Sunny wasn't far behind. Placing a spyglass onto a waiting tripod, he focused in on the four riders bunched in front of the gatehouse doors.

Sunny turned to Tallhelm, and with regret in his voice announced, "It's not Walt."

"Do you know who it is?" asked Nate, a little confused by his seeming inability to stifle his uncharacteristic curiosity.

Before Sunny answered the question, he rang a cradled ship's bell next to the tripod twice. "It's Bill Liecaster and Tubby Flint. The other two I don't know. One's a woman. Liecaster and Flint get through here about once a year. We tolerate them for a week or so, then they move on. I don't know what they're doing here, but I'm sure we'll find out." Sunny delivered this information hurriedly to Nate as he made his way off the deck and down to the stables.

Nate remained on the deck and watched the four riders for several minutes as they rode their horses out of the rear gatehouse doors and made their way to the ramp below him.

The temperature had been rising all day, and the late afternoon air no longer held a chill. Nate could see whatever snow the shovelers missed was all but melted. He could definitely see why Keith chose this spot. The view from this deck left him all but spellbound. Tallhelm lingered as the fading light of the day came streaming out of the west. He watched as the haze above the snow-covered peaks filtered the light from the setting sun and filled the sky with every shade of color one could imagine.

Nate looked down in time to see the four riders clomp up the ramp and into the stable. As the last rider, the woman, passed below him, she looked up and caught Tallhelm's eye. For an instant, their gazes met. The human alchemy that binds one person to another is mysterious. What turns one union into gold and another lead? It would seem that the former was at play here between Tallhelm and this woman. To say his curiosity was piqued would grossly understate the situation. Tallhelm shook his head out of its momentary paralysis.

Watching the horses disappear into the stable reminded him of the dun and his mule. What wonderful beasts. Nate's admiration for his animals was boundless. Before heading back into the bar to get his truck, Nate turned again to take in the sky. In that short time, the colors had faded. Now only grays and dark purples spilled out of the western sky.

Nate made his way back to the room off the kitchen, retrieved his saddlebags, and headed back out to the bar. He wondered how long Sunny would be with those new arrivals. He didn't have to wonder long because just then, Lucien came out from the kitchen and said, "Nate, I show you to your berth. Sunny's tied up. Here, I'll carry those. You grab your rifles."

Tallhelm glanced back as they left the bar. The two men were still sitting in the booth at the far end. Now they were talking.

8

BARKING IRONS

Tallhelm followed Lucien out of the bar and back along the hall-way, passed the stairs down to the stables and up a flight to the third floor. Here a corridor ran from one side of the building across to the other. In the middle of this landing was a hallway that could take you to either the front or the back of the building. Lucien turned right into the hallway, off of which were several rooms either side. Two doors down on the right was room no. 6.

Lucien put a large pewter key in the lock, turned it twice, and swung the door open, bidding Tallhelm to go inside. "Here you go, Nate. We got all your gear up here. There's a barrel of fresh water down the end of this hall. You can just put your privy bucket out here and one of the crew will get it for you. If you run low on firewood, there's plenty down the hallway and out that back door." Lucien led Tallhelm back out into the hall and pointed to a door at the end of the corridor. "There's firewood stacked either side of that door. Also, God forbid if there's a fire, there's two staircases out back. Either one will take you down to the ground."

Back in the room, Lucien looked around for a second, cracked open the casement window, and pointed to a small potbelly stove, red coals showing through the slots in its cast-iron door. "It's best leave this window cracked a mite. Let that fire breathe. I know I speak for the Captain and Sunny. It's sure good to have you here, Nate." With that, Lucien shook his hand, handed him the key, and left the room. Halfway down the hall, he stopped and came back to tell Nate, "That bowl of soup should keep the wolf from the door, but if you're still hungry, just come back downstairs and we'll fix you up."

As he nodded to Lucien, Nate thought of something himself. "Hold on a second. I almost forgot. Here, take this downstairs." Nate untied one of the packs that the mule had been carrying and took out a piece of oilcloth. Inside it was a three-quarter wheel of cheddar cheese.

"Why, thank you, Nate. Boy is Sunny gonna love this," Lucien said as he made his way out the door and down the hall.

The light from four whale-oil lamps, each placed on a small shelf in the corners of the room, flickered and slowly danced with each soft breeze that made its way through the casement window. The window was set chest high and recessed deep into the wall. Tallhelm, captivated by the unparalleled views from every deck and through every window of the Crow's Nest, pushed open the casement and peered into the deep river valley. The nearly full moon, still low on the horizon, shone brightly over the eastern rim.

The room was small but more than adequate to hold its sparse furnishings: a bed with three drawers, one next to the other, built in underneath, a plain table with a pitcher and basin atop, and a larger table and chair. A half dozen pegs were arrayed along one wall on which Tallhelm hung his canvas trail coat, retrieving the brace of double-barreled pistols from its inner lining.

Tallhelm had been wanting to do one thing since back up on the cut, and that was to clean and oil his revolver. Undoing the side flap on one of his saddlebags, he took out a small package wrapped in sackcloth and placed it on the table. Inside, neatly arranged, were the few tools Nate carried to clean and maintain his weapons. Shucking his revolver, he seated himself at the table and set to cleaning his guns. He cleaned the six-gun, and although he hadn't used them, cleaned his rifle and his uncle's Sharps fifty.

Nate had once seen a dirty rifle blow up in a man's face. The doomed man's face looked every bit like it had been dipped in stewed rhubarb. After enduring a lifetime's worth of agony, the man drew his sidearm and took his own life. None of the men present could have done anything to help the man. None offered any argument as the man probed his skull for a spot on which to brace the pistol and pull off a firm shot. Something died in Nate and all the men that held witness. To this day, that vision and its gruesome aftermath remain burnt into Tallhelm's memory.

"A man can only do so much" is a phrase that's used more as an excuse than an axiom. Nate knew the man was doomed, yet his sense of helplessness had temporarily paralyzed his soul. Relief eventually came, but not until he had to begrudgingly acknowledge the fickle and ruthless hand of fate.

Nathan Tallhelm tried never to let his gunpowder get wet or his weapons go uncleaned.

Tired but not ready to sleep, satisfied with the soup but not sated, Nate figured to go down and check on the dun and mule then make his way to the dining room. And maybe get a better gander at that woman he glimpsed earlier. Strapping on his gun belt and automatically drawing out the pistol, Tallhelm checked the heft of the big revolver in his hand. The new Smith and Wesson .44 his uncle had given him was an improvement on his old Army Colt given the fact it used cartridges rather than a cap and ball. Nate took the time to practice his draw, a discipline he adhered to and one that could easily mean the difference between life and death. Satisfied, he took the key with its green enameled 6 molded into the bow, locked the door, and made his way down to the stables.

"Which one are you, Ernest or Everett?" asked Tallhelm as he got to the bottom of the double flight of stairs.

"I'm Everett. I'm the oldest," answered the Samms boy, who had watched Tallhelm come down the stairs and was ready at the bottom with a lantern. Everett handed Nate the lantern and grabbing a spare, lit it and beckoned Nate to follow. Nate followed him past a series of stalls along the eastern wall.

The dun and mule, sensing Tallhelm nearby, were alert and poised as the lantern light caught their turned heads. "Hey, boys," Tallhelm greeted his mounts like the old friends they were.

"Mister, I'm leaving this lantern. You fetch it back, okay?" said Everett.

"Here. Take this for you and your brother." Nate handed the boy two silver dollars.

"You don't hafta do that, mister." The boy's tone was genuine.

"Nah, take that as a little extra for looking after my beasts so well."

"Thanks, Mister Nate," the grateful Everett responded as he walked back toward the front, to the light shining out of a tack room doorway. As he walked, he jangled the silver dollars in his pocket, anxious to tell his brother and add them to the five-dollar gold piece his mother had given them earlier.

Tallhelm wasn't accustomed to other people doing for him. Whatever he needed, he mostly rustled for himself. He rarely had much use for money. What little bit he had to buy was limited to ammo, basic provisions, and feed for the mounts, maybe an occasional wool shirt and trousers. Fact was, over the last several years, he had been able to save better than a thousand dollars. Bill Darcy kept this in a strongbox, hidden somewhere at the ranch.

Tallhelm, satisfied that the animals were being well taken care of, fetched the spare lantern off the wooden peg and made his way back to the staircase.

The energy he got from the bowl of soup earlier was beginning to fade; some supper would do just fine. Making his way back up to the bar, Nate stopped for a moment at the door. Again, reaching up and gently pushing the hanging lantern, he noticed how noisy the bar had become compared to the time before. Evidently, the Crow's Nest had more denizens than Tallhelm was aware of. As it was second nature to him, Nate checked the feel of his .44 in its holster and entered the room.

Tallhelm's green eyes were met by those of a dozen men. Sunny, who was standing behind the bar, gave Nate a big smile and beckoned him to have a seat.

"Hey, Sunny, did I miss supper?"

The evening had grown later than Nate realized. Looking past the bar and into the dining room, Nate saw Evie clearing off the last of the dirty plates and setting out coffee cups in preparation for breakfast.

"Yeah, but I'm sure Evie can rustle up something for ya."

Of the six stools in front of the bar, only one was occupied, and that only by a man getting another bottle to bring back to one of the tables.

Three of the four booths were occupied. The booth closest to the deck, whose glass doors at night now appeared like frosted black mirrors, was still home to the two men from earlier in the day. In the next booth were two men, one very tall and stocky and one tall and very thin, almost gaunt. These two were Bill Liecaster and Tubby Flint, two of the four who arrived in the late afternoon. The next booth was empty, and in the last one, closest to the bar, sat the woman and an older man, who appeared to be her father.

At one of two large round tables in the middle of the room sat five men playing poker. At the other table sat one man who was joined by the man who was returning from the bar with a bottle of whiskey.

When Tallhelm entered the room, a distinct murmur went up from the men at the poker table, occasionally giving sidelong glances toward Tallhelm. Those in the booths gave Nate a cursory look and then returned to their conversations.

"What you drinking, Nate?" asked Sunny as he cleaned a fresh glass, looked at it in the light, and set it in front of Tallhelm.

"Is that a bottle of Scotch whiskey I see there?" asked Nate.

"Sure is. Some of the finest sipping whiskey west of the Mississippi."

"I'll have some of that, thank you. I must say, I don't know how Keith does it, but that shelf of brown goods could rival anything I ever saw in St. Louis or Kansas City," an obviously impressed Tallhelm responded.

"The Captain likes the best and doesn't mind paying to get it here. Ah, here's your grub," announced Sunny as Evie Samms placed a plate with a large venison steak with baked yams and stewed tomatoes alongside.

"Thank you, Mrs. Samms. Man, does that smell good," said Nate.

"I thought you might be coming back down, so I had this steak ready in case. We want to keep you well fed. Don't want to give a Tallhelm anything to complain about, right, Sunny?" said Evie as she gave Nate and Sunny a smile.

"Looks like these dogs like the smell of this steak too," said Nate as he looked down at the two terriers, who were no doubt hoping Nate would drop them a morsel. "Evie, are these your boys' dogs?" asked Nate.

"No, them dogs are the captain's, but they think they belong to whoever got food in front of them. Don't worry about givin' them anything. They get plenty." Satisfied that Nate had what he needed, Evie nodded and retreated back through the curtain and into the kitchen.

Nate had scarcely sliced into his steak when one of the poker players came up to him and said, "I'm Brow Herman. I've known your brother Walt longer than I can rightly recall, and I must say it's a genuine pleasure to meet you, Nate. It is Nate, right?" The burly man extended his right hand to Tallhelm, a hand that Nate thought was about as big as a ham hock, and placed the other on Nate's back.

Nate, compelled to put down his knife, gave Brow Herman a firm handshake. "Well, you've seen a lot more of my brother lately than I have. I haven't seen him in nigh on twenty years." Before Nate had a chance to cut another piece of steak, two more men from the table crowded around Nate, wanting to shake his hand.

Sunny made the introductions and then implored the men to let Nate finish his supper. There was no way anyone in the room could miss the stir Nate's arrival at the bar had occasioned. As Nate went about finishing his food, one voice could be heard above the others.

"Hey, Fritz, who is this big celebrity?" asked one of the two men sitting at a table, the scoffing voice heavy with an unmistakable German accent.

"I don't know, Conrad. He must be someone special," answered Fritz. His words, however, lacked both the bravado and scorn of his partner's.

"He doesn't look like much of anything special to me," continued the man who Nate later learned was Conrad Drager, supposedly a famous hunter visiting the American Northwest in search of rare game. Evidently, he had some blank spots on the walls of his trophy room and sought to remedy that.

Nate couldn't help but take notice and looked to Sunny to somehow gauge whether this was shaping up to be a threat or just some loudmouth who had had too much to drink.

Sunny just shook his head, indicating he didn't think much would come of it, and added, "Nah, we just ignore him."

"Where you from, friend? We don't get many legends up this way," continued Conrad, his tone missing the sarcasm he had intended.

Tallhelm, no longer able to ignore the man, turned and looked Conrad Drager straight in the eye and said, "It would seem there's one too many legends hereabouts."

"Easy, Conrad. Don't get yourself shot. We're impressed. Leave it at that," leveled Sunny, annoyance more than apparent in his voice.

"Yeah, Conrad, there's room in the cemetery for everyone." This bit of information was offered by one of the dark figures slouching in the end booth. One of the two men Tallhelm had seen there earlier in the day. He appeared to be both young and deadly.

"Who you talking about, Dean?" asked the slouching man's friend as he returned from the bar with a fresh bottle of whiskey.

"Krautface and his friend," answered Dean.

"For Christ's sake, Dean, have some respect for the dearly departed," sarcastically chided Aldo Severman, Dean's equally deadly but more sober friend.

"Who are you calling dearly departed?" asked Conrad, all of a sudden real concern evident in his voice.

"Aldo, who are you calling the dearly departed anyway?" asked Dean.

"These two," Aldo Severman, using the bottom end of the bottle as a pointer in his outstretched arm, indicated Conrad and Fritz.

"Yeah, Conrad. Herzog is looking for men. Why don't you boys slope? If you leave now, maybe you could get there by dawn." The sarcastic Severman was caught up in the sound of his own voice and comfortable in the knowledge that he could draw on either of the Germans before they could even think about clearing leather.

When Conrad opened his mouth, he didn't figure on buying into anything with Severman or Dean.

Sunny, for his part, was intrigued by what Severman had said about. "Herzog looking for men?"

The old man and younger woman sitting in the booth near the bar were similarly intrigued by the mention of Herzog's name. They abruptly stopped their conversation and leaned out of the booth to get a look at who had mentioned his name.

Severman continued with the taunts. "You two can leave now or not. You call it," he said as he placed the bottle carefully and precisely over one of the many water-stained rings on the tabletop.

Tallhelm didn't like this at all. Big louts like Conrad were always overloading their mouths. Too bad he might get killed for it. Conrad Drager may have killed a man, maybe several. But most likely his killing was done formally, either in the military or a gentleman's duel. That was a hemisphere away from Severman and Dean. They were killers. Their disregard for human life was apparent in every manner and movement. Every situation was seen through the hungry eye. This deadly banter was only for the spectators. These men communicated to one another silently, like sharks cruising a lagoon, circling a kill.

Severman wore a long-barreled sidearm, holstered to his right leg. As Dean slid out of the booth and stood up, the blood rushed to his head and caused the thin gunfighter to stumble, only regaining his balance after staggering into two men seated at the poker table. Mild protest went up from the gamblers. Not enough protest, however, to cause the deadly pair to redirect their ire. Tallhelm could easily see why they hadn't been braced before. They were setting to kill Conrad Drager and Fritz, seemingly for no other reason than boredom.

Tallhelm saw Dean was wearing a double rig. The revolvers were short-barreled and lashed low to his hips.

"Okay, Drager, you Kraut-faced piece of dog shit, get up!" The weaving Dean delivered this command while the tall menacing Severman stood dead still and watched every move Fritz Langer made. Or didn't make, as it appeared Fritz Langer was frozen to his chair.

When Conrad continued to ignore Dean, Dean screeched, "Get up!"

With that, Conrad slowly turned to face Dean, the German's fair skin turning several shades lighter as all the blood in his body sought his pounding heart.

"Hell, I wasn't buying into nothing with you, Dean," stammered the man as he looked quickly to his lifelong friend Fritz Langer.

"Here's the deal, Conrad. I put my trigger fingers into these bottles." With that, Dean stuffed the forefinger of each hand into two empty whiskey bottles that sat on the table. Dean dangled his arms, the whiskey bottles reaching well past the short gunfighter's boot tops.

"You figured it out yet, Drager, you goddamn Kraut? Aldo, get me a blindfold. Conrad don't think it's fair yet," scoffed Dean, obviously enjoying his sinister high jinks.

Tallhelm had no doubt Dean could shuck the bottles and have his guns drawn before Conrad could even start to move his sidearm. Dean was a killer. In his mind, Conrad's body was already on the floor.

Tallhelm looked to Sunny to see if he had any play of his own in mind. "Goddamn you, Dean. Don't you break those bottles. You know Keith's particular about saving bottles."

"Forget the bottles. I got money." All of a sudden, Dean's voice was level and sober.

Up to this point, the poker game had continued at its own even pace. There had been no break in the deal of the cards and the clink of the gold and silver coins. But once Dean had risen to his feet, the men at the table stopped their game and intently watched as the drama unfolded.

As Tallhelm looked past Sunny toward the bulge coming through the kitchen curtain, Fritz Langer rose to his feet. "Captain Keith, do something. Do some…"

Fritz didn't get to finish the word.

Dean had dropped the bottles off his fingers and had his irons out and barking before Conrad even touched his piece. Dean's first shot went straight through Conrad's neck, and the bullet caught Fritz Langer in the cheek. The wide-eyed Fritz moved his mouth for a moment then spit the bullet out as Conrad reached for his throat. Dean's next two shots drove Conrad backward. Fritz, vainly trying to keep his dying friend upright but unable to, went sprawling to the floor, the dead and bloody Conrad landing face up on top of him.

"Enough! Stay put, Fritz," bellowed Keith. As Keith hollered *enough*, Severman drew his piece. Tallhelm couldn't believe a man could be so fast. One moment Severman was watching Conrad die, the next he was drawing a bead on Keith's chest.

Keith was ready. His big deep mortise chisel flew out of his hand, his outstretched arm pointing the direction of flight. The chisel's wooden handle cracked into the back of Severman's wrist as he instinctively turned to avoid it. His gun, jarred loose from his grip, hit the floor. The bullet in the chamber struck by the firing pin zinged across the room, lodging itself in the ceiling after passing through the parchment shade of the lamp hanging over the poker table. Thankfully, the bullet missed its glass kerosene globe on its way to the ceiling.

Dean whirled on Keith, disbelief and rage burning from his bloodshot eyes. "Keith, you bastard." Dean spit the words at the stocky but agile Keith.

"Move, Keith!" Tallhelm shouted as he pushed himself away from the bar. Keith had turned just in time to hear a bullet whiz past his face. Dean's second and third bullets splintered the back of the barstool Tallhelm had just vacated.

Nate fisted his six-gun and started sending lead into Dean's body. His first two shots exploded the pouch of tobacco in Dean's breast pocket. His second two shots shattered the firing pins on Dean's guns, tearing off the wan gunfighter's thumbs in the process. Dean had little time to contemplate his empty hands as images of his short life flashed through his brain.

Staggering toward the bar, he managed to remain erect long enough to find Severman's eyes. Severman, frozen by the dying man's stare, watched Dean back himself up to the bar and remain there, casually standing for the briefest of moments, before his lifeless body slid to the floor, cracking the back of his limp head on the bar as he crumpled to the floor.

Tallhelm didn't like killing one bit, but Dean had opened the ball. The room, thick with gun smoke, began to smart Tallhelm's eyes. Nevertheless, as he delivered his message to Dean, he had kept a watchful eye on Aldo Severman.

The man was a study in human conflict. One thing was certain in Severman's mind. He was going to kill this stranger whatever it takes. As sure as the sun rises, he was going to kill this man. Severman just looked at Sunny, then Keith, then Tallhelm as he sat heavily in a chair.

Severman didn't quite know who he was without Dean. The two had been together since they left Memphis some fifteen years before. Dean had been nothing more than a kid then. Severman, who was older by twenty years, had talked Dean into sticking up his uncle's store. In the bungled caper, Dean's aunt and uncle were killed, and his young cousin was trampled by the horses the escaping men had stampeded. The poor boy never recovered his faculties. From that day on, he never ventured farther than the two lots his father's store was built on. Dean, on the other hand, ranged far and wide. He and Severman fled Memphis and began a spree of robbery, rape, and murder. The volatile Dean, haunted by the look in his young cousin's eyes, was almost too much for even Severman to handle. Dean had turned on him a few times, blaming him for his torturous headaches and ceaseless life on the run.

Severman hated Tallhelm more than he thought he could hate. Dean, for all his hot-tempered ways, was all the homicidal gunslinger had.

Tallhelm walked over to Severman's gun lying on the floor as he dropped the spent casings from his revolver. One by one, he reloaded each chamber, flipping the gun back closed. He then kicked Severman's gun across the floor. It stopped at the man's feet.

"I don't know you, but whoever you are, I don't want to be watching my back for the rest of my life, so why don't we just finish this now?" said Nate.

"Yeah, you'd like that, you son of a bitch. My goddamned wrist is broken!" a near-hysterical Severman screamed, hate and anguish cracking his voice.

"Shut up, you bastard," cautioned Keith. "You could be lying there with your friend real quick if you don't watch your mouth."

Sunny had retrieved Keith's heavy squared-bodied chisel. The old man stuffed it back into its sheath, which was sown into his wide black leather belt. Keith had perfected throwing the long deep-set mortising chisel while on his many sea voyages. Depending on the desired result, he could have it hit its target blade first or handle first. He wasn't trying to kill Severman, just knock the gun out of his hand. Which was what it did.

"What's it going to be, Severman?" Keith leveled as he watched the gunfighter rise from his chair and shuffle to Dean's lifeless body.

Severman reached down and closed the eyes of his young friend. "Stranger, if I was you, I'd be enjoying my next couple of meals. They'll be your last." With that, he stepped over Dean's crumpled body and made for the door.

"Not so fast, Aldo. You're going to have to pay to bury Dean."

"Let him do it. He's the one what kilt him," responded Aldo Severman as he tilted his head in Nate's direction.

"Sage, you and Johnny need some money?" asked Keith of two of the five men who had been playing poker.

"Yeah, Captain, we'll bury Dean," answered the young Sage Heck, who evidently could speak for Johnny Dollars.

"Okay then. Check his pockets and take off that double rig. That can be part of the pay. One of you can have his horse as well. That should cover it." Keith spoke all this with a purposely matter-of-fact tone, sending the message to Severman that he could expect no compassion from him or anyone else at the Crow's Nest.

"Aldo, I'm gonna need that pistol. I can't have you back shooting Tallhelm here. Sunny, get that weapon," instructed Keith.

Severman, who had awkwardly placed his gun back in its holster with his left hand, simply turned to the side and let Sunny remove it. The rage burning in his eyes could have lit a rock on fire. With one last attempt to salvage some pride, he backed out the door and spit on the floor as he did so.

"Captain. We can't do this till the morning," stated Sage.

"I know that. Get him down to the stables and out to the oil shed. I don't want that body in here overnight." A note of weariness had crept into Keith's voice.

"Fritz, you come over here and let Evie have a look at your face. I'll get some men to help you bury Conrad, but we want his body down in the oil shed tonight," said Sunny.

Fritz Langer, in a state of shock, simply nodded his reply as he sat on one of the barstools and hardly winced as Evie Samms swabbed the hole in his cheek with some whiskey.

Bill Liecaster and Tubby Flint, who must have gotten his nickname sometime before the ravages of consumption had reduced him to a rail-thin wraith, had simply watched the whole incident with little more than bored curiosity.

The old man and younger woman, however, watched every second of the gunfight with riveted attention. There was a lot more going on here than either Keith, Sunny, or Tallhelm knew about. And it all involved the man Severman had mentioned—Herzog.

Once Severman had left the room, the pair approached Keith and asked if there was someplace they could speak in private. Since arriving earlier in the evening, Keith had learned little about why they had hired Liecaster and Flint to bring them to the Crow's Nest.

Now it seemed that was to change.

9

EVIL'S AFOOT

M iles Haverstraw and his daughter, Lorraine, were not the usual travelers who showed up at the Crow's Nest. And Keith said as much when they first met earlier in the evening. But then again, Keith had learned not to rule out much of anything when it came to the why and what for in people's personal lives. The pair simply said they were looking for a relative and had heard he might have come this way. Keith had been around long enough to know when someone was being less than forthright. He figured the old man and his daughter had their reasons and left it at that.

Now, as they requested a private moment, he escorted them to the same room off the kitchen where he had met with Nate. Before leaving the bar, he asked Sunny to bring their drinks back. The pair seemed grateful for Keith's gracious hospitality, but the last thing on their minds was drinks.

"Mister Keith, my father and I owe you an apology. We've learned it best to give as little information as possible until we're sure just who's who and what's what. That man said, 'Herzog is looking for men.' Do you know what he meant?" asked Lorraine Haverstraw as her father busied himself whittling a piece wood he picked off the pile of firewood stacked next to the potbelly stove sitting in the corner of the room.

"Can't say I do. But we suspect this Herzog has something to do with a friend of ours being bushwhacked," answered Keith.

"Then you know Bertram Herzog?" asked Lorraine, a heightened note of curiosity in her voice as she and her father exchanged glances. "Is this the man you know as Herzog?" With that, Lorraine produced two Wanted posters from inside her vest pocket. "Was this woman with him?"

"Yes, that's the man. I only met him once. He and a man named Parker, whom I do know, they were through here about six weeks ago. They stayed a few days and left, saying they were heading to Missoula. They weren't traveling with a woman, leastwise not when they were here. I've never seen the woman. I know the man he was with, Chance Parker. He's a no good. Why, what do you know about this Herzog?" asked Keith, his curiosity piqued by the apparent knowledge of Herzog these two possessed.

"My father and I have been tracking Bertram Herzog and Marlene Scabbe for the better part of eleven years. I'm not sure if way out here you would have heard of the Lautenburg fire?"

"Of course I've heard of the Lautenburg fire. Who hasn't? Fifty some people killed when a grain elevator exploded," answered Keith, uncharacteristically brusque in defense of his knowledge of the general goings-on in the rest of the country. Keith privately bristled when he was labeled a recluse, or worse yet, a hermit.

"Well, it was sixty-five people that were killed, and it wasn't any accident. Bertram Herzog and this Marlene Scabbe caused the explosion that started the fire. Mister Keith, Bertram Herzog and this woman are evil incarnate. You said your friend was bushwhacked. Well, I'd say Herzog would most likely be the one responsible. That man Severman, we have to find out what he knows, and soon. Whatever Herzog is up to doesn't bode well for you or any of these people here. You can be sure of that," said Lorraine.

"Let me get this straight. You and your father have been trailing this man and woman for eleven years. Can I ask why?" said Keith.

"That explosion killed my mother, two of my brothers and my sister, an aunt, an uncle, and three cousins, plus most of our friends and neighbors." Lorraine reached over and touched her father on the knee as he continued to whittle the piece of wood into the figure of a man.

"We were farmers, Mister Keith. We had a good life. We were happy. Then Bertram Herzog and Marlene Scabbe came to town and destroyed our lives forever. We're not farmers anymore. We're man-hunters. And we're going to see this man Herzog dangle from the end of a rope." Lorraine had remained fairly calm while delivering this information to Keith, but anger and bile had overtaken that composure, and she fairly spit out these last words.

"My father and I want to question this Severman and do it at gunpoint if necessary." Lorraine, to accent her statement, produced a short-barreled pistol from a shoulder holster and placed it on the table. "If he is duplicitous with Herzog, he's as guilty as he is and liable to answer to the full extent of the law."

Keith thought to himself, sure enough, these two were no longer farmers. They sounded more like lawmen than lawmen.

"I heard this Severman say he was going to avenge his friend's death. Do you think he meant it?" asked Lorraine.

"Oh, he meant it, all right. No doubt about that," said Keith.

"Well, in that case, he'll be here as long as that other man sticks around. Who is he anyway?" asked a more than mildly curious Lorraine.

"That's Nathan Tallhelm. He's cousin to Trader Darcy, the one who got bushwhacked. About talking to Severman, let's hold off on that for a day or so. He's not going anywhere, and right now we're waiting for two of my men to return from a reconnoiter. Maybe we won't need anything from him after all. Most likely he'd just lie to us anyway."

"As with so many places I've been, I wish the circumstances were different. Your place here is quite a sight to behold."

"Thank you. I trust your accommodations are suitable. We don't get too many ladies up this way."

"More than suitable. Thank you."

"How exactly did you know Herzog had come this way?"

"We tracked him to San Francisco, and from there to Portland. It took some doing, but we got word he paid someone to get him to Lewiston. It seems he was in search of this man Clayton Pealeday."

"Did you say Clayton Pealeday?"

"Yes, Clayton Pealeday. We were lucky in Portland. Herzog was asking around about this Pealeday, so we just went to Pealeday's place on the Snake. We missed him there by about a month. Herzog must be getting either reckless or emboldened because he's usually much more careful about covering his tracks. We've heard rumors that this Pealeday wants to start some kind of legal action to keep up around here Canadian territory."

"Well, I imagine you've heard of the Pealeday Cascades. That was disputed territory when Clayton Pealeday put his name to it. Now it's part of the Idaho Territory. He's not happy about it and hasn't been for years. He was a military man and makes no bones about using force to get his way. Maybe he's cooking something up with this Bertram Herzog. I don't know. I've had a few run-ins with Pealeday. There's still bad blood. Chance Parker is no prize either, as bad as they come.

"In any event, we can't do much about this tonight. And I've got to see what's going on out front. If you need anything, just ask Sunny. If he can't help you, he'll get someone who can."

As Keith, Lorraine, and Miles got up from the table, Miles Haverstraw, who had been silent the whole time while he whittled the piece of firewood into the shape of a perfect miniature man, opened the door to the stove and tossed the figure into the fire. As he watched it burn, and without turning toward Keith asked, "When did you say your men would be back?"

"I don't rightly know. They're expected anytime."

"I don't think it was just random gunplay when that man took a shot at you. This has Herzog's stench all over it. If I were you, I'd check to see if that man Severman has more money in his caboodle than what a man of his means should. Trust me on this, Keith. When either Herzog or Scabbe are close by, believe me, evil is afoot."

With that, Keith escorted Lorraine and Miles back out to the bar and told Sunny, "Whatever Miles and Miss Haverstraw here need, please make sure they get it. Also, keep an eye on Severman. We got to get a handle on this. Tell the men to keep their wits about 'em. We're heading into rough waters."

Jonathan Keith stopped and stood next to Nate and asked, "You okay? I'm not used to owing people, but I expect I owe you my life. Thank you, son." Keith, not waiting for an answer, poured himself a short drink, drank it down, parted the curtain to the kitchen, and could be heard asking, "Evie, how bad is that fella's bullet wound?"

"He'll be okay, Cap. Lot better than his friend," said Evie, evidently able to muster a bit of cynicism on occasion. "Cap, should I be worried about my boys?"

"Well, Evie, tell your boys to do what I just told Sunny. Just keep their wits about 'em." Having issued his last word on the matter, he headed out the rear door of the kitchen and up the private staircases that led to his quarters on the uppermost floor of the Crow's Nest.

10

POKER AND PRAISE

Tallhelm watched Sage Heck and Johnny Dollars undo Dean's double rig of six-shooters and empty his pockets.

"Sunny, look here," said Sage, holding up a leather poke with a bit of heft to it, wondering if the contents would also be part of their pay, along with Dean's guns and horse.

"Whaddya got, Sage?" asked Sunny as he and Brow Herman wrapped a towel around Conrad Drager's neck in an effort to prevent more blood from spilling onto the floor.

"Dean had this poke on him, bunch of double eagles," answered Sage.

"Here, let me see that. Your deal was for the guns and horse, but we'll let the Cap decide. Maybe we should spread it around. Hell, we all should get paid for just being around that son of…" Sunny broke off his comment, catching himself before he crossed some ethical line he had personally drawn. "Wasn't a lucky day for Dean, but just might be a lucky day for you two. Anyway, we'll see.

"Johnny, go downstairs and get Dean's trail blanket. We'll wrap him in that. Lahr, can you see if Evie needs any help with Fritz? Bill, come here and see about cleaning up this floor. Nate, you just sit there and help yourself to whatever you want. We owe you a lot. I swear Dean was gunning for the captain." Sunny hollered this from across the room as he opened the doors out to the deck to help let the smoke clear.

Once Severman had left the room, Nate retook a seat at the bar. Not the one from before. The back of that one was all shot to hell, thanks to Dean. No part of Nate liked killing. But true as that may be, he sure as hell liked living a lot more. Dean chose his play. No one to blame but himself.

"Where they gonna bury those men?" asked Nate as Lucien came through the curtain behind the bar and poured Nate another glass of whiskey.

"We got a cemetery up by the cut. First on, we'd toss bodies over the side. But you could only do that in the spring when the river fills the valley. Any other time, the body would just lay on the rocks till what it got ate up. No, we don't do that anymore. We have a cemetery now. Looks like we be adding to it some. I heard what Sunny said. We owe you, son. We're all powerful keen on keeping the Captain alive. You want anything, you just let me or you let Sunny know."

"I will, Lucien. I will," said Tallhelm.

Nate's mind was awash with thoughts and emotions, two men dead, Walt could show up anytime, that woman and her father, where'd they go, this Crow's Nest, Diving Hawk, what time is it…? Nate sat at the bar and finished one drink and poured himself another. He should be dead tired, but he wasn't. Nothing like facing down a trigger-happy gunslinger to get ya keyed up. Nate felt the cool air coming in from the porch and found its freshness begin to settle his mind. Leaving half a glass of whiskey on the bar, he walked out to the deck and up to the railing.

The moon was full risen and bright as could be. Looking down below, he watched as Sage and Johnny brought Dean's body out of the stable and over to a little stone building. Evidently, this is where the whale oil and kerosene were stored. Nate doubted there were many critters around, given the Nest's accessibility, or rather lack of it. But either way, you wouldn't want to be leaving dead bodies laying out in the open.

Soon, Sunny and Brow Herman came out carrying Conrad Drager. Conrad was a much bigger man than Dean, and he could see Brow Herman was relieved when Sage and Johnny each took a leg and left Brow to hold open the oil shed door. These men worked together like the crew on a ship, pitching in wherever needed without having to be told. Keith must have been one of those benign captains, relying on trust and respect rather than the lash.

Aside from the macabre shuffling of the dead bodies, the night itself couldn't be nicer. The crisp air of the day had turned into a clear and balmy night. Tallhelm could only think of one thing that would make the moment better, and that would be the company of that young lady he saw arrive earlier and only glimpsed for an instant this evening, as she sat in that booth, before all the shooting started. He hoped she wouldn't hold that against him. Nate wouldn't have too long to wait to find out because just then, he got the gentlest of taps on his shoulder.

"I want to thank you, Mister Tallhelm, for stopping that man before he killed anyone else. I don't even know you, yet somehow I feel your being alive is of grave importance to my father and myself. I'm usually not this forward. I'm Lorraine Haverstraw, and this is my father, Miles."

Miles Haverstraw nodded and shook Nate's hand. "I understand your cousin has come to no good," said Miles.

"It's more like no good had come and found him," said Nate, as he instantly wasn't quite sure what he had said, transfixed as he was with the warm sadness in Lorraine's eyes.

"Lorraine, I'm headed upstairs. I trust you won't be too long. Night, Mister Tallhelm." Miles touched his worn flat-brimmed hat and wearily walked across the deck and back into the bar.

"My, but I think I've never seen stars so bright or so many of them. This Captain Keith sure built him some kind of place here," said Lorraine as she leaned against the railing and stared up at the sky. "I wonder just how he was able to get this place built."

"I asked Lucien that same thing. Turns out, Captain Keith, when he puts his mind to something, not much can thwart him."

Nate walked over to the eastern railing of the deck and motioned Lorraine to come take a look. He pointed to the northern rim with its wide waterfall spilling into the basin below, feeding the river that flowed past the bottom of the towering crag the Crow's Nest was built on.

"Turns out building the Nest wasn't as impossible as it might seem. Lucien told me the captain and his men built a water-wheel sawmill up above those falls and logged timber out of the forest north of there. They floated the logs down to the mill, cut 'em, sent them over the falls, floated them to right below us, and hoisted them up. He had a crew of twenty. Sure looks like they knew what they were doin'."

Tallhelm and Lorraine stood next to one another in silence, enjoying the view and the evening air. Eventually, Lorraine spoke. "Somewhere out there is the man my father and I have been chasing for nigh on eleven years. There was a woman involved, too, but she seems to be elsewhere. Sometimes we'd only miss them by a month, a week, a day. This time, I think we at last got him." Lorraine's chest heaved as she gave a deep sigh. "Mister Tallhelm…"

"Please call me Nate."

"Well, Nate, I hope everything works out for your cousin and my father and I get to end this nightmare we're in. I'll see that man Herzog swing from the end of a rope if it's the last thing I do on this earth. You have a good night." Lorraine's tone was all of a sudden world-weary and sad as she turned away from Nate and headed back into the bar.

Tallhelm remained on the deck and watched Lorraine navigate the men returning to the poker table. He didn't quite know what to make of Lorraine Haverstraw. She was soft-spoken yet carried a pistol in a shoulder holster. One minute she was gazing at the stars, the next talking about hanging a man. He promised himself he would endeavor to find out just who this woman was.

"Hey, Nate, how about a little poker? We could always use some new blood in the game," came a voice from inside the bar.

Hearing this, Thaedell Lahr quickly cuffed Johnny Dollars lightly on the back of the head, evidently for his insensitive use of the word *blood*.

"Don't mind if I do," answered Nate. More than happy to turn his mind to something other than the plight of Trader and Veronica, which had consumed his very being for the last ten days.

Lucien brought Nate's half-finished glass of whiskey over to the table and cautioned, "Nate, if you shook hands with any of these boys, you better count your fingers. They got a way of making what's yours theirs."

"Nate, don't pay Lucien no mind. He just gots to be the worst poker player what ever drew a hand of cards," said Brow Herman.

"That ain't what keeps me from joining you boys. I just like to know what I got today, I'll have tomorrow" was Lucien's retort as he looked at the red stain on the floor before returning to the bar.

"Nate, you've met Lahr here and Bill Diehl. These two are Sage Heck and Jerome Corwell, but we just call him Johnny, Johnny Dollars." Brow Herman, having finished with the introductions, announced, "Draw, five card. Boys, we got some fresh money in the game tonight."

Tallhelm quickly emphasized that point by putting a five-dollar gold piece in the pot and drawing out four silver ones. For now, he put aside the business about Trader. Keith was calling the shots here. All Nate had to concern himself with was the lousy hand of cards Brow Herman had just dealt him. As Tallhelm arranged his cards, Severman returned to the bar, causing the air in the room to grow still. He retook his place at the booth from earlier, and with his right arm in a sling and his left firmly gripping the neck of a whiskey bottle, kept himself on a slow boil, occasionally looking toward Nate and the others at the poker table.

The men looked at the steely-eyed figure of Aldo Severman and then to Tallhelm, then back to Severman.

Speculation on the eventual outcome of the matter between these two added an additional measure of drama to an already charged atmosphere at the Crow's Nest. Everyone knew one of these men would be dead before too long. Bets would have been placed, but no one wanted to bet against Nate, and surely no one wanted to bet on Aldo Severman.

Although, betting on Severman would not have been a bad bet. A few years back, Sage Heck and Thaedell Lahr had seen him in action at the Settlement Bar, a bucket-of-blood saloon on the outskirts of Lewiston.

Who knows how it started, but before you knew it, Dean had upset a table, drew his two pistols and while ducking and diving, shot four men, two fatally. Severman, on the other hand, stood dead still, eyeballing the whole room, waiting to see if anyone was looking to join in. Well, three friends of whoever Dean had shot went for their pieces, and before you could blink, Severman had his long-barreled revolver out and shot all three. It wasn't nothing fancy, just light-ning-fast and slick. "Slick as a peeled onion," according to Sage Heck.

Nate Tallhelm was fast, but Severman could very well be faster.

Although everyone had known Severman as a menace, they feared with Dean gone he was like dynamite waiting to be lit. The hate burning in his eyes prevented him from seeing anything but a neat bullet hole between Tallhelm's thick brows.

Nate moved his place at the table so he was facing the end booth. He didn't expect Severman to make a play tonight, but just the same he wasn't going to expose his back either in an effort to prove himself wrong.

The conversation at the table was good-natured and limited to the play of the cards. Any player who had the skill or good fortune to win several hands was ridiculed for being in covenant with the devil or, worse yet, had solicited the Lord Almighty on behalf of his meager stake. By the same token, the player down on his luck was facetiously accorded the sympathy reserved for the absent of wit.

The play of the cards gave Nate the respite he had hoped for. The easy rhythm of the game, with its good-natured jokes and jibes, was a tonic Tallhelm drank in. He had never stayed one place long enough to be part of any group. But tonight, he felt a part of this. These men, although strangers, made Nate feel at home. He knew his trail would fork soon enough, but tonight the warmth of the softly lit room and the friendly banter was all he needed.

With each rotation of the deal, Nate found his tumultuous thoughts dropping away from him. The chance turn of a card was gladly exchanged for the life-and-death drama that had brought him here. Tallhelm had never stayed close to whiskey, but tonight he found himself topping off the black tar Sunny swore was coffee with an upturned bottle of Irish more than a few times.

The bar was empty except for the men at the poker table and Aldo Severman. Bill Liecaster and Tubby Flint had left not too long after the gunfight. The two hadn't spoken a word to anyone either upon their arrival or departure. Judging from the scowl on Liecaster's face, Nate could see the man was trouble with a capital *T*. He also wondered how Lorraine and her father had fared with these two as their guide on their way here. Sunny would make an appearance now and then, mostly to jam another piece of firewood into one of the two large stoves in the room. Sunny liked to keep the stoves well-fed and burning hot.

It turns out Sunny had been shipwrecked years ago off the tip of South America. For two weeks, he was marooned on an ice floe hardly bigger than the bed of a flat wagon. Stranded on the floe, the splintered remnant of a small shore boat his only protection from the incessant wind, the man came close to losing his mind. With the tortured economy of a crazed miser, he scraped enough tinder off the shore boat to keep the smallest of fires burning. Each small splinter helped sustain not only the fire but Sunny's mind as well. After two weeks, what was left of the boat could no longer shield his curled-up body from the wind. The buffeting left him drawn, leaving his raw nerves enraged and his mind no longer in check.

As the wind quashed the last of his fire, the flame no bigger than that of a candle wick, he lashed out at his fate. He had long passed praying. His prayers were more raw than prayers should be, but prayer still. Are prayers followed by curses any less worthy of heavenly attention? Sunny believed his were the truest form of supplications a man could make. Had they fallen on deaf ears?

The fire was out, night was but an hour off, and he knew darkness would bring death.

The merchant Captain blown off course by the same storm as the one that sank the ship Sunny had been on was cursing his luck when he spotted a dark speck clinging to an ice floe. He had no other thought than it must be a seal. But even in the skimming glare of the setting sun, something the Captain saw hinted that it might be a man.

The Captain was astounded to find the shipwrecked sailor alive, if not altogether fit. The sailor recovered from his ordeal. He had managed to keep all his fingers and toes, but his life would never be the same. His will to live had been tested and had triumphed. The victory was tinged by a cautious foreboding. It seemed that before he spotted the lights of the ship, Sunny had firmly wed his mind to the handmaiden of despair. Try as he might, she would never be far from his side.

Swearing off the sea, Sunny confided in the captain his new landlubber status. The captain asked him if he had ever heard of Jonathan Keith, the shipbuilder captain. The question scarcely called for a reply. Anyone sailing blue water knew of Keith, but Sunny had thought him long dead. This very ship, with its race-day rigging and low-to-the-water aft deck, bore the unmistakable look of a vessel crafted by Keith.

The captain, a close friend of Keith's through his shipbuilding and sailing days, had helped Keith ferry men and equipment up the Snake when he first embarked on his Crow's Nest adventure. He knew where the Crow's Nest was and drew a map showing the route.

When Sunny arrived at Keith's two years later, his letter of introduction was placed in a small drawer along with a dozen others. Sunny had found what he was looking for, a home where the footing was firm and the horizon steady.

Nate's attention drifted away from the card game as he thought of the prospect of seeing his brother, Walt, sometime soon. How long had it been since that day years ago that Walt bid the family adieu and headed west? That was 1849. *In three months it will be 1871, twenty-two years. I wonder what he looks like. I wonder if he's still got that burr under his saddle, I wonder if...*

Some comment Johnny Dollars made brought Tallhelm out of his speculation on Walt.

"What's that, Johnny?" Bill Diehl asked, disbelief and disgust in his voice.

"I said iffen your fingers weren't so thick, I'd say you was working the cards," repeated Johnny, adding a bit of force to the statement.

"Christ, Johnny, last night it was Brow. The night before that, it was Sage who was the card shark," said Diehl.

"Bill ain't making you keep shovin' your money into the pot," added Sage, the disgust in his voice favoring humor rather than wrath.

"Yeah, you know Thaedell is the card shark at this table," said Brow.

"Sage, you better tell your friend most people consider them fighting words," cautioned Thaedell. His voice carried the same humorous lilt as Sage's.

"Hell, I know that," defended Johnny. "I didn't mean nothin' by it, you know that. It just seems I can't hardly win a hand."

The near-desperate tone of Johnny's words made it clear he hadn't won too many hands in the poker game of life.

Tallhelm knew there was no malice in what Johnny said. Most times the cards he held would have won the hand. His full house, aces, and jacks lost to four deuces. Two hands later, in a game of seven-card stud, Johnny's four kings lost to a low straight flush Tallhelm caught on the last card. You couldn't hardly blame the man for being miffed.

It would seem Jerome Corwell, affably known as Johnny Dollars, was one of those individuals who could never catch a break when he needed it, his aims and ambitions always falling just short of success. He was successful at one thing though, and that was failure.

Johnny reached into his worn deacon's coat and produced a sheaf of bills that could choke a horse. "Nate, could you see your way to changing a bit of this folding money for something with a little clink to it? I scarcely have a half-dozen silver dollars to remind me where my pockets are," he said.

Nate was getting to see a new side of Johnny. But before he had time to even peruse the scrip, a roar rose up from the group, loud and swift enough to have him redeposit the bills back from whence that had come, posthaste.

"Forget that, Johnny. Nate's a friend here. Anyway, you got enough men chasing after you as it is. Don't add another one to it.

That Missouri scrip you got was worthless when they printed it, and worse yet, what you got is counterfeit," said Brow Herman.

Sunny, missing little of what went on in the room, asked, "What, don't tell me Johnny tried playing with them shin plasters again?"

"No," answered Sage. "But he did have a mind to foist 'em off on Nate here. I guess that's just about as ignorant."

The responsibility Sage Heck felt toward Johnny was evident in his voice, although Sage and Johnny hadn't met but six months ago. In the frontier, the recipe for partnership knew no time, convention, nor scribe.

"Hell, *ignorant* ain't the word. Suicidal's more like it," added Bill Diehl.

"Nate coulda plugged him on general principles," began Brow Herman as he readied himself to lecture Johnny on what was expected of one to engender respect amongst friends.

"Nate wouldn't gun Johnny," stated Sage who, in spite of his assured tone, found himself looking to Tallhelm for confirmation.

Properly chided, Johnny apologized, "No disrespect intended, Mister Tallhelm. Believe me."

Nate, for his part, was mildly amused by the concern, feigned or otherwise, afforded him at Johnny's expense. There was no malice in these words. This joking was the mortar that bound these men one to the other.

"No, Sage, I wouldn't gun Johnny. But I gotta tell ya, the last man that tried to cheat me, well, let's just say his cheating days are over," offered Nate with a tone that made Johnny swallow hard. The others shook their heads in slight embarrassment.

"Hell," interjected Sage in Johnny's defense. "Iffen a couple of those cards woulda fell different, Johnny woulda won big."

"Yeah, Sage. I guess you're right. But on the other hand, if my aunt had balls, she'd be my uncle," reasoned Brow Herman.

"Ahh, you're full of kadewey dust, ya old fart," countered Sage.

"Here, Johnny, I'll deal you a winner." With that, Lahr, next in turn for the deal, gathered the cards and announced, "Seven-card stud for Johnny." Lahr shuffled and dealt the cards with the fluid ease of a magician, each card floating from the deck with the grace of a falling leaf, settling on the green baize in a rhythm that mesmerized the circle of players. Johnny won the hand and established the meter of his departure from the table by slowly pouring himself another glass of whiskey.

Earlier, Sunny had brought two bottles to the table and announced with a small flourish, "Compliments of the Captain. Help yourselves, boys."

The group showed themselves to be either most obliging by nature or great lovers of whiskey as the one bottle was emptied and the second was well on its way to joining the first. Johnny, savoring the last vapors in his empty glass, rose from the table and arranged his pants and coat, seeking a general comportment that for him was never quite attainable. "Gentlemen. Later, Sage," said Johnny.

"Johnny," the group answered in unison.

"Later, Johnny," said Sage Heck.

Nate later learned from Lahr that whenever Johnny got so low as to resort to the bogus scrip, he would deal him a winning hand. Evidently, Thaedell Lahr could shuffle, arrange, and deal the cards in whatever manner he wanted them to fall. The other players were in on it as well. It was better than outright charity, and Johnny managed to salvage a bit of respect, an important consideration amongst these men. Lahr refrained from employing these particular skills, except when Johnny's desperation was too painful to endure. A curious but harmless wrinkle to the game, as far as Nate was concerned.

The hour was late, very late. Severman was either passed out or dead asleep in the end booth, which was just what Keith and Lucien wanted. The two men emerged from out of the kitchen and said something to Sunny, who then gave a conspiratorial nod toward Brow Herman, beckoning him to quietly come over to the bar.

"Brow, come back in here," Sunny whispered, leading Brow Herman through the curtain behind the bar and into the kitchen. "Lucien and the Captain want to search Severman's gear. Don't you boys make any noise and wake him up before they get back up here. Got it?"

Brow Herman nodded and rejoined the group. Of course, they all wanted to know what was afoot, their wide eyes and upturned palms silently communicating their curiosity. They were savvy enough to know it involved Severman and the desire to keep him asleep.

Brow made a back-and-forth gesture with his hands, one over the other, which was understood to mean "Keep quiet and just play some cards." Watching Brow Herman do this with his fat ham-hock hands had a comical quality to it, but no one dared laugh.

Returning from the transient quarters of the Crow's Nest, a closed mezzanine above the tack room referred to as the rope hotel, Keith and Lucien conferred with Sunny and then called Brow Herman back over to the bar.

"We found twenty double eagles in Severman's kit, and with that poke Dean had on him, that makes more than forty altogether. Where in the hell did those two get that kind of money?" asked an increasingly angry Jonathan Keith.

"That old man Haverstraw had the situation pegged right. These two are in league with that bastard Herzog. Before he wakes up, get him down and into the brig. If he wakes up, sap him." With that, Keith produced a lead-filled leather sap from behind the bar and handed it to Sunny. "No sense talking to him tonight." Keith delivered this information while keeping a steady eye on Severman.

"Sunny, he may have had an extra pistol in his saddlebag. Don't take chances with that snake. Got me?" cautioned Keith.

"Got ya, boss."

"Brow, don't mention anything about the money to the boys. Just tell them I'm worried he might backshoot Nate over there. That's why I'm having him locked up. Got that?"

"Got it, Captain."

"It's late. Why don't you boys call it a night and help Sunny get him down to the brig?" said Keith.

"Sure thing, Captain," answered Brow.

Brow Herman delivered the information to the poker table, and in short order, four of the men were carrying a passed-out Aldo Severman out the barroom door and down to the brig. Nate chuckled to himself as he noticed that Bill Diehl was fulfilling his part of the task seemingly without the aid of vision.

Normally in a few hours, Tallhelm would be stirring himself awake. He was usually up and at it at first light, the finest part of the day to his reckoning. Watching the sun come up made him thankful for the day that every dawn heralded. If nature is a mystery to be solved, he believed that solution was best sought at daybreak.

At dusk, when men gather to burn night fires, rising smoke carries their eyes to the heavens, and their hearts and minds to all manner of speculation and romance. But with the graying light of day, what at night looked to be soft and smooth now appears to be hard and jagged. What was seen as a divine altar the previous night now appeared more like a broken dais, requiring keen and immediate repair.

Whether the dawn of a new day breaks cloudy or brilliant, Tallhelm knew the product of a day's work to be worth more than the fanciful thoughts of a thousand nights.

As the men carried Severman down the stairs to the brig, Nate went up the stairs to his room, slid the bolt on the door, undid his gun belt, and hung it off the back of the chair next to his bed. Nate pulled off his boots, stretched out, and passed into a deep and well-earned sleep.

11

KINDLING AND A KISS

"Nate, you awake in there? Nate, wake up. You in there?" Tallhelm heard Sunny's voice, but it took him a moment to realize just where he was.

"Yeah, sure, I'm in here. What's the ruckus?" answered Nate as he quickly pulled on his boots and strapped on his gun belt. Drawing his revolver, he wondered if Sunny might not have a gun to his head. "What's up?" asked Tallhelm, hoping to get a clearer idea of what was afoot.

"Hell, nothing much, now that we know you're alive." Sunny's tone had changed and now was more matter-of-fact, almost regrettably anticlimactic. Sliding the bolt, Nate pulled open the door and was greeted by Sunny, Keith, and the two Samms boys.

"I didn't know there was a limited sleeping policy at this place. What time is it anyway?" asked Nate.

"Just past eight in the morning. You slept clear around the clock and then some," answered Keith.

"Eight o'clock in the morning" was the only comment the not quite awake Tallhelm could muster.

"We figured with the distance you traveled and that gunfight, you had a right to be tired, but when we didn't see you last night, we got a little concerned," offered Keith, relief evident in his voice.

"Hell, I can't believe it. I must have been right tuckered out," said Nate.

"Yeah, we was just fixing to lower Everett here down the side of the place and have him climb in your window," explained Sunny as Nate lit one of the whale-oil lamps.

"Sorry to cause such a stir. That's hardly like me to sleep that sound," said Nate as he filled the basin with water.

"Hell, that ain't nothing," replied Sunny. "When I was at sea, after battling this one storm, the whole crew slept for two days. Only the captain and his parrot stayed awake. He said we had the parrot to thank for waking him up before we ran aground."

"Thanks for being ready, boys. We should excuse Mr. Tallhelm now," announced Jonathan Keith. "I expect he'll be wanting some breakfast."

"We'll see you downstairs," said Sunny as he went to follow Keith and the boys out the door and down the hall.

As the boys were turning to leave, Nate asked, "How's my horse and mule doing, boys?"

"They're doin' good, mister. They're doin' real good," answered both boys in unison. "That mule's a caution. Pa says he's part devil and to keep shy of him. But he don't scare me none."

"I believe he could run," added Ernest, the younger of the boys. The fact that Keith had enlisted the boys for the dangerous job of getting in Nate's room made then feel almost like men.

"Well, son, I reckon you know good mule flesh, 'cause he is a runner." Nate reached into his pocket and brought out two silver dollars, which he flipped to the boys on their way down the hall.

"Nate, you don't have to tip those boys like that. Lucien pays those boys good," said Sunny.

"Looks like they got a good home and ain't wanting for get-about, but a little silver to jingle means a lot to young boys like that. Anyhow, that money came out of that poker game the other night. Ain't like I broke my back getting it."

"Oh yeah, the poker game," began Sunny as Nate ducked his head out the window in an effort to judge the weather. There was no wind to speak of, and the air was very mild for this time of year.

"Yeah, ha," Sunny went on. "Those boys couldn't figure how comes you didn't join the game last night. They could understand you maybe not wanting to play poker, but they reckoned you'd come through the bar. Them boys speculated on every which way to explain it. Johnny Dollars even said that maybe you was some kind of apparition and that you were never here to begin with. Brow Herman called Johnny near enough to an idiot to be called one. Adding that it wasn't no apparition what killed Dean."

Sunny went on for what seemed like an eternity about Nate's absence from the bar the night before. Nate had to laugh to himself and remembered why he preferred the solitary trail.

"So what's up with that Aldo Severman? You still got him in the brig?" asked Nate, no particular concern evident in his voice.

"Yeah, he's still locked up, and we're in no hurry to let him out either. Boy, will the Cap and me be glad when Sarusha and your brother get back. Maybe today's the day. Anyway, Nate, I'll see you downstairs," said Sunny.

Twenty minutes later, Nate came into the bar and made a bee-line for the dining room.

"Lucien, what the hell's that noise I'm hearing?" asked Sunny.

"You mean what sounds like somebody squishing through muck then choking a bullfrog, that sound?" replied Lucien Samms.

"Yeah, that's it. A damn big bullfrog," answered Sunny in feigned confusion as he and Lucien looked first up toward the ceiling then down to the floor.

"Okay, I get it. What you're hearing is my stomach growling, and as much as I'd like to stand here and let you boys have your fun, if I don't get some of whatever that is I smell coming out of that kitchen, I'm gonna faint!" Nate said this half jokingly as he made his way past the bar and into the dining room and closer to the wonderful aroma of Evie Samms's buttermilk hotcakes.

"Yeah, I imagine you're a bit hungry, seeing as you haven't eaten in a day and a half," said Sunny as he motioned to Nate to sit at the table closest to the kitchen door. "Sit here, Nate. Evie don't take kindly to anyone just walking into her kitchen. Here's some coffee. Flapjacks will be out in a minute."

Nate sat down and began a long stretch of his cramped arms and back muscles, yawned and rubbed the rest of the sleep out of his face as he awaited Sunny's return from the kitchen.

"Here you go, Nate. Evie must like you. She broke out one of Lucien's salt-cured hams and fried you some eggs to go along with these hotcakes. Maybe I should try sleeping for two days if this is the breakfast I can expect!"

"Don't kid yourself, Sunny. It's my good looks that Evie's thinking about," Nate joked.

"You're both wrong. I told Lucien and Evie to treat Nate like he was one of ours. The way he handles that shoots pistol, we want him on our side." This came from Jonathan Keith, who wasn't usually given to humorous comments.

"Thank you both. Whatever the reason, I greatly appreciate these vittles. Boy, am I hungry," said Nate as he folded over a flapjack and sopped up a bit of fried egg.

Evie came out of the kitchen and poured Nate another cup of coffee and began to top it off with some Irish whiskey when Nate waved her off.

"Word has it you like your coffee spiced up some," said Evie.

"No thanks, Evie. This coffee can take the curl out of my boots all by itself." Tallhelm gave Sunny an accusatory look and added, "A man could leave the Nest with a reputation about as low as a yellow skunk found passed in a barrel of sour mash."

Sunny shook his head and tried unsuccessfully to remove the sheepish look off his face.

"Sunny, I'm figuring on taking my horse and mule out for a stretch, maybe look for some game. Any ideas?"

"Fact is, I was gonna send Everett and Ernest out to collect some kindling from up on the cut. If you care to go with them, they could load up your mule. That'd be a big help. As far as any game you see, that's always welcome," responded Sunny.

Nate remembered back to the masses of fallen tree limbs he and the three Indians encountered on their way down the mountain. He also thought to himself that that seemed like a month ago, but it was only a matter of a few days.

"Sure thing. That sounds just about right. How soon those boys heading out?"

"Pretty much anytime, but I'm sure they'll be more than glad to be accommodating to your schedule. Seems those boys would fall one over the other to help you whatever way they could."

"Well, I'll be ready directly. Thank you very much, Mrs. Samms, for that great breakfast!" Nate hollered back to the kitchen.

"Oh, you be more than welcome, Mr. Nate," Evie answered.

Tallhelm returned to his room and opened the window to again check what the day's weather was likely to be. The day was bright, clear, and mild. He extended his hand out the window and caught a few of the water drops melting off the roof as they fell past his window. Lingering for a moment, he dared himself to stop and take note of this one moment in time, much like the drip, drip of the melting snow, the relentless passing of time, and his place in it. But life was carrying him along from one circumstance to another, with little chance to step outside and contemplate life as a whole. Now wasn't that time either.

Nate turned away from the window and checked the cylinder in his revolver. He didn't think he had to worry about Aldo Severman since Keith had him locked up in the brig. Nevertheless, when someone says, "I'm gonna kill you before the week is out," it definitely gets your attention.

Nate holstered his revolver, closed and locked the door, and headed down to the stable.

The Samms boys, having gotten word from Sunny, had his horse saddled and the mule ready to go.

"Hey, boys, I guess we're going to get some firewood. How's this work?"

"Well, what we do—"

"What we do—"

The two boys began talking at the same time till Tallhelm held up his hand and pointed to Everett. "Okay, one at a time."

"What we do is take these ropes and make bundles. Then we lays them over our horses and walk 'em back here to the stable. then

Mister Sunny tells us where to bring 'em," explained Everett in a slow and deliberate manner as if Tallhelm was somewhat slow-witted.

This brought the biggest grin to Nate's face that he had in some time. Just then, footsteps could be heard coming down the staircase, and out of the shadows emerged Lorraine Haverstraw.

"I was hoping to take my horse and father's out for a stretch. Mind if I tag along?"

"No, we don't mind," the boys answered in unison, giving one another a look that fell somewhere between surprise and bewilderment.

Nate chimed in with an additional, "No, we don't mind. Do we, boys?" Trying as best he could not to betray his joy at being able to spend some time with the alluring Lorraine.

"Let me saddle your horse," Nate offered.

"I'd appreciate that very much, thank you," answered Lorraine.

As Nate busied himself saddling the horse, the two brothers gave sidelong glances to one another, rolling their eyes and making faces that only young brothers could share.

Lorraine Haverstraw wore men's black wool trousers, a beige cotton blouse, and a brown quilted leather vest, buttoned up to just below her ample bosom. Over this, she wore a fleece-lined canvas coat. She stood about one head shorter than Tallhelm. Nate watched as Lorraine gathered her blond hair tinged with silver into a ponytail and tucked it beneath her flat-brimmed hat. Even in the dim light of the stable, Tallhelm could see that her brown eyes betrayed little emotion save an unmistakable seriousness. The trials and travails that Lorraine Haverstraw had endured had molded her into a strong and resolute woman, a force unto herself.

"You're not afraid of riding along with a man who killed someone?" asked Tallhelm, making sure there was no awkward residue from the other night.

"I'd be afraid if you weren't that man. You know I was there. I saw what happened. If you hadn't shot that man, you wouldn't be here right now, and then what?" answered Lorraine as Nate handed her the reins to her horse.

"Mister Nate, we'll be walking our horses back once they're loaded. You be wantin' to bring along a couple of these horse blankets and these pieces of rope. Don't worry. Everett and me will show you and Miss Lorraine just what to do," Ernest directed as he handed Nate the blankets and several hanks of rope.

"Whatever you say, Ernest. Looks like we're working for you boys now. Hope we can catch on. Are the dogs coming along?" asked Nate, seeing as Star and Maggie seemed to be in on everything that went on at the Nest.

"No. Cap don't like them to get past the gatehouse. One went missing once and had the Cap worried sick."

Before Everett pulled open the large stable doors, he gave two yanks on a knotted rope hanging next to the door. A bell rang twice, which evidently signaled Ghosty to open the gatehouse doors. They were slowly swinging open by the time the boys, Nate, and Lorraine approached.

The group made their way through the gatehouse corridor, out the open doors, and rode single file up the switchback. Nate looked back and watched as the massive entry door swung back closed as if by the magic of an unseen hand.

Jonathan Keith had engineered a weight-and-pulley system that allowed for the heavy doors to swing open and close with very little effort on the part of the person manning the gatehouse. That person was, and had been for the last several years, an old man they call Ghosty and his equally mysterious mother.

The pair had shown up at the Crow's Nest with little more than the clothes on their backs and two large Bibles. They told Jonathan Keith they were on a pilgrimage of some sort and had exhausted their provisions, but that "God would provide." In this case, "God" was Jonathan Keith. He put them up in the gatehouse as a way of shielding his men from their constant proselytizing and Bible quoting, and they have been there ever since.

From all reports, they spend their days taking turns reading scripture to one another and the several cats with whom they shared the gatehouse. Their only other activity, apparently, is the opening and closing of the gate when they hear the bell ring.

One strange rumor concerning Ghosty and his mother was that pressed into the pages of their Bibles were any number of hundred-dollar greenback notes. No one really knew how this rumor got started or if in fact it were true. All in all, this only added to the spookiness of the lore surrounding the two.

Nate's body gave a slight shudder as he turned his gaze away from the gatehouse and focused on staying in single file as the four made their way up the narrow switchback. Sunny had told him about Ghosty and his mother the night he arrived at the Crow's Nest. Nate could stare down a panther, but something like Ghosty and his mother gave him the willies.

Although Trader Darcy and Veronica's fate was never far from his thoughts, right now, though, Nate's thoughts were on the visage of Lorraine Haverstraw as he watched her handily guide her horse up the precarious switchback. She obviously knew how to handle a horse and, from her assured bearing, probably most any other thing she put her mind to. He had noticed, when she was getting on her horse, she still had her small shoulder holster under her coat. This woman would not be one to trifle with. But beyond that, in the full light of day, Nate couldn't help but be struck by an unmistakable weariness that shaded her countenance.

On seeing this and the inherent vulnerability on Lorraine's face, Nate Tallhelm wanted to do everything he could to relieve the pain that had so affected her life since that fateful day back in Lautenburg, Ohio, twelve years past.

Once on level ground, Nate brought his horse next to hers and began what he hoped would be friendly small talk. She, however, spoke first.

"You're really concerned for your cousin. I can see that. Did you grow up together?" asked Lorraine, not turning to Nate but keeping her eyes focused on the ground and the footing for her horse. The horse had been stable bound and was slow to find its natural gait.

"Yes, we did. Back in Pennsylvania."

Nate went on to give a short account of his life and ended with the arrival of Guyer and Bowersox at Bill Darcy's place and his subsequent trip up to the Crow's Nest.

"Sunny told me about you and your father surviving the Lautenburg fire. I can't imagine how bad that must have been. I wasn't back East when that happened, but it was in all the papers. What a tragedy."

Nate didn't know if he should have brought up the subject of the Lautenburg fire, and now that he had, cursed himself. He had figured on keeping the conversation to small talk, avoiding any unpleasant memories. Well, the hope of sticking to small talk was all but gone. Again he cursed himself. What was he thinking?

Everett and Ernest, who had been leading the way, slowed their gate, which allowed Nate and Lorraine to come alongside. Here on the open expanse between the switchback and the foot of the cut, the four could ride abreast of one another.

"What we do is ride on up the cut and see what deadfall there is and collect it on our way down. We only want to go up as far as need be, 'cause we be walkin' on the way back." Everett explained the routine as they approached the bottom of the cut.

The group rode on in silence, with nods to one another as they pointed out deadfall that had gathered in tangled heaps along the bank.

Nate thought back to the night spent with Diving Hawk and the others, the harrowing flight from the stampeding bighorn, and the falling body of Snarling Wolf. Again, he was struck by how long in the past that night seemed, yet it was only two days ago. He also wondered how the trio was getting on and how their small village would fare over the winter.

"You hear that sound? That's my favorite sound in all the world," Lorraine announced as she looked up to the tops of the pines and let the sound of the wind blowing through the swaying treetops wash over her. The sound must have resonated with some long-ago memory, because Nate noticed the slightest of smiles transform her face from melancholy seriousness to almost wistful joy in an instant.

"Yeah, I like that sound as well. It brings me back to when I was a kid. Our house in Virginia had pines all around. See those hawks up there? They're riding the heat that comes off the face of the canyon, and with the cooler air off the forest, you get the wind," explained Nate.

"Well, I knew that," said Lorraine.

"No, you didn't," Nate responded playfully, glad to have Lorraine elide over his comment about Lautenburg.

Stopping their horses, the Samms boys dismounted and pointed to a large mass of tangled limbs farther up the trail. "We'll start bundling here. Maybe you and Miss Lorraine can go up yonder and work on that pile?"

"Well, Miss Lorraine, looks like we have our orders. What do you think?" asked Nate.

"I imagine we can handle this, Mister Nate," answered Lorraine. "Provided you don't slow me down," she added, much to Tallhelm's delight, as any respite from the gravity of both their situations was welcome.

"Mister Nate, we'll take the mule and her pa's horse and load 'em up. Make sure you drape yours with those horse blankets. We don't want them horses getting barbed by any sticks when we be coming down that switchback," cautioned Everett.

Nate and Lorraine rode on up the trail toward the large pile of entangled deadfall.

"I can't hardly remember the last time I worked alongside a woman," announced Tallhelm.

"Well, I can't remember the last time I worked beside a man," answered Lorraine.

"You suppose one of us has to be in charge?" queried Nate.

"Well, I imagine I could be in charge, seeing as women are naturally better at getting things organized," quipped Lorraine.

"Well, seeing as that's the case, you can be the foreman, oh, excuse me, the forewoman of this operation," answered Nate. "But I got to warn ya, I'm not used to taking orders, and I can't be responsible for how I may react to being told what to do," he joked, obviously enjoying this good-natured exchange.

Arriving at the deadfall, the two dismounted and tied their horses to an exposed root of one of the trees growing atop the bank.

"So let's see, what do you think we should do first?" asked Lorraine.

"If I was in charge, I say we'd lay out these ropes and lay these branches over them till we had enough stacked up to tie into a bundle about this big." With that, Tallhelm made a circle with his arms about three feet across.

"That sounds just like what I was going to suggest. Thank God I'm in charge," Lorraine said but couldn't hold a straight face any longer. She smiled and began to laugh. Nate did the same.

What happens between a man and a woman when they first meet can take any number of avenues. The morning's ride out of the Crow's Nest and up the trail to do something as simple as collect firewood had given the pair a chance to test the waters. At first blush, it would appear these waters could run deep.

The pair set about stacking and bundling the dried branches. Larger pieces Nate would prop against the bank and break with his foot. Most of the kindling, however, could just be picked up and laid across the two lengths of rope and then, when big enough, cinched up into a neat bundle. The pair worked in silence, intent on the task at hand.

After a time, they had three large bundles ready to go. The last stack took more time and effort as these pieces had to be yanked free from the tangled mass. It was while attempting to do just that, that a limb suddenly came loose, and Lorraine lost her footing and went reeling backward. Quick reaction by Nate saved her from falling. He caught her and brought her upright, holding her momentarily, motionless, her face within inches of his. Their eyes met, and for an instant, it seemed like their two souls mingled, possessed by but one thought.

Lorraine wanted more than anything to give herself over to this moment but found herself placing her hand between their lips and turning away her gaze.

Nate, for his part, felt a range of emotions roiling inside his heart and head that were heretofore unknown to him. This Lorraine Haverstraw must surely be the missing part to the puzzle of his life. That missing part that led him away from his fledgling homestead this spring and set him on the open trail. A trail that had ultimately led him here, to this moment.

The two avoided one another's eyes, concentrating on securing the bundles of kindling to their horses, two bundles on each horse, one each side.

"Nathan, my father and I have been chasing Herzog for eleven years. Now if I'm not mistaken, he's less than two days' ride south of here. I can't, as much as I like to, let anything interfere with us seeing this through. I hope you can understand," Lorraine said as she untethered her horse.

"No, I can understand what you're saying. This has to get resolved before you can get on with living your life," answered Nate, contemplating his own situation with regard to his cousin Trader and Veronica. "Lorraine, you don't have to explain anything to me," added Nate as he unhitched his horse and came alongside.

"Nathan, come here." As Tallhelm drew near, Lorraine reached up and took Nate by the back of the neck and pressed her lips to his. She closed her eyes and waited until she felt his body relax and the two become as one. As she drew away, she caressed his cheek and wiped a solitary tear away from her own.

The pair walked in silence and soon joined up with the Samms boys. Before continuing on, Nate had the boys hold their horses and walked Lorraine over to a gap in the pines, which allowed for an unobstructed view into the upper valley and a bird's-eye view of the granite peninsula on which sat the Crow's Nest.

"You can see why the Indians called that outcrop Wishpush Walwas Nez for beaver tail," said Nate. It was clear from this vantage point how it narrowed at the southern end where the switchback met the gatehouse and how, as it went north, widened out. Every bit the shape of a beaver's tail. Going from south to north, first there was the gatehouse, then the Crow's Nest, then an open area out back, the outdoor stable, the hogpens, a large garden plot, now fallow, an area where several cows grazed, and finally at the uppermost end a large stand of old-growth oaks and pines. You could see why Jonathan Keith had chosen this spot to build his retreat from the world. He easily could have called it the Citadel. Set apart as it was by a deep and wide chasm bridged only by the perilously narrow switchback, its sheer granite sides leaving no room for a misstep by man or beast.

Tallhelm could usually judge distances fairly well, but from this perspective, he couldn't rightly figure how wide the chasm was between him and the Nest. Nate hollered to Everett and Ernest, "One of you boys bring me your bow and a quiver of arrows."

The Samms boys never left the Nest without at least a bow and some arrows, on the off chance they might come across some game. Today they also each had a rifle, added security given the possible threat occasioned by Herzog being in the area.

"You never hit the Nest from here, Mister Nate," informed Everett as he handed Tallhelm his bow and an arrow out of the quiver.

"Yeah, I know that. I'm just wondering how close I can get," answered Tallhelm.

"Mister Nate, you just be wasting an arrow," said Everett.

"Yeah, I guess you're right." Nate handed Everett back his bow and the arrow.

"Maybe on down the cut, you might get halfway, but not up here." Everett was pretty emphatic about it.

"Mister Sunny and the Captain came up here once with the Captain's Henry. It could reach the Nest, but they never hit what they was aiming at."

Tallhelm knew, from using his uncle's Sharps, that he could hit a target at eight hundred paces. That told him that from here, the Nest must be about half a mile. If it came to someone trying to lay siege to the Crow's Nest, they wouldn't be able to do it from up here. This far up the cut, you could look down on the Nest, but that'd be about it. Farther down, you'd be about eye level, farther still where the cut leveled out. The Nest proper held the higher ground. Anyone not welcome or with evil intent would make an easy target from most any vantage point on the Crow's Nest.

Keith years ago had to fight off two assaults. One from some French trappers, who had run out of supplies and had made a half-hearted attempt. The other was the great Nez Perce chief Black Eagle. Keith wouldn't go into it, but Sunny later told Nate that it was a personal affair between the two. Something about Black Eagle's sister.

Even Sarusha and Lucien didn't know exactly what had started it. In any event, Black Eagle was unsuccessful. And some years later, the two men buried the hatchet.

Tallhelm and Lorraine paused for a last look down to the Crow's Nest and the surrounding gorge. The stark remoteness of the setting made Lorraine wonder why Jonathan Keith had chosen to retreat from the world in the first place. However, long ago, she gave up trying to figure why most men did any of what they did.

With these thoughts and her recent kiss with this Nathan Tallhelm on her mind, she turned back toward the Samms boys. As she turned, she touched Nate's sleeve and said, "The Nez would say, 'Yixa walwas.'"

Nate Tallhelm could only look at Lorraine's back as she walked toward the Samms boys, speechless and wondering what the depth of this woman Lorraine Haverstraw was.

12

TURKEY SHOOT

"Lorraine, did you get breakfast? You were down to the stables pretty early," asked Tallhelm as he offered her his canteen. She waved it off as she lifted her own off the saddle horn and took a long swallow.

"I did. Mrs. Samms fixed me some ham and eggs right after you left. Why, do you have something in that saddlebag?" asked Lorraine.

Before Tallhelm could answer, Everett Samms announced, "Ma never lets us leave the Nest what we don't have food packed. Should be enough for us all."

With that, Everett untied a cloth sack from his saddle and motioned for everyone to gather around and see just what Evie Samms had provided for their midday meal.

By now, it was well past one, and the work of the morning had given everyone a good appetite.

"What'd Ma pack for us?" asked Ernest as the four gathered together. Nate took an extra tarp and laid it on the ground next to the bank in the warmth of the early afternoon sun.

"Well, we got some biscuits, apples, some of Mister Nate's cheese, and some salt fish," answered Everett as the group sat on the tarp, divvied up what was in the poke, and using the bank as a back rest, began to eat. They ate in silence.

Nate could see from the expression on Lorraine's face that she was enjoying this break from whatever else was going on in her life.

A good morning's work, a mild October day, the as-yet-unknown path her relationship with this Nathan Tallhelm would take, and the thoughtfulness of Evie Samms all made for an almost sublime moment. Tallhelm felt the same way.

Just as Nate began to shut his eyes for a brief after-lunch siesta, Ernest announced, "We best be getting back. Pa said with this Herzog man around, we shouldn't be dawdlin'. He cautioned us not to get too far or be gone too long."

"Yes sir, from what Miss Lorraine and her Pa told the Captain, he is no man to be triflin' with. Ernie and I will lead these horses back single file. If you and Miss Lorraine follow along, we should be okay," added Everett.

Nate rose up from where he'd been sitting, looked left and right, removed his rifle from his horse, and waited for the Samms boys to lead the five horses and mule down the trail and fell in behind with Lorraine at his side.

"I guess I missed out on that palaver. What did you and your Pa have to say about this Herzog?" asked Nate.

"Well, the other night, when Father and I heard that man Severman say Herzog was looking for men, that told us we were surely on the right track. You were out at the bar when we told Captain Keith about our pursuit of Bertram Herzog and what he had done back in Lautenburg. So yesterday, when they were out burying those men, we sat down and told them what went on back in Lautenburg, leastwise what we think went on."

"They had a mind to wake you up, but Mister Jonathan," Lorraine said, mimicking the pronunciation of the Samms boys, trying to recapture the lighter mood that the day had held, "said to let you sleep, figuring you needed your rest and he'd fill you in on it later."

"Remember a while ago you said you read about the Lautenburg fire in the paper. What you read had very little to do with what really happened," continued Lorraine as she and Nate kept an even pace with the boys and the loaded horses.

"I imagine you read it was an accidental silo explosion that started the fire and that sixty some lives were lost. Well, there was a silo explosion, really a grain elevator, and many people died, but as sure as night follows day, that explosion was no accident. No, it was no accident," repeated Lorraine Haverstraw as she stared absently into the distance, reluctantly allowing her memory to administer another lash to her tortured heart.

"For the longest time, I wasn't even able to talk about that damn night. Time does not heal all, as people like to say, but time does give you the chance to plan your revenge, and that's what I do now. I know that doesn't sound very ladylike, but now all I think about is revenge and justice. Hopefully, when this thing is done, I can begin my life, and Father can finally escape from his personal hell." Lorraine's voice betrayed little emotion, which made her words that much more striking.

"My hurt and sorrow is about what I lost, my mother, my dear brothers, my sister. My father's another story. He's racked with guilt, and that torments him to no end. His torment is that he played right into Marlene's hands, and once he and the others were in her grip, she turned the job over to Bertram Herzog. Hell, Nathan, my father wasn't alone. The whole damn town was taken in by her."

"Was this Marlene Herzog's wife?"

"They weren't married, leastwise not in the usual sense, but they had a covenant stronger than any wedding vows. This was a union fashioned by the hand of the Devil. Nathan, these people are as bad as they come. This Marlene Scabbe came to town pretending to be a heartbroken widow. Married the widower Slottower, who owned the mill and elevator. Once she was in his will, Lamar had a so-called 'accident.' After that, she took over the business. She talked my father and the other farmers into banding together and buying the mill. Sounded great at the time…oh, God, I can't talk about it."

If Lorraine could talk, she would describe what, at first, would appear to be a cut-and-dried case of a gold digger going after a widower's money. A quaint scenario compared to what was really going on. The full story still remains hidden from all save two, Marlene Scabbe and Bertram Herzog.

Nate was glad to see the group nearing the bottom of the cut. Lorraine had grown silent. The trauma of that night could always render her mute, as the love she felt for her lost family parried with a smoldering rage she was as yet unable to extinguish.

The Samms boys had stopped, and Ernest walked back to Nate and Lorraine and whispered, "Bunch of turkeys up yonder." He motioned for Lorraine to stay put and for Nate to come on forward.

Everett, standing dead still behind the lead horse, had his bow out and an arrow ready to fly. Ernest readied his bow and inched his way a bit closer.

The wind coming out of the west was working in their favor, but Nate knew, and maybe the boys did as well, that being quiet would be what would determine success or failure. Nate loved this. Hunting wild turkey with a bow and arrow was something much more familiar to him than all the business about Trader and Herzog, Severman and Dean.

The boys were close enough, and on Everett's signal, let their arrows fly, two arrows, two dead turkeys. Nate motioned to Ernest to hand him his bow and an arrow, and as the birds began to run to the shelter of the woods, Nate let go with a shot and bagged another bird.

Nate and Ernest retrieved the birds and after binding their legs, hung them over the saddle horn of Nate's horse and proceeded to the switchback and down to the Nest.

Evie Samms, along with her husband Lucien, were responsible for keeping everyone at the Crow's Nest properly fed. So the addition to the larder of the three fat turkeys was welcome news. However, Evie did have an aversion to plucking the feathers of any fowl. Evidently, this arose from some experience she had as a child in Antigua. So before she had a chance to temper her words, she announced to Lucien, Sunny, and anyone else within earshot, "If you men think I'm plucking and roasting three turkeys for a bunch of belly worshipers, you got another thing coming!"

Lucien quickly assured his wife that the birds would be ready for the oven before she ever had to lay eyes on them.

Evangeline Addashay had first met Lucien Samms years ago, when Jonathan Keith's ship the *Celine* made port in Antigua to take on fresh water and provisions before heading back up the East coast and across the Atlantic. Evie was the oldest daughter of the purveyor who supplied Keith with whatever foodstuffs he needed.

When they first met, Evie was but a young girl helping her father load goods dockside. But over the years, and on every subsequent visit to the port, Lucien watched Evie grow from that young girl into a beautiful woman. It was on their last stop in Antigua before heading around the Horn and up the west coast to Portland that Lucien asked Evie's father for his daughter's hand.

The father agreed, and Evie did as well, more than willing to leave her island life and marry the man she had been secretly hoping would take her away, as he had already taken her heart.

Jonathan Keith was happy to provide a proper and generous dowry. So while the ship was still in Falmouth Harbor, the wedding party gathered on the deck of the *Celine,* and as a gentle sea breeze playfully toyed with Evangeline Addashay's wedding veil, Captain Keith performed the ceremony.

That night, the rum flowed freely.

Lucien cherished his wife, and if she didn't want to pluck turkeys, it was okay with him.

"Evie, I never much liked plucking chickens myself," said Lorraine as she and Nate sat at the bar and watched Ernest and Everett ferry small bundles of kindling out onto the deck.

"I hear that," hollered Evie back through the kitchen curtain.

Lorraine enjoyed her time with Evie, and for her part, Evie was delighted to have another woman to help her in the kitchen. Also, Lorraine provided a sympathetic ear when Evie found need to complain about the uncivilized habits most men seemed to possess and of which they were totally unaware.

Lorraine's skills in the kitchen had gone for so many years unused. She liked kneading the dough and watching Evie make a sauce, something that she used to do with her mother and sister.

Thinking out loud, Lorraine said, "That's something else Herzog and Marlene took from me, all what I was supposed to learn. Sure, I can speak five languages and have been hither and yon. I don't even know if I can bake a loaf of bread."

"I keep hearing about Herzog. Where's Marlene?" asked Nate.

"We lost track of Marlene some time back. Herzog, we were able to pick up his trail in San Francisco. Maybe they had a falling out. Father and I don't know. Alone or together, it doesn't matter. Where they go, death follows. Nathan, your cousin is lucky to be alive. Herzog doesn't usually fail when he wants someone dead," said Lorraine.

"You two want something to eat? Supper won't be for a while," asked Evie as she came out from the kitchen.

"I'm all right. How about you, Lorraine?" asked Nate.

"Nah, I can hold out till supper."

"I could go for something to eat." This from Bill Liecaster, who was sitting in one of the booths with his partner, Tubby Flint.

"I wasn't asking you," said Evie with an acrid tone which left no doubts as to how she felt about Bill Liecaster.

"Well, why not?" was Liecaster's retort.

Sunny Martin, who had come into the bar in time to catch the tail end of this exchange, told Liecaster, "You and Tubby can slope anytime. Far as I'm concerned, the sooner the better."

"No need to get your back up. I was just hungry," said Liecaster.

"Well, the way you're talking, it sounds like you're hungry for some trouble. If that's the case, just see me," answered Sunny Martin, a man who definitely took no guff from anyone.

Liecaster gave no response to this, and Sunny let it drop.

"Sunny, I guess you're tired of me asking, but you got any better idea when my brother and Sarusha will be back?"

"Sorry, Nate. Can't really say. Seems this waiting got me a wee bit agitated. Thanks for working with the boys getting that kindling. Every bit helps."

Sunny checked the stacks of kindling on the deck and once again took a look up to the switchback. Nothing.

The wait for Walt and Sarusha to return with news of Trader Darcy and Veronica had everyone on edge.

But there was little they could do but wait.

13

FIGHT SCENE

The kindling Nate, the Samms boys, and Lorraine collected yesterday would do to start the fires, but keeping them going would take split logs, and lots of them. Sunny always made sure there was a ready supply of felled trees waiting to be sawn and split. Nate was more than willing to lend a hand.

A loud crack echoed off the granite walls of the upper valley. The late afternoon sun had long since retreated over the pine forest that sat atop the promontory, south and to the west, the dark shadow it cast seemingly in concert with Nate Tallhelm's darkening mood.

Another crack and another echo resonated off the wall and then faded into the valley. Nate had busied himself for most of the afternoon splitting wood. The large wedge of iron smashed through the dry oak logs in one fell swoop. The Samms boys had been setting the logs on the wide flat stump for Nate to split, barely keeping up with his machinelike rhythm. Two huge pyramids of split logs flanked the chopping block, soon to be neatly racked alongside several other rows of cured firewood. The first stop on their one-way journey to the fireplaces and stoves that kept the Crow's Nest warm throughout the cold winter months. Winters could be harsh in these parts. Cured firewood and lots of it were an imperative.

Tallhelm carried his weight in whatever situation he found himself and was glad to do his part. But more to the point, he had been at Keith's now for four days and had grown restless. The physical activity and the good-natured banter he enjoyed with the Samms boys had done little to get his mind off the concern he had for his cousin's fate. Trader and Veronica were holed up somewhere, and God only knew how bad their situation was. Rather than ease his mood, the work had only added to his smoldering fury. With each thunderous crack of the maul, his resolve sharpened, his anger roiled.

Darkness came early, and Evie Samms had already called the hungry boys in for supper. Nate should have been hungry himself, but his mood had gone sour, and with it his appetite. He planted the iron maul firmly into the chopping block and made his way to the rear of the building.

The back of the Crow's Nest looked every bit like the rear of a five-story boarding house. The ground floor, which was the height of two stories, held the stables and mezzanine "rope hotel." Framing the two massive doors which opened into the stables were wooden staircases, either side, which zigzagged their way to the top of the building, passing through railed balconies at each floor. Off the top balcony, a catwalk ran down the western side of the building. On the catwalk, Keith had erected an eight-foot-high wall, with openings for gun emplacements spaced every several feet. This provided the perfect position to return fire to anyone across the chasm which separated the Nest from the flat.

The Crow's Nest had withstood the two sieges. Those failed attempts taught Keith what were the weaknesses in his fortifications. These weaknesses were addressed with enhanced defenses, defenses which would be sorely tested before the year was out.

Anger wasn't something that sat well with Tallhelm. Just like steel, you lose your temper, you lose your strength. No, frustration and anger were emotions Nate cared not to coddle. Those were things that Nate knew how to control. He knew what to watch out for, what pitfalls to anticipate, how to act beforehand rather than only react. But now other emotions were in play, emotions that could be more perilous than either anger or frustration. The thoughts percolating in his brain came not from his head but from his heart. Lorraine Haverstraw had captured a part of Nate's and wouldn't let go. She was very much in his thoughts, and he seemed powerless to control them.

Her physical beauty was undeniable, but it was the nature of her being that captivated his heart. She had an assured air about her that Nate found disarming yet endearing. She had been through so much in the last several years, the horrible death of her family and virtually all her kin. She had watched her father devolve into a near stranger as they pursued Herzog clear across the country and back again. Now that the quarry was finally within reach, she feared he may completely lose his grip and do something that would have dire consequences for all concerned. These concerns she shared with Tallhelm, finding him easy to talk to, even though she never quite knew what his thoughts were. All Nate knew was that he wanted more than anything to protect Lorraine and keep her safe.

These were the thoughts rumbling through his brain as he walked back through the stable to see his horse and mule before heading upstairs. The Samms boys took care to see that the two were properly fed and groomed. Keith had a well-organized place here, as you would figure an ex-ship captain would. Satisfied all was well with his mounts, he made his way up to his room.

Tallhelm heard the usual noise and goings-on as he approached the second-floor landing. Suddenly, he felt energized after the day of splitting wood. The work was tonic to his body if not his mind. As he felt the tautness return to his muscles and limbs, he wondered, *Maybe I am hungry after all.*

As he passed the barroom door on his way upstairs, above the chatter, he could hear Bill Liecaster's voice. Although the words were unclear, the volume and meter bore the unmistakable resonance of a complaint.

Bill Liecaster was a man bigger than most. His large frame carried more muscle than fat. His head, seemingly meant to be square at birth, had misshapen itself into something that resembled a crushed box. Atop his head, a thick coif of black hair defied gravity, helped in this questionable effort by liberal applications of bear grease. It was just such grotesque fancy that made this otherwise dolt of a man the dangerous character he was. As his appearance had been constructed with little regard for normalcy, so likewise had his brain.

Tubby Flint was nearly as tall as Liecaster but a third his weight. His body hung about its frame like a potato sack draped over a ladder-back chair. It took only one glance to tell the man possessed an unslakable thirst for alcohol, at once the relief and ruination of the consumptive. Flint's days of being a brute were gone, but as Liecaster's sidekick, his sense of self-worth was buoyed, giving meager succor to his broken soul.

Nate's senses naturally went on alert as he listened to the voices coming through the door. He heard Sage Heck say something. Then like a roar from a wild beast, he heard Bill Liecaster bellow, "I'll kill you, boy! Nobody tells me what to do." The next noise coming through the door were tables crashing and glass breaking.

Then Nate heard Lorraine scream.

He was through the door and across the room in the blink of an eye. Just in time to see Liecaster grab Sage Heck by the shirt collar and rear back to give him another right hook.

Nate caught Liecaster's fist midflight, stopping the punch cold. The brute was taken by surprise, and for a moment didn't quite know what was happening. But he was quickly brought back to reality when Nate began pummeling his face and head in a torrent of blows. Liecaster was big, he was mean, but he was surely no match for the quicker, more agile, Tallhelm.

The first sound that reached Nate brain was Sunny hollering, "Nate, stop! You're gonna kill him, Nate!"

Nate shook his head for a second, and when he regained his focus, all he saw was a bloody lump of pulp that had been Bill Liecaster's face.

There was no joy here. In an instant, horror filled his mind. He looked about the room. He saw Lorraine begin to move toward Sage Heck, whose face was swollen and red. Nate's gaze met hers, and he was struck by the unfathomable pain he saw there. Nate had killed Dean the first night here, and now he nearly beat a man to death within an arm's reach from where she stood. The anguish and confusion he saw there pained his heart.

"The killing, this," gesturing toward Liecaster, "this endless vendetta that's made my father a stranger, will it ever end, ever?"

123

Lorraine screamed her lament as she sat heavily in a chair and sobbed uncontrollably. Years of holding her emotions in check gushed forward like water through a ruptured dike. Evie Samms sat next to her and held her, providing what little comfort she could. Helping her to her feet, Evie led her over to the door and out of the room.

"Sunny, what the hell happened?" Nate asked as he looked from Liecaster, to the upturned table, to Lorraine, as Evie led her away.

"You just beat the hell out of Bill Liecaster, if that's what you're asking," Sunny said as he motioned to Johnny and Brow to drag Liecaster off to the side of the room. "Tubby, get over here and see about cleaning up your friend. And you, Sage, better get a piece of meat on that face," Sunny said as Brow and Johnny, grumbling, dragged Liecaster off to the side and propped him up against the wall.

"Sunny, I don't mean that," Nate stated as he gestured toward Liecaster. "I mean what happened before? How was Lorraine involved?"

"Well, Bill had been drinking most of the afternoon and he got this notion that Miss Haverstraw would like to share his company. Sage had just stopped by the booth to say hello, and whilst they were exchanging pleasantries, Liecaster staggers over, and before you could say ahoy, he grabs ahold of Sage and wallops him. Miss Haverstraw hollered, and the next thing you were through the door and here we are."

"Thanks for stepping in, Nate. He got me by surprise," Sage offered as Lucien Samms emerged from the kitchen and handed him a thin venison steak to put on his face.

"Anytime, Sage, and thank you for standing up for Miss Haverstraw."

"No thanks needed, Nate. Any of us would have done the same. It's just I was the one close by."

Jonathan Keith, who had followed Lucien out from the kitchen, took one look at Bill Liecaster and said, "I don't think we'll be having much trouble from Mister Liecaster for quite a while."

The occasional scuffle between men was something Keith took pretty much in stride, but this involved a lady, and that could not be tolerated. Miles Haverstraw and his daughter were special guests of his, and any slight or inconvenience on their part, he took personally. Keith had a bad feeling in his gut that somehow he was losing control of what went on at the Nest. A situation he was unfamiliar with. Matter of fact, the tension that presently enveloped the Crow's Nest was growing palpable. Tonight's incident and the shootings the other night were only harbingers of things to come.

"Here, Nate, have a drink. I can see why your cousin had those trappers seek you out. You can shoot and fight." With that Keith poured Nate a tall glass of whiskey. Tallhelm took a big swallow and poured what was left slowly over the knuckles of his right hand.

"Cap, I just happened to be at the Darcy's when Peep and Carl showed up. Truth be told, Trader didn't know that I'd be at his Pa's place, just worked out that way. All the same, I'm glad I was.

"I'm sure it goes without saying, there would be hell to pay if anything were to happen to Miss Haverstraw. What about him?" asked Tallhelm as he pointed toward Liecaster, who just now was coming to.

Keith didn't like being put on the defensive, but he could easily tell Nate had genuine affection for Miss Haverstraw. "Like I said before, I don't expect we'll have any more trouble out of him, leastwise not tonight."

He began to pour another drink, but Nate waved it off. "I think I'll have some supper first."

Soon, the chatter in the room and the friendly insults at the poker table returned to normal. Sunny thanked Nate for all the firewood he split. The Nest had more than a half dozen fireplaces and twice as many stoves, and in the winter they ate the firewood at a pretty good pace.

Lucien brought out a large bowl of venison stew, a half loaf of bread, and a big slice of elderberry pie and set them on the bar in front of Nate. "There's more where that came from, if you're still hungry."

"No, Lucien, I think this should do just fine," answered Nate.

"Man, you sure as hell beat the tar out of that bastard. I never much cared for him. He's been through here a few times. Stays a couple days and moves on. His friend Tubby Flint isn't a bad sort, but it's like they say, 'You're known by the company you keep.' Can I get you anything else?" added Lucien.

"Matter of fact, a pitcher of cold water would suit me just fine," replied Nate.

"Coming right up," answered Lucien.

"Lucien, I was wondering, just how do you get your water up here?"

"Well, we catch whatever rainwater we can, but mostly we got a ready supply out of a little spring in the gatehouse. It must be fed from what comes down from the woods on the promontory. We haven't run dry yet."

"So what I gather is that some people come, stay for a while then go. Others appear to be permanent fixtures. What gives?" asked Nate as he tore off a chunk of bread and dipped it into his stew.

"Well, you see that group at the poker table, Brow Herman and them? They're like the crew on a ship. They have jobs to do, and for that they live here and are taken care of. Get a little pay put aside. The others who come and go do just that. They come and they go.

"See those lanterns over there?" Nate turned his head in the direction of the booths and barroom proper. "There was an artist through here maybe ten years ago. Stayed a year. He didn't have any money to speak of, but he sure could draw. Painted those parchment shades, all those scenes, right from his memory.

"Same kind of thing with those carved columns." Nate looked at the red bark-less cedar poles which were the main supports throughout the building. Each pole in the bar sported intricate carvings of grape and ivy vines, and the faces of every woodland creature you could imagine woven in and around the vines.

"Two Russians showed up here one day. Again, no money. But as you can very well see, they could carve. They stayed 'bout half a year." An obviously proud Lucien Samms pointed out to Nate several other unique features of the bar and adjacent dining room. Lucien, who rarely took the time to dwell on what Jonathan Keith had created here at the Crow's Nest, allowed himself in this moment to look about him as if he were seeing it all for the first time.

"Mister Jonathan is what you might call a student of mankind. He don't mind seeing all kinds. And I'm here to tell ya, we see all kinds come through the Nest. Some get here and find a home, a home they never had. Everybody pitches in and does their part. The Nest takes a bit of work to keep the whole place shipshape, as it were. If you weren't so good at splitting wood, Sunny might have you swabbing hallways and wiping down mopboards.

"The crew changes from time to time. We got a pretty good bunch right now.

"Take Sage, for example. His folks were killed by Indians when he and his twin sister were but a couple years old. An army patrol, out of Fort Union found their folks' place burnt to the ground. His Ma and Pa dead, most likely scalped. The major in command saw signs there might be young ones about. Well, he had the company form a line and circle the house. After each rotation, they moved farther out. On the third go-around, they found Sage and his sister, Clover, hid under the trunk of a big tree their folks had dug out for a hiding spot.

"One of the soldiers kept goin' on, 'Heck, Major, this and heck, Major, that. Heck, Major, what will we call 'em?' The major had no clue what the family's name was. So he gave them the last name Heck. And 'cause they found them where all this sage and clover was growing, he named them Sage and Clover.

"They were raised by the quartermaster and his wife back at the fort. Sage left out of there when he was sixteen. Clover, I understand, eventually married a corporal and has the life of an army wife. Sage, growing up, trained with the soldiers, and I gotta tell ya, what that boy can't do, well, I haven't seen it yet. He's been here at the Nest probably six, seven years.

"Brow Herman and Bill Diehl, they're a couple of old knockabouts. They met in the California gold fields in '49 and have been together ever since. When things didn't pan out for them in California, they headed north. What haven't they done? Hunt, trap, loggin', salmon fishing, you name it, they've done it. I hear they even used to train greenhorns on how to load a rifle and skin a deer. They're good friends of your brother. I understand he saved their lives about ten years back. Well, they're getting old now, and it looks like they found a home here at the Nest.

"Thaedell Lahr, now he's another story. He came to San Francisco in '49, but as I understand it, he had no real taste for the work it took to prospect and instead got involved in real estate. Made some real money on lease options and such. The town was growing fast, and he knew, one step ahead of everyone else, which direction it was going.

"It turns out, when they filled in part of the harbor, he owned the only way to get down to it. Long story short, there was a court battle, and he had to make a settlement. He came away with a good bit of money, though. But then he lost most of that when he opened a hotel and gambling emporium that burnt to the ground two years in. Anyway, he managed to hold onto some cash, moved to Portland, and bought a couple of properties. He heads back down there every couple of years. But he always comes back to the Nest. I think he likes Evie's cooking.

"Don't even ask me about Johnny Dollars. I'm pretty sure he's on the run for something what happened back East. He doesn't say much about his past. Sage is the only one what knows much about him.

"That's the crew. Good men all, and ready to dampen the fires of hell for the Captain, if need be. They just may have to do that, 'cause right now there's some kind of storm a-brewing. I can feel it in my bones. And my bones don't lie." This last comment from Lucien Samms was accented with a look skyward and an inquisitive rolling of eyeballs that Nate had never seen the likes of before.

"I got to agree with ya. There will be a reckoning, sure as hell. I'll be glad when Walt and your Indian friend get back. They been gone how long now?" asked Nate.

"They left out of here about four or five days before you got here, and you been here, what, four days. So I say about nine days. They should be back just about any time. If I were you, I'd relax. No sense anyone heading out till they're back and we have a better idea of what's going on," cautioned Lucien.

"Yeah, you're right. Thank the missus for the delicious stew and this pie. Maybe I'll see about taking some more of their money like I did the other night. I was so tired after coming off the trail. I don't rightly know how I read what cards I was holdin'. I believe they wanted to take advantage of my compromised state, but I got the better of them instead," joked Tallhelm.

As Nate picked up his glass of whiskey and went to leave the bar to join the poker game, he asked Lucien, "Is it just me, or does a lot of drinking go on here at the Nest?"

"Yeah, I know it seems that way, but that's 'cause everything's out of kilter. Plus it's wintertime. Most of the year those boys be busy doing one thing or another well into the night. Not now though, with it getting dark so soon. You be here in July, it'd be different."

"Well, what the hell. I ain't lost my face yet," said Nate as he let Lucien fill his glass and went over to the poker table and took a seat.

"You boys want to win back some of your money? Good luck," a smiling Nate announced to the group, feeling very much like a regular here at the Nest.

14

STALKING DUEL

The evening twilight that filtered into the room had already yielded to lamplight while Nate sat at the end of the bar and listened to Lucien explain the backgrounds of the crew. The men gathered around the poker table were knee-deep in tall stories and unbelievable anecdotes made believable by the warmth of the friendship these men shared.

When Nate came to the table, he caught the tail end of a story Brow Herman was telling about a run-in Walt and Bill Diehl had with a whiskey vendor up on the Columbia.

Nate was intrigued by the stories these two old friends of Walt's were telling, and they related them with such passion and poignancy. Herman and Diehl evidently had spent years in close contact with Walt in the California gold field, trapping on the Columbia, and even a few winters down in the Baja.

Ever since a fateful night years back, the Tallhelm family had scant word of Walt's whereabouts or well-being. Hearsay and rumor were the only bits of news that made their way back East. Small comfort to his kin. But now Nate got to hear, firsthand, stories of his legendary brother's exploits.

"Maybe you can clear up something for us, Nate. How'd it come about your brother headed west in the first place?" asked Brow Herman.

"Walt never told you two about what happened back home?" queried Nate.

"No, I can't say it ever came up," answered Herman.

"Well, one thing I know is your brother is pretty sparing when it comes to using words. He don't go on much," offered Bill Diehl.

"Go on much! Hell, Walt could make a dumb mute seem like a jabber bird," countered Herman. "But to answer your question, no, he never said a word. Of course out here it's not real polite to delve into a man's why or what for. Could be he was running after a woman or more likely running away from one. Or maybe looking to get shy of the law or hoping to strike it rich. Striking it rich, yeah, hitting the damn El Dorado. That's what brought me and Diehl here out West, striking it rich. Yeah, we was gonna be rich men!" From the detached gaze that came over Brow Herman's face, one could see things didn't quite turn out that way, and the drink and late autumn night had brought on a lapse into regretful melancholia.

"Enough about that crap, you old farts. Let Nate tell us why Walt come out here anyways," Sage Heck blared, rousting the group back to the topic at hand. "Leastwise I thought he was going to tell us," continued Sage, a slight note of hopeful anticipation in his voice.

"I hadn't given it much thought before this, but now the burden of this curiosity is weighting upon my brain," interjected Johnny Dollars with a note of eloquence that brought all the men to stop what they were doing, gaze momentarily at Johnny, then back to Nate.

"Well, it is quite a story. Would you like to hear it?" teased Nate.

The men's reply came as a series of snorts and nodding heads.

"Yes, Nate, if you would," came the voice of Jonathan Keith, who had been sitting silently in one of the booths off to the side.

"Well, fellas, I remember it like it was yesterday."

With that, Nate took a slow drink of whiskey, brushed back his hair, and began his narrative.

"It was early spring. One of those days when the air lets you know winter is for sure gone. Everywhere you look, things are pushing up out of the ground, the creeks running fast and full from the spring thaw, all the birds making a racket. You could smell the ground coming back to life after the winter. Life started out fine that morning, but it sure as hell didn't turn out that way.

"We learned one thing that day, and that was that Walt was every bit like a coiled rattler ready to strike. And as fast as a rattler can strike is as fast as life can change. What happened that day goes back to how come we came to move to the Shenandoah in the first place.

"Our family had lived and grown up back in the Cumberland Valley just north of the Mason-Dixon. My grandpa was the head caretaker for a man name of Howlander, a finer man you would never meet. His farm was big, biggest in the whole valley. It had everything—dairy cows, horses, timber, a fishery, apple, cherry, peach orchards. He even had an acre of flower gardens that he kept just 'cause he knew his wife liked fresh flowers.

"Mr. Howlander was often away on business, and he needed someone he could trust to run things, whether he was there or not. That someone was my granddad. For this, he was given a nice house to live in, as if it were his own, and a per annum that usually went right into the bank.

"When Gramps died, Pa and my Aunt Ruth, Trader's mom, took over running the place. Eventually, my father met and married my mother, and Aunt Ruth tied the knot with Bill Darcy. We all lived in that one house. It was more than big enough for both families, and Bill Darcy's work as a surveyor had him everywhere but to home. A lot of living happened in that house.

"Hell, my cousin Trader and me, we were raised up like brothers. We had a good life. Sure, there was no end to the chores, and once out of school, straight up man's work. Reckon I've dug enough tree stumps to last a lifetime. Anyway, we didn't get everything we wanted, but then again, we didn't want for anything either."

"Boy, amen to that, Nate, about digging stumps. Got to be damn hard work." This from Johnny Dollars.

"Hell, Johnny, you never did a damn good day's work in your life. Don't tell me about digging stumps. I've dug my fair share, I'll tell ya," Brow Herman declared.

"Hell, I think I still got the calluses from when I was digging stumps!" said Bill Diehl.

"Me too, damnit," added Thaedell Lahr. Everyone at the table gave Lahr the same sarcastic grimace that such an absurd statement deserved. A chorus of "Oh yeah, sure, right" accompanied these looks. It was more than well-known that Lahr was definitely not one for physical labor.

Nate, seemingly transfixed, didn't hear any of this banter as he gazed absently into his whiskey glass lost in a long-forgotten memory until Sage Heck implored him to go on with the story.

"Oh, where was I? Right, sorry, fellas. Long time ago. Anyway."

Nate paused for a moment, turned to Jonathan Keith and, as if they were the only two people in the room, asked, "You sure Miss Haverstraw is all right?"

"Don't worry, Nate. I gave Lorraine my duck's foot, just in case any unwanted visitors got a notion to come callin'. If she lets go with that five-barreled pistol, we'll be cleaning up blood for a week."

Jonathan Keith's duck's foot pistol was a weapon ship captains carried that could fire a five-shot fusillade all at once. For a sea captain, a duck's foot could prove right handy to repel attacking pirates or thwart a mutiny. Jonathan Keith never had to worry about a mutiny. Pirates, though, were always a concern.

Satisfied as to Lorraine's safety, Nate nodded to Keith and went on with the story. "Okay, so where was I? I gotta tell you, fellas, memories are like opening an old trunk. You don't quite know what was put in there. I haven't really thought about these things in some time.

"Ah, right, Mr. and Mrs. Howlander didn't have any children of their own. I suspect Mrs. Howlander was barren, but that was never talked about. So when all us kids came along, they treated us almost like we was their own.

"They were fine people who enjoyed life and helped us enjoy it as well. Every fall, once the crops were in and the apple orchards picked, they'd throw a big party. Most of the townsfolk would come. There were long tables covered with plates of fried chicken, baked hams, cakes, candied fruit, copper tubs full of kegs of beer for the men, bottled root beer for us kids, the whole affair lit with Chinese lanterns strung between the trees.

"There were horseshoe contests for the men, pie-baking contests for the women. For the younger girls they even had a peach turnover competition. The youngsters had hoop and stick races. For the older boys they set up colored canvas archery targets. All the prizes were real money, and anyone who competed came away with at least a ten-dollars gold piece.

"Thinking about it now, it was kinda like a potlatch, white man style. At the end of the night, there was a big fireworks show which, I might add, Pa was in charge of.

"One thing that was nice to see were the Howlanders, who never drank much. But on this night they joined in with everybody. Later on, they could be seen sitting next to each other in these big rocking chairs on their front porch, holding hands and laughing.

"Every winter they would take us into town to the Emporium and buy us any one thing we wanted. Walt, Lonnie, and me always got the newest rifle or pistol that had come in. The girls, of course, would get Sunday dresses and such.

"So life went along. But then, as I've learned, nothing lasts forever. And eventually life as we knew it went the way of all things.

"First, Mrs. H grew ill and soon passed. Then Mr. Howlander began feeling poorly, and it became clear his time was drawing nigh as well. He called my Pa in and thanked him for all my family's hard work over the many years. And to show his gratitude, he was leaving us the house we lived in and several acres of land to farm and do with as we pleased. He also said he had no blood kin and was leaving a good bit of the estate to his wife's brother.

"My Pa always said Arthur Howlander's humanity began where most people's left off. A finer human being was not to be found. Unfortunately, his brother-in-law was no such man.

"Mr. H died, and the town had an official week of mourning. All the flags about town flew at half-mast. So loved was this man. When the will was read, two of the local churches, the school, library, the orphanage, and everyone who worked for him was generously remembered. As promised Pa was left the house and nine acres, along with six horses, a draft team, a number of cows, and a couple dozen sows.

"Although the brother-in-law came away with the lion's share of the estate, he was not satisfied. Some people are never happy. Long story short, he contested the will. Most of it held up, but for some reason, the judge ruled against us. We were left only the horses and livestock, not the house and land. People raised a stink, but the judge couldn't be swayed. He was adamant. We was given the option of renting the house and continuing on as workers or moving on. That was too hard a pill to swallow. We had never had to pay rent and had improved the property as if it were our own. No, we couldn't abide by this. We were given thirty days to decide or move out.

"You know you talk about Walt being quiet. Well, the day that ruling came down about the house is the day Walt changed. From that day on, you never knew what he was thinking, where he went, or when was he coming back. He was never seen unless he wanted you to see him. But he never complained. We had a lot of work to do, and he set right to it. Pa said Walt had become resolute, but Pa added that being resolute could go different ways. Resolute is one thing. Bitter is another.

"One casualty of all this was Walt was fixing to marry this one gal, but that all went to hell. Without any real property or ready prospects of making a good living, she broke it off. Yeah, boys, Walt was once set to be hitched. He always did have a way with the girls. He liked them, and they liked him. Losing that girl was one more cut that fertilized that seed of rage growing in my brother."

Tallhelm paused and took another swallow of whiskey. As if on cue, all the others took a drink as well. Not wanting to interrupt the discourse, Jonathan Keith motioned to Sunny to fetch another bottle from behind the bar. Sunny obliged, and as each man silently refilled his glass, Nate continued.

"There was one bright spot in all of this. Pa always saved most of his money. We grew nearly all our food. Any supplies we needed, feed and such, was always on hand just as part of running the farm. Pa was right frugal. So when he went to the bank to close out the account, he knew the family had saved a decent sum. What we hadn't known was that Mr. Howlander had matched every deposit my Pa and granddad had ever made over all those many years. Well, I gotta tell ya, it nearly brought my Pa to tears. Ma, for her part, bawled like a baby when she heard what Mr. Howlander had done. For us, it was as if the sun had finally come out after a month of rain. This man, Arthur Howlander, was truly beneficent.

"This money was more than enough to pull up stakes and move somewheres away from what had become every bit like a poisoned well. Start a new life."

"Bill Darcy, Trader's Pa, being a surveyor, had traveled all over. He had talked about a beautiful little valley down to the Shenandoah. Land could be had, and depending where you chose, you could be as near or as far from a town as you like. Pa, Walt, and me rode down into Virginia and scouted around for a nice piece of land. Ma and the girls were hoping to settle close to a town, but Pa was set on something a bit more off-the-beaten track.

"Well, we found it. Seventy-five acres of land from the ridge on down to the road. There was enough level ground, once fenced, to graze some cows and pasture the horses. There was a spring that fed a little creek that cut through the property. It was nice, really nice, and after two years of damn hard work, we had built a right respectable home for ourselves. We had grubbed out enough field stone for the house and put in a fine stone fireplace and chimney. For the outbuildings, the hog pen and lean-to stable, we used timber we had to hand. We had brought what we could from back home, but even so we found ourselves going to town for one thing or another. It was on one of those trips to town that all hell broke loose.

"The lumber mill where we had gotten our floorboards and millwork was closing down. There had been an accident where the owner's son had gotten tangled up in the feed chain, and it mangled him something fierce. It took more than a week for him to die. The father damn near lost his mind listening to the agony of his dying boy. He wanted nothing to do with the mill ever again. Matter of fact, he never set foot back on the property. He turned the whole operation over to the local auctioneer to liquidate.

"So there was going to be a big auction. As chance would have it, we were ready to build the paddock and a proper stable and needed a good bit of lumber ourselves.

"Earlier that week, we went to the mill and saw what was to be had. We needed a few good lots of dressed boards, squared timbers, and some fenceposts. This they had.

"The day of the auction, like I said before, was as nice a day as you could want. Ma and the girls came along, and all in all, we was pretty keyed up. Matter of fact, the whole town was keyed up. People from all up and down the valley were crowding into town for this auction. For our part, we were surprised that there were that many people living about.

"Ma and my sisters went off on their way. And Pa, Walt, Lonnie, and me went to the auction. Looking about at so many people, we were wondering if we would come away with any lumber at all. The bidding got a little heated at times, and we had to check out of some of our first choices, but we prevailed on two stacks of good lumber and some fenceposts. I remember the lot numbers we bought, number 18 and number 49, 'cause that was the same as the year, 1849.

"Walt and Pa go down to the office to settle up, and Lonnie and me go fetch the wagons and look to gather up Ma and the girls. Needless to say, there was a lot going on. Yeah, it seemed like the whole valley had turned out for this auction. Men and rigs coming and going, kids running about, dogs barking at horses. I even caught Walt giving a few ladies a nod and a wink. As I said, the girls liked Walt.

"Anyway, we get ready to load our boards and notice they were not the ones what we had paid for. Someone had switched lot numbers, and what we were left with was little better than slabwood. Pa went to the auctioneer and said, 'Some kind of mistake had been made and let's get it cleared up.' The auctioneer said it was out of his hands and then wondered aloud that maybe we were mistaken. After all, one stack of boards looks pretty much like another.

"Well, I could see this grated on Pa no end. It was obvious the people gathered about were having a bit of fun at our expense. Walt hadn't said so much as one word as all this was going on. Pa said if this doesn't get straightened out, he was expecting his money back. Again, the auctioneer said it wasn't his problem. With that, Walt had heard enough and said, 'Well, it's going be someone's problem, and it sure as hell won't be ours.' Walt voiced this in low and even tones that let me and everyone know these weren't empty words.

"It was fairly obvious that we were working against a stacked deck. Being we were on our own, the first order of business was to find the lumber lots that were rightly ours. Well, we found them. They were being loaded onto a couple of wagons by the Pogue brothers. The Pogues were a family that worked for a local farmer name of Harold Garbbler.

"Garbbler had the biggest farm there about and had his hand in one thing or another. But the word about town was he wasn't as rich or as legal as he would like people to think. Seems like most every town has a Harold Garbbler.

"We never had reason to deal with the man before, but straight off, we could see that what people was saying was every bit to true.

"Walt didn't raise his voice, but you could tell he meant business when he told the Pogues, 'I don't know what you think you're doing, but that's our lumber you're loading.'

"Pa added that some kind of mistake must have been made and...Pa never got to finish, but that old man Pogue cut him short. 'You're damn right someone made a mistake. It's when you people moved here in the first place!'

"All of a sudden, we knew there was more to this than a couple stacks of lumber. What exactly that was, we hadn't a clue."

"'Keep loading that lumber, boys.' This now from Harold Garbbler, who had been lurking nearby in the shadow of a large warehouse.

"'You touch another one of those boards and it will be the last thing you do.' This time Walt's voice was louder, but still slow, clear, and resolute. Then in one motion, he drew his pistol, grabbed ahold of old man Pogue, and shoved him backward so hard, the old man and two of his boys went sprawling onto the ground.

"I suppose out of instinct, they had gathered close. Well, all the better, 'cause Walt held his pistol on three of them, and Lonnie, who had quietly reached his rifle from under the wagon seat, held a bead on Butch Pogue, the oldest of the three brothers.

"'I'm calling all you out right here, right now!' You could feel the air grow still and all about get quiet. The only sound we heard were the clicks of the hammers on Walt's double-barreled pistol as he drew them back. Then he said, 'You're nothing but a bunch of rotten lying, thieving skunks, and I'm not having it. One or all of ya. I don't care.'

"Walt was slow to boil, but once there, watch out. Pa and me were as surprised as the Pogues about how quickly the situation had become dire and maybe deadly. But really, in some way, this started that day back in Pennsylvania when that judge voided Mr. Howlander's will.

"'You crazy son of a bitch, put that gun away or I'll have it out with you right here,' screeched Butch Pogue.

"'Fine by me' was Walt's reply. 'How's about those woods right there. We both go in and only one comes out.'

"'Hell, yeah, Tallhelm. I hunted and killed about everything that's ever been in them woods. Suits me fine,' countered Pogue.

"With all this going on, people started crowding around. Then one of 'em pushed his way to the front and hollered, 'Everybody hold on now! Nobody's gonna shoot nobody. Harold, what the hell is all this about?' This was from a man who we figured was the local law officer. He had arrived on the scene just as the Pogues were getting up off the ground.

"'Nothing here to concern you, Hank. This is just a misunderstanding that got a little out of hand, that's all.' This Garbbler tried to sound matter-of-fact, but you could hear the fear in his voice.

"'It's gone too far, Sheriff. I'm going settle this here and now and there's no stopping it,' Walt said, and you could tell he wasn't fooling.

"'Okay, Tallhelm, you want a stalk, that's fine by me' was all Butch could say.

"'Now hold on. That's your boy there, Jed. You sure you want this to go on?' the sheriff was asking Jedidiah Pogue, the father to the Pogue spawn.

"'Butch is full growd. If he got a notion to brace Tallhelm, ain't my place to stop 'em,' answered Pogue.

"The sheriff just shook his head and said, 'All right, if you two are set on doing this, you'll do it right. You both go in them damn woods, and but one comes out. Each man will have his rifle and a pistol.'

"'And a knife,' added Walt.

"'And a knife,' agreed the sheriff.

"'What about our lumber, Sheriff?' Pa asked.

"'To hell with the lumber! Let 'em have it. Maybe it'll catch fire someday!' bellowed old man Pogue.

"'Okay, Pogue, it's three o'clock now. We're going to load our lumber, and I'll meet you back here at six o'clock sharp. That should leave enough daylight for me to find ya and shoot ya.'

"The tone of Walt's voice clearly unnerved this Butch Pogue. Evidently, he was the local bully who could get away with more bluster than bite, and now he had to deliver on one of his threats. We could see he was starting to wonder about just what the hell he got himself into.

"So we loaded our boards and tried not to appear too distraught by the prospect of Walt not being with us for supper that night or any other for that matter.

"Ma and the girls were fretful and in anguish over the whole situation. The two little ones clung to either side of Ma like potholders to a hot skillet.

"Pa could only give his encouragement by giving no encouragement at all, but finally he asked Walt what he planned to do.

"'Don't worry, Pa. Pogue may have hunted those woods, I'll give him that, but nothing he was shooting at could shoot back. Things change when the quarry you're hunting got a gun. Also, Nate, where do you think I've been going when I'm gone at night?'

"I told him, 'Hell, I never know where you go or where you been.'

"He tells us, 'Well, for the last two years, I've been going through these woods day and night on my way to keep company with more than a few of these gals here about. None of the Pogue women, though, but I expect they think I have, and that's the burr under these boys' saddles. So be it. That's one thing, them worrying about me taking their women, but stealing our lumber and laughing about it is another.

"'Don't you concern yourself. Truth be told, I expect the three of them will come after me. That's all the better. It's pretty clear we can't live in this valley with these Pogues lurking about. You heard what he said about maybe our lumber will catch on fire. That's to say our house may catch fire. Ain't having it. Ain't having it no way, no how. This will be settled tonight and that's it.'

"Walt's words went little way to comfort our minds, especially Ma and the girls. They didn't have much to say, but the fear that showed in their fretful eyes spoke for 'em.

"We had loaded the lumber on the wagons, and Lonnie, with the girls, headed back to home. Ma wasn't about to leave, saying she wouldn't draw an even breath till this whole damn thing was settled. First time I'd ever heard Ma cuss.

"Anyway, come six o'clock, Walt and Butch Pogue stood on the road that ran alongside the woods. I'd say they were maybe a quarter mile apart. They both had their rifle, a pistol, and a hunting knife. You could tell the sheriff was disgusted with the whole thing. But at six o'clock, he threw up his hands, the signal to start the stalk.

"Pogue and Walt took off into the woods. Walt took off a hellin' straight up toward the ridge. Pogue did the same, at least that's what Walt reasoned Pogue would do. So Walt stopped quick and made a beeline for about halfway to where Butch came in and where he figured him to be. Not twenty minutes had gone by, but that Walt had gotten in behind Pogue and was shadowing him at about twenty paces. When they got into some tall pines, Walt saw his chance. Where the oaks and maples grew, there was lots of underbrush, but here under these pines, it was open. Nothing but pine needles.

"Walt stopped next to one of the taller of these pine trees and calls out to Pogue. The man stopped dead in his tracks. All the time he thought Walt was somewhere in front of him. Well, you could only imagine how surprised the bastard was when he realized it was the other way around, 'cause the next thing he did was whirl on Walt and took a rifle shot. Well, that shot coulda hit someone in the next county 'cause it came nowheres near Walt.

"'You can back out of here, Pogue. You and your trash can leave the valley and never come back, or you can stay here and die. I'll give you that choice. I'm damn fed up with the likes of you, cheating and conniving. What will it be?' Walt called.

"Walt hadn't seen a need to duck behind the tree as Pogue's bullet had gone so far astray. Dropping his spent rifle, Pogue reached his pistol out of a belly holster and, taking aim, fired a shot that splashed some bark off the tree next to Walt's head, but nothing more.

"'How you at knife throwing, Butch?' With that, Walt steps out in front of the tree and gave Pogue an open target.

"Walt was expecting Pogue to draw his knife from his coat, instead he pulls out another pistol. Seeing this, Walt had had enough. He hit the ground, rolled hard to his right, got himself prone, cocked his rifle, and shot. The bullet caught Pogue square in the heart. He was dead before he hit the ground.

"Walt figured the other Pogues would have heard the shots and been coming that way. Quick as he could, he took off his coat and switched his coat and hat with the one Butch Pogue was wearing and propped the dead man into the crotch of a tree. Walt made sure to put the man's back toward the sound of the approaching Pogue brothers. He then grabbed up Pogue's pistols and rifle and sprinted toward the ridge and circled back around.

"Well, sure enough, wasn't no time till Walt could see the other brothers working their way through the woods. Walt inched down in behind them and waited.

Once the two brothers saw who they thought was Walt, they leveled their rifles and shot. Both bullets would have killed Butch Pogue if he hadn't already been dead. But for good measure, each drew their pistol and shot again. As the two warily approached the body, they reloaded and, with cocked hammers, kept them at the ready. Just then, a winded old man Pogue appeared at the edge of the stand of pines.

"'We got him, Pa. We got that bastard!' Walt said he could hear the relief and joy in their voices.

"'Where's Butch?' shouted the old man.

"'He must be down the way. Butch!' the one brother called out. Then the other. 'Butch.' The old man got close in, just as the two were ready to turn Walt around.

"'Turn that son of a bitch over. Butch, we got him. Butch!' hollered old man Pogue.

"God only knows what horror those sorry bastards went through once they realized they had been pumping lead into the back of their own brother Butch and not Walt. Whatever their anguish and confusion was, it didn't last long 'cause just then, Walt steps out and tells them to 'turn around and meet your Maker.' Walt had his and one of Butch Pogue's pistols loaded and cocked. Now he was facing three but just as well, he thought. Why not clean up the whole damn bunch right here?

"Each of the brothers fired. One slug caught Walt just aside his left shoulder, more like a bee sting than a gunshot.

The others' shot went astray. Walt let loose with the two pistols, and both brothers fell. Old man Pogue shouldered his rifle and took his shot. The bullet grazed the side of Walt's forehead just above his right eye. A little bit of blood got in Walt's eye which he wiped away then hollered out, 'I hope you're happy now, you crude bastard. Go join your boys.'

"Walt then drew his hunting knife, and quick as you can blink, flung it about twenty yards and planted it deep into Jedediah Pogue's chest. As he was falling, old man Pogue made an awkward attempt not to fall onto the bodies of his dead sons, but failed.

"That was the end of the Pogue boys pushing people around. By the time Walt got back to where Pa and us were waiting, seemed like most of the town had gathered about."

"'Heard a lot shooting. Where's the Pogues?' asked the sheriff.

"'You can find them up yonder, Sheriff. They're dead,' answered Walt.

"'All of 'em?' asked the sheriff.

"'Yup, all of 'em.'

"At first the people there didn't believe Walt.

"Then the sheriff said something to Mrs. Pogue, and she starts wailing and going on. That's when the people knew what Walt was saying was true.

"Garbbler shouts, 'Arrest this man!'

"'I ain't arresting nobody. If I arrest anyone, I'll arrest you. Maybe if I had done that a long time ago, this wouldn't never of happened. You're done here, Harold, and it's time you realized it.' You could tell the sheriff meant it.

"Old man Garbbler just stood there. His day had started out fine, but now here he was, disgraced, humiliated, and exposed for the four-flusher he was.

"For us, the relief we all felt was beyond ebullient."

"Beyond what?" asked Sage Heck.

"Ebullient, Sage. Another word for happy, but real happy." Lahr offered this clarification as he and the others looked at one another, almost transfixed not only by the story but by the fact that Walt had never mentioned so much as a word of it during all the years they'd known one another.

"Damn, kilt all four of 'em," blurted Johnny Dollars.

"Was that the end of it, Nate?" asked Jonathan Keith.

"Well, yeah, I suppose. The end and the beginning. By the time we were headed out of town on our way back home, a couple dozen townsfolk stopped us and wouldn't let us go, but that we agreed to let them help us in any way they could. They would have it no other way.'

"This pleased Ma no end. She knew the girls had to have friends in town if they were going to have a full life and proper schooling. Something they hadn't had since we left back home. Yeah, Ma was ebullient. Ebullient, I say, Sage, ebullient." With that, Nate smiled and looked about the table.

Silent awe settled upon the group till Sunny cracked open another bottle and poured each man a drink and solemnly offered a toast to "Walt Tallhelm, one damn good man to ride the river with!"

"To Walt!" echoed all the men at the table.

"So, Nate, you said before that Walt headed west that night?" asked Brow Herman.

"Yeah, Brow. Not that night but just a few days later. He told me that taking care of what Garbbler and the Pogues were trying to do gave him back his footing. He likened it to going from quicksand to solid ground. Pa understood, and I guess I did as well. That business back in Pennsylvania had left a world of bile in our guts. Too bad so much blood had to be shed, but to Walt, they had started it, and this time Walt could do something about finishing it.

"A couple days later he headed out West. Back when we left out of Pennsylvania, Bill Darcy, Aunt Ruth, Trader, and the twins headed out to Colorado. Uncle Bill had been hired on to do a long-term surveying job for the railroad. Walt figured to head there first. Turns out, it wasn't till about six years later that he caught up with them."

"I've seen that scar on Walt's forehead. Can't get much closer to being shot dead than that, I suppose," said Sunny.

"Damn lucky," offered Johnny Dollars.

"Hell, what are you taking about? That bullet coulda hit him square in the forehead and most likely just bounce off. You know how hardheaded Walt is!" Brow Herman added.

"I gotta tell ya, boys, I ain't talked this much since I don't know when. Anyway, I can't wait to see that bear dog of a brother of mine. That is iffen he don't get himself all shot up before then. I understand this Herzog, from what Miles and Lorraine say, is as ruthless a son of a bitch what ever drew a breath."

"Don't you worry, Nate. Walt and Sarusha can handle that bastard Herzog and whatever trash is riding with him," stated Bill Diehl.

Herman's matter-of-fact tone was reassuring to Nate. Nevertheless, not until he was standing face-to-face with his brother would Nate's apprehension be assuaged.

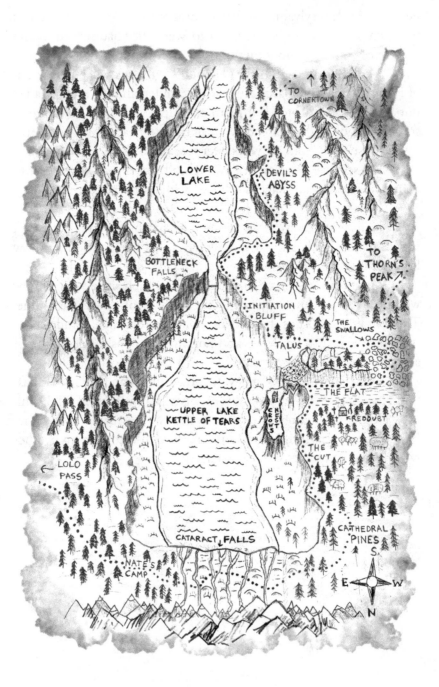

15

THE RECONNOITER

B row Herman and Bill Diehl would have tempered their pronouncements about Walt's and Sarusha's invincibility had they been aware of what the men encountered on the trail leading up to Initiation Bluff. The men following Johnathan Keith's order to see if they could find out what had become of Trader had left out of the Nest eight days ago. Late morning of their second day out, they came across the first indication that all was not as it should be—the burnt and animal-ravaged remains of Marcel Dagget.

"Dagget," Sarusha grunted with a disdainful sneer, indicating only contempt for the man.

"How can you tell?" Walt asked, since all that remained of Dagget, once the wolves were finished, was a pair of bare leg bones sticking out of his boots. Vultures had picked the bones clean and were frantically trying to get to what meat remained inside the boots when Sarusha scattered the birds with a pistol shot into the ground.

"Those are his boots."

Walt Tallhelm didn't know Dagget, having only seen him briefly at the Crow's Nest. He didn't know if he was as low a skunk as Sarusha evidently believed, but he felt any man deserved better than this.

Dagget, along with Tice and the two Johnson brothers, had left the Nest a day before Walt and Sarusha. They told Sunny they were heading to Missoula to find some women. Well, Missoula was in the opposite direction, and Tice knew this. So whatever plot was the genesis of that deception was yet to play out.

Whoever did Dagget in—and that most likely was Tice—didn't care if anyone found the body, or more to the point, wanted it to be found. Because any rider on the rim trail would have had to come this way. If it was meant to scare people off, it wasn't working.

When Walt and Sarusha left the Nest, they were headed south to Initiation Bluff and farther on to the Bottleneck Falls. Trader's map indicated the cave of gold was located somewhere south of a place known as the Devil's Abyss. In Indian lore, the place was also known as the scene of the "night of the widest eyes," the location where two centuries before, the Indians had extracted their gruesome revenge on the Spaniards who had plundered the cave of Stone Eyes and forever poisoned the area for the local tribes.

It would appear Tice and company were headed in that same direction. Walt and Sarusha hadn't started out tracking Tice, but once they picked up their trail the previous afternoon, that's just what they were doing.

Although only thirty miles due south of the Crow's Nest, the route to Initiation Bluff required a trip through the Swallows and made the journey almost three times that distance. Any rider heading south from the Crow's Nest had to first head west to get around the talus shelf that blocked the rim trail. The quarter-mile swatch of steep shale talus ran from the very edge of the rim west to the face of a high forested promontory. Anyone wanting to head south would risk almost certain death crossing the rock-strewn talus as steep as a church roof. Which meant the only way south was first to head west to dreaded Swallows—a vast maze of boulders and stone outcroppings that created a deadly labyrinth—then wend your way south. By the same token, anyone coming north on the rim trail toward the Crow's Nest would also have to head west and through the Swallows. This talus barrier added yet another strategic advantage to the Nest's unique location.

Sarusha was very familiar with the route he and Walt had to take on the first leg of the journey. The near constant wind that swirled through the Swallows obliterated any hoof tracks almost as soon as they had been made. The complex labyrinth had spelled doom for any number of animals and scores of men, men who became hopelessly lost once they ventured in. The aptly named Swallows did just that—swallowed up man and beast.

Fortunately, Sarusha knew the right ways in and out. South of the Swallows, there were two trails through the forest: one bent to the west, and after a three-day ride would bring you under the shadow of Thorn's Peak. The other headed south and east and eventually led back to the rim, just north of Initiation Bluff.

Sarusha and Walt, once through the Swallows, took the trail south and east. Soon they came across the hoof tracks of Tice and company and, in time, the gruesome remains of Marcel Dagget.

Walt and Sarusha were good at reading sign and were able to put together most of what took place, except just why Dagget had been shot in the first place.

The trail around the rim was at times as wide and welcoming as a country road. Other times, little more than the width of a garden path. Sometimes the trail meandered away from the rim, weaving its way through scruffy chaparral, other times returning to the rim where it could be nothing more than a narrow ledge, where one false step would send a rider over the edge to his doom.

It was at one of these points that Tice was forced to put down his horse. The mount had gone lame farther back the trail and had been making its way with a broken gait. Unable to go on and blocking the narrow trail, it had to be put down and pushed over the edge. The buzzards circling the canyon floor far below identified the final resting place for the unfortunate beast.

Two of the riders doubled up, and shortly after that, where the trail widened, the men struck their camp.

Sarusha knew Tice and Dagget but very little about the Johnson brothers, other than that they had no business being away from a town. More used to high-kicking dancehall girls than high mountain trails, the brothers were clearly out of their element. Tice and Dagget weren't all that good at being out of doors either, but their feral nature held them in better stead.

Tice, a gunslinger with a fairly strong resumé in that regard, usually left town only when forced by the law or pressure from an overwrought public. Dagget was nothing more than a shiftless no-good who clung to any scant opportunity to get himself through one day and onto the next.

How—or more to the point, why—the four of them ended up here in the first place was a question that needed to be answered. And most likely that answer had something to do with Trader and Veronica going missing.

Reading what sign was available, they could see that the men, with scant experience to guide them, had made a fire from scrub pine hastily gathered as night approached. The sap from the bushy pines would have sputtered as the needle-covered branches erupted into flames, then quickly died.

Between the fact that there were four men and only three horses and the near constant task of feeding a fire that never quite became a fire, plus the concern for their general welfare, the Johnson brothers had questions that needed answers.

"Tice, what's the deal? Dagget here just told Lee that this Herzog may not have any women in his camp. Now what is it? The only reason we left out of the Settlement was to get some new women. And now he says there are no women. What the hell's going on?" Ray Johnson asked.

"You said Dagget told you what?" asked Jack Tice, the anger more than apparent in his voice.

"Dagget said, Herzog…didn't…have…any…women…in… his…camp."

"Don't you boys worry about that. Sure Herzog got women. I saw them myself," the deceitful Tice answered. "Why don't you Johnson boys go see about getting something more to put on the fire? I gotta have a talk with Marcel in private."

Dagget, meanwhile, was trying to figure what of his gear he could keep after Tice had commandeered his horse and was told he'd have to double up with one of the Johnsons. He needn't have bothered.

"Marcel, don't worry with that. Come over here by the fire," directed Tice.

Marcel paused to finish off the last of the whiskey bottle he and the Johnson brothers had been passing around since attempting to make a camp. It would be the last whiskey to pass his lips in this lifetime. No sooner had Dagget come into the firelight than Tice started filling him full of bullet holes.

Momentarily bewildered, Dagget looked down at his sievelike body before falling dead into the fire, a fire that was just getting large enough to provide some decent warmth for the normally saloon-bound men. Tice watched as Dagget's body sputtered and burned in the soon-to-be-abandoned fire. He was slowly reloading his revolver as the Johnson brothers returned with two small armfuls of firewood.

"What's all the shooting?" asked Ray Johnson.

Seeing Dagget's body in the fire, Lee Johnson's only comment was "Christ, Tice, you didn't have to outen' the fire with the son of a bitch."

The emphasis was placed on the word *fire* and tinged with concern.

"To hell with him. That squirrelly bastard was always getting me pissed off for one thing or another. Now we don't have to ride doubled up. Good riddance to that useless sot," announced Jack Tice as he wondered to himself how the Johnson brothers could take the fact of his plugging Dagget so calmly.

"I didn't know much about that man, but what I did know, I didn't like," chimed in Ray Johnson as he salvaged the few larger pieces of firewood from what had become a pathetic and half-assed funeral pyre for Marcel Dagget.

"We should have been to Herzog's camp by now. If there were any wind tonight, we'd all be dead ducks," continued Ray.

As if on cue, from some mischievous deity, a whirlwind blew about the fire, carrying all the light-gray ash up and into a tall funnel that danced about the men for several moments, then collapsed.

"Hell, we're nowheres from Herzog's. That lame horse of mine held us up. This camp is okay," offered Tice feebly.

"What camp?" ridiculed Lee Johnson as he moved away from where Dagget lay and set to making a new fire.

"This was a mistake, Ray," Lee continued. "The only reason we left down the Settlement was 'cause what Dagget said about women. Yeah, Dagget's dead now, and we're camped out with this trigger-happy bastard and a goddamn half-lit fire." The anger in Lee's voice rose with each word.

"Hell, if you boys don't like the setup, slope," responded Tice, knowing full well the Johnson brothers couldn't go anywhere till dawn.

"What about the women?" pressed Ray Johnson, looking for some confirmation of what had enticed him and his brother away from the chancy but relative comfort back at the Settlement Bar in the first place.

"Dagget was wrong about the women. I don't know what the hell he was talking about. But Herzog is putting together an outfit, and there's women. And I'm supposed to be in charge. So if it comes to getting women, I'll be the one to see," Tice smugly stated, his tone indicating an end to the conversation.

"Damn it, Ray, what'd we get ourselves into? As soon as we get..." Lee Johnson's voice trailed off as he thought he heard something move off in the darkness. All three men had revolvers in their hands before they finished turning in the direction of Lee's gaze.

Out of the darkness, the red eyes of one coyote appeared, then another and another. The eyes and bared teeth of the animals gathered what little light the fire possessed. In all, a dozen hungry coyotes stood peering at the motionless trio for several moments.

The wind changed slightly, blowing the stench of Dagget's half-burnt body past the pack. The one closest to the men turned first. Then, turning as one, the pack, at a lope, disappeared into the darkness.

"Ray, I don't care if you never get your nubbin skint again. We're g'tting' back up to that Crow's Nest, then on down to the Settlement," an obviously agitated Lee Johnson announced.

"Hell, don't let a couple coyotes spook ya. How in the hell did you boys ever end up this far from a whorehouse anyway?" added Jack Tice in an attempt to introduce some levity to the situation.

"Hell if I know," answered both men in unison.

"I'll be damn sure it won't happen again," added Lee.

The Johnson brothers spent a restless night wondering what they had gotten themselves into. Tice, on the other hand, had no trouble sleeping through the night and had to be jostled awake in the morning, well past dawn. The men broke camp in silence, went through Dagget's gear, took what they wanted, kicked the rest into the dirt, saddled up, and continued heading south on the rim trail.

Sarusha and Walt figured the three riders were less than a few hours ahead of them. They looked about one last time, shook their heads, guided their horses around Dagget's discarded saddle, and continued up the trail to Initiation Bluff, some five miles on.

"I wonder how many more trail markers like that we'll find?" asked Sarusha, cocking his head back in the direction of Dagget's remains where the vultures had regathered to finish their meal.

"Seems like a right cold bunch. If this is what they'd do to one of their own, hate to think what they'd have in store for a stranger," Walt reflected as he unsheathed his rifle and checked to make sure a bullet was ready in the chamber.

"When we get to the bluff, if those men stay to the rim trail, which I think they will, we should get a good look at 'em."

After two or three miles on the trail up to the bluff, Walt turned and asked, "You see what I see?"

"Yeah, seems like Tice wants to stay in behind those two brothers."

Walt and Sarusha, when they originally picked up the men's trail, had quickly figured out what horses the brothers were riding, since they usually rode next to one another. Tice's horse was the one gone lame, and now he rode the late Marcel Dagget's mount. So when they saw the hoof tracks of Dagget's horse always following behind the brothers, it wasn't hard to put two and two together.

The bluff where the men were headed was clearly visible up the trail, a straight and steady uphill grade. Initiation Bluff was the highest point anywhere around the rim and would afford the men an unbroken vantage point of the whole of the Kettle of Tears.

The name Initiation Bluff had survived long after the rituals that gave the place its name had come to an end. Centuries ago, braves who had come of age and proven their courage individually were brought to this bluff and, as a group, were given one final task: hollow out a cedar log, carry it down to the upper lake, and paddle it across.

The job seemed simple enough, but every step of the process required keen judgment and skillful execution. If the log they chose was too big, getting it down the perilous path to the lake could be calamitous in any number of ways. If the dugout ended up being too small, it would become overloaded and swamp itself.

As in many initiation rituals, the behavior of the initiates at all stages of the process brings to light otherwise hidden character traits. Who are the leaders? Who are the followers? Who shows ingenuity? Who is a contrarian? A tribal leader cannot teach cohesion or bestow esprit de corps upon a group, but a task like this could. Working together as a group, in the small context, reinforced in the initiates a greater sense of tribal unity.

The elders, for their part, would always step in before any fatal miscues took place. Again, reinforcing the good of the tribe even at the expense of some bruised egos.

Walt and Sarusha crested the trail and stood upon the bluff.

"There they are, just like I said. Let's get back out of sight. If we can see them, they can see us," cautioned Sarusha.

Hidden from view, the men watched the three riders make their way past the overlook above the Bottleneck Falls and out of sight. Beyond the falls, the trail wove its way west for a stretch and then continued south.

"If we follow them on this trail, once we round that bend, we'd be as naked as the gospel bird on Sunday morning. We don't want that bunch to know we be trailing 'em," added Sarusha.

"Sounds like you been spending too much time talking to Lucien," commented Walt, noting Sarusha's use of Caribbean vernacular.

"I don't know if what Lucien and I do could pass for talking. I can't understand half of what he says," admitted Sarusha.

"Yeah, and the other half ain't worth hearing," joked Walt, showing a rare grin, as the two had a small laugh at Lucien Samms' expense.

Coming back out from cover, they stood on Initiation Bluff. The panoramic view that presented itself was humbling. Far to the north, the cataract spilled over the edge of the rim and into the upper lake. South of that, just off the west wall, was the Crow's Nest, perched upon its rocky crag. Rather than appear out of place, the Crow's Nest highlighted the natural grandeur of the scene—the defiant and resolute edifice striking a deep harmonic chord in anyone who cast their gaze upon it.

Just south of where they stood was the Bottleneck Falls, its moss-covered palisades perpetually shrouded in mist. Sunk into the valley below lay the blue lower lake. Tranquil and serene, it enjoyed the soft light of the late autumn sun. Along the eastern shore, the men caught the only bit of movement to disturb the scene—a giant sliver of stone crashed silently into the lake, broken from the cliff face by the ceaseless work of weather and root.

"From here on, we'll take a trail I know through the woods. We'll get on ahead of them by tomorrow noon. Those boys don't know it yet, but they'll be camping out in the open again tonight. There's no way to get off that trail and under cover before dark, the sorry sons of bitches," Sarusha said as he looked about one last time before reining his horse into the woods that abutted the bluff. Sarusha had never been cavalier about the Indian blood of his mixed heritage. Standing on this bluff, that fact was attested to by the pain in his heart that rang through his body like a bell.

His father, the great Nez chief Anahuy, at first had decided to keep an open mind concerning the white man. So much so that he took as his wife a Frenchwoman whose strength and empathetic nature made her worthy of respect in all quarters.

Anahuy never regretted the decision to marry Sarusha's mother, but while Sarusha was still a young man, he took his son aside and said, "Don't trust white men. Their so-called sacred word lasts no longer than the shadow of the clouds as they pass over the hillside."

Sarusha judged each man on his own merit and gave no quarter once slighted. You didn't get a second chance with Sarusha.

The trail through the forest was dim but defined enough that the men were able to ride at a good pace the rest of the afternoon, until darkness forced them to stop. They found a small creek and struck their camp close by.

"We'll head back toward the rim in the morning. That map of Trader's has that damn cave somewheres just south of Devil's Abyss. I think tomorrow we'll get some answers," Sarusha announced as Walt dropped a fishing line into the creek, hoping to catch something to add to their regular fare of dried fruit, jerked beef, and trail biscuits.

"Sounds good to me. The longer this goes on, the worse it gets," said Walt. And with a rare bit of luck, no sooner had he put the line in water than he was pulling out a two-foot trout.

16

FOUND OUT

"Damn nice camp. I could see spending a few days right here. Too bad we gotta be chasing these bastards," Walt Tallhelm opined as Sarusha fried up the last of the trout.

"We'll find something out today. We can't go back and tell the Captain all we found was a shot-up Marcel Dagget and a good place to catch trout," said Sarusha, looking to see what Walt was up to.

"I ain't had a bath since I don't know when. Sometimes I get a little too ripe even for my own damn self," announced Walt as he stripped down and got in the creek.

"Thank God you caught those fish last night, 'cause sure as hell they'd be floating up dead any minute now," joked Sarusha.

Once Walt was finished his monthly bath, the men packed up their gear and were on the trail just as the morning sun started to filter through the thinning aspen leaves, the cool autumn air reminding them their time was done.

"Reckon we'll get ahead of those boys and wait for them somewheres below the Abyss," suggested Sarusha.

"I wonder if there's still three of 'em."

The cynical speculation in Walt's voice made Sarusha shake his head and respond, "Something tells me they'll be a lot more men dead before this whole thing's over. Gold has a way of taking over men's better judgment." Keeping to the forested trail and riding at a brisk pace, by noon they were south of Devil's Abyss and planned on

157

awaiting the arrival of Tice and the Johnson brothers. Just then, they saw smoke over toward the rim.

"I think we found where Tice and them were headed. Something tells me that fire ain't Trader's," offered Walt as he dismounted and gently stroked his horse's face, settling the natural apprehension the steed may have had, given its keen sense when varmints were about, both the four-legged and two-legged kind.

Sarusha dismounted and sniffed the wind, tilting his head in the direction from whence they had come and, in a low voice, suggested they leave their horses back a ways and make their way on foot. Walt silently agreed.

As he led his horse away, Walt felt the location of each of his throwing hatchets inside his vest—at the ready. He unsheathed his rifle, took out an extra box of shells from his saddlebag, and waited for Sarusha to decide how far from the campfire smoke they should go before tying up their horses.

The two men hadn't lived this long in these mountains by taking unnecessary chances. They found a little hollow, out of the wind and well off the trail, where their horses would keep and made their way back toward that camp. Twenty minutes later, they were looking down on a ramshackle assemblage of tents and lean-tos. Two deer and a turkey hung from the low branches of a nearby tree. The fire that had originally alerted the men was all but out, its listless plume of smoke rising straight up in the still noonday air. The camp appeared to be all but deserted.

From the safety of their hidden perch, they kept watched, not quite certain what their next move was. That question was answered when they saw Tice and the Johnson brothers ride into camp, fresh off the rim trail.

Tice rode behind the brothers and had his rifle trained on their backs. "You boys tie your horses up over there and get over to the side of that canyon pronto," directed Tice.

Walt and Sarusha could see one of the brothers had a large welt on the side of his face, and both their gun belts were slung over the saddle horn of Tice's horse.

"No big mystery what's going on here," whispered Walt to Sarusha. As Tice herded the two brothers over toward the rim, Walt suggested one of them should circle around and come up from the south and get a better idea of exactly what was what.

Sarusha agreed and crept backward, disappearing deeper into the woods. The Indian made a wide circle to the west and soon was coming up from the south. Sarusha was familiar with the hoofprints of both Trader's and Veronica's horses. Veronica's mount was, in fact, a wedding gift from Jonathan Keith and a horse Sarusha knew well. Ever aware, he was looking for those hoof marks like a hound to a scent.

Sarusha carefully crossed over the rim trail and climbed partway down the canyon wall. A thin ledge provided footing, and some short shrubbery gave him something to hold to. He looked northward, where he could clearly see the opening to a cave, then inched his way closer, getting near enough to hear the voices of several men. He couldn't make out exactly what they were saying, but it was more than apparent what they were doing. Each man came to the front of the cave and emptied a bucket of rocks over the side and down to the canyon floor, one after another after another. The only break in the activity was when a boatswain's chair was lowered down with one of the Johnson brothers in it. He was immediately put to work.

When he leaned forward to get a better look, the shrub Sarusha was holding onto gave way. Momentarily teetering on the ledge, he managed to regain his balance and clung tight to the canyon wall. No one had seen him. But Sarusha had seen enough. He inched himself backward, double-checking the strength of every handhold as he went. He regained the edge of the rim and quickly crossed back over the trail and into the woods.

As he circled back around toward Walt's position, he took time to belly-up to the very edge of the encampment. He had just folded himself into a low spot and pulled some leaves over top as someone came through the woods and into the camp, missing Sarusha by inches.

The man, intent on the movement in the camp, didn't take notice of Sarusha, and a good thing too. It was Chance Parker, a bloodthirsty and trigger-happy son of a bitch for sure.

"I was wondering who was in the camp. When you get back?" Parker asked Tice, who had just finished tying a rope around Ray Johnson's legs.

"'Bout an hour ago. How's come youse the one fetching water?" asked Tice.

"Everybody's working the cave," answered Parker as he hung the dozen or so canteens he'd been carrying on a picket tripod. "How many men you get?"

"I left outa Keith's with three, but one of 'em suddenly came down with lead poisoning and died," answered Tice, not caring one way or another if Parker wanted more information than that.

"Lead poisoning, when did that come on?" asked Parker, figuring he knew what Tice was saying but wanting to be sure.

"I guess that started when I put six bullets into the thieving son of a bitch," carped Tice, aware that Chance Parker put a lower value on human life than even he did.

"What's with him?" asked Parker as he thrust his jaw in the direction of Ray Johnson.

"He and his brother had been volunteers, but after that thing with Dagget, they got a little squirrelly. I didn't know if I could trust 'em anymore. His brother agreed to work. This one figured he got principles."

"Tice, take off that gag," instructed Parker. "What's your name?"

"Ray Johnson."

"This is the setup here, Ray. You and your brother...where is his brother, by the way?"

"He got lowered down to the cave."

"Anyway, this is the setup. You and your brother help us do what we're doing and you could end up with more money than you ever dreamed of. That's one choice. The other choice is, I put a bullet between your eyes and make your brother drag your dead body over to that cliff and throw it off. Your choice."

Chance Parker finished giving Johnson this ultimatum as he broke his pistol and sighted through the gun barrel at Johnson's head.

"My brother and me had a deal with Dagget and Tice here. I don't—"

"Whatever deal you had with Dagget ain't my worry. You heard what deal you got with me. Now what's it gonna be?" Parker said this last part in a voice that could make a demon shudder.

"What the hell. Not much of a choice, is it?" answered an ash-en-faced Ray Johnson.

"No it ain't, but it's the only one you're gonna get," pressed Parker.

"You got a deal," answered Ray as he lifted up his hands, allowing Tice to cut the rope bindings.

"Don't you try anything foolish. I'm just about fed up with this whole damn mess. Now make your way over to the rim. Somebody will lower you down. You got a pair of gloves? If you do, I'd take 'em. While you're at it, take these with ya." Parker handed Ray Johnson a half dozen canteens and waited for him to be out of earshot before asking Tice, "You see Severman and Dean up at the Nest?"

"Yeah. As a matter of fact, they were just getting there when we was leaving. They in on this?" asked Tice.

"Nah, Dean owes me some money," answered Parker, not interested in giving Tice the true answer.

"What about the woman? Any sign of her?"

"No, we gave up looking for her. I don't see how she could make it in these woods for too long. I figure her scalp is hanging from some lodgepole or she's keeping some big buck happy."

Sarusha was hard-pressed to stop himself from springing up and attacking these two. But his mind was awash with questions. The two hadn't mentioned Trader, but why would they only be looking for the woman and not Trader? Sarusha rightly figured he best not make any snap decisions till he found out more.

"What was going on up at the Nest? Old man Keith wasn't all that hospitable to me and Herzog when we was there. He didn't know from nothing about all this. And I still think he don't," Parker said as he watched Ray Johnson reach the canyon rim.

"Nothing much. No one was saying anything about this Trader Darcy or his woman. Leastwise, I didn't hear no one say anything. Some big hombre showed up couple days before we left. Tallhelm, Walt Tallhelm."

"Walt Tallhelm. Did you say Walt Tallhelm?" an obviously agitated Chance Parker asked.

"Yeah, Walt Tallhelm. You know him?"

"Damn right I know him. I had a run-in with him some years back. Him being around is not good news. But what the hell, the Colonel's about half ready to forget this damn gold and just go kick that old bastard Keith out of his damn Crow's Nest, him and his damn half-breed."

Parker fairly spit out these words, using as much disgust and disdain as his voice could muster. "Tallhelm being there might just do it. Two birds, make that three birds, with one stone. That might be how this goes. That beaner wife of Darcy's should be dead, just like her old man. Damn it all!" Parker then spit on the ground, the only outlet for his annoyance with the whole situation.

"How the hell did that happen anyway, her getting away?"

"Oh, hell, we came up on them real quiet-like, me and Herzog. She was on her horse lowering Darcy down over the edge to the cave when Herzog cuts the rope before I had a chance to grab ahold of her horse. I got off a couple shots, but she was in the woods too damn quick. Stupid son of a bitch Herzog anyway. Our only play might be taking over the Nest, but again this Herzog, he's got gold fever, and ain't no stopping him."

"Where is Herzog, anyway?"

"Where he is every day. In that cave working those men. I've seen gold fever. It ain't pretty."

"Where's Pealeday?"

"He's still down to Lewiston, trying to work some of those diehards into a frenzy. Ain't going to work, though. Gone on too long. That border's staying right where it is. I figure I'll stick and see this thing through. What the hell, why not?"

Chance Parker knew Clayton Pealeday's problems were more complicated than he let on, but again he didn't care to share all the facts with Jack Tice.

"Talking about gold, how much they get out so far?" asked Tice.

"Herzog ain't saying, and I got tired of asking. If I was you, I wouldn't ask either."

Sarusha had heard enough. He had a mind to get back to Walt, get the horses, and head south looking for any sign left by Veronica. If Parker looked for her and couldn't find her, it didn't mean he and Walt couldn't. Sarusha was a good tracker, and Walt, for his part, could track a jackrabbit through a briar patch.

Sarusha slithered backward and made his way to where Walt had been keeping vigil.

"What'd ya see?" asked Walt.

"More like what did I hear. After I saw where the cave was, on my way back, I got close enough to hear what those two were saying." A thirsty Sarusha delivered this information as he took a long drink from the waterskin he had forgotten earlier.

"I see Chance Parker's in on this. That means Clayton Pealeday is as well. What ya hear?"

"What I heard didn't sound good."

Sarusha told Walt everything the men had said. Walt listened to Sarusha, but his inner voice was what he heard the loudest. Again, darkness from the depth of his soul began again to eclipse the light. In an instant, the deep disgust he had for those that embraced murderous greed came flooding back. Much like how a smell can transport you back decades to another time, what these men had done to Trader had brought back all that bile from years past. For Walt, it crystallized the one and only task he had ahead of him. If nothing more in this lifetime, he would see these men dead.

Sarusha had grown to consider Walt almost like kin. The pain and anger he must be feeling right now showed clearly on his face. At a loss as to what else to add, he said, "Oh, maybe you already know, but Parker and Pealeday don't like you. Some kind of bad blood between you and them?"

"Hell yeah. How can there not be bad blood when you got people like Pealeday and that son of a bitch Parker?" Walt had to catch himself as he felt his voice getting louder. "There was bad blood, and now the only good blood will be theirs when I see it spouting out of their necks after I slice 'em open."

Walt delivered this resolve as he stared off into space and absently felt the bumps in his vest where his hatchets resided.

"Let's get back to the horses. Veronica might still be alive. I want to start looking for tracks while there's still some light," said Sarusha.

Walt nodded.

With a new sense of urgency, the men were back on their horses, and with a few good hours of daylight remaining, they combed the forest south of the encampment, looking for any sign left by Veronica Darcy. As the day turned to dusk, their vision adjusted to the dimming light, and they were able to look for tracks in near darkness. Eventually, the only place where there was enough light to see was the rim trail. The three-quarter moon was low on the horizon but bright enough to light their way. By now, the men were well south of the camp, far enough south not to be seen.

As fate, providence, or just pure luck would have it, the rim trail would prove to be just where the men needed to be looking. On foot, they led their horses slowly down the trail, silently searching. Sarusha's head snapped hard to the right as out of the corner of his eye, he caught the faintest remnant of a hoofprint from Veronica's horse. "Whoa, look here." Sarusha gave Walt the reins of his horse, and in the blink of an eye, he was crouching on one knee, intently scrutinizing the hoofprint.

"There's two people on this horse," announced Sarusha. As he stood up, he looked Walt in the eye, the two silently sharing the impact of the find.

Walt and Sarusha followed the tracks, lost them, then found them again, but with the moonlight failing, blocked by passing clouds, the men decided to strike a dark camp and continue the search in the morning.

They had trouble finding sleep as their minds worked to analyze every scenario possible. They conjectured between themselves what they would have done had they been in Trader's shoes. Cornertown was the closest and most logical destination. Parker would have known this. But those men thought they were looking for a Mexican woman, new to the area, who had just seen the rope holding her husband from falling to his death get cut and disappear over the edge of the rim. They must have figured that she probably didn't even know there was a Cornertown. And even if she did, she'd have scant chance of finding her way there.

Once Herzog and Parker gave up looking, they concluded hopefully that Veronica had fallen victim to starvation, animal attack, or hostiles.

"We gotta think like Trader would," said Sarusha.

"Riding double, that horse would get tired sooner than later. If I was them, I'd be looking for a downhill trail and some good grass," surmised Walt.

"Thorn's Peak!" both men said the name at the same time.

"Yeah, to the foot of the Thorn, it's all downhill from here, and the tree line this side has plenty of graze to it. Let's hope we can keep their trail. But hell, Trader would be most likely trying not to leave any trail," said Sarusha.

"I figured that. Maybe one of us should head to Cornertown and see if Nelson heard anything and the other head over toward the Thorn. We could rendezvous somewhere between," said Walt.

"Sounds like a plan. If we find Trader and Veronica alive, you still gonna slit Parker and Herzog's throats?" asked Sarusha.

"I don't know. Maybe I'll just shoot 'em. But one way or another, they're dead men," Walt said as he settled into his upturned saddle and beckoned the dawn to come quickly.

Part Two

SAFE BUT NOT SECURE

17

REUNITED

Walt and Sarusha woke the next morning with hopeful hearts. The men, maybe overly cautious, went without a fire and coffee, figuring on putting a little more distance between them and the nasty bunch working the so-called cave of gold before building a fire.

Troubling as Parker and Pealeday's intentions concerning Jonathan Keith were, their focus was on finding Trader and Veronica. Their battle with Herzog and his outfit would come in due time.

Tracking Veronica's horse proved to be an almost impossible task. Trader knew every trick there was to hide tracks. Also, the trees, shedding their leaves, covered the few tracks that were unwillingly left. They kept to their plan of working downhill toward the narrow valley that sat in the eastern shadow of Thorn's Peak. The so-called trails were really dim paths that game had worn into the forest floor. More times than not, these trails led to water, and it was at one of these junctures that the men finally found a hoofprint in the dried mud of a creek bank.

Their hunch was proving to be true. Trader and his wife were headed toward the Thorn. As they rode on, they lost the trail and found it again several times. By late morning, having lost the trail again, they decided that one of them should break off and head directly to Cornertown.

The plan was simple enough. Sarusha would go to see if there was anything Nelson in Cornertown knew. Walt would ride west toward Thorn's Peak. If he picked up their trail, all the better. He just may, as he was heading to the Indian villages that Trader would know of.

Sarusha was well-respected in most native quarters. In some, though, his mixed-breed background was a source of contention and acrimony. But not in the villages where Walt was headed. Matter of fact, Sarusha might still have some relatives there. He had, however, known Delbert Nelson in Cornertown for better than twenty years, which was why he was chosen to check whether Nelson knew anything of Trader and Veronica.

Walt was always greeted with respectful caution in all but the most bellicose of tribal villages. He was, or at least had been, on good terms with the two tribes where he was headed. If they knew anything, he was sure they would be more than forthcoming.

Before parting ways, the men agreed to rendezvous in two days at a point halfway between Cornertown and the Thorn. If either didn't show by the day after that—a development the men were loath to contemplate—the one should search out the other. Both men fully expected to keep the rendezvous, but they also knew enough not take anything for granted. The West was full of stories of someone going out at night to use the privy and never being heard of again.

Before splitting up, they took time to make a good noonday meal and rethink if there was anything they missed. Uncertainty and suspicion had been replaced with anticipation and a growing sense of immediacy. Trying to find comfort in a very troubling situation had soured there mood, but not so much that Walt couldn't joke with Sarusha about his cooking.

"Usually iffen someone's gonna poison me, they'd do it secret-like. With this food of yours, you're right out front about it."

"Can't poison a dying snake" was Sarusha's response, leaving Walt to chew on the fact that he'd not only been called a snake but a dying one at that.

Being men of action, more used to confrontation than calibration, they found themselves going over the events of the last several days and assuring themselves they'd made the right choices. In the four days since leaving the Crow's Nest. The second day out, they discovered Dagget's remains. Later that same day, they espied Tice and the Johnson brothers on the rim trail. The next day, finding the encampment of Herzog and Chance Parker answered some questions but at the same time gave them tough choices to make. Either try to find Veronica or attack Parker and Tice while everyone else was over the rim, working the cave. It was a tough choice, and maybe an opportunity lost.

Walt and Sarusha were not men who second-guessed themselves. The decision they made gambled with the chance that Pealeday and Parker, along with Pealeday's personal militia of diehard Canadians, would attack the Crow's Nest before they were able to get back and warn Keith. All in all, a very unsettling state of affairs.

After taking a keener appraisal of how much ground each man would have to cover, they decided to rendezvous the next day rather than two days hence. It would mean some hard riding, but sometimes hard riding was what had to be done. They finished their meal, checked their firearms—something they did without even realizing it—and hit the road. Sarusha to Cornertown, Walt to the Indian villages strung along the foothills of Thorn's Peak.

Cornertown was really not a town at all. In reality, it was, like so many broken dreams, simply the tattered remnant of one man's idea of the future. When he'd originally opened his modest trading post, Delbert Nelson had envisioned Cornertown growing into a busy juncture for travelers on the road west. It had a freshwater spring, a treeless expanse that lay at the foot of a gap in the mountains to the west, and a large creek that flowed down from the north.

All this pointed to a promising spot to plant one's flag. But alas, although the gap to the west was an opening in the mountains, the route proved to be difficult for a rider and impossible for a wagon. The creek did flow swiftly from the north to the south, but no frontier-bound travelers were ever coming from the north.

Soon Cornertown became, rather than a juncture, just another empty terminus—the end of the trail for a motley assortment of itinerants who had nowhere else to travel.

The weatherworn sign read Cornertown Pop. 14." It had originally read "Pop. 17," but the 7 had been altered to look like a 4. Truth be told, the population of Cornertown was more like eight.

Sarusha tarried none and got to Nelson's just as night was upon him. People originally referred to Delbert Nelson as simply Nelson, then old man Nelson, finally only as Pop.

Pop Nelson was standing on his porch with a rifle at the ready as he watched the rider crest the creek trail and bring his horse onto the thin, gravelly creek-side beach.

"Boy, am I glad to see you. Get in here as soon as he's done!" shouted Nelson to Sarusha who was letting his horse drink his fill.

Sarusha undid the saddle and bridle, flung them over the porch railing, and grabbed his saddlebags. Nelson, ever one to know just what to do, handed Sarusha a hard-canvas feedbag. After draping it over his horse's head, he headed up the steps and across the wide roofed-over porch, which was all but covered with black walnuts drying in the air.

Forlorn and weather-beaten as Nelson's old trading post appeared from the outside, once inside the place was clean, well-lit, and welcoming.

"So what news you got about Trader? How's he doing?" asked Nelson as he tried to decide which to do first, fetch a jug for Sarusha or finish lighting the evening fire. He chose to fetch a jug.

"Whoa, what you mean how's Trader? Me and Walt Tallhelm have been out trying to find him and his woman. What do you know?"

"Well, hell, Trader's woman was through here about a month ago, and I sent Peepsight Guyer and his partner Carl down to Bill Darcy's to get help. Bill Darcy was supposed to get up to the Nest, get help, and then come a-running. You didn't see Bill Darcy?"

"No. Bill Darcy never got to the Nest, leastwise not as of four days ago." Sarusha, confusion evident on his face, poured himself a drink and asked Nelson to sit down and go over everything from the very beginning.

Midway through the account, two men came in and awkwardly pretended to be surprised that Nelson was not alone. Nelson smiled at this artifice and introduced Sarusha as an old friend and left it at that. The men each retrieved a small jug of hooch and made some gesture that they would pay for it later, when Nelson wasn't encumbered with a guest. Nelson smiled wryly, knowing the men had seized on an opportunity to get some of his hooch without money or barter. No harm done. Just such guile and feigned ignorance was what breathed the little life there was into Cornertown.

Nelson finished his account of Veronica's visit, and in turn Sarusha told him all of what had transpired since he and Walt had left the Nest.

"You said about seeing Chance Parker. He was here a couple weeks back. Bought about everything I had, which wasn't all that much. I had to send two men down to Clearwater to get me resupplied." Nelson speared four quail onto a spit rod and set it over the fire. "Parker also hired two men out of here. Paid them in advance with a couple of double eagles each. They left without clearing up their bill with me. No matter. They left some stuff here. I figure they'll be back this way."

"I wouldn't expect to see those boys again or whatever money you were owed." Sarusha was well aware of how things were being handled by Parker and Tice up the way.

Nelson had no comment.

"You said Trader's woman headed out that trail I just rode in on?" asked Sarusha.

"Yeah. Like I said, Peepsight offered to go with her, but she said no. I wondered about Parker. I know he usually stays down to Lewiston. You gotta understand, I had no play. If I let on I suspected anything, we wouldn't be having this conversation," a slightly embarrassed Delbert Nelson explained.

"Don't worry, Pop. You did the right thing. No sense getting shot for nothing. After all, who would be left to make this good shine?" Sarusha poured himself another drink out of the earthen jug the men had been pushing back and forth between themselves. "I'll be leaving out of here first thing in the morning. From what I can tell, until this whole thing gets straightened out, I'd be extra careful about any strangers coming and going. Pealeday's got something brewing, and it doesn't look good. Can you trust these men, Pop?" Sarusha made a gesture in the direction of the two men who had come and gone earlier.

"Don't worry about them. Truth be told, we've become more like family than any family I ever had. They wouldn't do for the long haul, but they're okay to break bread with," Nelson said while he pushed some contraption with his foot that rotated the spit slowly over the fire. "How's Keith and them up the Nest?" He was not so intent on hearing Sarusha's answer but instead thinking to himself how it had been too long a time since he had seen his friend Keith and the others.

"Not too good. We gotta get this thing straightened out before any of us can draw an even breath."

"And Walt?"

"Well, with all this going on, he's liable to become too mean to be around. Once we get the chance to set things right, he'll be a lot better," said Sarusha as he made his way over to an easy chair and closed his eyes. "Pop, I'm gonna rest my eyes. You'll let me know when the quail are ready, okay?"

"Sure thing."

Sarusha didn't hear Pop Nelson's response as he had already fallen asleep. The days of hard tracking had all but exhausted the man. And now the combination of being indoors, a warm fire, and the hooch had sapped the last of his energy. Nelson let him sleep and waited till close to midnight before stirring him awake so he could eat his supper and return to resting his tired bones with the added comfort of a full stomach.

When Walt and Sarusha split up, Walt wasn't far from his first destination, so while the sun was still on his face, he was approaching the village where he hoped to find some information about Trader. The village, however, was long abandoned. All that remained were faded ruts left by wishbone sleds as they were dragged north. Walt knew where they were headed. He'd be hard-pressed to get there by dark, but his horse was as strong and tough as they come. So he rode hard and, just as twilight was fading, reined his horse out of the forest and saw the Indian village in the distance.

He lingered at the lower edge of the tree line and watched as one by one the campfires that dotted the grassy plateau came alive. The scene appeared idyllic, almost romantic, but Walt Tallhelm knew all was not well with the tribes here, as was the case most everywhere. The deserted village he'd visited earlier hadn't relocated by choice. Tribes were being forced to gather together, reluctantly putting aside internecine disputes and resettle under one banner, sacrificing their tribal identities—victims of ham-handed treaties written by their enemies. While they were now forced to unite physically, they were not always united in their response to their common threat: the relentless western movement of white men.

This village had been here in the shadow of Thorn's Peak far longer than memory allowed. The snowcapped summit was unchanged in all that time, not so the village. Gone were the many longhouses that anchored these natives and their traditions. Now fewer than a half dozen remained scattered among the teepees.

Walt sat his horse and took in the scene. Thorn's Peak may have been misnamed. It wasn't just one high spire of a summit but rather a massive wall of saw-toothed peaks, each trying to outdo the other in magnificence. The giant wall of granite that ran for twenty miles from north to south was snow-covered year-round. Its towering height trapped any clouds moving from the west. The rain clouds that found their way through dumped their burden into the ravines and gorges on the eastern slopes, giving rise to a lush forest of pine, fir, and cedar. Several waterfalls cascaded down these narrow gorges, cut into the rock over millennia, feeding as many fast running streams, several of which gathered together into one and emerged from the forest and flowed out and around the grassy plateau that lay at the foot of the Thorn.

Walt Tallhelm knew these people and allowed his memories to stir his mind and heart to bygone days. If she was still alive, he had a most dear friend there across the way.

Between him and the long grassy plateau lay the creek and its steep bank. As Walt rode down from the tree line and made his way through the creek and up the bank, he was first flanked by two braves, then four, then six, until a virtual gauntlet defined the path he and his horse must take.

The grim faces of those lining his way concerned him not. What concerned him was whether or not they knew anything of Trader. Also, there was another reality that had been gnawing at him ever since Jonathan Keith told him about Trader's map. If where Herzog and those men were working was in fact a cave of gold, it would be bad news for everyone, especially the Nez. Unfortunately, his cousin Trader would be front and center in bringing that about.

Unknown to Walt was the fact that Jonathan Keith had offered Trader and Veronica any amount of money they wanted if they would let him destroy the saddlebag and its burnt-on map. Trader considered Keith's offer but was undeterred. The pair were not consumed with gold fever but rather were on a treasure hunt that had in some ways begun two centuries before.

Walt didn't know one way or another if the Indians here were aware of what was taking place over at the Kettle of Tears. He hoped not.

Walt had spent time in this village years before. Back then, it was a happy place. Now, though, the look in the eyes of those he saw were fearful and guarded. The village itself was half as big as it had been, even with the influx from the other village.

The braves escorted Walt past unadorned buffalo-hide teepees as wide-eyed children hid behind their mothers and old men watched in silence. As they neared one longhouse, several Indians came out and stood facing one another, awaiting the person inside, who was obviously the tribal leader, to emerge and greet Walt Tallhelm.

Two braves took the reins of Walt's horse as he swung down from the saddle and made an effort to straighten his clothes and generally improve his appearance. Walt expected to see the Chief, a man he had known for years and was on good terms with. Who came out, though, was not the Chief but his daughter, Quiet Bird.

"K'aplash [tomahawk], I know why you come." Quiet Bird spoke English and knew that those gathered about did not. "I would have hoped that you were here for another reason, but that is not so. But beguile me one more time, and tell me it is I you seek."

"I would gladly lie, but you and I don't lie to one another. But trust that my being here will afford us the chance to share what of life we know. The Chief?" Walt feared that the question may have already been answered by the fact that the chief's daughter was the one in charge.

"My father is inside. Come greet him."

Walt was relieved that the Chief was still alive but was anxious to ask about Trader. However, he knew not to press his host, or rather, hostess. Patience was not Walt's long suit, but patient he must be.

The longhouse was dimly lit and possessed a mixture of aromas which he was sure the occupants had grown so accustomed to that they were unaware. Several women tended two firepits, the smoke from which rose straight up and escaped through square holes cut into the roof.

The Chief sat in a large chair and beckoned Walt to come closer.

"Ah, K'aplash, they told me you were coming. Come closer. My eyes are now always in twilight. I can see time has not been kind to you. Maybe now my daughter's heart will glow brightly for a younger native man," The Chief said half in jest, but the words carried the eternal concern a father had for the happiness of a daughter. "I will let her answer the questions you have. We will speak again tomorrow."

"Chief, as always, you are the teacher of all things. Tomorrow we shall speak of the times that were and the times that shall be," Walt said as he bowed and backed up several feet, following Quiet Bird out of the longhouse.

Once out in the open, Quiet Bird pointed to a teepee off to the west, along the tree line at the very edge of the plateau. "Your cousin is there. He is better now, not so before. Bring him this." With that, Quiet Bird said something to one of the women standing close by, who then went into the longhouse and returned with a doeskin bag stuffed with herbs.

"Thank you. I had hoped you would still be here."

"Your cousin's teepee is small. My teepee is large. It is there."

The two looked at one another, and what passed between their eyes was known only to them and the ether.

18

TWO SPOONS

Quiet Bird, with little more than a few words and hand gestures, had four braves mounted with torches in hand ready to escort Walt to Trader's teepee. In the shadow of the mountain, the twilight hour was brief, but a cloudless sky and a nearly full moon, just now rising, provided more than enough light to see by.

Quiet Bird had provided the torch-bearing escort as a measure of respect for her long-absent lover.

"K'aplash, your cousin may still not be well," Quiet Bird said as she touched the side of her head, clearly implying that Trader's mental state was questionable.

Standing next to Walt's horse, and with her hands on the slack reins, Quiet Bird barked out a few more orders. A woman scurried away and came back carrying a branch that had several fish strung along it.

"We call your cousin and his woman Two Spoons. Give these to One Spoon. Make sure she feeds you well," Quiet Bird said as she stepped aside and gently touched Walt's leg as he began to ride away.

The lead brave rode up to the front of Trader's teepee and, while still on his horse, shouted through the closed flap in passable English, "Spoon! Spoon!" The brave then turned to Walt and put his hand up in a gesture that told Walt to be patient and let someone in the teepee come out before approaching any closer.

Seeing how careful the brave was not to spook his cousin, Walt began to wonder just how critical Trader's mental state was. A good minute went by before a hand reached out and undid the flap on the teepee and pushed it aside. Standing there was Trader, remaining erect with the help of a crutch and Veronica's stiff body.

"Spoon, Quiet Bird says this man is your kin."

Trader took his one free hand, rubbed his face several times, looked at Walt for a moment before smiling weakly, and as his eyes filled with tears said, "Walt, Walt Tallhelm. Ronnie, it's my cousin Walt."

Veronica clutched Trader's arm tighter as tears began to stream down her face. The four braves quickly swung down from their horses, and two of them went about building a fire atop the charcoal remains in a firepit that fronted the teepee. The brave in charge took the string of fish from Walt and undid the leather bag of herbs from Walt's saddle horn and told something to one of the men, who then quickly rode off.

Walt got down from his horse and went over to Trader and gave him and Veronica as strong a hug as Trader's delicate condition would allow. "Boy, if you ain't a caution. We've been looking for you and was wondering if we'd ever find ya. I'm not a praying man, but thank God in heaven."

"Trust me, cousin, I wasn't much of a praying man myself, but you being here sure is an answer to my prayers," Trader said while adjusting his footing, momentarily losing his balance as Walt tried as best he could to steady his frail cousin.

"Here, come on in. Walt, this is my wife, Veronica. I call her Ronnie. She is one hell of a woman. That Quiet Bird is one hell of a woman too. We got her to thank for me being alive," Trader said as Veronica helped him over to a knee-high sleeping platform on which Trader gingerly sat.

Inside the teepee, it was nearly pitch-black, the only light coming in from the newly lit firepit outside the teepee. Veronica went about lighting several tallow candles, and soon the inside glowed with their amber light.

"Boy, you look pretty busted up. Hell, I don't know where to begin," Walt said as he dragged a stool over to Trader's bed and sat down.

"You can start by telling me how's Ma and Pa."

"Your Ma and Pa? I wouldn't know straight off. I haven't seen them in what, three, four years."

Trader closed his eyes and in his confusion tried to put together what exactly to ask next. "Ah, how comes you came looking for me? You wasn't down to Jackson and saw those trappers, Peepsight and Bowersox? That's who Nelson sent down there."

"Nah, I was up at the Nest, and Keith sent me and Sarusha out to look for ya. Seeing how's you hadn't signaled back to him like you was supposed to. I don't know nothing about Peep and Bowersox."

"Sarusha, where's he?" Trader craned his neck to see if Sarusha was somewhere outside the teepee.

"He's down to Cornertown. We figured Pop Nelson might know something. I'm supposed to rendezvous with him tomorrow down to Flat Rock. Boy, will he be relieved. Anyway, what the hell happened up there on the Kettle?"

"What happened up on the Kettle? To be honest, sometimes I can remember, sometimes I can't. One thing I know is those sons of bitches tried to kill me. Ronnie here could tell you better. My head is sore," Trader said this as he laid out on the bed and Veronica gently stroked his forehead.

Veronica got set to explain to Walt what had taken place. But before she had a chance, Walt broke in, "Oh, by the way, they think you're dead."

Without opening his eyes, Trader said, "Damn right they think I'm dead. Why wouldn't they? The sons of bitches cut the damn rope!"

Walt could see that if he wanted to get the whole story, he should just let Veronica tell it and try not to interrupt. Before Veronica could start, however, the brave in charge motioned to Walt to come outside. The brave who had been sent away returned with two waterskins, a basket of bread, and a tall woven bag with a clay pot inside.

Inside the clay pot was squash and corn soup. The fish were already cooking, suspended over the fire on a spit rod.

In his native tongue, the brave explained, "Sometimes we cook for Two Spoons." He handed Walt one of the waterskins and hung the other on a tall tripod along with the bag of herbs from before. The Indian pointed to the fire and gestured that he would let him know when supper would be ready.

Returning inside, Walt handed the waterskin to Veronica, who promptly filled a cup and handed it to Trader.

"You got another one of those?" asked Walt as he nodded toward the cup of water.

Veronica, showing she still had her sense of humor, went to take the cup from Trader and give it to Walt. After everyone had a smile, she reached around and produced another cup, filled it, and gave it to Walt.

Walt sat down and waited for Veronica to start her narrative.

In better English than Walt had anticipated, Veronica began, "I was lowering Tray down over the side like we do many times. That was how we did. The rope tied to the horse. I back to lower Tray down the side. Before I saw them, one man, a man we had seen in this town Lewistown."

Veronica mispronounced *Lewiston*, but Walt was not going to interrupt. He also thought this account was going to take a lot longer than he figured.

Veronica went on, "He runs out from the trees and cuts the rope. The other man, I never see him before in Lewistown, he go to grab my horse, but I make the horse run quick and he shoots at me, but my angel guardian moves the bullet, and I get into the woods. I could hear Tray scream, but then I could not. That day I ride till I don't think they find me. That night, I don't want night like that night. That night I cry. I only cry."

"She's some woman, my Ronnie," interjected Trader, who all of a sudden, from the force of his voice, seemed to be as strong and lucid as ever. "Two things saved me. One, the rope had a big knot tied into it so Ronnie knew when to stop backing up. After they cut the damn rope, I went sliding about halfway down the side of that cliff. Then that knot got caught on a shrub and jerked me to a stop. I was messed up something fierce. I had hit my head. My one leg was broke, my collarbone was broke, some ribs, and I had a good-sized gash on my arm. You ever have any broken ribs?" Trader asked this but didn't really expect an answer.

"Anyway, I was pretty damn woozy for a while, but then I started to be able to think straight. My first thought was what the hell happened up top? I thought that the rope had come loose from Ronnie's saddle, then I looked up and could see the end of rope had been cut. That's when I put two and two together. First thing I did was get tight to the wall. I didn't want those bastards seeing me. Then I tore some of my shirt and made into a bandage of sorts and tied it around my arm." Trader stopped and took a small drink of water.

"Well, the second thing that saved me was we had a plan if by accident the rope did come loose and I survived the fall. I was to work my way along one of the ledges that run along that cliff. Climbing straight up would have been impossible, plus I didn't know who was up top. I sure as hell wanted to find out, but not right then. Anyway, working along one of those ledges, which go south and angle up toward the rim, could eventually get me back up to the rim. I tied some scrub branches tight to my leg in a half-assed splint and slowly worked my way along toward the rim.

"It took me all that day and most of the next, but I finally made it. Ronnie had remembered our plan and prayed to God I'd survived. She had circled back around to the rim trail and stayed in the woods out of sight, and that next evening when it was just getting dark, she saw me climb up onto the trail. I got into the woods, somehow got onto that horse, and we hightailed it."

"I not know if Tray was alive. I pray and pray. God hear my pray."

Where was God when that bastard Herzog cut the damn rope? Walt thought, but he quickly clenched his jaw and remonstrated himself. *That's no way to be thinking.*

Looking kindly toward Veronica, Walt said, "Maybe your prayers were answered. When Sarusha and me saw where you came up onto the rim, we knew you was alive." Turning to Trader, he continued, "Sarusha knows Ronnie's horse pretty well and could see it had two riders." Just then, the brave interrupted and indicated that the food was ready.

Veronica got out three large wooden bowls, splashed a little water in and out of each one, handed one to Walt, and went out to the firepit and served up a bowl of the squash and corn soup for Trader. The fish and bread she put on a flat board for all three to eat off. Walt got himself a bowl of the soup and returned to the teepee. While Veronica and Walt were serving themselves, the two braves who were cooking the fish and heating up the soup gave Walt a nod then rode off.

Walt could see that Quiet Bird was making sure he was well taken care of. He must find some way to return the favor.

The trio ate in silence. It was obvious Trader needed all the sustenance he could handle. But halfway through the meal, he set his bowl aside and said, "I'll finish that later. I just don't have much of an appetite."

"Hell, I guess not. Boy, all you been doing is laying about. I'll get you up and going. Don't you worry," Walt said while he polished off the last of his soup, half the bread, and all but three of the fish.

"What were you doing up to the Nest anyway?" asked Trader.

"I can't really say. I was doing some loggin' work up above the Spokane when I just got a notion to get myself down to the Nest. Now I know why," Walt said as he eyeballed the remaining fish but controlled himself. After all, Trader, bad appetite or not, had to get his strength up. Sooner or later, they had to get back to Keith's.

"By the way, you find any gold in that cave?"

"Not a nugget. But there was more than a half dozen cave openings right around where I was." What Trader didn't tell Walt was that while he was inching his way across that ledge, he found what looked to be a sealed-up cave. There was no one thing that told him that. But with his face but inches from the cliff face, he could see that here it had a different look to it. This was probably the covered-over entrance to the cave of gold. It was a good half mile from where he had been looking. Trader hadn't even told Veronica, more than willing to put the whole business behind them. Seems like looking death in the eye can change a man's idea of what's important in life and what's not.

"How's Nate? When the last time you seen him?" asked Trader.

"I ain't seen him since I left Virginia. Your Pa said after you got back from the war, he come by their place. I missed running into him a couple years back. Your Pa said he was doing good. Wonder where he is now?"

"I kept missing him myself. Maybe someday we'll all be in the same place at the same time." Trader's hopeful speculation was more prescient than he knew.

"I'm going to head down to Quiet Bird's and thank her for the grub and looking after you. When did you get here anyway?"

"Been now about two, three weeks. I sort of lost track of time there for a while. Funny you mentioned Flat Rock. That's where I holed up when Ronnie went down to Nelson's. When she got back, we headed for here. I wasn't sure what kind of reception we'd get, but I took a chance. We couldn't stay out in the open a day longer."

"What all you tell Quiet Bird about how's come you was all busted up?"

"I told her a rattler spooked my horse and I got caught in the stirrup. Dragged me a ways. I got free, but the horse ran off."

"You think she believed you?"

"I don't know. She didn't say anything one way or t'other. She's smart. I didn't want to lie to her, but hell, I don't know. Captain Keith offered me any amount of money I wanted for that map. Now I wish I had taken him up on it. Maybe that bunch what bushwhacked me will get tired of looking and just go back home. I hope I didn't queer things between you and Quiet Bird. She's powerful fond of you."

"Yeah, I reckon so." Walt searched his heart and wondered if he should feel guilty about how things were left between him and Quiet Bird when they parted ways some years back. He was much younger then. Truth be told, he hadn't felt the same way about any woman he'd been with as how he felt with her.

"Veronica, you keep taking good care of him. I'll see you two in the morning," Walt said as he left the teepee and made apologies to his horse and told him, "I'll get you fed directly."

Quiet Bird's teepee glowed with the soft light of a half dozen candles. "How are Two Spoons?" asked Quiet Bird as Walt entered her teepee and took off his hat. She pointed to a place where he could put his saddlebags and beckoned him to come near.

"They're doing about as good as can be expected. Thank you for the vittles and everything else you've done. I've missed you," Walt said as he went to where Quiet Bird was standing, took her in his arms, and kissed her.

Quiet Bird did not resist.

19

FULL CIRCLE

The predawn chill of late autumn made the warmth of Quiet Bird's teepee that much more welcoming. Entwined as they were, Walt couldn't quite tell where his body ended and hers began. Lying there with his eyes closed, he wondered what fate awaited Quiet Bird and her tribe.

Last night as they lay awake, Quiet Bird told him, "Before the white man, we hunted and fished from the great ocean to the mountains of the Bitterroot. Now in less time for the sun to reach late day, we can ride across all the land that the whites say is ours. And even now this little bit of land sees more settlers come. Some of our tribe will fight. This I know. Between you and me, there is understanding, but not so with others. My heart is heavy."

Walt Tallhelm had no argument to give Quiet Bird. The honesty between them forced him to tell her what really was what with his cousin. He laid out all that he knew: the old Spanish map, the Kettle of Tears, Herzog, the whole scenario. She said she was aware of most all of this. Her love for Walt allowed her to overlook Trader's lies. She said that the white man was not the only enemy, but that time itself was as mighty a foe for her people as well. She finished her lament by telling Walt, "Let us pretend all is well and enjoy the time we have together, be it a day, a week, or if your heart is willing, the rest of our lives."

As the sun rose and chased away the morning mist, the two held each other tight and agreed to find what joy they could for as long as they could.

"I have to rendezvous with Sarusha today down at Flat Rock. Would you like to ride along?" asked Walt.

"Sarusha has two cousins in this village. They can go and meet him. You should tend to your cousin if he is to travel soon."

What Quiet Bird had said about Trader made sense to Walt. The sooner they got back to the Crow's Nest the better, he thought. If they rode full out, it would still be better than a three-day ride, but practically speaking, with Trader in the shape he was, more like four or five. Maybe the plan would be for Sarusha to set out on his own for the Nest to warn Keith about Pealeday and Parker's planned attack. He would follow later with Trader and Veronica at a more leisurely pace.

It also occurred to him that while his group was on the way back to the Nest, if Pealeday set out from Lewiston to hook up with Herzog, they would definitely cross paths with Pealeday at some point. That could be a problem.

All in all, a lot to chew on.

The first thing Walt had to find out was just how well Trader would do atop a horse. But that could wait. Walt, although no stranger to roughing it, didn't mind enjoying the comfort Quiet Bird's teepee afforded his tired bones. Also, Trader wasn't likely to be up at the crack of dawn anyway.

Walt was wise to get as much rest as he could. He didn't know it yet, but this day would challenge his strength and stamina in ways that they hadn't been tested in some time. His legendary reputation as a great warrior was well-known to braves in Quiet Bird's village. Were a brave to best this Walt Tallhelm in a contest of strength and warrior skills, their reputation would be equally as great.

Quiet Bird and her father held sway over their tribe, but only to a point. Whatever contest any braves had in mind, short of being lethal, would have to be tolerated. And in some ways, this could prove beneficial, proof that their respect for Walt was well-placed.

Walt finally roused himself and asked Quiet Bird about Sarusha's cousins. "If they're gonna meet Sarusha at Flat Rock, they should leave soon."

"They shall be on their way within the hour."

The early morning sun had begun to disappear behind a milky white screen of clouds. The dampness in the air and the cooling temperature signaled the arrival of the first snowfall of the year. It hadn't started to snow yet, but surely by the end of the day it would. Walt thought that if he was going to see if Trader could sit a horse, he'd best get to it.

As he made his way to Trader's teepee, a group of braves blocked his path. The largest of them came forward, scored a line in the ground, and stood on one side, brought his foot to the line, and challenged Walt to do the same. Walt knew what this was about and knew he had no choice but to accept the challenge.

Walt unencumbered himself of his coat and vest, placed his foot alongside the Indian's, grabbed his outstretched hand, and the contest was on. The Indian was big and equal in height and girth to Walt. So there was no ready advantage for either one in that regard. Walt had Indian-wrestled before and employed a tactic that usually worked. His first move was to squeeze his opponent's hand with everything he had and, in that instant, crouch and pull his opponent down and behind him. It had usually been a successful maneuver, but not so today. The brave did not falter, and Walt almost did.

Equally matched in strength, the two were soon engaged in a contest of balance and will. They wrangled in silence for a good two minutes, eventually the brave weakened. Walt had just spent several months doing ax and double-buck work in a logging camp. That extra muscle seemed to carry the day, as Walt eventually bested the Indian with his brute strength.

The brave smiled and gave Walt a slight bow, turned to the assemblage, and motioned for them to honor the winner. As Walt went to put his vest back on, the Indian couldn't help but notice the hatchets lining the inside. He smiled again and pointed to the hatchets, then to himself, then to Walt. Walt didn't know if the brave wanted to have a hatchet fight or rather, as he hoped, a contest of hatchet throwing.

Walt could understand most of the Nez language, but he didn't care to risk saying the wrong thing, so he turned and pointed to one of the trees that dotted the plateau and made the motion of throwing a hatchet. The Indian nodded in assent. Walt pointed to where he figured the sun to be, then pointed straight up, indicating noontime. The brave nodded again. As Walt made his way on to Trader's, he thought, I *guess I'm going to be in a hatchet-throwing contest later.*

Though Walt saw smoke rising through the opening at the top of the teepee, he nevertheless hollered out, "Hey, Trader, you awake in there?"

"Hell yeah, I'm awake. Come on in. You want some coffee?"

"That'd be good. I could drink coffee all day." Walt nodded to Veronica as she retrieved the pot off the fire and poured him a cup. "You think you can ride a horse? How's that leg healing up, anyway?"

Trader had broken his shin bone. He was fortunate that when he originally set the break while on that ledge, he set it right. The splint he fashioned from his torn shirt and some shrub branches did the job. When he got to the village, the twigs were replaced with thin slats, and after that it was just a matter of time.

"I don't know, but we can give it a try. I can't put much weight on this leg. My ribs finally quit hurting, though." Walt and Veronica helped Trader out to Walt's horse. Trader shivered a little. "Looks like snow's coming. If I can't ride, maybe you could pull me on a sled," said Trader half-jokingly.

"We ain't going over a prairie, cousin," answered Walt, knowing full well that the trail back to the Swallows and onto the Crow's Nest was through some pretty rough country.

"Here, step up." Walt interlocked his fingers and hoisted Trader up, who winced in pain but was able to get into the saddle, albeit awkwardly.

"How's that feel?" asked Walt, knowing all too well how painful broken ribs can be.

"Let me ride around a piece and I'll tell ya then," responded Trader, who remembered back to the excruciating pain he was in on the ride from the rim to Flat Rock and then to here. "I guess my ribs haven't stopped hurting after all, but I can do this. I don't know for how long at a stretch. But we can make it. I don't have a horse. I guess you know that."

"Don't worry about that. I'm sure I can work out something with the Chief."

Now that Trader was up on the horse, he didn't relish the idea of having to get down, knowing it would be at least as painful as getting on, if not more. "Let me just ride around for a bit. We better make sure we bring along some of that tea Quiet Bird's been giving us. It helps the pain." As Trader rode about, Walt could see from the look on his cousin's face that he was feeling good about finally not being bedridden.

With the morning getting on, he told Trader, "Come on over here. Let me help you down. I got to get back yonder. You and Ronnie start thinking about getting your truck together. I'm hoping we can leave out of here in the morning."

Being realistic, though, leaving tomorrow wasn't really going to happen. Snow was coming, and he knew he and Quiet Bird wanted to spend more time together. Just better relax and allow Quiet Bird to extend her hospitality. Trader and Veronica were alive and generally well. Keith, Sunny, Lucien, and the crew up at the Nest could take care of themselves. *Quit fretting like an old woman*, Walt thought. Also, he hadn't even sat down with the Chief. Worst thing you could do was insult the Chief. Indians can be powerful keen about what is and what isn't an insult. Beyond that, all Walt had to think about now was how good he was at throwing his tomahawks.

Quiet Bird, given the age and failing health of her father, was charged with organizing the generally unorganizable inhabitants of the village. To that end, today she was seeing to whatever had to be done in preparation for the coming snowfall. She had already sent men into the forest that skirted the plateau to drag out any new dead-fall. Whatever firewood had to be covered or brought inside was seen to. Cut hay was brought up to the remuda, which had been moved into high lean-tos just inside the tree line. The waterskins and gourds were filled. The women were sent to forage before snow covered the forest floor.

With preparations proceeding as best they could, Quiet Bird stood in front of her father's longhouse and welcomed Walt inside. "How are Two Spoons?"

"They're okay. He can sit a horse now. Of course, he doesn't have one. I hope we can work out a good trade," Walt said, realizing he didn't have much with him to trade, or for that matter, he didn't own much of anything at all. But he trusted that Quiet Bird and the Chief would see to it that he got what he needed.

"Someone's going to have to ride bareback." A mischievous grin added the slightest glint to the look in Quiet Bird's eye. "I understand you made some friends this morning," she continued as she held back the flap to the longhouse.

"I don't know if they saw it that way or not. You tell me. I think he wants to even the score by showing me how to throw a tomahawk."

"Buffalo Horn is a very proud warrior, but he respects you. He knows we call you K'aplash [tomahawk], so maybe he wants to see if your name is well-earned. It should be interesting. The Chief wants to come and watch. I'm glad. It's hard to get him up and out anymore." With that, Quiet Bird ushered Walt over to her father, who had momentarily fallen asleep.

"You hungry? These women make me jealous. They're more interested in feeding you than the Chief. Ah, he doesn't eat much anyway," Quiet Bird said as she lovingly looked at her aging father.

"Sit over here, K'aplash." Quiet Bird motioned Walt to a table that sat along one of the two firepits in the longhouse. Two women giggled as they ladled a thick meat stew into a large wooden bowl and arrayed some finger cakes and dried fish on a board.

"I better not eat too much. I gotta be sharp when I go up against, you said, Buffalo Horn?"

"Yes, Buffalo Horn. This should be quite the contest. You saw for yourself how capable a warrior he is. I'm sure the whole of the Nez Nation wants to watch this. I don't think you know what kind of a reputation you have with my people," a somewhat bemused Quiet Bird explained.

Walt, before he had a chance to catch himself, was struck with a tinge of jealousy that must have shown on his face.

"I see that look. No, Buffalo Horn is not interested in my company. He and his woman are very happy. No, his concern lies with the blue coats. He's one of the braves that wants war."

"Can't hardly blame him. I'd feel the same way. When I was a kid, we had someone take a house and some land from us. You can get used to it, but you never get over it. That was just my family and Trader's. You're talking about a whole tribal nation," said Walt, suddenly wanting to talk about anything other than this. "Where you have your hatchet-throwing contests, anyway?"

"Up by the woods, not far from where Two Spoons are," answered Quiet Bird, happy to be off the subject of her tribe and the white man as well. "Here my father's awake. Come."

Walt had nothing but unbounded respect for the Chief. The world the Chief grew up in, Walt could only imagine. How do you make any assumptions of a man whose world was so different from the one you know?

Quiet Bird's father, Chief Ironwood, was born in 1795 and had been witness to the complete upending of all the traditions his people knew—traditions that had endured for millennia. When elders like Chief Ironwood die, knowledge of the world they knew dies with them. To a certain extent, that's true of all generations, but in this case, the saeculum these men lived and breathed will never again come to pass. It will exist only in their memories. When they are gone and the memories they possess are gone along with them, knowledge of what that world was will be forever lost.

In quiet moments, the Chief allows his memory to weave a tapestry, threads of joy woven with threads of sorrow. The joy, the majesty of his people; the sorrow, the pain of what they had and will never have again.

The Chief shared his lament with Walt and Quiet Bird. "When I was a young man, this time of year we would be preparing to leave our summer lodges to go over the Bitterroot to hunt the buffalo out on the open range. Now if we do that, we become the hunted ones. We become the prey.

"I remember it like it were only yesterday. Quiet Bird's mother and I watched a little finch that seemed to protest a brook its babble. We laughed and laughed at that little bird. The brook, of course, kept babbling, and the finch squawked on and on and flew about. Eventually the bird tired and quietly sat a limb. My people are like the finch and the brook is like the White Man. They kept coming, and we squawked and squawked, but of course to no avail. That's why your mother and I named you Quiet Bird. So you would not waste your life in a useless caterwaul." The Chief sat up, reached over, and touched his daughter on the cheek.

Chief Ironwood could arrive begrudgingly at a resignation bordering on acceptance—and pass it on to Quiet Bird—only because his tribe could still cling to a semblance of the old ways, albeit tenuously. For future generations, however, the relentless incursion of the white man's modern ways would obliterate their way of life and turn their sacred objects into little more than roadside trinkets and their rituals into farcical fodder for an exploitive motion picture industry. All this would stoke a righteous anger that no amount of acceptance could extinguish.

"Now let's go see if this man you are so fond of cannot embarrass you," the Chief said. "I've seen Buffalo Horn throw a hatchet, K'aplash. Even you may not be as good. I understand you need a horse. You will have a horse, but how good a horse..." The Chief did not finish the sentence, but Walt knew what he was saying. The Nez Perce bred the best horses in the West. Their Appaloosa would be any rider's prized possession. How well Walt did in this contest would decide how good a horse he would be given.

"I'm gonna get up that way. I'll see you up there," Walt said as he went to help the Chief up but was waved off. The chief got up on his own and appeared to be more hale than Walt would have thought.

"You know where you're going?" asked Quiet Bird.

"I think so. Up along the tree line, right?" As Walt went to leave the longhouse, he could see small groups of three and four Indians heading up that way. He turned back toward Quiet Bird. "Or I could just follow where everyone is going."

It would appear anyone who wasn't busy preparing for the first snow would be on hand to watch this hatchet-throwing contest. Walt thought, *I'm better when I'm heaving my hatchet at an enemy. I hope I still have that edge when it's not life or death.*

Walt first made his way to the teepee of Two Spoons. Trader and Veronica were standing outside. "Can you make it over there okay?" asked Walt.

"Yeah, I'll be okay. We'll be right along," answered Trader.

Thankfully, the target was set up just down the way from Trader. It was a round oak tabletop that had been discarded by some family on their way West. The trails going westward were strewn with cast-off belongings too heavy or cumbersome to carry any farther. Black lacquered spinet pianos with their veneers peeling up after being left exposed to the elements, tall wardrobe mirrors, round oak kitchen tables like this one, all sacrificed to allow the pioneers to trudge on. One of those discarded tabletops somehow found its way to this village.

Wedged into the crotch of a double-trunked oak tree, the target was just now getting a fresh set of concentric rings whitewashed onto its face. The center was indicated by a bright red dot the size of a walnut. Buffalo Horn greeted Walt with the slightest of nods. Walt was unable to judge much from Buffalo Horn's demeanor. Quiet Bird had said that he wasn't an enemy, but sometimes in competition even friends can become enemies.

Nothing was going to happen until the Chief arrived, so Walt took the time to walk to the tree line, pick out a tree, and get in a few practice throws. Whatever it took to be good at this was much more than pure mechanics. In combat, all the senses are keyed and primed to function almost devoid of thought. Walt didn't think he could muster that kind of concentration in a simple throwing contest. Time would tell.

The Chief and Quiet Bird had arrived, and behind them in a giant semicircle, most of the village stood silently. Buffalo Horn walked off ten paces from the target and scored a line in the ground.

Each man had four hatchets to throw and would take turns throwing their four. Walt went first, and in the time it took to count to four, he had planted one hatchet next to the other across the red dot. Buffalo Horn did the same.

The men moved back another ten paces. At twenty paces, Walt put a little arc into his throw. All four hit their mark. Again Buffalo Horn did the same. As Buffalo Horn began to mark off another ten paces, the two men heard some rustling and low shouts coming from the woods. Walt and Buffalo Horn heard this noise before anyone else since the sounds were coming from the woods up and to the left of the target. Both men looked that way, and what they saw raised the hair on the back of their necks. Fighting their way through the briars that grew thick at the edge of the woods were two women and a girl, their faces scratched and bleeding. Not three feet behind them, a heaving grizzly bear was in full-out pursuit.

Walt sprang into action, closing the distance between him and the women in the blink of an eye. In that short time, he had thrown two of his hatchets, one of which had planted itself in the side of the bear, but with little consequence. Buffalo Horn was but a step behind Walt and had done the same, but neither of his weapons stuck.

The young girl tripped and while on her back was trying for all her life to scramble backward away from the giant bear. Buffalo Horn, who was fast on his feet, got between the girl and the bear and began to swipe at it with his tomahawks, one in each hand. The bear reared back, and as Buffalo Horn moved in, it clawed him across the temple, sending him reeling with blood running down his face.

Now it was Walt's turn, somersaulting over Buffalo Horn, who lay on the ground half-conscious. Walt sprung up inside the bear's reach, so close he could feel the animal's hot breath. He planted the hatchet in his right hand deep into the bear's neck. Enraged, the bear reared back, and Walt took the opportunity to duck underneath and get in behind.

Walt couldn't believe the size of the bear, half again, as tall as any man. Knowing he had to do something, Walt took a few steps back, switched his last hatchet to his right hand, got a running start, and leaped up and onto the back of the bear. Holding on for dear life, he hacked away at the bear's neck with all he had. Walt didn't realize it, but the bear's claw had caught him across the face. Small beads of blood began to appear along the scratches.

By now, other braves had joined in the battle and stabbed at the bear with spears. The bear swatted them away and, in primal rage, whirled about, bent forward, reached back, grabbed Walt, and flung him over his head onto the ground, barely missing the girl, who just now was being pulled safely away.

Walt, slightly dazed, began to become a bit enraged himself. Wiping some blood and dirt out of his eyes, he grabbed two spears off the ground and charged the beast. As he taunted the bear with the spear in his left hand, he looked for an opening to plant the other spear into the bear's heart. It seemed like nothing short of that would stop the marauding grizzly.

The bear had something else in mind. Seeing Buffalo Horn crouching on the ground, trying to regain his feet, the bear pushed past Walt, but not before Walt was able to thrust a spear deep into its left side. A bloodcurdling yelp went up from the animal as it went to pounce onto Buffalo Horn. Walt shouted a warning, and in the nick of time, Buffalo Horn grabbed a hatchet off the ground. As the beast was all but on him, he planted it into the bear's forehead. The bear let out an ungodly roar and fell to the ground. The bear knelt up and vainly tried to claw Buffalo Horn but finally collapsed into a dead heap, one of its lifeless limbs laying across Buffalo Horn's face.

The assemblage was awed and dumbstruck.

"Can I get some water?" asked Walt, suddenly as thirsty as he could ever remember. The next several minutes were a blur as the adrenalin was still coursing through his body like a runaway train. He remembered the women looking after the three who had been fleeing the bear, their arms and faces scratched up something fierce from their run through the briars. Buffalo Horn, bleeding from his face wound, was helped up and led over to Walt. The men shook hands and pulled one another close, smiled, and patted each other on the back. Little kids poked at the dead bear with spears, then quickly ran away, only to come close and do the same again.

"K'aplash, you are my man!" Quiet Bird said as she took off Walt's gray bandana and cleaned the blood and dirt from his face.

The Chief had a quick meeting with several braves as they were deciding what to do with the bear. It would appear fresh bear meat was going to be on everyone's menu.

"K'aplash, come here," called out the Chief. "You shall have your pick of two of my best horses, and we will escort you, Two Spoons, and Sarusha up as far as the Swallows. You are indeed a great warrior. My daughter has chosen wisely. Please do not betray her." Chief Ironwood spoke as a chief and a father.

Walt took Quiet Bird aside and told her, "When I'm done with this business up at the Nest, I'll be back. I don't know how you hardly got along without me."

When Walt felt that hankering to get down to the Crow's Nest, he had no idea it would lead him back to his old lover Quiet Bird.

Now that it had, he wasn't going to fight it. All that remained now was seeing that Pealeday and Herzog ended up dead or in irons.

Trader and Veronica had watched the throwing contest from the back of the gathering and couldn't see much of what was going until they saw Walt up on the back of the bear. At first he wondered if that was part of the contest, but quickly figured out what was really happening. But in that instant, Trader was profoundly saddened. He had once been as full of vim and vigor as any man. But enduring the physical and mental wounds of war, and now this broken leg and the business with his head, had him wondering, was he ever going to be back up to snuff? He knew he was made of tough stuff. He looked at his wife and was grateful that she was made of pretty tough stuff as well.

Trader shook off his melancholia, gripped Veronica's hand, heaved a sigh, and refocused on his cousin Walt as he was being flung off the back of the bear. Trader, with the aid of his crutch and Veronica's help, worked his way a bit closer, and they were able to see Buffalo Horn finish off the bear.

Thankfully, Walt had come out of the encounter with little more than a few scratches. Buffalo Horn had gotten the worst of it, but even though he was savagely clawed by the bear, no permanent damage resulted. What did result for Buffalo Horn was an unbreakable bond forged between himself and this white man. Walt was enthusiastically welcomed by all into the tribe of this Nez village. As it turned out, one of the women and the girl being chased by the bear were Buffalo Horn's sister and niece, making his gratitude even that much greater.

Eventually, the shouts and murmuring of the gathering faded, and as the bear was being dragged away, the snow began to fall.

Quiet Bird and Walt made their way over to Trader and Veronica. Walt gave his cousin and Veronica a big hug. "Son of a bitch, you Two Spoons, I guess you never know what a day will bring, do ya?"

Trader shook his crutch, indicating that he couldn't agree more. One minute he was on the search for a cave of gold, the next he was sliding down a cliff face.

"We're going back to Quiet Bird's. Why don't you two join us? I still got a good bit of a bottle of whiskey I've been toting along," Walt said as Quiet Bird reached up and daubed the blood that had beaded out of the scratches on Walt's face.

"Sounds good to me."

"When do Sarusha get here?" asked Veronica, wanting the question answered but mostly wanting to be part of the conversation.

"Should be here by sundown. Of course, with this snow, who can really tell when the sun goes down?" Quiet Bird's answer was tinged with a bit of humor as the relief of Walt surviving the battle with the bear had left her feeling a bit giddy.

"Can you make it down to Quiet Bird's okay?" asked Walt.

"Yeah, I'll be all right. Don't worry, we'll get there," answered Trader.

The rest of that afternoon was spent with the four of them gathered around the fire in Quiet Bird's teepee, telling stories and sharing memories. As the snow began to pile up in front of the teepee and darkness approached, a hand pulled back the flap on the teepee, and Sarusha's smiling face appeared in the opening.

"Did I miss anything?" he asked, unsuccessfully feigning ignorance. He and his cousins had been told the whole story of the bear attack within minutes of crossing the creek and entering the village.

"I've got to tend to my horse. Don't worry about saving any of that for me," said Sarusha, and he pointed to the near empty whiskey bottle. "Nelson gave me something to take along. I'll be back."

Sarusha returned and joined the party, which eventually moved to the Chief's longhouse and went long into the night.

The snow continued to fall. Tomorrow, plans could be made, but tonight all took a brief respite from the cares that lay so heavily on each one's head and heart.

20

Promises Made, Promises Kept

Over the next few days, preparation for the ride back to the Crow's Nest proceeded at a pace both too slow and too fast for all concerned. Sarusha was anxious to get back to aid Jonathan Keith, but also enjoyed being in the company of his native tribe and especially his cousins, whom he hadn't seen in years.

Trader was ready to hit the trail, but he had some reservations about how well he could travel. A few trots around the teepee was a long way from six or seven hours in the saddle. Plus, he had to consider Veronica. She was game for most anything, but then again, most anything could happen. Veronica, for her part, had become used to Quiet Bird's hospitality and didn't relish the thought of leaving the warmth of a teepee for the open trail. But all that aside, she would be ready to leave anytime Trader was. Walt was on a mission, and not much could deter him from that. But he cherished his time with Quiet Bird and his talks with Chief Ironwood. He also spent time picking out two Appaloosas from several he was given to choose from.

On top of that, Walt made time for Buffalo Horn, who had a bandage across his forehead and one side of his face. He was lucky the swipe of the bear's claw wasn't an inch lower. Otherwise, he would be a blind man. The two spoke of where they had been and where they expected to be. Strange that Walt expected to be back in this village, and Buffalo Horn expected, more likely than not, to be gone from the village and somewhere on a warpath.

Quiet Bird was the most conflicted of all. She wished it were two months in the future and K'aplash was back here, safe and sound. She, too, cherished the time they spent with one another. But she also knew the sooner Walt got on the trail, the sooner he would return, if he were even able to return. She knew of Clayton Pealeday and knew him to be trouble. One of the many who chose to be friends of the Indian when it suited them and an enemy when it did not. Quiet Bird didn't know this man Herzog, but from what she understood from Walt and Two Spoons, he was no man to trifle with. The only way all this would be resolved was through bloodshed— no doubt about it. Quiet Bird prayed none of that blood would be Walt's. She knew what Walt meant to her, and all other men paled in comparison.

So preparations proceeded. The snow, rather than a hindrance, became a boon, a respite of sorts. It signaled the end of one thing and the beginning of another. A punctuation mark on the march of time. Like any heavy snow, it gave the sensation of a suspension of time—brief but real.

Early on the third morning after the snowfall, the party left Quiet Bird's village. Sarusha's cousins and two other braves made up the escort. The Chief was more than happy to provide this escort, grateful to K'aplash for his quickness and courage. He was proud that he was in a position to reward Walt with two of his prized horses, and also secretly pleased that Buffalo Horn was the one to finish off the bear. Everyone shared in the glory. The harmony in the village was tonic to the aging Chief.

Sarusha lent Trader his horse and saddle and rode one of the Appaloosas bareback. The Appaloosa wouldn't be accustomed to a saddle anyway. That was something that would take some time and the hand of an expert saddle-maker. The Appaloosas were so prized that they deserved nothing less.

The trail from Quiet Bird's village to the Swallows should take three days, but most likely four. It was a steady uphill climb most of the way. Plenty of oats and grain were packed for the horses. There would be precious little grass to graze on even at the best of times. Where the snow remained on the ground, little to none.

Walt didn't know if Trader and Sarusha felt the same way, but he felt a bit foolish with all the fanfare that rose up when the group prepared to ride out of the village. Evidently, for some reason, the killing of that bear was seen as a good omen. It wasn't much of a good omen for Buffalo Horn. But then again, he was now the undisputed bravest of the brave, which had to be a good thing.

Quiet Bird bid farewell to Walt in the privacy of her teepee, sensitive to his generally stoic nature. The Chief, however, was at the front of those assembled, and the last one the group saw as they crossed back over the creek and disappeared into the forest, heading north and to the east.

Shortly after hitting the trail, Trader wondered aloud more than once about the prospect of seeing his father at the Crow's Nest. Again he was a little hazy on figuring how much time had passed since this whole drama had begun, but he was sure Peepsight Guyer and Carl Bowersox, men he knew to be true blue, would have delivered his message to his Ma and Pa. Already enough time would have passed for them to get down to his folks' place and for his Pa to then get up to Keith's. Walt and Sarusha agreed, but all they knew for sure was that Bill Darcy hadn't been there a week ago.

Of course, what they didn't know was that Walt's brother and Trader's cousin Nathan had arrived at the Crow's Nest two days ago, and he keenly awaited their return.

The trail the group took out of Quiet Bird's village skirted the Lochsa River for the first leg of the journey then cut off to the north. First night out, they camped under the shelter of an overhang back up from the river, which at some time in the long-forgotten past had sculpted away anything that couldn't withstand its raging current— as it coursed through the narrow river valley—leaving in its wake giant overhangs, the faces of which were polished as smooth as glass.

The snow had all but disappeared from anywhere touched by the sun, but it remained as deep as ever in the shadowy areas of the forest. Here, under the overhang, the party spread their bedrolls on dry ground and spent the brief hour of twilight fishing the river while the horses grazed on lush grasses in an open clearing nearby.

Although the party was concerned about the impending future, that concern didn't eclipse their appreciation of the beauty and tranquility of this camp and the trail up to it. Whatever their current concerns, these men were also simply living their lives, and to do so without enjoying the better parts of what life presented would be nothing short of forfeiture and defeat. So they fished when they could and warmed themselves in the glow of their campfires, laughed and retold stories, repaired their gear, and tended their horses.

In the course of their journey, they would linger and look back to take in the beauty of a valley they were just leaving before they crested the summit of a mountain trail, only to be presented with another breathtaking vista, humbling them with the majesty of what Mother Nature had wrought, artistry so divine that the crucible of a man's heart had no recourse but to overflow, too limited to contain such overwhelming beauty. A guileless tease by Nature, who created a flower whose nectar was too sweet to consume.

On the second day out, the party cut the tracks of four riders heading toward where Herzog and Chance Parker would be on the Kettle. The tracks were only a few hours old, and all agreed they were glad to have avoided an encounter. A fight was to be had, no doubt about that. But a clearer picture of just who would be involved in that fight was needed.

Surely some of those working the so-called cave of gold were doing so against their will. The Johnson brothers and the two Chance Parker had recruited from Nelson's in Cornertown were surely by now having second thoughts. For those men, it would be one thing if they were actually finding gold and could look forward to a payday, but everything known up to this point would say otherwise. Most likely the pay they would get would be a bullet in the back, gold or no gold.

The group was making good progress, and it turned out Trader was able to keep up with the others with a manageable level of pain. The camp they struck on the evening of the third day was only a half-day's ride from the Swallows. There was talk of the escort heading back to their village in the morning, but the braves would hear none of it. They had been instructed to stick with K'aplash till they reached the Swallows, and that was what they fully intended to do. The braves had even discussed among themselves whether or not to go all the way to the Crow's Nest. None of them had ever ventured this close to the Kettle of Tears. The Chief hadn't stipulated that they go no farther than the Swallows. The choice was theirs. It remained an open question.

That question was answered, late morning the following day, when the group reached the edge of the Swallows. The braves had decided to head back to their village. The bond this group had forged over the last four days was more than apparent by the heartfelt embraces shared by all.

Walt, Sarusha, and Trader had wished they had some gift or token to give these men, but alas, all they had to give was their respect. Veronica gave one of Sarusha's cousins her necklace to give to Quiet Bird. The party of eight divided itself—four heading into the Swallows and four heading back up the trail from whence they had come.

Walt and party reached the switchback down to the Crow's Nest shortly before sunset. The group had wound their way through the Swallows in silence, each one lost in their own thoughts, their anticipation bubbling one thought to the surface only to be quickly replaced by another. One thing was sure: the relief on the part of those at the Nest was guaranteed, but how the different parties digested the information they had to impart was another matter.

Sarusha took the lead going down the switchback and at the gatehouse reached up and rang the bell. The window above hinged open, and Ghosty peered down. His face betrayed no emotion as he pulled the window closed and awaited the sound of two bells. Sarusha was sure Ghosty recognized him. Why he had to wait to open the gate made him wonder. In as long a time as it took to have that thought, someone up on the deck rang the bell twice.

Hearing the gatehouse bell, Keith assumed it was Sunny and Lucien. He had sent them up to the cemetery, not to bury someone but to resupply a redoubt he had below the shed up there. Keith had it built when he still had his original work crew on hand. It was hidden underground and could shelter eight men. It was stocked with everything you would need to hunker down, along with enough guns and ammo to equip a small army. It hadn't been seen as necessary in some time, but with all that was going on, no precaution could be viewed as excessive. The only people who knew about it other than himself were Sunny, Sarusha, and Lucien and Evie Samms. The crew didn't know it was there. It was secret and an ace in the hole if needed.

When Keith looked down to the gatehouse and saw Trader and Veronica along with Sarusha and Walt, he couldn't have been happier had he been witnessing the Second Coming. Shedding the yoke of concern, his spirit was reenergized. After ringing the signal bell, he went back into the bar and called out, "Evie, put on some coffee and get out some extra grub. That bell was Sarusha and them."

Keith got back out to the deck and watched as the group came out the rear door of the gatehouse and made the steady climb up to the Nest. He hollered down, "We're not taking on any new men. Go back!" Keith was a man whose sense of humor was more subtle than this, but he couldn't help himself.

Sarusha, still in the lead, called his bluff and hollered back, "Okay!" and began to feign turning his horse around. The two just smiled at one another.

Evie quickly made her way through the kitchen and out to the back balcony and shouted, "Nate Tallhelm, your brother just rode up!"

Nate planted the ax into the chopping block and told the Samms boys, "That's it for today, boys. I gotta go see my brother."

The boys looked at each other and then told Nate, "We're coming too, Mister Nate. We be wanting to see this ourselves."

"I wonder if he gonna be mean to his brother?" asked the younger Ernest of his older brother Everett.

"I wouldn't know why not," answered Everett as he reached over and jostled his brother's head.

Keith was down to the stables and was pulling open the doors as the four riders neared the top of the ramp.

"Look who we found," said Sarusha.

One by one, the riders clomped into the stable with Walt bringing up the rear, leading the rider-less Appaloosa.

"Trader, looks like you ran into some trouble. Oh, and, Walt, do we got a surprise for you," Keith said as he went to help Veronica down off her horse.

"Not much would surprise me right now, seeing as what I just been through." Walt was referring to either the fight with the bear or his rekindled relationship with Quiet Bird, the reality of which was just starting to sink in.

Nate, with the Samms boys trying to keep up, strode through the dark stable and appeared amid the group as if out of thin air. As the Samms boys began to take the reins of the horses, Walt handed his to Nate thinking he was someone helping Ernest and Everett.

"I guess you gone blind and stupid since I seen you last," Nate said.

The familiar sound of Nate's voice turned Walt's head slowly around, thinking that voice sounded just like his one brother. While peering at the man holding the reins of his horse, all Walt could muster was "I'll be damned." The two brothers came together, shook hands and embraced, pushed away, looked at each other—more like inspected each other—and embraced again.

"Hey, Trader, this must be Veronica. Your folks told me about her," said Nate.

"Ah, were you down to Jackson and saw Peep and..."

Nate interrupted Trader before he could finish the sentence. "Yeah, Peepsight and Bowersox. I was at your folks when they showed up. You okay? You look sorta okay."

"I've been better," answered Trader as he waited for Sarusha to help him down from his horse, a routine the two had perfected over the last four days.

Walt and Nate just looked at one another, and Nate thought about all the living both of them had done since they last saw one another. When you're young, you can gauge a sibling's makeup, because you know pretty much what world he's lived in. Not so now for Walt and Nate. From all reports, Walt had been over the mountain and around the bend. Nate hoped his brother hadn't become a stranger.

"My, oh, my, look at these horses," exclaimed Jonathan Keith. "Look at these horses, boys. I doubt they're used to being inside. Why don't you take them out back?"

Before the boys led the horses away, Walt took time to stroke and say a few words to each one. Bonding with the animals was a slow and deliberate process. This was highlighted by the fact that the Appaloosa Sarusha had been riding turned back toward Sarusha as he was led away. Maybe that horse had already chosen Sarusha as his master. Walt might have no choice but to gift the steed to Sarusha, an eventuality he'd be more than willing to accept. Over the last several days, an unbreakable bond had been forged between the two men, respect and well-earned trust, the mortar of that bond.

The group had no sooner unburdened their horses of their saddles and saddlebags than the gatehouse bell rang. "That's got to be Sunny and Lucien. Hey, Brow, go see if that's Sunny. If it is, ring the bell!" Keith hollered up to Brow Herman and Bill Diehl, who had been silently watching from the top of the stairs.

"Why didn't Ghosty just let me in? I'm sure he saw it was me," asked Sarusha.

"Ghosty has new instructions. Don't open that door unless he gets the okay from up top, no exceptions. Evidently, he's doing just what I told him. I know a storm's brewing, and I'm waiting to hear if it's just a squall or a full-blown typhoon."

Sarusha didn't hesitate with his answer. "It's gonna to be a typhoon, Cap. No doubt about it."

Just then, the bell from up on the deck rang twice. Ten minutes later, Sunny and Lucien were clomping into the stable. In that time, Bill Diehl and Sage Heck had come down and were helping carry some of the gear upstairs.

Bill Diehl looked at Walt, shook his head, and said, "Boy, you're like a bad penny. Just can't get rid of ya."

"This bad penny pulled your bacon out of the fire more than once, you old coot," Walt said with a big smile on his face. Surprised by how relieved he felt, having gotten back here with his cousin Trader and his wife Veronica all in one piece.

A promise made and a promise kept.

21

NOW WHAT?

Nate and Walt caught up with each other as they tended to the horses.

Before Jonathan Keith headed upstairs, Sarusha pulled him aside and gave him an appraisal of what he figured was afoot concerning Pealeday and Parker.

Sunny helped Trader up the stairs as Evie Samms came down to escort Veronica to her room.

Keith wanted to get everyone together, find out exactly what was what, and plot a course forward. Even with what Sarusha had told him, he still wondered if it was a squall or typhoon on the horizon. He had faced choppy waters before. Sometimes they settled out on their own, other times they grew to where they could sink the ship, sending all on board to their death. A captain doesn't call all hands to battle stations at the first sign of trouble. Keith had to get all the facts before doing that.

The meeting he needed would have to wait. It was getting toward suppertime. Plus, after coming off four days on the trail, Trader and the others would have to get settled and rest up a bit.

On the way up the stairs, Sarusha passed Johnny Dollars coming down carrying a plate of food. "Where you going with that?"

"Down to the brig. The Captain got that snake Aldo Severman locked up," answered Johnny.

Sarusha's mind flashed back to what he had heard Chance Parker ask Tice back at their camp: "You see Severman and Dean up at the Nest?" So he asked Johnny, "Just what did Severman do to get locked up?"

"Well, the Cap will have to fill you in on all what happened, but it looks like him and Dean was gunnin' for the Captain. Dean got into something with that Kraut Conrad. Ended up killing him. That's when Nate had to draw on Dean and shot him dead. A lot been going on since you left outa here."

"Nate Tallhelm shot and killed Dean?"

"Yeah, that's what I said." Johnny got past Sarusha and made his way to the brig, a solid windowless room way in the back of the stable.

Sarusha wondered what else he and Walt had missed in the time they'd been gone.

The dining room was abuzz as the crew, eating their supper, would stop and regreet each recent arrival as they came to the bar and got a drink. Normally the goings-on at the Nest were routine, not a whole lot to distinguish one day from the next. Now, though, speculation and anticipation filled almost every waking moment.

There was the whole situation with Aldo Severman. No one really knew how that would turn out. If he was in league with Herzog, he would have to answer to law for that. The territory wasn't without law, but just who and where that was wasn't all that clear. More times than not, justice was served up at the end of a six-gun.

Then there was Bill Liecaster, who was still licking his wounds from the beating Nate put on him. He and Tubby Flint were keeping themselves pretty scarce. But when they did show up, they could readily see that Liecaster—his face swollen and the whites of one eye a solid red, red as Japanese lacquer—was having trouble dealing with his anger and confusion. Those two emotions whirled about his untethered mind.

Also, who really knew how and when Miles Haverstraw and his daughter, Lorraine, would get their revenge on the malevolent Bertram Herzog? Word had reached the crew that Herzog was the one who set the Lautenburg fire, news that elicited long low whistles of disbelief from Brow Herman, Diehl, and Thaedell Lahr.

Plus, the cat was out of the bag as far as what Trader and Veronica were up to. Keith had relented when asked for the tenth time just what Sarusha and Walt Tallhelm were doing away from the Nest for so long. It didn't really matter much, considering the fact that Pealeday and Parker were recruiting men to help excavate the so-called cave of gold. That secret might still be limited to those actually at the site, but most likely not for long.

Keith thought, *Hell, in the matter of a few months, my world has gone from routine and tranquil to unpredictable and chaotic.* Jonathan Keith ate his supper in the back room off the kitchen. He ate alone, trying to envision the best path forward. He expected to have a general meeting with the whole crew, but not before he had a chance to hear everything that Trader, Sarusha, and Walt Tallhelm had learned.

Keith was surprised Clayton Pealeday was spoiling for a fight. Pealeday's whole myopic obsession with making the Idaho territory a Canadian province was a ship that had sailed a long time ago. But he had seen this before: all rational thought, sacrificed in the name of an idea whose viability existed only in the warped vision of a zealous few. Nevertheless, that fact did not diminish the destruction that could be wrought. More to the point, such a harebrained crusade can be much more damaging than an enemy with defined, and if not reachable at least negotiable, goals.

Keith would have to sharpen his wits and face the facts: blood would be shed. In the meantime, he had to do what captains do— keep a steady hand on the tiller. As he mulled over his options, he heard Nate from out front ask, "What's on the menu, Evie? My brother's hungry as a trencherman."

"Well, tonight we got roast turkey, thanks to you and my boys."

"Sounds good to me. I've been eating Sarusha's cooking one too many days… Oh, hey, I didn't see you there," added Walt with a sidelong glance at Sarusha, who he'd been clearly aware was standing right next to him.

"You boys just sit tight and stop bothering me," said Evie.

The trio had lingered at the bar waiting for the dining room to clear out. As they were going in, they were joined by Lorraine and her father.

"Lorraine, this is my brother, Walt. Walt, this is Lorraine Haverstraw and her father, Miles."

Miles Haverstraw, direct as always, wasted no time asking him the only question he really cared about: "Did you see Herzog?"

"No, can't say we did, but he was close by. Nate told me what that man did back in Ohio. My condolences for your loss. Believe me, after what he did to my cousin, we're gunning for him with all we got."

Miles Haverstraw looked toward the south and asked, "How far south of here did you say he was?"

"Due south about fifty some miles," answered Sarusha. "We realize you're anxious to get this thing moving along, but just trust that the Captain will come up with a plan to see him and his whole bunch either dead or swinging from a rope. No sense going off half-cocked." Sarusha's tone had become more forceful than he'd intended, but he knew what he said was right.

"You men can say what you want and think what you want, but I've been tracking that Satan for the last eleven years. Eleven years, mind ya, clear across the country and back again. So don't be telling me what and what not to do, damn you! We lost track of that harpy Marlene Scabbe. I swear by God we're not going to lose this bastard." Miles Haverstraw fairly spit out the words and, realizing he had lost his temper, got up from the table and left the room.

Lorraine remained at the table, knowing there was no consoling her father when he was like this. She also didn't feel obliged to apologize for what he said and how he said it.

Her father had not only lost his family and kin but almost every friend he ever had. Trying to piece together the series of events that led up to the fateful night of the Lautenburg fire was a torturous exercise for Miles. Why hadn't he seen what was going on? The answer to that question is simple. No moral person would have conjectured what was afoot between the widow Marlene Scabbe Slottower and the teamster Bertram Herzog, who, frankly, no one had ever noticed.

Few words carry the specter of malicious intrigue as the word *seduction*, the unsuspecting gradually lulled and lured, only to realize too late the trap they find themselves in. Marlene Scabbe was able to seduce the whole town of Lautenburg with what appeared to be a magnanimous plan to benefit the small farming community, a plan Miles Haverstraw wholeheartedly endorsed and was instrumental in convincing some others to do the same—a decision that has haunted him day and night for the last eleven years. His anger mixed with his personal shame could set his mind seething with a tumult of emotion no man should have to endure. Yet he did, day after day, year after year.

"My, but doesn't that turkey smell good," said Lorraine, choosing to elide over the angry outburst by her father.

"Boy, you got that right. I don't know how you do it, Evie, on what little help you get," Nate told Evie Samms as she was returning to the kitchen after bringing out a platter of roast turkey.

"I was there when Nate and Evie's boys shot these turkeys. You could call your brother deadeye Nate," said Lorraine.

"Oh, I called him a lot of things when we was young. I don't believe deadeye was one of them, though," said Walt as he made a boardinghouse reach across the table and grabbed the bowl of baked yams.

"You'll have to excuse my brother. Working a logging camp doesn't exactly cultivate you with the finer points of dining etiquette," said Nate.

Hearing this, Walt looked to his right and left then sheepishly said, "Oh."

Lorraine smiled and said, "I've spent a good part of the last ten years in boardinghouses, and believe me, you fellas could eat at the Queen's table compared to what I've seen." It put a smile on Nate's face as well.

His respect and ardor for this woman grew with every word that came past her beautiful lips.

"Boardinghouses? I guess so, traveling around like you did," said Nate, hoping to get Lorraine to elaborate some on her odyssey in pursuit of Bertram Herzog.

"After the fire, it took Father and me a good year to be able to even think straight. That's about the time we read that this insurance agent in Columbus, the one who was involved with Marlene Scabbe, had committed suicide. This got us to thinking, Why would the man do that? I don't know if you know the geography of Ohio, but Columbus is about fifty miles north of Lautenburg. So we made the trip up there and started looking into the insurance agent's background.

"That was my first stay in a boardinghouse. After a month or so spent doing detective work, it became pretty clear that the fire that killed my family was no accident. Well, the next thing..." Lorraine didn't finish her sentence, because just then her father returned to the dining room.

"I owe you men and my daughter an apology. It's not easy for me to think about this man without losing my temper. I hope you can understand," Miles said as he retook his seat at the table and asked Nate to pass him the plate of biscuits.

"You men look like you can handle yourselves, but I must caution you. Bertram Herzog is like no other man you have ever faced. Believe me," Miles said as he gently placed his hand over that of his daughter's.

"Lorraine tells me you boys grew up in the Cumberland Valley. We've been through there. Haven't we, Lorrie?"

"More than once, Father."

"Well, look who's here. Lorraine, Miles, this is my cousin Trader. Where's Veronica?" asked Nate.

"She's up getting herself a bath, something a few other people might think about doing," Trader said as he moved the chair next to Nate a foot away, then moved it back. "Just joshin', cousin. Don't pay me no mind." Trader sat down and nodded toward the platter of turkey that had found a permanent home in front of Walt Tallhelm.

"Sunny told me the Captain wanted to get us all together and figure out what we're gonna do next. Whatever it is, I should be ready. I'm looking forward to trying out my new Smith and Wesson that Pa sent up with Nate. I'm still sore as hell. Oh, excuse me, miss. I'm still sore as all get out, but my trigger finger still works just fine."

Trader then demonstrated that fact by pretending to shoot a pistol a half dozen times.

"Hell, yeah, you can," said Lorraine, giving a slight wink to Nate who was sitting across from her at the table.

"Let me see that gun, if you don't mind," said Miles.

Trader drew the gun out of its holster and handed it across the table to Miles. He inspected the firearm closely, then passed it back to Trader. "Takes cartridges. That's quite an improvement. Only gun I ever owned, before all this started, was a shotgun for scaring crows from the corn. Never killed one thing other than butchering a hog now and then. Chickens, of course. Now I can't hardly think of anything else but killing that man Herzog." Miles then went silent and stared absently into his glass of water before taking a sip.

"Well, you just may get your chance," Trader declared. "But enough of that. After supper, I'm treating everybody to drinks at the bar to celebrate my return from the dead. Leastwise Herzog and Chance Parker think I'm dead. I can just picture his gravestone. Here lies Bertram Herzog, shot dead by a dead man."

"Easy, Trader, sounds like you been at the bar already." This good-natured chide came from Sunny Martin, who had been standing in the doorway.

"Ah, Sunny, I'm just happy me and Ronnie are back here in one piece. Anyway, my offer still stands."

The group spent the next hour eating and talking about nothing in particular. Walt talked a bit about him and Quiet Bird. Someone asked Trader how he and Veronica met. What was it like where she came from?

Nate asked Lorraine how come she knew some of the Nez language, only to learn that Lorraine had a working knowledge of several languages and spoke five fluently. Early on in their search for Herzog and Marlene, the Haverstraws learned that people were more forthcoming with information when asked in their native tongue. Lorraine made it her job to spend much of her time in libraries, searching newspapers for any mention of Herzog and Marlene and learning languages.

Nate asked Sarusha what he thought about the Appaloosa he rode on the way here from Quiet Bird's village.

Veronica arrived from upstairs and was introduced to Lorraine and Miles. Evie Samms, knowing Veronica would be late, had put aside a plate of food for her and brought the piping hot dish out from the kitchen and joined the group.

Sunny, enjoying the mood in the dining room, brought over a round of drinks from the bar, and the group was soon joined by Lucien and the Captain. Out at the bar, the crew were at their usual poker table, joined now by Fritz Langer, whose cheek sported a bandage from the hole Dean's bullet put in it.

Everyone in the two rooms seemed to be in a good mood except Bill Liecaster and, by extension, Tubby Flint. Those two, as was their habit, were guzzling alcohol just about as quickly as they could. The only thing that removed the scowl from Liecaster's face was opening his mouth to slam down another shot of whiskey.

Eventually Jonathan Keith excused himself, but before leaving, told everyone that tomorrow they'd have a meeting and plan a way forward. "So enjoy yourselves 'cause after tonight, we'll most likely be going to battle stations."

Shortly after the Captain's departure, Lucien and Evie bid the group goodnight, as did Miles Haverstraw.

Nate asked Lorraine, "Would you like to get some air?"

"I'd like that very much."

On their way out to the deck, the pair couldn't help but pass the booth occupied by Liecaster and Flint. Liecaster could be heard making some low grumbling sounds without looking up from his drink. Normally, Nate wouldn't tolerate this sort of baiting on the part of Liecaster or anyone else. But with Lorraine right there, he thought better of it. No doubt about it, Liecaster was damn near out of his wits. The man was seething with anger. What avenue that anger would take remained to be seen.

Nate wondered to himself, *Do I have to worry about being back shot by this bastard? Like I don't have enough to concern myself with.* As he did so, he just kept walking and opened the door out to the deck for Lorraine. The fresh air was a welcome change after being inside all evening.

Nate and Lorraine leaned against the railing where they first met. Again, the light from the moon illuminated a breathtaking view. The view south showed high billowing clouds moving from the east. Clouds that were suffered to wait above the Bottleneck Falls as the snow-laden mountains to the west extended the chill of their greeting.

Simply being next to one another warmed their hearts. And as Nate turned and took Lorraine in his embrace, the ardor of their desire for one another banished any chill in the air. Their pent-up passion was almost too much for propriety to control, yet control it they did. Again, Lorraine put her hand between their lips. "Please, Nathan, not here. Not now. But soon."

Nate could understand this. He could understand it for a number of reasons. That understanding made it no less painful, as every ounce of his being wanted to possess Lorraine and wanted to be possessed by her.

Not now, but soon.

22

THE TASTE OF BLOOD

The sound of the five-barreled duck's-foot pistol reverberated through the Crow's Nest like a cannon blast. The stillness of the wee hours shattered as the walls of the building did little to muffle the gun's report that echoed down through the valley.

Every door in the Nest flew open as all parties sought the origin of the blast.

"You boys stay put," Lucien Samms hollered into the boys' room as he quickly pulled on his trousers and boots. He was no sooner through the door and up the back stairs than he was joined in the hallway by Sunny and Sarusha as they rushed to Lorraine and Miles's room. Just inside the doorway was the crumpled body of Bill Liecaster, his face all but blown off.

Lorraine sat there wide-eyed and motionless as the shock of what had just happened rendered her dumbstruck and paralyzed.

Miles Haverstraw, returning from the outdoor privy, arrived a moment later. Fear and disbelief rendered him speechless as well. Soon the hallway in front of Lorraine's room was jam-packed with almost everyone in the building. Nate pushed his way through the crowd, took Lorraine in his arms, and led her back out the door and down the hallway. Neither spoke a word.

Nate had hastily dressed himself, buckled on his gun belt, and grabbed his trail coat, sans its brace of double-barreled pistols. He now draped that coat around Lorraine, who had begun to shiver uncontrollably.

Keith, arriving on the scene, took control of the situation. "Nate, take her down to the bar. Lucien, get back downstairs and have Evie meet us in the bar. The rest of you see about cleaning up that mess. Where's Tubby Flint? Sunny, you and Walt see to Haverstraw. Get him down to the bar as soon as you can."

Nate poured Lorraine and himself a stiff drink. There weren't many things that could put a scare into Nate, but seeing Lorraine shivering and in a state of shock evidently was one of them.

"Here, Lorraine, drink this."

With her hands shaking so much, she spilled half her drink on the way to her lips. Nate poured a bit more in the glass and Lorraine, holding it with both hands, steadied herself, paused for moment, then drank it down. Her body then went limp as she laid her head on Nate's chest and closed her eyes.

"I killed that man, didn't I?" asked Lorraine.

Nate carefully weighed his answer. "That man is dead. That's what he wanted."

"Where's Father? He'd gone out to the privy and next thing I know, that man was in the room and coming at me."

"I'm right here, Lorrie," said Miles, who had gotten himself dressed and down to the bar along with Sunny.

"Here, Miles, drink this," directed Sunny as he poured Miles and himself a glass of whiskey.

"I can see thinking about killing is one thing. Killing is another," said Lorraine, who had started to regain some measure of composure.

Evie and Veronica were also in the room and stood close by, ready to help in any way they could.

"Nate, why don't you take her over to that booth?" instructed Jonathan Keith.

Nate guided Lorraine over to the closest booth and sat her down. There she sat with Nate holding her tight. Just six hours ago, Nate would had enjoyed nothing more than holding Lorraine like this, but now, given the circumstances, he had to silently curse the devilish hand of fate.

Keith and Sunny huddled with Miles Haverstraw and told him they were going to move their things out of that room and into another, a rarely used room on the top floor, next to his own. This would spare Miles and Lorraine the need to walk past the blood-spattered doorway.

"Veronica, go ask Lorraine if there is something she could get for her to put on. The sooner she gets to deciding things the better," said Keith.

"God, what next?" he said as he sat on one of the stools at the bar and rubbed his face. "What the hell time is it anyway?"

"Not quite five, Cap," answered Sunny.

"Evie, could you make some coffee, please? I'm going up to get dressed. Sunny, get Sarusha, Trader, and Walt and meet me back here in half an hour. Have Sage and Johnny get the Haverstraws' things up to their new room. See to it that Brow, Diehl, and Lahr know they're responsible for getting Liecaster down to the oil shed. Oh yeah, tell Flint he's got till noon to clear out of here. He can have Liecaster's stuff. The horse and saddle stay. I've had it." An obviously exasperated Keith barked out these orders as the time for contemplation had come and gone. Now it was all action.

Sunny rarely questioned what the Captain had decided, but in this case found himself saying, "Cap, I'd think twice about letting Tubby leave outa here. I got no sympathy for him, but when you think about it, Pealeday and that man Herzog, they don't know Trader's alive. Also from what Sarusha and Tallhelm say, they think Veronica's probably dead. The other thing is, why risk letting Herzog know the Haverstraws are this close on his trail? I'm not saying Flint would head right to where they are. Most likely he'd get himself back down to Lewiston. Hell, when you think about it, the condition he's in, he might be dead before he gets up the switchback, but hell, I don't know."

"I see what you're saying. Just tell him we're taking Bill's horse and saddle for the cost of burying him. While you're at it, take any guns they got. I know Liecaster had a rifle and a sidearm. I think Flint has some kinda saddle gun, but I'm not sure. Whatever they got, take 'em. Good thinking."

"So he can stay for the time being?"

"Yeah, for the time being."

It was almost noon till any semblance of normalcy returned to the Nest. For breakfast, Evie Samms just made a big pot of porridge and left it at that.

Keith had his meeting with Sunny, Sarusha, Trader, and Walt. The product of that meeting was a general strategy on how to move forward. The first thing to do was to find out just what Aldo Severman had been up to.

Keith had decided he didn't want Liecaster's body in the oil shed after all and had the crew take him up to the cemetery plot straight off and plant him right after they got their breakfast. The Nest had gone three or four years without a burial. Now in little more than a week, there would be three.

"Sunny, you and Walt go down to the brig and get Severman. Bring him up here to the bar. Now that I think about it, take him out back and wash him down. I don't want him stinking up the place any more than he already does," directed Keith.

"I got ya, Cap," answered Sunny.

"Lucien, did they get that room cleaned up yet?" asked Keith.

"No, not yet, Cap. That was some godawful mess. It's gonna take a little doing."

"While you're at it, get my duck's foot back up to my room. I'm gonna want to clean and reload that. Who the hell knows what might happen next?"

"Boy, Cap, we ain't seen this kind of business in quite a while."

"No, we haven't. No, we haven't."

Nate had taken Lorraine up to her and Miles's new room and gotten Veronica to join them. Keith had suggested a little laudanum wouldn't be a bad idea, and Miles agreed. Soon the drug's effect had Lorraine in a light but fitful sleep. Nate took his leave and joined his brother along with the others in the bar as they waited to see what Aldo Severman had to say.

"Severman, I'll make this simple for you. Tell us what we want to know and I won't take you out back and make you walk the plank," said Keith in a very matter-of-fact tone, one that made you think he would actually do it.

"I ain't saying a damn thing till I get a drink," a combative Severman answered.

"Get him a drink," said Keith.

Aldo drank that down and held up the glass and wiggled it. Keith nodded to Sunny his assent.

Aldo drank that and did the same thing again.

"Okay, that's enough. No more till we get some answers. Now what the hell were you and Dean up to?" asked an increasingly angry Jonathan Keith.

"First off, you bastards..." began Severman.

"Watch your mouth, you homicidal son of a bitch," said Sunny as he grabbed ahold of Severman, yanked him out of his chair, and was considering whether or not to slap him around.

"No need for that, leastwise not yet," said Keith.

Sunny let go of Severman and shoved him back into his chair.

"As I was about to say, you wouldn't throw me off a cliff, 'cause y'all are God-fearing Christians. That wouldn't sit well with the Man upstairs," said Severman.

"Don't toy with me. God just may just consider that I was doing Him a favor. So don't be so damn cocksure of yourself. Now what the hell were you and Dean doing with all those double eagles? I happen to know you and Chance Parker were cooking something up. Now what was it?"

Keith said this but wasn't 100 percent sure if there had been a deal between Severman and Parker.

"Big time Captain Jonathan Keith, you're like an old blind rat, hiding up in some corner. You should get out more often, then you'd might know what's going on." Aldo Severman said this in such a way that told the group something was afoot, and it wasn't just about Chance Parker.

"What's in it for me, iffen I tell ya what I know?" continued Aldo.

"First off, how about us letting you live? Is that reason enough?" said Sunny.

This whole time, Sarusha, Trader, Walt, and Nate were sitting quietly by, trying to figure out, along with Sunny and Keith, just what was Severman's game.

"That's not enough. I still got some unfinished business with him over there." Severman looked at Nate and thrust his chin in his direction. "Pour me another drink."

Keith nodded to Sunny. "One more and that's it."

"I'll tell you everything, and I mean everything, if you let me draw on him over there." Again, Aldo indicated Nate.

"That ain't gonna happen," said Keith.

"Cap, let me have him for a half hour. I'll get him to talk," offered Walt Tallhelm.

Severman, feeling an opening, continued his taunt, "Why, you yella, you Yankee son of a bitch."

This time, Sunny lifted Severman out of his chair, held him up off the floor, and slapped him back and forth a couple of times, then shoved him back down so hard the chair and Severman went flying.

"One more time, I'm warning ya." Sunny obviously was having trouble keeping his temper, and for good reason.

"I'll do it," said Nate. "If that's the only way we're gonna get him to talk, I'll face him."

"Now hold on. No need for that, Nate. Let's everyone settle down," cautioned Keith.

"Yeah, just like I figured, yella," carped Aldo.

"Shut up, you," said Walt, not enjoying the prospect of his younger brother getting killed in a gunfight after only seeing him for less than a day after a twenty-year absence.

"I thought you said your wrist was broke?" Nate put in.

"Naah, it just smarted a bit. Thanks for your concern, but I'll be just fine," said a sarcastic and increasingly bold Aldo Severman.

"Look, Cap, there's a lot at stake here. We really have no idea what Herzog, Pealeday, and Parker are cooking up. Also, I can't be worrying about being back shot by this bastard unless you plan on keeping him locked up in that room downstairs forever," said Nate.

"What do you men think?" asked Keith.

"I'm not for it, but in some ways, it's Nate's call," said Sunny.

"That's how I see it, Cap," said Sarusha.

"I still say give him to me for, forget half an hour, fifteen minutes, and I'll get him to talk," said Walt.

Aldo Severman, weighing the uncertainty in the voices of his inquisitors, was emboldened enough to say, "I don't even know why you got me locked up in the first place. Me and Dean won that money in a poker game down to the Settlement Bar for all you know. That's the problem up here. No damn law."

"Boy, that's rich coming from you, you lying pile of fish guts," said Sunny.

"What's it gonna be, Caaap?" Severman asked, openly ridiculing Captain Jonathan Keith. "We got a deal?"

During this back and forth, Nate rubbed the handle of his .44, sometimes drawing it in and out of its holster an inch or two.

"Do we need to know what he knows?" asked Keith of the men gathered about.

"I gotta say, Cap, it's tempting," said Sarusha.

"The hell with it. I said I'd do it," repeated Nate, all the frustration of the last two weeks coming to a near boiling point.

"What about him?" asked Severman, pointing toward Walt. "Once I kill his brother, I don't wanna get shot by this one."

"Nate, you sure?" asked Walt.

"Yeah, I'm sure," answered Nate.

Walt wasn't asking Nate if he wanted to face Severman. He was asking him if he could outdraw the reputedly fast Aldo Severman.

"It's settled then. Okay, Aldo, you got my word. Now what do you know?" asked Keith.

"Not so fast. I wanna be able to leave outa here when this is all done," said Severman.

"Sure, you can leave here. You can go tell Chance Parker to give you some more money 'cause you didn't get the job done. This was a bit of supposition on Sarusha's part, who, along with Walt Tallhelm, had been trying to put all the pieces of the puzzle together since the afternoon they were looking down at Herzog and Chance Parker's camp.

"What was that explosion before?" asked Severman.

"Nothing to concern you. You got your deal, now let's hear it. What the hell is going on?" demanded Sunny.

"Well, where should I begin?" asked Aldo Severman, obviously enjoying the power his inside information gave him. "You should know, Tice and Dagget are in on this," said Aldo.

"We know that. Tell us something we don't know," said Sarusha.

"You can begin with what did you and Chance Parker have cooked up and take it from there," said Keith.

"Yeah, Pealeday and Parker paid Dean and me each four hundred to come here and see about gunnin' you and the half-breed and your man Sunny here, if we got lucky. We asked about the darky, but Chance said he wasn't worried about him. We didn't figure this one would be here." Severman pointed to Nate.

"Anyway, the deal is Clayton Pealeday's got to clear out of Lewiston, and fast. Some people got together and decided enough was enough. Word got up to the Canucks that something had to be done. It got back to Pealeday that he's gonna be arrested for stirring up all that trouble about the border. That's one thing you didn't know about," an almost boastful Severman said as he pointed to the whiskey bottle, figuring every tidbit of information should be worth another drink.

Keith nodded okay. Once Severman got his drink, Keith said, "Go on."

"Well, right about the time this information got down to Lewiston, this man Herzog arrives and is there looking to throw in with Pealeday. Seems like this Herzog is on the run, and he had somehow gotten word about Pealeday being a malcontent and troublemaker. Hell, no big surprise there. Anybody up this way knows that.

"Anyway, Pealeday asks him, 'Why should I have anything to do with you? What's in it for me?' Just so happened Herzog saw your boy here and his beaner wife with surveying equipment and some mining tools at the same stable where he had his horse. He's pretty cagey, this Herzog, and he went and got a room next to yours wheres you were staying. He must have heard enough to convince Parker and Pealeday to join up with him and jump whatever gold claim the two of them knew about. Once they heard they were coming up here to the Crow's Nest and the Kettle, of course with the old legend, that's all they needed.

"Pealeday's got something against you, Keith. I don't know what it is, but he figured he could even the score and take over this place and ride out the storm. Herzog followed Darcy and his woman on up to here. Dean and me was paid and told to wait a couple of weeks and come here directly from down Lewiston. Dean and me was having a good time at the Settlement on Chance's money, and I guess we got a late start. Anyway, we got here and saw our opening when that loudmouthed Kraut started carping about your friend. You know the rest," Severman finished and pointed to the bottle of whiskey.

"You telling me Clayton Pealeday is going to get arrested?" asked Keith.

"He'll get arrested if they can find him. The law in Lewiston wasn't gonna do anything till they got something official from up in Canada. That's who wants him. Pealeday got a lot of friends in Lewiston. Hell, he all but founded the damn town," answered Aldo.

"Yeah, I can see that," said Keith, trying to figure out all of what Severman had just said. "Besides you and Dean, who else is supposed to be coming this way?"

"Hell, I don't know everything. You're supposed to be the smart one. This Herzog had plenty of money and wasn't afraid to let some people know there was money to be made if they threw in with him. There's some lean and hungry boys down that way. Some bloody ones, that's for sure. I believe that war got some of them liking the taste of blood. I myself never cared for the military."

"Yeah, you son of a bitch, you didn't need no war as an excuse to shed blood, did ya? Don't bother answering that," said Sunny.

"How many horses did you and Walt see at that camp?" asked Keith.

"Seven, maybe eight," answered Sarusha.

"Yeah, and we saw those four riders heading that way on our ride up here from Quiet Bird's," said Walt.

"Damn, we're talking at least a dozen or so, and that's if no one else joins up."

"How was you to let Parker know if you got the job done?" asked Sarusha.

"We never got it figured that far ahead," answered Aldo.

"Can you men think of anything else?" asked Keith.

"Nope, only thing I guess is what this bastard wants for his last meal," said Trader. He then added, "They'll be a lot of men waiting for you on the other side, I can guarantee ya that. Walt here knows all about that kind of thing."

Walt didn't quite know what Trader was talking about, but just the same, got a stern look on his face and nodded.

"Lucien, go get this man a plate of food. Doesn't have to be anything special, if you don't mind," directed Keith, who was racking his brain to come up with something else to ask Aldo Severman. There's always more to find out.

"Lucien, get him some coffee too. I don't want to feel guilty for plugging a drunk," said Nate.

"You ain't gonna be feeling nothing once I'm done with ya," said Severman.

"Sunny, go get his rig. I got it upstairs. You load it. I don't want him getting any funny ideas," instructed Keith.

While Lucien got Severman his food and some coffee, the men sat around the table in silence, each one hoping for one outcome but knowing when two men faced each other, nothing was ever guaranteed.

Trader Darcy, for his part, was thinking back to when he and Veronica were in Lewiston and wondering just how Herzog got on to them. Regardless, he was angry at himself for being careless, if in fact carelessness on his part was what led them to be found out.

"Cap, I expect we'll do this out back. I'll meet you all down there," said Nate in a quiet and somber tone. No bravado, just resolve.

The weather, in keeping with the drama of the situation, was overcast and gloomy. A damp chill greeted the men as they made their way down the back staircase.

Nate didn't relish having to draw on another man, but it was something he was no stranger to. One time in the Mogollon, in Arizona, he was part of a posse going after a gang of cattle rustlers and horse thieves. He got separated from the posse and found himself facing off with the ringleader of the bunch. Nate had him in his rifle sights, but some deep-seated sense of fairness let him give the man an open play. They faced each other at twenty paces, and Nate managed to put two bullets in the man's shoulder before he even cleared leather. The rustler lived and eventually stretched out a hangman's rope.

The other time was in a barroom in Cheyenne, when a man was on the prod for some reason and accused Nate of cheating at poker and called him out. Nate tried to convince him otherwise, but he wouldn't listen to reason. Out in the street, Nate gave him one more chance to back away and said he was willing to forget the whole thing. No dice. He should have taken the offer and walked away. After Nate's entreaties fell on deaf ears, the man went for his gun. Nate didn't fool around, put three bullets right in the man's heart. Nate didn't care to be called a cheater but would have let it go by. But the malcontent was on the prod and just looking for trouble. He found it.

Severman strapped on his gun belt and, using the chopping block as a support, tied the bottom of the holster to his leg.

Keith didn't approve of it, but word had spread, and the whole of the Nest was arrayed on the two back staircases and the upper balconies to witness the duel.

Nate looked up and was glad to see that Lorraine was not among them.

"Okay, Severman, here's your piece. You can check the loads if you want." Sunny's tone was flat and betrayed no emotion as he handed Severman his long-barreled six-gun. Aldo Severman broke the pistol, checked the loads, closed it, and let it slide gently into its holster.

Severman stood next to the chopping block as Nate backed up twenty paces, keeping his eyes on Severman the whole time.

For what seemed like an eternity, the men faced each in silence. It almost felt like the wind itself held its breath. So still was the moment.

Nate saw Severman's eye twitch a split second before the gunslinger drew his revolver, slapped back the hammer, and went to squeeze the trigger. Severman was fast, but not fast enough. The impact of Nate's first bullet spun the gunfighter half around, causing his shot to go awry, missing Nate's head by inches. Nate's second bullet caught Severman in the side of the neck. His black kerchief soon became blacker, soaked with blood.

Severman staggered forward a few wobbly steps, turned his head sideways, and caught Tallhelm's eyes as he crashed to the ground, dead.

There was no cheering from the onlookers. Only silence. Nate automatically gave his revolver one twirl and redeposited it in its holster.

He looked up to the uppermost balcony and saw Lorraine standing there, the kindest of smiles on her face.

Nate looked around and, to no one in particular, commented, "It looks like rain."

23

WAR POSTURE

Sunny motioned to Sage Heck and Johnny to come down from their perch on the balcony as he commented to Lucien, "I remember one of them. I don't know if it was Dean or Severman saying, 'There's room in the cemetery for everyone.' Well, looks like they found that out for themselves."

"With all these bodies we be burying, we gonna need some new shovels for them boys" was Lucien's response.

"Brow, do me a favor and get Severman's blanket out of the brig. And while you're at it, make sure you leave that door open. Sage, it looks like you and Johnny got yourselves another horse to argue over. This rig goes back up to the Cap's quarters," Sunny said as he reached down and closed Severman's milky gray eyes, undid his gun belt, and emptied the loads of his six-gun. "Just so you know, Nate, they were all good."

"Well, that didn't make much of a difference, did it?"

There was no real joy in Nate's voice. Of course, he was glad it was Aldo Severman lying dead in the dirt rather than himself. But all this going on had left him a bit weary. "Sunny, I'm going upstairs and rest a bit. Walt, I'll catch you up later."

"Sure, Nate. I'll most likely be in the bar or up in my room. Good shooting by the way." Although he hadn't seen Nate in years, Walt could easily tell when his younger brother was feeling blue. And why shouldn't he? Killing another man was about as absolute an

231

experience as one man could have. Even when that man is human vermin like Aldo Severman. At least Nate was still alive enough inside to be bothered. Some men aren't.

No sooner had Nate entered his room and shucked his gun belt than there was a light rap on the door. It was Veronica and Lorraine. "Nate, Lorraine's still a bit woozy from that laudanum. She asked me to bring her down here."

Lorraine went to Nate, put her head on his chest, and held him tight.

"Thank you, Ronnie." As Veronica went to leave, Nate added, "Tell Trader I owe his Pa another thank you for giving me that .44. Severman was fast. I think that gun made the difference."

"I tell him. You want door open?"

"You can leave it open."

Although the bed in Nate's room was narrow, it was wide enough for him and Lorraine to lie next to one another. And they did, in a loving embrace, and were soon asleep.

It was just early afternoon, but given the fact that Nate had been up since about four-thirty in the morning and had endured the stress of a gunfight, no wonder he was tired. Lorraine, of course, had been fairly traumatized by having killed Bill Liecaster. On top of that, later on, she watched as the man she loved faced off against the vile gunslinger Aldo Severman. Her exhausted mind was more than willing to seek the warm bosom of slumber.

Matter of fact, the whole of the Nest was in a miasma of sorts. Strangely, the only aspect of the goings-on that seemed to be cut and dried was the task of burying Liecaster and now Severman. Nate was right about the rain coming, and the burial detail, consisting of the whole of the crew, was rushing to complete their task before the rain started.

The men were thankful that the loamy earth of the forest floor was easy to dig.

"Wonder how many more we gonna have to plant before this whole thing is over?" asked Johnny Dollars.

"Who the hell knows," responded Brow Herman and Bill Diehl both at once.

"Damn. Nate's fast. I was watching, and I swear, he had that piece out before you could blink," commented Thaedell Lahr, who was using his shovel more as a prop than a tool.

"Aldo was fast too, but not fast enough," said Sage.

"Well, anyone want to say some words over these two?" asked Brow Herman.

"I will," said Lahr. "Dear Lord, thank you for getting these two down to hell. Now maybe we can get some rest. Amen."

A chorus of Amens went up from the group.

"Who wants to get a drink?" asked Johnny Dollars.

"Johnny, I think that's your first stupid question of the day," quipped Bill Diehl.

As the men left the cemetery, Brow asked Sage and Johnny, "What are you two gonna do with those extra horses? You know you got to pay Everett and Ernie to look after them."

"Yeah, we know. The Cap will work it out. Maybe he'll trade for some of those double eagles Severman and Dean had," Sage wondered aloud.

Jonathan Keith had a lot more on his mind than who had to pay for feeding a couple of horses. From what Severman said, the Nest could expect to be attacked by Clayton Pealeday and as many mercenary ex-soldiers as he could hire. Not a very comforting thought. He wasn't quite sure what to expect from Bertram Herzog, but from what the Haverstraws described, it surely pointed to something potentially cataclysmic. Now with this Herzog in league with Pealeday, that spelled real trouble.

Clayton Pealeday was a man with many faults who, over the years, had nurtured those into as many tragic flaws. Nothing, however, interfered with his abilities as a military tactician. In that regard, Keith was most concerned. Between the Canadian diehards and Pealeday's paid gunmen, there was no way to judge just how big a threat the Nest was facing. This was shaping up to be a battle nothing short of straight-up root hog or die.

Keith was not without options. He had fought pitched battles with Barbary pirates and survived. He had withstood two sieges upon the Nest and had triumphed. Keith was both inventive and resourceful. No doubt about it, he and his crew along with the Tallhelms and Trader Darcy were facing a challenge. He knew that for sure.

He also knew that if it was war Pealeday and Herzog wanted, it was war they would get.

Only Sarusha, Sunny, and Lucien really knew the kind of arsenal the Crow's Nest possessed. There was a magazine, chockablock full of black powder, grapeshot, and more. There were also some deck cannon held over from Keith's seafaring days that could be deployed.

Keith, the remoteness of the Crow's Nest notwithstanding, kept abreast of any new developments in the area of arms and explosives. To that end, on their last supply trip down to Lewiston, he had Sunny and Sarusha, along with the usual resupply for the Nest, return with three cases of high-grade dynamite.

Also, a year ago, he made a trip himself along with Thaedell Lahr down to Portland and came back with two cases of brand-new Spencer carbines and three cases of ammunition.

They also had that fully stocked redoubt under the cemetery shed. Keith never wanted to be without the option of fighting an attacker on two fronts. Also, behind the old-growth stand of pines and oak at the uppermost end of the Nest was a way down off the crag and back up to the cut. Although it was an arduous climb, men could make their way to that redoubt without having to expose themselves going up the switchback. Keith had plenty of strong hemp rope to aid in that effort.

The rain began to fall just as the burial crew made their way back down the switchback and up to the stable. All in all, a right gloomy bunch. "Let's get that drink," suggested Bill Diehl.

"Drink? I think you mean drinks" was a weary Johnny Dollars' response.

Keith normally frowned on the crew drinking in the afternoon. However, he was also a man well aware that being flexible was also a strength unto itself. The two burials, plus the cold steady rain, made an afternoon spent in the bar seem completely apropos. Sunny kept the two big potbellied stoves well-fed, and just as they warmed the room, so did the whiskey do its part to warm the spirits of the men.

Although none of the crew spoke openly about it, nevertheless the same thing was very much on everyone's mind. Just how was the Cap going to deal with Clayton Pealeday and this man Herzog? The longer that remained a question the more it ate away at the intangible strength the Captain imbued in his men.

Keith was aware of this as well. He had to figure out a strategy and articulate it to the crew with force and conviction. That strategy, distilled into its simplest elements, came down to being either on the offensive or the defensive. Keith had begun to concoct a plan that incorporated both. Parts of the plan were bold, and parts of it were basic in their simplicity. Keith hadn't had to be shrewd in his approach to a problem in some time. But the challenge he and the men faced would call into play every ounce of ingenuity, cunning, and courage they could muster.

"Johnny, do me a favor and see about getting Sarusha, Trader, and Walt down here. I'll be in the back room."

"You got it, Cap," answered Johnny as he gulped down whatever whiskey remained in his glass.

His plan involved more than a bit of danger, and Keith wanted to be sure the men would be on board for it. Ten minutes later, Sarusha, Trader, Walt, and Sunny were gathered in the back room off the kitchen.

"Sit down, men. Sunny, get us a bottle. God, what a day. I wasn't too thrilled with Nate going up against Severman. Thank God that went the way it did," Keith said as he spread a hand-drawn map out on the table.

"I don't want to wait until that bunch that bushwhacked Trader and Ronnie get to the top of the switchback before we do something. Plus we got Pealeday to contend with. It's hard to say just how he's going to come at us. Whatever way it is, I want us to be ready.

"Here, look at this map Evie drew. So here, from the top of the switchback to the Swallows, is roughly eight miles, and it's all open going. On the flat is where we can whittle down their numbers. To the south, you got the promontory. I imagine they could try getting up into those woods and making their way here, but there's no way to get down from up there on a horse.

"Now the promontory is the high ground, granted, but even its closest point to the Nest is still three-quarters of a mile, too far out of range to do any damage. I suppose they could try sliding down the talus and hope they get stopped before going over the rim, but I doubt they'd risk that. There's really no way to get down from that promontory till you're almost back to the Swallows. That face is forty feet of sheer rock. One way or another, they got to come along that flat.

"This is where you three come in. Between the promontory to the south and the forest to the north, the flat is what maybe three, four hundred yards wide. Narrow enough for you three to hit anything you're aiming at from the cover of those trees. Or am I wrong?" Keith stopped his explaining, took a drink of whiskey, and continued. He really didn't expect an answer to his question.

"Once we find out they're on their way, let's hope there's enough time to get you three up into those woods. There's more than enough food, water, and ammo up in the redoubt to keep you three as long as this goes on. Which, I want to tell you, I hope is not all that long. We don't want this thing dragging out. We got to hit them fast and hit 'em hard."

"No argument there, Cap," said Sarusha as Walt, Sunny, and Trader nodded in agreement.

Keith continued with what he was thinking. "Pealeday is smart enough not to just ride into an ambush. If he comes straight from Lewiston, he'll pick up the trail that would bring him to the Swallows. But I don't think he'll wanna to do that. Too risky.

"I figure before he gets anywhere near there, he'll break off and stay well west of the flat, swing around north, and get up on the cut. From there, he could keep us busy while he has some of his men come across the flat and try to get down the switchback."

"Cap, what about us having a few men up in those promontory woods south of the flat?" asked Trader.

"I thought of that. I thought of maybe having Fritz, who was military, and Johnny up there. They'd have to be on foot. No sense having horses up there. I think we got time to set them up in a camp."

"That would make for a nice crossfire," said Walt.

236

Sarusha stood up, leaned over the table, and pressed out the creases in the map and repositioned the turned-over coffee cups holding down the four corners. "Cap, what about this? Without too much work, we could move some of the skeletons of those buffalo and elk that got trapped in the Swallow's dead ends to the few good ways through. Some of those passageways are so tight, a horse has no room to even turn around. You get that bunch either lost or trapped in amongst them rocks for a day or two. Once they do get out and onto the flat and are met with some hot lead, they may just call it quits."

Keith turned to Walt and Trader. "What do you think?"

"Hell, Cap, nobody knows the Swallows better than Sarusha. I say why not. It should put that bunch in a pretty ripe state of mind," said Trader.

"We could even be in among them rocks ourselves and get in some target practice before we head out and get across the flat to that north wood." This suggestion from Walt Tallhelm might have seemed cold and homicidal, but when someone opens the ball, you got to be ready to dance. Walt Tallhelm stayed ready.

"Cap, with the three of us out there and Fritz and, say, Johnny up in the promontory woods, are you going to have enough men left at the Nest?" asked Trader, the concern heavy in his voice. Trader, after all, showing up at the Nest with Veronica's centuries-old saddlebag map, was partially responsible for at least Herzog's part in all this. The bad blood between Clayton Pealeday and the Captain was another matter. In any event, Trader knew he'd do whatever it took to set things straight. He looked upon Jonathan Keith as a mentor, favorite uncle, and old friend all rolled into one. It was Keith's kind and reassuring counsel that helped Trader come out of his postwar depression. He wasn't going to let him down now. Trader Darcy had also decided, although he hadn't spoken to anyone about it, to forget about the cave of gold. Once this whole affair was over, he and Ronnie planned to head down to his folks' place and make a simple life for themselves there.

Keith responded to Trader's concern without hesitation. "Don't you men worry about that. Brow and Bill Diehl are crack shots. Sage will be up top on the parapet. Everett and Ernie can shoot. I figure on putting Thaedell in the gatehouse. Anyone coming down the switchback would make a wide-open target even Lahr couldn't miss. And don't forget, we got myself, Lucien, Sunny, and Nate. That's plenty of firepower. Hell, maybe even Ghosty will want to get into the act. Remember the Bible, an eye for an eye. I doubt it, but who knows.

"Anyway, at some point, we'd get you three back down the switchback and into the Nest once you did your damage. Also, Lucien and me talked about making up some gunpowder and grapeshot 'pineapples.' We can put them out on the flat or up the cut and detonate 'em with a rifle shot."

"I like the sound of that," said Walt.

"Trader, you were cavalry. Any suggestions?" asked Jonathan Keith, not one too proud to seek advice when he needed it.

"I don't know, Cap. How well do you know this Clayton Pealeday? Is he the kind to come straight at ya or try something else?" asked Trader.

"Well, usually he's been one to just ramrod through anything in his way. He just made the wrong choice in thinking he could keep part of the Idaho Territory for Canada. So now he's painted himself into a corner. We all know a cornered man is unpredictable, damn near liable to do anything. I tell ya, men, I needed this like I needed a hole in my head."

The weariness in Keith's voice betrayed the exasperation at having to deal with any of this business. He knew there were no guarantees in life, but he also thought that at this stage, he wouldn't be facing decisions where the lives of a dozen people hung in the balance. He begrudgingly knew he couldn't let it get to him. He could do this. It just angered him that he had to. But just that anger was what was going to give him the edge he needed.

Trader, seeing this weariness in the Captain, took a resolute tone when he said, "This is nothing I ain't seen before. One of the main parts of our job in the cavalry was finding where the Rebs were and which way they were moving. That's just what we got here. The question is, once we find them, what do we do then?

"Look here on the map. If I was him, I'd loop around the north woods and get to the cut north of the Nest. He can't come through those woods to get to the cut. That forest is about as thick as quills on a porcupine. That would be tough going. If Pealeday does stay to the west, the only real trail over that way—Sarusha, correct me if I'm wrong—is right about here." Trader pointed to a place on the map west of where the flat ended and a forest began. "I say we have a scout watching that trail. From the western edge of the flat to the Nest, there's an open sightline. Whoever is out there could signal back to the Nest." Trader's suggestion was met with silence as the men were trying to weigh all the variables.

Jonathan Keith decided it was time to let the strategic thoughts settle. "Men, let's chew on this for a while. I'm calling a general meeting for after supper. We'll flesh out our plans then. Meanwhile, I know you all have your own rifles, but I got those new Spencers and plenty of shells. You'll each get one. No harm in having an extra rifle.

"Sunny, on your way out, ask Johnny to come back."

"Sure, Cap."

Three minutes later, Johnny arrived, making a vain effort to straighten his trousers and tuck in his shirt.

"What's up Captain?" asked Johnny quickly adding, "If it's about me trying to get Mr. Haverstraw to buy some of my scrip, that was more of a joke than a real offer. Well, maybe a little bit."

"No, Johnny, this isn't about that dumb scrip of yours. Why don't you just give all that to Sunny? He could use it to light a fire. No, I got to ask you something. You know sooner or later, most likely sooner considering the hard weather coming, those that bushwhacked Trader are coming this way. I want you and the Austrian to be up on the promontory and help set up a crossfire. From up there, you could shoot down. Plus you'd have the cover of the trees and be able to pretty much pick your target."

Keith went on, "We'd set up a camp, plenty of grub, and you would each have a Spencer and more than enough ammo. The only problem—well, not the only one—would be you'd be on foot. Once we know they're on their way, we'll get you two up that bank with some rope ladders we'll have ready to go. Depending on how it goes, you two may have to be up there for a couple of days."

"Cap, what about me and Sage doing this? You know he can shoot," asked Johnny.

"Well, it just may be Sage and you. But I was hoping to have him up top on the parapet. We're figuring Pealeday may come at us from up on the cut, and Sage is about as good a long-rifle snipe as there is. We'll need him there more than on the promontory. You get along with Fritz Langer?" asked Keith.

"Yeah, Cap, we get along okay, I suppose. He can't play poker worth a damn."

"Tell ya what, you do this for me and I'll buy that scrip off ya. How's that?"

"Hell, Cap, you don't have to do that. You been real good to me since I got here. I'll do it. Fritz and me will do it," said Johnny as he felt a renewed sense of self-worth.

"That's good, but I wanted to know where you were before I asked Langer. So don't say anything until I get a chance to see where he's at."

"You got it, Cap."

"Tell Fritz to come back, okay? By the way, how'd it go burying those two?"

"No real problems, 'cept I'm getting these hard places on my hands."

"You're joking, right?" asked Keith. "They're calluses in case you weren't"

"Oh" was all Johnny replied.

As Johnny left the room, Keith had to admit to himself that all the quips and comments made at Johnny's expense were most likely well-deserved.

To say Fritz Langer was a man lost and adrift would be to understate the situation. When his lifelong friend Conrad Drager was shot dead by Dean, his purpose in life drained out of him like a canteen with a hole in the bottom. Fritz had served under Conrad Drager in the Austrian army and had Conrad to thank for saving his life more than once. After the latest war between Austria and Prussia ended, the two set out together for the American West.

Fritz Langer was a friend, companion, confidant, and servant of sorts to the wealthy and unapologetically arrogant Conrad Drager. In the wake of Conrad's death, Fritz had tried to anesthetize himself with alcohol, but to no avail. He knew eventually he'd have to get back to San Francisco and return to Europe. But for now, here he was, holed up in this place called the Crow's Nest, doing whatever it took to make it from one day and onto the next.

When Jonathan Keith called him aside, he had no idea that his request would give his life purpose again and finally break the paralytic grip his melancholia had on his soul.

"Fritz," Keith began. "I never really conveyed my condolences about you losing your friend. But I was hoping that with Dean gone and now Severman, maybe we can start putting that all behind us."

Keith had more than enough experience in counseling men, something he had to do regularly as a ship's captain.

"Fritz, I'll get right to it. We need your help. I don't know if you're aware of it, but we're looking to be attacked sometime soon."

"I have heard such talk at the evening table of cards. It would appear a vendetta is in play. Your men here seem more than able to handle whatever threat may face you. Do you really need my help, or does my pathetic moue force your empathy?"

Obviously, Fritz Langer had placed himself on his own torture rack, which unfortunately did no good for anyone concerned.

"Fritz, I truly do need your help. Hear me out. I want you and Johnny Dollars to man the high ground on the promontory woods. Come out here. I'll show you."

Keith and Fritz made their way out of Keith's office, through the pantry, the dining room, and out to the deck off the bar. Keith pointed out to Fritz the promontory wood that rose up above the talus. "I want you and Johnny up in those woods. Sarusha knows a way to get up there from down by the Swallows. We'd set you up with a couple of camps back along that wall. No one can get up there on horseback, and it's damn near impossible to get up there on foot."

"How do we get up there?"

"I got a couple of rope ladders left over from before. We'll have them in place. Once you're up, you can pull 'em up and there you go."

"I'll do it" was all Fritz replied, more than happy to have some purpose to his life other than his lackluster effort to craft a letter to Conrad Drager's relatives back in Europe.

Now Jonathan Keith had in place the first two parts of his strategy: Sarusha, Trader, and Walt Tallhelm in the woods north of the flat, Fritz and Johnny Dollars in the promontory woods to the south. Clayton Pealeday would most likely engineer a more robust assault on the Crow's Nest than the two that Keith had previously beaten back, but Keith was prepared to respond in kind. It portended to be a battle royale.

It could not be overstated, however, how angry Keith was about the invasion of his sanctuary. Over many years, he had been more than willing to offer any wayward traveler refuge and sustenance, asking no more than that they respect the most basic of codes known to man. But yet here he was, having to wage a battle to the death, for no other reason than to counter the greed, warped ambitions, pride, and jealously of Bertram Herzog and Clayton Pealeday.

Well, those two were not going to trap Jonathan Keith in their web of desperation. The all but predictable venality of mankind was the reason why Keith secluded himself from the world in the first place. He knew the world for what it was. Why it was that way was the smoldering question that vexed him so. Be that as it may, avoiding the world was no longer an option. He must meet it head on and give it no quarter.

After supper, Keith asked everyone to remain close by. Soon the bar was filled with every habitué of the Nest. The Haverstraws sat in the booth closest to the bar. Fritz Langer, although welcome at the poker table in the evening, still was pretty much a solitary figure, and he sat in the next booth by himself.

Nate, Walt, and Sarusha, along with Trader and Veronica, sat at one of the large round tables, and the crew arrayed themselves around their usual poker table. Lucien, Evie, and the boys sat on the stools at the bar. Sunny Martin stood next to one of the stoves, ever ready to shove another split log into its glowing maw.

"Where's Tubby Flint?" asked Keith.

"He's been down in the rope hotel all day," answered Johnny Dollars.

"I expect that's a good place for him. Let the sleeping dog lie," said Keith.

"Some of you may know by now what we learned from the late Aldo Severman. For those who don't, I'll lay it out for you. Clayton Pealeday has an arrest warrant out against him, and he has no plans of letting anyone serve it. What he plans to do is hire a bunch of out-of-work soldiers and try to take over the Nest. Now add into the mix this man Bertram Herzog and the fact that he's working with Chance Parker. Trader and Ronnie can tell you what those two are capable of. Miles and Lorraine here can attest to that as well. We don't know when they're going to make their move. Hell, it could be tomorrow for all we know. Anyway, we got to get ready, and there's no time to waste.

"I put my long-range scope out here on the deck, so from now on, in daylight hours, we'll have someone eyeballing Initiation Bluff. Up top, we'll have someone keeping an eye on the flat and as far up the cut as we can see. You won't need the scope to see movement on the Bluff, but when you do see something, the scope can tell us how many and who. We'll take two-hour shifts, dawn to dusk. Sunny has the watch schedule."

The sober reality took a few moments to sink in, but there it was. The outside world had come knocking, and life as these men knew it was going to change. As each man contemplated this change, Keith's voice brought them back to the moment.

"From what Trader says, Herzog, Parker, and whoever else is searching that cave down by the Abyss are not going to find any gold. That should get them just about fit to be tied. Now from what I understand, not all those boys are bad actors, so who knows how that will play out. We know from firsthand experience on the part of Miles here, Herzog has no problem killing anyone, anytime. Right now, by our best count, there are ten, maybe a dozen men, down there. Eventually, they'll be coming this way. Just when, we don't know. That's the reason to keep an eye on the Bluff.

"We could of course hunker down and hope to outlast a siege. We may have to do that anyway, but it would be better if we did some damage to them before that eventuality. I've come up with a plan. We know those coming at us from the south can't come over the talus. So from the south, one way or another, they're going to have to come through the Swallows. Now hear me out. It may sound far-fetched, but we need every advantage we can get.

"Tomorrow, Sarusha's going to take you men into the Swallows and rearrange some of those animal bones. Even someone who knows the Swallows can get lost in there, so maybe with the good pathways through looking like dead ends and dead ends looking like the good ways, just maybe they'll get hopelessly lost in there and all die.

"Anyway, if they make it out, we'll give them a good reception, that's for damn sure. Once out and on the flat, they'll be in the open. What is that, eight, ten miles from the Swallows to the switchback? We'll take advantage of that eight or ten miles to kill as many of those bastards as possible."

Sunny and Lucien looked at one another. Rarely had they heard the Captain speak with such unvarnished language.

"Men, I'm only going to say this once, and hear me out. This most likely will be a full-on fight to the death, theirs or ours. This Herzog is looking at the hangman's noose. Clayton Pealeday has painted himself into a corner, and the only way out for him, in his mind, is taking over the Nest. Well, dammit, it ain't going to happen. So what I'm saying is, we give no quarter. This is war. This is root hog or die."

24

ABLE AND READY

The next few days in and around the Nest were spent in frenzied preparation for the expected arrival of Herzog and Pealeday. Lucien remarked to Keith, more than once, how it was like old times, his barking out orders and focusing every ounce of physical and mental energy to one end, readiness. Keith racked his brain to come up with every possible advantage.

Sarusha and the crew rearranged the plethora of animal skeletons in the Swallows to misdirect anyone trying to make their way through. Upon Lucien Samms's suggestion, charred logs were used to mark certain rocks so those from the Nest wouldn't get lost themselves.

Keith had extra barrels of water arrayed on all the decks and the back balconies in case of fire. Deck cannon were placed, sighted in, and tested. Albeit small, Keith's two deck cannons could hurl an iron ball and grapeshot across the chasm and well out onto the flat. These were positioned on either end of the western parapet, and a third larger cannon was on the deck off the bar. That cannon was trained on the top of the switchback.

Sunny, along with Brow Herman and Bill Diehl, set up the two camps for Fritz and Johnny Dollars. The camps were a piece of artistry. They were well hidden, well supplied, and strategically located. From these well-protected perches, anyone coming along the flat, some forty feet below, would be an easy target. Access up to the promontory was provided by two rope ladders. When the time came, they could be brought down from up top with a hard yank on repurposed liana vines, innocent in appearance to anyone except the men from the Nest. Once up and on the promontory, the rope ladders would be pulled up. Hopefully they would remember to pull up the vines as well.

Keith and Lucien took on the delicate job of fabricating the crude but extremely lethal pineapples. These were made by filling earthen jugs with gunpowder and grapeshot, corked, then wrapped in several sticks of dynamite.

Keith had Sarusha and Sunny dig out a half dozen alcoves along the bank next to the cut where Sage Heck would have a clear shot from the parapet on the top floor. A pineapple was placed in each alcove camouflaged with mud to make it all but invisible.

Keith, as in any campaign, didn't want to leave any opportunity not taken. To that end, he had Walt and Nate lop off the last twenty feet of the tallest of the lofty pines at the uppermost end of the Nest. They then cobbled together a standing platform five feet below the top. This put the marksman at the perfect height to rest his rifle on the flat top of the tree. The top was covered over with a tied down tarp to minimize the problem of sticky pinesap. This perch was by far the tallest point on the Nest and well above the adjacent cut. Once the platform was constructed, Keith had Sunny put two more pineapples farther up the cut. With any luck between Sage on the parapet and Nate atop that pine, anyone coming down the cut would be blown to smithereens. Literally blown to smithereens.

The more Keith got prepared for the assault, the more his primal being came to the fore. Back in New Bedford in his youth, he had been an unapologetic and successful barroom brawler. Now he was remembering the mantra that played in his head back then: "I can beat you." Now of course it was "We can beat you."

And to that end, every man in the Nest along with Lorraine, Veronica, Evie, and her two boys were given a brand-new lever-action Spencer. Brow Herman, Bill Diehl, and Sage Heck were all expert marksmen. Of course, the Tallhelms and Trader Darcy were as well. When the time came for the lead to start flying, the Nest would be ready.

Sunny, Lucien, and Keith, although each was fairly good with a rifle, were all much better at sighting in and firing cannons, useful in their seafaring days. Unfortunately for Keith and crew, Clayton Pealeday was also very capable of sighting in and firing a cannon. Whether he would show up with any was an open question. If he did, hopefully, they could be disabled before inflicting any appreciable damage.

After three days of intense preparation, Keith and crew felt as ready as they could be. Now the nerve-racking ordeal of awaiting the attack began.

The late afternoon sun was casting long shadows across the deck outside the bar as Walt Tallhelm was finishing his two-hour shift at the spyglass trained on Imitation Bluff.

"See anything, Walt?" asked Lahr, his replacement.

"Just saw a herd of elk. I tell ya, when this is over, I'm gonna do me some long-overdue hunting."

Nate and Lorraine were out on the deck keeping Walt company, and Nate commented to Walt, "Yeah, Walt, that'd be nice. Me and you out hunting together again. Just like old times." Nate said this, but in reality, he had never spent near enough time with his older brother. Nate and his younger brother, Lonnie, were the ones who mostly hunted together.

"The Shenandoah was good for deer and small game, but out here you got those elk I just saw, bighorn sheep, bears, buffalo, bobcats, you name it," said Walt.

"Sure enough. You know, Walt, we was never ones to sit a tree stand and wait for game. Maybe we shouldn't wait for them what's down the way," Nate said as he tilted his head toward Initiation Bluff and beyond.

The three continued their conversation as they came in from outside and took seats at the bar. Gathered about were Sunny, Sarusha, Brow Herman, and Bill Diehl, taking advantage of the first opportunity to have a leisurely late-afternoon drink in three days. Soon they were joined by Trader and Veronica.

As Jonathan Keith came out from the kitchen, Walt Tallhelm offered a suggestion. "Cap, why don't Nate and me head south and take care of that bunch straight off? We know where they are, and I've seen the layout. I'd feel a lot better if we'd get rid of them, and then we'd only have to worry about Pealeday."

"Don't think you're gonna grab all the glory. Bill and me, we're up for that too. It'll be like old times," chimed in Brow Herman.

"Yeah, old times. Me saving your tired old ass again. Hell, why not? Maybe we could use you two old farts as bait. What do you say, Cap?" asked Walt.

"I don't rightly know. I imagine we could change our strategy a bit. What do you think, Sarusha?"

"Well, Walt and me saw where their camp is, or leastwise was. It'd be easy enough to attack, being there is some high ground where we was looking down on them. But hell, Trader says the cave they were searching probably didn't have any gold to begin with. So they might have moved on down the rim. Attacking that camp might be chancy. One thing we know for sure is when they do decide to come at us, they got to come over the Bluff."

Sarusha's words clearly pointed out some of the problems with the idea of Walt, Nate, Brow, and Bill Diehl taking the fight to Herzog. But he also pointed out a key element that might work in their favor—notably, Herzog had to come over Initiation Bluff.

The Bluff had been watched religiously from dawn to dusk for the last three days. No movement whatsoever had been seen, except the occasional herd of deer or elk moving along the rim trail.

"Cap, you're running this show, but hey, where's that map?" asked Walt. "Once we set out, if you see any movement on the Bluff, light off that cannon. We'll hear it and know they're coming. If we pushed it, we could make our first camp just this side of the Bluff."

"We don't need the map," Sarusha said and pointed to the cannon out on the bar deck. "I know that from the Nest here through the Swallows and up to the Bluff is well within earshot of that cannon. Remember, once that shot starts bouncing off the rim, you can hear it near the whole way down to the Bottleneck."

"Sounds good to me," agreed Keith.

"If you men are looking to do that, I'm coming along. I wanna see Herzog die." This pronouncement came from Miles Haverstraw, who had been sitting by himself in the booth closest to the bar. Evidently, this was where he could be found late afternoon, usually whittling a piece of wood into the image of a man, careful to have the chips fall into an empty coal scuttle Sunny had given him.

"Miles, we appreciate how you'd be keen on being along, but it could be rough going. I think we better leave it to the younger ones," Jonathan Keith's replied.

"Younger ones! These two don't look all that young to me. I'm as fit as they are, maybe more so," answered Miles as he pointed to Brow Herman and Bill Diehl, who really weren't all that old, maybe in their midfifties. It's just that etched on their faces were the outer and inner scars of having endured the rigors of frontier life.

"What do you think, Lorraine?" asked Keith. "He's your father after all. Damn, this is a tough one."

"Father, I know it's tempting. I wouldn't mind being along myself. But let's be practical. These men can't be worried about you when they're out there. I say let's see if they can get him back here alive and then we'll deal with that Satan," said Lorraine, trying to be sympathetic and diplomatic at the same time.

Hearing what Lorraine said, Keith added, "Miles, I have to be firm on this one. I'm gonna ask you to stay here and help out on this end. Like Lorraine said, if they get back here with Herzog alive, he's all yours."

Miles nodded in agreement.

"Okay, we'll do this. We'll get ready tonight and head out first light," said Walt.

A question on everyone's mind but never spoken was whether or not these four by themselves could get the job done. It was a quick enough process to figure out who couldn't go. Sarusha was the most logical one to go along but he wasn't about to leave the Captain with Pealeday liable to show up any time. that went for Lucien and Sunny as well. Trader wasn't 100 percent yet. So that left only Sage and Johnny. Sage could have gone, but Keith was counting on him to be up top on the parapet when trouble started. Johnny, well...

So no one brought it up. It was going to be Walt, Nate, Brow, and Bill Diehl.

The men knew there was danger involved. No sense dwelling on it.

"I'll have Evie pack up enough grub for four, five days. That should do it." Lucien didn't mention that supplies in the Nest were running low. But that concern would have to be addressed at a later time.

"While we're here, let's make a quick toast to the demise and death of Bertram Herzog and Clayton Pealeday," announced Keith, who could feel visceral relief from the decision to go on the offensive. A man well aware of the power of esprit de corps, Keith looked around to see who was missing. "Sunny, see about getting Sage and Johnny up here. Fritz too." Ten minutes later, all of the Nest's habitués were gathered about. The setting sun freed Thaedell Lahr from his post at the spyglass, and he joined the group.

With Lucien, Evie, and the boys behind the bar, and the rest of the group gathered in front and with glasses filled, Keith said. "Here's to us and the strength we give and the strength we get from one another. May it carry the day!"

Shouts of "hear, hear!" reverberated through the bar. Each one, as they drank down the toast, thought about the last part of the Captain's toast: "May it carry the day."

Early next morning in lantern light, the men saddled their horses and packed horse feed and extra gear on Nate's mule and Bill Liecaster's horse, an oversized steed who was by far the best of the mounts of which Sage and Johnny had been paid. Silent and somber, the men came through the gatehouse and up the switchback on their way to the Swallows. The night had been unseasonably warm, and a thin fog shrouded the trail, making the trip up the switchback even more perilous than usual.

As the group approached the Swallows, Walt voiced a logical concern. "I'm just wondering whether we're gonna have a problem finding our way through these rocks. Maybe Sarusha did too good a job messing with the right way through."

"Don't worry, Winifried. You ain't gonna get lost. Bill and me marked the way," said Brow Herman.

"What the hell is that?" asked Bill Diehl, alarm in his voice.

"Not what the hell but who the hell," answered Brow Herman as the image of two riders emerged out of the wisps of fog.

"The way they ride, I say they was Injuns," said Nate.

Each man had his rifle cocked and ready, waiting for the two riders to get close enough to get a clear look.

"Injuns, that's for sure. Now I wonder, are they friendly?" asked Bill Diehl.

"Friendly, hell yeah they're friendly. They're friends of mine." Nate's voice got louder as each word left his mouth.

"Tarlton, the man who shoots once. We meet again." Diving Hawk spoke this in his native tongue as he and Drum Face emerged out of the fog and rode up to the group.

"My Indian brother, meet my brother Walt," said Nate.

Walt's knowledge of the Nez Perce dialect of Quiet Bird's tribe allowed him to understand most everything Diving Hawk said.

"Our people know of this man. We know him as Bear Face," said Diving Hawk.

In a low stage whisper, Walt asked Nate, "Who the hell is Tarlton?"

"Don't ask why, but it's me," answered Nate in as low a voice as possible.

"Our hunting party found much game, and the others are now returning to our village. Drum Face and I are looking for a new winter home closer to the game. We said, let us find Tarlton. He knows these things."

"Well, Diving Hawk, I'd like to help you, but right now we are hunting the men who would do us harm," said Nate.

"We will join you. We owe you much, Tarlton. Your enemies are our enemies. It would be our honor to ride in your party." Diving Hawk's voice had the note of finality that Nate and the others knew meant the issue was not to be debated.

As Bill and Brow led the way through the Swallows, Nate and the two Indians brought up the rear. By midmorning, the party of six had made their way out of the rocky maze, and after another three hours, they were well on their way to the rim trail. That's when they heard the faint echo of the cannon blast off the canyon walls.

"Someone's come over the Bluff." Brow Herman was the first to say this, but the words were on the lips of each man.

"How far to the rim trail?" asked Nate.

"An hour or so to the rim. Another hour to the Bluff," answered Bill Diehl.

"That gives us about an hour to find the right spot for our welcoming party." Nate's cynical comment was a bit out of character for him, but soon the moment he'd been thinking about for the last month would be upon him, and all that bile was boiling to the top.

"I know just the place about a half hour up the trail," said Brow Herman. "It's a part of the trail that for them will be uphill. Also, the trail gets narrow through there, so they got to ride single file. It'd be our best spot to keep this from turning into a running skirmish."

As the men momentarily clustered about, Nate asked, "What exactly is our plan? I'm not one to ambush someone in cold blood."

"Nate, I know what you mean, but they didn't give Trader any advance warning when they cut that rope and sent him down that cliffside. And I doubt Jack Tice had a sit-down with Marcel Dagget before he shot him to doll rags. No, this bunch are coming to kill us and take everything we got. No sense waiting for that.

"Also, if they gets in and takes over the Nest, how long you think it would be before them boys was passing around Lorraine like some backstreet whore on Saturday night? I wouldn't give…" Walt went on, but Nate didn't hear a word. His mind was paralyzed with the thought of what Walt had just said about Lorraine. Well, this put the set to Nate's jaw, that's for damn sure. Now there was no doubt what had to be done, no doubt whatsoever.

Walt knew his words were harsh, but he also knew now was not the time for any second thoughts about what had to be done and how to do it.

Bill Diehl chimed in as he and the others began rechecking their sidearms and rifles. "The Cap said no quarter given. That's our orders, and by God we're gonna follow them through."

Walt explained to Diving Hark and Drum Face what was going on and offered Diving Hawk his extra Spencer Carbine. The Indian waved it off and instead held up his bow, the weapon he was most comfortable with.

Seeing this gave Nate an idea. "Thinking about it, if they're gonna be riding single file, Diving Hawk and Drum here could pick off the last riders one by one before we start the lead flying. What do you think?" Nate had started calling Drum Face simply Drum, and now so did all the others.

"If Diving Hawk and Drum are up for it, I'd say that makes a lot of sense. They could at least peel off the last two or three before anyone was the wiser," agreed Walt.

"Well, let's get up there and get our spot. Wonder how many there is?" asked Brow Herman. In all their time on the frontier, neither Brow Herman nor Bill Diehl had actually killed anyone. The prospect of doing so now made their palms begin to sweat some, but they didn't let on. They didn't savor the idea, but they also knew it had to be done.

A half hour at a brisk pace brought the men to the spot Brow Herman had been describing, a narrow tree-lined section of the trail with a steady uphill grade for those on the way. The corridor through the trees even had a five-foot-high bank on the west side. This left as the only option for those coming down the trail, once the shooting starts, to either keep on the trail or bolt into the woods and back toward the rim.

The men hitched their horses well back from the trail. No need for a horse's whinny to alert anyone. Nate and the Indians positioned themselves first in line to "greet" those coming, but they would wait for the group to pass before Diving Hawk and Drum got the signal to pick off the last of the riders. Diehl and Herman were in the middle. Walt was the last man they'd have to get by.

One hour later, a rider came into view on up the trail. As he got closer, Nate could see it was only one horse, and there were two men riding bareback. This surely didn't look like much of a threat, so Nate came out of the woods onto the trail, his rifle ready.

"Don't shoot. We got no guns. Don't shoot!" the men hollered out in unison.

Nate didn't recognize the pair, but Bill Diehl did. He called up the trail to Nate, "That's the Johnson brothers. What the hell?"

The men looked gaunt and half-crazed. They had no coats on, and one was only wearing long johns and nothing else. "Don't shoot!" the pair repeated.

"We ain't gonna shoot ya. What the hell happened to you two?" asked Brow Herman, who along with Bill Diehl gathered around the men as the Johnson brothers all but fell off their horse. Walt Tallhelm remained hidden where he was, not trusting that this wasn't some kind of trick.

"You got water?" asked Lee Johnson as he held onto the neck of the horse for support.

"Here, drink this. Are you being chased?" asked Nate.

"Yeah," answered Ray Johnson as he almost choked on the canteen of water.

"How far behind you figure they are?" asked Brow Herman as he looked back up the trail.

"They're back a ways, at least an hour, maybe more like two. They had come around that bend down by those falls and well on their way to that bluff when we was coming over the top," answered Lee Johnson.

"How many are there?" asked Brow.

"Best we can figure about ten. Could be more," answered Ray.

"I seen you two before. You were the two that tangled with Jack Tice. How many you say there are, and just who the hell are they?" This question from Walt Tallhelm, who had come back up the trail and joined the group. Nate turned his head to look at Walt because he had heard that tone in his brother's voice before. It didn't bode well for those coming this way, that's for sure.

"Well, there's Herzog, Chance Parker, Tice. Ray and me never got no names of the others. Four got into camp about a week ago and three more the day before yesterday," answered Lee Johnson.

"All them boys was well-armed, and some of 'em were leading pack horses. Them boys are loaded for bear, that's for damn sure," added Ray Johnson.

"We know about Herzog and Parker. What about Pealeday? You hear anything about him?" asked Walt.

"Don't know nothing about Pealeday, but I'll tell ya, those boys what just joined up look plenty hungry and plenty mean. What you fellas got in mind? Whatever it is, it better be good, 'cause they mean business," said Lee.

Pealeday and Herzog had no problem finding men whose guns were for hire. Their allegiance as well as their guns could be bought for the price of a ball of opium or enough money to drink away their pain. They were willing to kill for no reason other than to seek a murky vengeance for what had been taken from them. You could find these men as faithful patrons of nearly every saloon from the gray Atlantic to the blue Pacific, their withered souls clinging to life like so many marcescent leaves, dead but not yet fallen.

"Looks like you and your brother here left that camp in a bit of a hurry," said Bill Diehl, stating the obvious.

"Hell yeah. That bastard Herzog is about half crazy. Only reason we're alive is 'cause we played along real good. Anyone who didn't had an 'accident' when they was being hoisted back up from one of them caves. Two that we know of had 'accidents.' One boy couldn't take it anymore, and hell, he just jumped. Ray and me saw our chance and took it. There was two others with us, but one got shot dead. The other got away, and I believe he headed south. I think to Cornertown. Leastwise he had talked about being from Cornertown, so we figured that's where he headed. You boys got any grub?" asked Lee Johnson.

"Yeah, we'll get you some. Let's get this horse off the trail and back in the woods. You think you boys could shoot a rifle?" asked Nate.

"Damn right we can shoot a rifle. We got some scores to settle. I want Tice. I owe him for this." Ray brushed his hand gently over a dark purple bruise that bulged out from his right cheekbone.

This whole time, Diving Hawk and Drum stood by, silent and still.

"Whatever your plan is, we're with you all the way," said Ray.

"Well, we expect to pick off a few of the ones bringing up the rear with some arrows from my friends here. After that, we're going open up on 'em. Nothing too fancy. What do ya think, Walt? Where should we put these two?" asked Nate.

"There's some thick pines down my end. They can be in there. Nate, you give the one your extra Spencer and I'll give the other one mine. I expect to do a little work with these," answered Walt as his pulled open his vest and looked down at the hatchets tucked into the lining.

"Tell your Injun friends to get as many as they can before the shooting starts. We'll leave it to you, Nate, to open the ball. Brow, you and Bill work together. Each one of you pick a man. Make sure it ain't the same one. Me and these two will be down the way. You boys come with me. Bring that horse along. I'll get you a shirt and some britches."

"How about that grub?" asked Lee.

"Yeah, I got something," answered Walt.

Before the group broke up, Brow Herman asked a question that had become almost an afterthought. "By the way, did they ever find any gold?"

"None that we ever saw," answered Lee.

"Nah, they didn't find no gold, and it put that bastard Herzog near out of his mind," added Ray.

Everyone was no sooner back in place than the faint echo of a cannon could be heard. This meant the men had about an hour till they could expect to see Herzog and the men riding with him. After what Walt had said, Nate didn't have to remind himself that there was no other way to do this. The other day, he was able to take up Aldo Severman on his challenge and meet him face-to-face. No such chance here. In his heart of hearts, he hoped this would be the last of the killing, but reality told him otherwise.

Herzog and his group, of course, heard the cannon blast, and Chance Parker commented to Tice, "Looks like Clayton beat us to the dance."

"I wonder if that darky's woman likes white meat." Crude and deadly, Jack Tice never made an effort to have a decent thought.

"I wonder how Aldo and Dean made out. Our work might be all but done," a hopeful Chance Parker wondered.

The group of ten thundered on over the Bluff and down the rim trail, intent on catching up to the Johnson brothers and sending them to meet their Maker. The Johnson brothers, though, were but a minor annoyance. Parker and the others were on their way to fulfill the task that was paramount in their thoughts—taking over the Crow's Nest and killing Keith and anyone else they had to.

They rode on, leaving the rim and following the trail as it cut through the thick forest. Eventually, they came to a stretch where the trail narrowed, and they were forced to ride single file.

25

BLOOD ON THE TRAIL

Chance Parker sensed something was not quite right, but he didn't fully grasp what was going on until he turned around and saw the man behind him slumped over the neck of his horse with an arrow sticking out of his back. "Injuns!" he hollered. "Injuns!"

Instinctively, he spurred his horse forward, nearly causing it to flounder as it ran up onto the horse in front of him. No sooner had he steadied his mount than he felt a bullet rip through his shoulder, sending him crashing to the ground. Rolling to the side, he barely missed being trampled by the packhorse he was leading. Quickly doubling up the flap on his coat, he attempted to stem the flow of blood spurting out of his chest, only to realize he'd been shot twice.

Parker saw the rider in front of him duck down and hold tight to his horse, trying to make a smaller target of himself. But in fact, the man had been shot dead, and after going forward a half dozen steps, fell off his horse and lay dead on the trail, his eyes wide open, looking skyward.

Rifle fire and the shouts of wounded and dying men were all but drowned out by the loud snorts and screeches of a dozen panicking horses. The riders who weren't lying dead on the trail tried to escape into the woods. Three of them made it. All were wounded, one of them Bertram Herzog.

Walt grabbed ahold of the reins of a horse that was dragging its rider. Freeing the dead man's leg from the stirrup, he swung up onto the horse and gave chase. When he caught up with two of the men, their pleas for mercy fell on deaf ears. Herzog, however, got away.

Returning to the trail, Walt took charge. "Anyone get hit?" When no one said they had, he began to bark out orders, clear and direct. "Bill, Brow, gather up their guns. You Johnson boys, you get hold of those pack horses. Nate, you and your Injuns see about rounding up all the horses you can. We don't want that one that got away coming back this way and getting an extra horse. I'll check if anyone's still breathing."

"That one that got away was Herzog," said Ray Johnson.

"Damn!" said Walt as he looked up and down the trail at the bodies lying about.

When Walt got to Chance Parker, he saw he was still alive, but barely. "Don't try to fight it, Chance. You're dying."

"You got a smoke?" asked Parker.

"Yeah, sure." Walt quickly rolled a cigarette and brought the lit smoke to Parker's lips.

"You know, I never had nothing against you, Tallhelm. I'm not as bad as everyone thinks. I just took a wrong turn somewheres," Chance Parker said as Walt held the cigarette for him, and he took another deep drag.

"That can happen. Sometimes it just comes down to who ya meet and when ya meet 'em. Can you tell me what Pealeday is up to? You got any kin?" asked Walt. "I could let 'em know you was right with the Lord at the end."

"Nah, I ain't got no kin. Nobody gonna miss me. As far as it goes with Clayton, all I know is he's coming to the Nest. Just when, I couldn't say. Hell, we thought that cannon we heard was him. But now I see it was most likely a warning shot for you all. He's coming, and he's got some men. How many, I don't know. He don't like that old man Keith." Parker coughed a bit and lifted his chin so Walt could give him another drag on the cigarette. He died before Walt could get it to his lips.

Walt closed the dead man's eyes and took Parker's unused revolver out of its holster. "Tie these bodies onto their horses and tie 'em tight. We don't need them falling off and holding us up. It'll be dark before long. Let's get back down the trail as close to the Swallows as we can and make camp there." He turned to one of the Johnson brothers and said, "I see you got Jack Tice. That sure as hell is no loss to humanity."

"Yeah, I got him, and now I'm gonna be riding my own horse again," smirked Ray Johnson, who had to steady himself as all the shooting and commotion had made him nauseous and a little dizzy.

"Hey, Johnson, get over here and look after your brother. We're moving out in ten minutes."

Walt wanted to get back to the Nest as soon as possible. This part of the plan had gone almost as well as could be expected. Herzog got away, but Walt was sure he was wounded as he was leaving a blood trail. He could probably track him, but right now getting back to the Nest was the best move.

The whole shooting affair was over in less than five minutes. Once the riders filed by and had passed Nate and the Indians, Diving Hawk and Drum put arrows in the last two riders. Nate was the one who shot Chance Parker and the rider in front of him.

Ray Johnson, from his position on the high bank, had held a bead on Jack Tice's head, and as soon as Nate let go with his rifle shot, Ray sent Tice into the afterlife and his grim reckoning. Bill Diehl and Brow Herman got their signals mixed up and ended up shooting the same man. Lee Johnson had no problem putting two bullets into Bertram Herzog, remembering all the pain and abuse he inflicted upon him and his brother. Unfortunately, Lee's shots weren't fatal, and Herzog bolted off the trail and into the woods.

Walt, seeing the lead rider was well ahead of the group, didn't wait for Nate's signal and decided to put one of his tomahawks into the lead man's forehead. Once the shooting started, Walt took his rifle and peppered the second and third riders with a half dozen bullets. Two riders in the middle of the procession were hit and made a vain attempt to escape into the woods, where Walt caught up to them and finished them off.

As fate or misfortune would have it, the only one to escape was Bertram Herzog. Nate, once he and the Indians had the horses under control and the bodies tied on, suggested, "Walt, why don't me, Diving Hawk, and Drum go after Herzog? He shouldn't be too hard to track."

Walt vetoed the idea.

"Getting back to Keith's, and as soon as possible, is what we should be doing. Parker said Pealeday is on his way. Hell, they thought that cannon fire was Pealeday starting in on the Nest. Let's try to make the Swallows before dark. We'll make camp there and see about burying these bodies. Don't have to be anything fancy. Just get 'em in the ground."

Frankly, no one had thought much about having to bury anyone, but they knew it just wasn't right to let dead bodies lay out in the open. Out on the prairie, vultures and coyotes would make short shrift of any body lying about. Enough bleached bones lying out there to attest to that. But here in the woods, not so.

Once everyone was organized, the men made their way back down the trail toward the Swallows as quickly as they could. It was not easy going leading the pack horses and all the others with their dead riders strapped over their saddles. The men rode in silence, each man finding his own peace with what had just taken place.

Bill Diehl and Brow Herman just weren't sure which one's rifle shot had killed the rider they were aiming at. This gave the two of them some sort of internal doubt as to whether or not they had killed a man. Much like a firing squad, when one or two members are given a nonlethal round. In any event, neither one of them was going out of their way to take credit.

Once it was too dark to go on, the group stopped and made camp, which was not easy. Three pack animals and all the horses, save two, had been rounded up. Shortly before they stopped to make camp, the two horses unaccounted for came loping down the trail and rejoined the others. All totaled, there were twenty-two horses and Nate's mule to deal with. They all had to be unburdened and fed. Thankfully, Chance Parker and his outfit had taken care to pack plenty of horse feed. They had also brought along a couple of well-worn shovels and a pickax from their aborted cave excavations. What else the packhorses carried was mostly grub, ammunition, and dynamite, all of which Nate and the others would be sure to put to good use.

The dead were laid in a line on the ground and in the light of a large bonfire. Working in teams of two, the men went about digging shallow graves and burying the bodies. This labor went well into the night, the last body being laid to rest sometime after midnight.

Every kind of exhaustion rendered the men speechless as they lay awake thinking of the events of the day. Soon, however, each man slept, save Nate, who was given the first one-hour guard shift.

During the night, the weather had turned cold, and in the morning the men wasted no time making a second campfire as they went about the task of reloading the pack horses and Nate's mule. With a thought to making better time, whatever the pack horses were carrying was evenly distributed onto the rider-less horses. No sense having overburdened pack horses slowing things down.

Nate made as big a pot of oatmeal as he could, which he shared with Walt, Diving Hawk, and Drum. The two Indians smiled to one another and nodded toward Nate, thinking back to the same meal they had first shared together while back up on the cut.

After breaking camp, and before they mounted up, the men stood next to the graves, and Brow Herman said a few words. "Lord, take these men and judge them as You would. They all started out as some mother's son. Now here they lay. Have mercy on their souls."

It took an hour to reach the Swallows and another three to work their way through. The day was clear and cold, and the smoke rising straight up from the chimneys of the Nest was a welcoming sight. The group had been keen and vigilant as they rode along the flat, expecting to see or hear Pealeday and his men. But all was quiet, and they made their way down the switchback and through the gatehouse without incident.

"Lordy, Lordy, Lordy" was all Lucien Samms could say as he watched the contingent come through the gatehouse and on up to the stable. Practically the whole of the Nest had watched from the deck off the bar as the men came into view on the flat, down the switchback, through the gatehouse, and up to the stable. It was quite a sight.

They had left the Nest early in the morning the day before as a group of four. Now they returned as eight, two of them Indians to boot. The fact that they returned leading five packhorses, a mule, and another eight horses carrying saddles but no riders made for a sobering procession.

A mixture of relief and solemnity greeted Nate and the others. "Sunny, you and Sarusha see to getting these horses unloaded. Once that's done, Lucien, have the boys take 'em out to the back stables," directed Jonathan Keith.

"Sunny, better let us help ya. Two of them is carrying dynamite," said Brow Herman as he and Bill Diehl took charge of leading those two horses back into the stable.

"Well, look here," exclaimed Trader as he saw his horse in among the others. "Never thought I'd be seeing you again, old boy." The smile on Trader's face went from ear to ear.

Lorraine stood to the side, waiting for Nate's undivided attention before giving him the embrace she was so relieved to be able to give. Everyone had been on tenterhooks since yesterday, having watched Parker and the others coming up and over the Bluff.

Lorraine was tough and had made herself tougher over the years spent pursuing Herzog. But now, with the love she felt for Nathan Tallhelm, she had something more important in her life than even her vendetta against Bertram Herzog. It was something precious and fragile, and the thought of losing it would be a pain too hard to bear. She almost regretted having this desire to love and be loved, but she was powerless to fight it. She prayed for the day when the sun would rise and the only thought she need have was what to cook for breakfast or which blouse to wear. Hopefully, that day would come. But for now, life was lived moment to moment, day to day.

Once the handshaking and head-nodding subsided, Keith took Walt Tallhelm aside and said in a low voice, "Good job. That couldn't have been easy." He said it as he and Walt looked at the horses with the empty saddles being led back into the stables.

"I tell ya, Cap, none of us liked doing it, but I wasn't gonna risk any of our men getting shot up. Nate wasn't too keen on it, but he came around. He's got Lorraine to worry about. Anyway, dammit, it had to be done. We got Chance Parker and the rest, but Herzog got away. He's wounded and might be dead by now. Hard to say. Parker told me before he died that Clayton would be coming this way. Didn't say just when, only that he was coming."

"Where'd those two come from?" Keith asked as he tilted his head toward Diving Hawk and Drum, who were standing quietly by, holding onto their horses and looking about the cavernous stables. This was probably the first time the men had ever been in a building any bigger than a long house.

"Hell, they're the Injuns Nate ran into up on the cut a couple weeks back. Don't pay it no mind, but they call Nate, Tarlton. Tell ya what, let's have a little fun and start calling him Tarlton ourselves," Walt said in an attempt to move from the grimness of what happened yesterday.

"Tarlton, you say." Keith took a moment for this strange bit of information to register, then went on. "I see those two Johnson brothers came back with you. We watched them come over the Bluff. What's the deal with them?"

"They was running from Parker and his boys when they rode up on us. I guess they saw an opening to escape and lit a shuck out of that camp. There was four of them that made a break for it. One of 'em got shot dead. As best they know, the one that got away headed to Cornertown. These two were running for their lives. Hell, the one was in nothing but long johns, and they was riding a horse bareback. I reckon they're still a little sore from that," Walt said as he went over to where Lorraine and Miles were standing.

"Sorry about Herzog getting away, Miles. He's wounded and may be dead by now. Once this thing with Pealeday is taken care of, we'll go out and look for him. I don't know what else to say."

Miles Haverstraw gave no reply. Instead, he just looked at Walt with an unfocused gaze, silent and far away.

Lorraine, sensing the awkwardness of the moment, quickly told Walt, "I'm sure you did the best you could, Walt. Seems like other than that, your mission was quite a success."

"Well, leastwise now all we got to worry about is Clayton Pealeday and what he's figuring on doing," answered Walt.

Sage Heck, having been spelled by Fritz Langer at his lookout post, came down to the stables and joined Lahr and Johnny Dollars in helping Brow Herman and Bill Diehl tend to the packhorses. But really, he was more interested in finding out all the details of what happened up on the trail yesterday.

"Bill, so what went down out there?" asked Sage.

"Sage, you know that narrow stretch of trail when you're getting up toward the rim? Well, once we heard that cannon blast, that's where we waited for 'em. Nate's Indian friends took out the last two in the column, then Nate opened up. Hell, it was over before ya knew it. This Herzog was wounded but got away. He's probably dinner for a wolf pack by now. Not much more to it," answered Bill Diehl.

"That's it?" asked Johnny Dollars, mildly annoyed that Bill didn't give a more elaborate account.

Thaedell Lahr sensed that the men didn't want to go into much detail and said to Johnny, "Veni, vidi, vici. I came, I saw, I conquered. Not much more to it. What do you say we get some drinks?"

No one offered any argument to that suggestion. Before the crew went upstairs, Brow and Bill took Lahr, Sage, and Johnny over and introduced them to Diving Hawk and Drum. They had been standing with Nate and Lorraine and appeared to be gradually adjusting to being inside the Nest.

Diving Hawk, who had become comfortable with Bill Diehl and Brow Herman, felt compelled to sing Nate's praises to these friends of theirs. In a combination of Nez and broken English, he announced, "Tarlton is my friend and blood brother. You should be honored to be in the company of such a great warrior. Tarlton, the man who shoots once."

The assemblage didn't quite know how to respond to this, so they all just nodded several times and backed away toward the staircase. Nate, for his part, just smiled and directed the Indians to follow everyone up the stairs.

The switchback was watched religiously throughout the day, but starting that evening, Keith initiated another tactic to ensure no surprises from anyone looking to come that way: boobytraps. He instructed Sarusha to go up onto the switchback and set a few trip wires tied to the triggers of two of Keith's old blunderbuss. These would provide ample warning if anyone had a notion to get to the gatehouse under the cloak of darkness. Also, where they were placed on an especially narrow stretch of the switchback, the surprise report from the loud blunderbuss would most likely panic the horse and send both horse and rider plunging to their deaths.

Now that the threat of an attack from Herzog and Chance Parker no longer existed, the bar was abuzz with speculation as to just when Clayton Pealeday was going to make his move. As the whiskey glasses began to be filled and conjecture mingled with bravado, Evie Samms had a more immediate problem to deal with. The arrival of the returning men had preempted the midday meal, and now the afternoon was well on and everyone was hungry, so she announced, "Only one big meal today and that's going to be in about two hours. So don't anyone get drunk on an empty stomach. Better wait till you can get some food on your gut. Lorraine, Ronnie, I'm gonna need some more help in here."

Veronica Darcy had, along with Lorraine, taken to helping Evie Samms in the kitchen. The three women were more than happy to share one another's company. Evie, of course, with the Nest at near capacity, could use all the help she could get.

The morning before, Sarusha and Sage, after shadowing Walt and the others halfway to the Swallows, spotted several deer at the edge of the flat up near the cut. Two rifle shots took down two deer. One of these was now being roasted out back. There were a lot of mouths to feed, and this venison was well appreciated.

Diving Hawk and Drum, along with Nate and Trader, eventually found their way out to the back staircases and down to where Lucien and Sunny were roasting the venison. The Indians surely felt more comfortable in this setting than up in the bar. At first, the group stood in the warmth of the early winter sun as they took turns turning the spit. But soon they stood in the shadow of the Nest and gathered closer to the fire. Mostly the men were silent, the only sound the fat from the roasting meat landing on the fire, hissing and erupting into so many brief flashes.

Diving Hawk and Drum had a few words between themselves and then asked Nate in a mix of Nez and broken English, "Tarlton, what would you have us do? We could leave tomorrow or stay and fight these other men."

Nate answered in his best Nez, "We could always use brave men like yourselves. But these men are my enemies, not yours."

"But these men, if they take this"—Diving Hawk cocked his head toward the edifice of the Nest—"then what of our plans to move our village close to here? Then these men will be our enemies. We stay and fight with you." Drum nodded in agreement. It was settled.

"We can sleep here or in there, not up there." It was clear the Indians would just as soon sleep outside or in the stables but not in the rope hotel or up in one of the rooms.

Nate hunched his shoulders and drew the collar up on his coat to indicate the night would be cold and there was no reason to sleep outside. "We'll make a place for you there," Nate said as he pointed to the stables.

"That woman yours?" Drum, who didn't say much, looked up to the second-floor balcony where Lorraine and Veronica were standing, the ladies having taken a break from the work in the kitchen.

"That she is, leastwise I sure hope so," answered Nate. The Indians smiled to one another.

"Hell yeah, she's his woman," chimed in Sunny, with Lucien and Trader nodding their agreement.

"Wait till the moon comes out tonight. Those two will be gazing at it like it could give them a wink." This bit of humor came from Trader Darcy, who had known Nate all his life and had never known him to be smitten. But now Trader, sure as hell, could see that he was.

"When's some of that venison gonna be done?" asked Nate, ready to change the conversation to a more comfortable subject.

"Be about two hours. Time enough for you to do some spooning," Sunny said.

This comment made Trader reach for the whiskey bottle Nate had in his hand. "Better let me hold that. You don't want to get all drunked up. Women don't like that."

Nate just smiled and shook his head. The Indians didn't quite know what was being said but got the general idea. Diving Hawk, who was standing right next to Nate, jostled him a bit and gave the group a big smile. Both of the Indians were probably ten years older than Nate, and both had been married for many years. Having a little fun at a bachelor's expense was a well-earned privilege of a married man.

"Tell Evie the meat will be done in a couple hours," Lucien hollered up to Veronica and Lorraine.

"Anything need you?" asked Veronica.

"Well, you could send down another bottle," answered Trader.

Veronica just started saying a bunch of stuff in Spanish and nodded to Lorraine to come back inside.

The men didn't say anything, but they all smiled and looked at Nate.

Nate didn't really mind. All the joking in the world couldn't change how he felt toward Lorraine. He just thought to himself, *Let 'em have their fun.* Frankly, any levity was welcome considering what he and the Indians had been doing this time yesterday.

Supper in the evening was a loud and raucous affair. The dining room was too small to handle everyone, and the tables in the bar were just about full. Keith was relieved Walt and his party's foray had been a success, but he wasn't ready to let his guard down one bit.

"Men, enjoy yourselves tonight, but no drinking after ten o'clock. Let's not forget this job is only half done. Clayton Pealeday is nobody's fool. What we got going for us now is he doesn't have Chance Parker to help him do his dirty work. Anyway, have your fun tonight. Tomorrow it's all hands on deck."

Jonathan Keith didn't let on, but he was more than elated that things went as well as they did for Walt and the others yesterday. As a captain, he had to maintain his personal feeling toward his men somewhat in check, but truth be told, he had profound affection for Brow Herman, Bill Diehl, and all the others. Any sternness on his part was for no other reason than to ensure everyone's safety and survival.

Soon after Keith finished his announcement/decree, Johnny Dollars returned to the bar from out on the deck (where he had been relieving himself over the railing, something that was verboten but nevertheless happened from time to time) and hollered, "I think someone is coming down the switchback!"

As quick as you can say, "how do," a dozen men were out on the deck, trying to make out just who it was. Miles Haverstraw spoke first. "That's Bertram Herzog."

Walt, who had only seen Herzog for a brief moment, agreed. "Damn if it ain't."

"Sarusha, are those trip wires set?" asked Jonathan Keith.

"Yeah, they're set all right."

Herzog was barely visible in the light from the moon, but enough so that everyone could see that attached to the end of his rifle was a white and red bandana.

"Well, either he's the trickiest son of a bitch to draw a breath or else he's coming in to die." This particular gem of conjecture came from Sunny Martin.

"Sarusha, come here. How close is he to that first trip wire?" asked Keith.

No sooner had the words come out of his mouth than the report from the blunderbuss reverberated off the canyon walls and sent up a cloud of gun smoke that took a good two minutes to clear.

As he peered into the clearing smoke, Keith turned and told Sarusha, "You and Walt get down there and see what's going on. Better tell Ghosty to keep a watchful eye. This could be some kind of damn trick."

Needless to say, Miles and Lorraine had nothing on their mind except the fact that their eleven-year odyssey might finally have come to an end. Neither one was much given to drink, but in this moment, they went into the bar and picked up the closest glass of whiskey they could find and drank it down.

The two looked at one another, and all the events of the last eleven years flashed through their minds. One image after another— the boarding houses, police stations, libraries, the desk clerks at fine hotels telling them, "No, we haven't seen this couple." All the images finally led back to one horrible image indelibly seared into their memory—the conflagration that was the Lautenburg fire.

Part Three

ALL SCORES SETTLED

26

THE LAUTENBURG FIRE

Miles and Lorraine returned to the deck and watched with riveted attention as Sarusha and Walt made their way through the gatehouse and up to where Herzog's crumpled body lay on the trail.

Miraculously, Herzog's horse didn't bolt down the switchback after throwing him and stood quietly by as Walt and Sarusha approached.

"Is he alive?" shouted Keith.

"They're too far away to hear you, Cap," said Sunny, who repeated the same question but much louder. "Is…he…alive?"

Walt heard this and shouted back, "Yes!"

"Sage, do you know how to reset those trip wires?" asked Keith.

"Yes, I do, Cap."

"Well, go do that. When that's done, you stay in the gatehouse with Ghosty till I give you the all clear. That will be three bells. Make sure you take that Spencer with you."

"Aye, aye, Cap."

"Hell, take Johnny with you. He's the one with the eagle eyes. Just keep your wits about ya." Keith didn't quite know what to make of Bertram Herzog's riding down the switchback. Maybe it's as simple as Sunny suggested: he's dying and he's looking for help. A dying man will do most anything to stay alive, even ride into the enemy camp.

If it was help and mercy he was looking for, he sure wouldn't be getting any from the Haverstraws. Keith knew that because when Walt hollered back that Herzog was alive, he could hear Miles curse under his breath, "Good. Damn that bastard. I wanna watch him die."

Walt and Sarusha got Herzog up and into the stable, and Keith took over.

"You men get him onto the worktable in the tack room. Lucien, go upstairs and get my doctoring bag. Sunny, see about getting some hot water down here. Everett, get some more lanterns into there."

Herzog was passing in and out of consciousness, and his breathing fluctuated between gurgling coughs and long, sickening rales. Keith could just let the man lie here and die or he could do something.

Keith's ship, the *Celine,* didn't carry a regular doctor, so whenever doctoring needed to be done, it was Jonathan Keith who did it. He had to try to save this life. After that, who knew what path things would take? Up on the trail yesterday, Walt and his men gave no quarter. Why try to save this man's life? Herzog no less. Ethical questions become murky in wartime. That being said, Keith knew he at least had to try to do what he could.

Two hours later and with two bullets removed, it was a tossup whether or not Herzog would live. Keith had done what he could and left the tack room with a clear conscience.

"Someone's got to keep an eye on him. Any volunteers?" asked Keith.

No one said a word till Sunny suggested, "Get Tubby Flint to watch him. They got something in common. They're both about half dead."

Keith shook his head, and with a wry smile to Sunny, said, "Sure, get Flint down here. All he does is lay about. Why not?"

Sunny hollered up to the rope hotel, which was right above the tack room. "Tubby Flint, we need you. Come down here."

The rope hotel was a long enclosed mezzanine that ran along the western wall above the tack room and stable stalls. It got its name from the dozen or so rope hammocks that berthed most of the itinerants who passed through the Crow's Nest. It wasn't the best lodging, but then again, it wasn't the worst.

While the men waited for Tubby Flint to come down, Sunny got the two rifles and handgun that were kept in the tack room. "Everett, take these upstairs."

"Tubby, come here. I'm going to lock this door. You sit out here and listen. If he wakes up, let someone know. Got it?" Sunny's orders were brusque, but there was little sophistication to Tubby Flint, and directness seemed to work best.

When Keith got back upstairs, he rang the signal bell three times, allowing Sage and Johnny to free themselves from the cringe-inducing company of Ghosty and his mother.

Returning to the bar, the pair were sarcastically asked to quote some scripture, which they responded to by saying, "It'll cost you bastards a drink."

"In that case, skip it," Lahr answered.

Since Herzog had been brought into the stables, Miles and Lorraine along with Nate, Trader, and Veronica sat quietly in the booth closest to the bar. They talked about one thing or another, waiting for Keith to finish doctoring Herzog and find out whether he would live.

Keith returned from downstairs and reported that whether Herzog would make it through the night was an open question. Now it was a waiting game.

Miles and Lorraine heard the harmless joking Brow Herman, Lahr, and the others were making about Herzog. "Fat bastard. How bad can he be?"

"He didn't find no gold, but he sure as hell found some lead," said Johnny Dollars.

"Nathan, those men shouldn't joke about Herzog that way. They have no idea what he's capable of," said Lorraine as she turned her head and looked at the men at the poker table.

Nate had learned enough about Herzog to know he was no man to joke about. "I think part of that joking is just nervous relief. They know Herzog is one bad hombre."

"Sometimes I almost wish Father and I had never learned the truth about that damn explosion and fire and never heard the name Bertram Herzog."

"How exactly was it you got onto the truth about what happened?" asked Trader.

"How'd we learn what really happened?" said Miles. "I remember that moment like it was yesterday. It was a news item I read in our local paper. The insurance agent in Columbus who had handled the policies for the bank and co-op had committed suicide. Lorrie and I both wondered why he did that and if it had anything to do with the what happened in Lautenburg.

"Since the fire, Lorrie and I had been hard-pressed to go on. It was an effort to get up every day when the first thought in your head was what we had witnessed that night. It was a nightmare we never woke up from. This piece of news gave our lives purpose again. We took the train up to Columbus and started to investigate this insurance agent, Parquet Dunn. Unfortunately, Dunn didn't leave a suicide note, but with a little effort, we learned that he had handled the life insurance policy for Marlene and the late Mr. Scabbe. This led us to investigate the accidental death of Mr. Scabbe, which turned out to not be accidental after all.

"It was only by dumb luck that we were put onto a relationship between the then Mrs. Scabbe and her handyman. We spoke with a neighbor who suspected Mr. Scabbe's death was not an accident but had nothing concrete to really go on. He suspected it involved the Scabbe's handyman, a man named Bertram. Once the neighbor described the man and I remembered one of the freight teamsters had a name like that, we began to put two and two together.

"We went to the man who had headed up the governor's investigation with this information and were told the case was closed and the commission's report stood. After a month in Columbus looking into everything we could find out about Dunn, Marlene, and Herzog, we got back to Lautenburg, only to learn Marlene had checked out of the hotel and left town. After that, our only purpose in life has been finding Mr. Bertram Herzog and Marlene Scabbe." Miles looked down to the floor as if he were looking through it to where Herzog lay on the table in the tack room and said, "We don't know where Marlene is, but at least we got Herzog."

In a rare moment of self-revelation, Miles added, "We, the whole town, were taken in by this Marlene. I curse myself every day for not seeing what was going on. Every day."

Miles could have saved himself his soul-numbing guilt had he known just how ruthless and cunning Marlene and Herzog really were. The way in which the events unfolded belied little of the true nature of what was taking place.

Lorraine and her father had firsthand knowledge of some of the particulars leading up to that fateful night; however, the full story still remains hidden from all save two, Bertram Herzog and Marlene Scabbe.

Lorraine was able to explain to Tallhelm and the others how Herzog and his cohort Marlene Scabbe had come to town and how Marlene had seduced the recently widowed Lamar Slottower, the owner and operator of the local grist mill, grain elevator, and implement company. That much Lorraine knew as a certainty. Beyond that, no moral person could ever have conjectured the true depth and ineffable depravity that guided Herzog and Scabbe on their path of destruction.

Seduction So Complete

Marlene Scabbe came to Lautenburg, checked into a suite of rooms at the Washington Hotel, and thus began her and Bertram Herzog's slow and methodical plot to wrest control of the feed and grain business from Mr. Slottower.

Slottower Feed and Grain was a solvent moneymaking enterprise. Not only was it a profitable day-to-day business, but it also benefited from monthly loan payments of several of the local farmers, who were routinely extended credit till their crops were harvested, or to purchase some implement that would allow them to be competitive where the yield per acre meant the difference between profit or loss.

In lean years, when drought, pests, floods, and all the elements that placed a farmer at the mercy of Mother Nature occurred, Lamar Slottower was more than willing to help. Such were the vicissitudes of farm life. Lamar Slottower's generous and fair-handed business practices helped make the small farming town of Lautenburg prosper and grow, and grow it had. What had started as a small cluster of farms at a bend in the Scioto River was now the county seat and home to a population of several thousand. One of those several thousand, however, was about to become the unsuspecting prey of Herzog and Scabbe—Lamar Slottower.

Marlene Scabbe, recently widowed and, thanks to the life insurance policy of her dead husband, easily donned the visage of a widow in mourning and lady of means.

She opened accounts in both of the local banks, informing the bank managers that she sought to open or buy an existing business and settle into a peaceful life. "A life far removed from the painful memories of the house and home I shared for far too short a time with the dearly departed Mr. Scabbe," she said.

The late Mr. Scabbe's life insurance policy provided the funds to finance the pair's new and more ambitious plot. A scheme that would take longer to execute, but one that would yield a payoff far greater than anything they'd realized to date. Success breeds power; power fuels ambition. Bertram Herzog and Marlene Scabbe had both in excess. In addition, their lack of moral restraint allowed them to divorce themselves from any guilt or remorse for the devastation they created.

The Washington Hotel, by far the best hotel in Lautenburg, was an imposing edifice. A building that, when originally built, appeared to be oversized. But, as planned, the town eventually grew, and soon enough, its marble lobby and grand dining room didn't seem incongruous at all. It was here in that dining room that a "chance" meeting of the widower Slottower and Marlene Scabbe was to take place.

On any given weekday, most of the professional men and business owners of Lautenburg could be found having lunch in the dining room of the Washington Hotel. Marlene Scabbe was also a regular patron during the lunch hour. She was always seen wearing either a traditional black or brown dress, the proper attire for a recent widow. And soon enough, once everyone who chose to notice (and everyone did) that this woman was a proper lady, she was extended every courtesy. So when at lunch one day, as Lamar Slottower walked by her table, her napkin just happened to slide off her lap. She bent down to pick it up just as Lamar did the same. Their eyes met.

The snare was baited.

Several days later, another "chance" meeting took place when Lamar Slottower, while making his weekly bank deposit, happened to encounter Marlene Scabbe conversing with the bank president about her business plans. As Lamar approached, the bank manager rose from his chair and introduced Marlene to Lamar. Marlene gave a nod to Mr. Slottower and commented that the two had "met before but were never properly introduced."

Lamar replied that "he had seen Mrs. Scabbe at lunch and was glad to make her acquaintance."

The trap was set.

Marlene knew how to play her part and played it well. She knew better than to flirt with men. She didn't have to. She assumed, and rightly so, that they would want her approval, as that was the case with most men concerning Marlene. So it was no surprise that when Lamar Slottower inquired of his old friend, the banker, as to Mrs. Scabbe's character, the response was a full-throated endorsement. After all, she had opened her account with a rather large deposit. Although it was unspecified, the banker assured Lamar that the sum was substantial.

That following Sunday, after attending services at the same church as Lamar Slottower and his two daughters, Marlene (once again, "by chance") found herself sitting in the dining room of the Washington Hotel at a table but a few feet away from that of Lamar's and his two daughters. Lamar, somewhat sheepishly, felt compelled to introduce his daughters, and to his surprise and relief, the girls suggested she join them at their table.

The trap was sprung.

The two were married in early spring, one year and a day from the death of the first Mrs. Slottower.

Lamar Slottower, at fifty-eight years of age, was a man just past his prime but in good health, and given his moderate use of alcohol and tobacco, he expected to live a long and happy life. Marlene Scabbe, however, had other plans for Lamar, and a long life was not one of them.

Fourteen years his junior, Marlene Scabbe felt the world was hers for the taking. She had had a successful life of breaking all the rules, playing by those defined only by Bertram Herzog and herself. This life had not eaten away at her peace of mind; rather, it had accorded her a sense of invincibility, and why not? She could count many conquests in her past, and she now saw Slottower and his two daughters as easy game.

The girls, although still acutely feeling the loss of their mother, were willing to accept Marlene into their family as they could see their father returning back to his more jocular self, a disposition the first Mrs. Slottower did not always enjoy.

Bertram Herzog arrived in Lautenburg in time to hear the church bells ring on the morning of Marlene and Lamar's nuptials. Marlene, once she was properly included in Lamar Slottower's will, would have completed the first part of the plan. Then it would be Herzog's job to bring this phase of the stratagem to its deadly conclusion.

Lamar Slottower and Bertram Herzog could not have been more different. Slottower was a genuinely caring human being, one more likely to give than to take, a man who counted most others as friends and was, himself, seen as such. Herzog, on the other hand, cared for no man. He always took and never gave. The idea of friendship was, frankly, anathema to him. He had no friends and preferred it that way. The two men did have one thing in common, however. Both were orphaned at a young age.

Lamar Slottower, a self-made man in every sense of the word, lost both parents to the Yellow Fever epidemic of 1803. He was raised in a state orphanage until the age of fourteen, at which time he struck out on his own. Hard work, coupled with an unfailing moral compass, kept him in good stead. Eventually, he became a very successful businessman, owner of the Slottower Feed and Grain company.

Bertram Herzog lost both parents as well. They perished in a house fire set by the young Bertram. The boy confessed to setting the blaze but could offer no reason as to why, other than it might be something that would give him a measure of enjoyment. Given his remorseless and defiant attitude, the authorities were at a loss as to how to deal with the young arsonist. After much debate and hand wringing, he was committed to a juvenile institution for the mentally ill. He was nine years old. Bertram Herzog was smart enough to eventually convince the staff that he was no longer a threat to society, which could not have been further from the truth. He emerged twelve years later, at the age of twenty-one.

Somewhere along the line, he teamed up with Marlene Wolf, and the pair executed one grift after another until they graduated to insurance fraud and eventually murder. Now their latest plot found Herzog, upon arriving in Lautenburg, renting a room for himself in one of the cheap hotels on the outskirts of town. The next morning, he took a laborer's job in the local freight yard. Herzog and the new Mrs. Slottower were never to be seen together. They had no need. Herzog needed only a gesture of assent from the new Mrs. Slottower, a signal that she was properly included in the Last Will and Testament of Mr. Lamar Slottower.

The plan was simple. Lamar Slottower was to die an "accidental" death. Marlene and the daughters would inherit the feed and grain business. After a proper length of time, Marlene would suggest the business be sold, and then "she could live her life in proper mourning, free of the overwhelming concerns and responsibility of maintaining such an operation."

It took but a few brief months for Marlene to solidify the trust of Lamar and his daughters, and by the end of that summer, she was the legal heir to half of the estate. In the event of Lamar's death, 50 percent was to go to Marlene, and 25 percent to each of his daughters.

Marlene, while waiting at the mill for Lamar to join her for lunch, wiped something off the side of her nose. This was a signal to Bertram Herzog, who was passing by driving a wagonload of barbed wire, that she was now included in Lamar's will.

Meanwhile, Marlene, the new Mrs. Slottower, happy to have shed the unfortunate last name Scabbe, was enjoying the comfortable style of living that the generous Mr. Slottower provided. Never having children of her own, it was difficult for her to take any interest in the lives of her stepdaughters. But she played her part as the caring stepmother as best she could.

The older of the two girls, Lydia, at twenty-three years, had no interest whatsoever in men or marriage. The younger daughter was the opposite. Laurie wanted to marry every man she met. But all the prospective suitors were rejected by her father out of hand. She was simply too young and irresponsible to become a wife and, in all probability, a mother. There would be plenty of time for both girls to find their way.

Marlene, although she was more than willing to robustly provide Lamar with all the pleasures that a loving wife could offer and had even grown fond of Lamar in a curious and bemused way, was not about to deviate from the master plan.

Lamar must go.

The job Bertram Herzog took at the freight yard gave him almost daily contact with the goings on at Slottower Feed and Grain. The railroad that came south from Columbus through Lautenburg at first was just a single line with a small passenger station. But as the town grew, so did the rail line. First one siding was added, then another, then two more, and out of those sidings, a spur line, then two. One of the spur lines serviced Lamar's feed and grain business. There were regularly scheduled rail freight pickups and deliveries to the grain elevator and loading docks. Also, Lamar, who was always looking to expand his business, had just added two storage tanks to the rail siding for the new product, kerosene. Business was brisk and booming.

Observation had always been one of Herzog's strongest skills. Although his perspective was jaundiced, it was unfailing and surgically precise. Within a matter of weeks, he knew Lamar's daily schedule down to the minute. He only had to choose the time and place for an "untimely accident" to befall the doomed Mr. Slottower. Several options presented themselves, like so many playing cards fanned out while playing a game of whist. Herzog would choose one, and rest assured it would be deadly.

No one could ever say Bertram Herzog was a virtuous man. However, one virtue he did possess was patience. He would bide his time and allow the rhythm of day-to-day life to settle upon the world of the recently remarried Lamar Slottower. The money he and Marlene had realized from the estate and insurance policy of the late Mr. Scabbe was adequate for financing their new plot to its deadly conclusion. In time, an opportunity would present itself.

Accidental Murder

And so it did on one unseasonably warm late October afternoon. A thunderstorm was brewing, and as the sky darkened, everyone was hurrying to load or offload their goods. Harvest season always saw more than the usual rail and teamster traffic at Slottower Feed and Grain, and this day was no different. The loading dock and rail siding were jammed with farmers delivering their goods. Lamar Slottower was central in directing traffic amid this maelstrom of activity.

Herzog, whose job occasioned him to be ever present at the rail siding and adjacent loading dock, saw his chance and took it. As the first thunderclap rang through the air, he took a lit cigar to the rump of one of a team of horses directly behind where Lamar Slottower stood. The horse reared up, and in a panic, the whole team and their fully loaded wagon lunged forward, trampling Slottower and pinning him under a wagon wheel. His chest was crushed. He died in the street.

No one thought anything other than it was a tragic accident and the lightning and thunder were to blame. Herzog had simply melted into the background amid all the hollering and confusion. No one was the wiser.

Marlene Slottower received the news and rushed to the scene too late to bid farewell to Lamar but soon enough to be seen as the distraught and heartbroken widow. As she had had some experience with this situation, she played her part to the hilt. Rain-drenched and weeping, the "grief-stricken" Marlene was led away from the gruesome scene, and as she made her way through the jostling crowd, no one noticed the turn of her head and the slightest of nods she gave to one of the teamsters. The deed was done!

Marlene now had to do a task she admittedly was loath to perform. It was that of comforting Lamar's devastated daughters. She must do so, though she had no genuine sympathy for the girls. She lacked the usual human ability to feel compassion for another, even her two stepdaughters in this, their time of unfathomable grief. She could make a show of compassion, but it would be a painful part to play.

The "accidental" death of Lamar Slottower, tragic and criminal as it was, simply served as a prelude to a much greater and far more heinous crime brewing in the mind of Bertram Herzog. His appetite for arson had gone unsatisfied for far too long, and this feed and grain business presented the perfect opportunity for a fiery conflagration large enough to sate the nearly insatiable.

Now that Slottower was dead, Marlene was in control of the business, a business that ran very well, thanks to the competence of Lamar's head foreman, Blaine Hockenberry. What the diabolical pair had to do now was by far the most difficult part of the plan to execute—the endgame. Of course they could just liquidate the assets and move on. But Bertram Herzog saw a way to double or even triple the amount of money to be gained by using one of their tried-and-true schemes: insurance claims. It had worked well before, and the pair were confident they could make it work again.

This time, however, the stakes were to be much higher, and the return promised to be that much greater. Then they would move on. Marlene, for her part, eventually would have to leave town, too overwrought with grief and pain, trying to put the "tragic memory of Lautenburg" out of her mind. Bertram Herzog, ever in the shadows, would simply be another itinerant laborer seeking work elsewhere, a laborer whose presence in and departure from Lautenburg would be scarcely noted.

Greed for some knows no bounds. Giving assent to his greed, coupled with a wanton disregard for human life, was the place where Bertram Herzog felt most comfortable.

Marlene Slottower, of course, could have lived a very comfortable life as the widow of Lamar Slottower. The feed and grain business was immensely profitable. Most of the townsfolk, due in large part to Marlene's excellent ability to play every part to perfection, had accepted her as one of their own, a feat not easily achieved in a small town such as Lautenburg. Nevertheless, they had, and there she was, living in the big house on the hill. She was greeted with deference and respect whenever she ventured out. As comfortable as life could be in that grand home, it was not part of the plan.

On the day Lamar Slottower was put in the ground, a procession of mourners shuffled past his daughters and the widow Slottower to offer their condolences. One of those was a lowly laborer who whispered four words to the black-veiled widow: "Columbus, Sunday a month."

A month and a day after Lamar's funeral, Marlene and Bertram Herzog had their rendezvous in a hotel in Columbus, Ohio. The meeting was, for the pair, a long-awaited tryst, where they toasted one another with champagne and congratulated themselves on a plan executed to perfection.

Ultimate success, as close at hand as it may have seemed, would only be achieved once Lautenburg was just another road marker on their trail of fraud, destruction, and murder. To achieve this, the pair would have to marshal all of their devious ingenuity and guile. What usually made their type of work easier was a belief, somewhat well-founded, that inside all men's bodies beats a heart not immune to compromise, larceny even. Lautenburg, however, might be the exception to that rule. Honest and true to the core were the farmers and merchants of this town. With this as a given, Marlene and Bertram planned accordingly.

Marlene, returning from Columbus, focused entirely on the job at hand. Part of that job was to appear to cherish the memory of Lamar and ensure the emotional well-being of the girls. To this end, she did whatever she had to do to allow life to return to some measure of normality.

Fall turned into winter; winter melted into spring. Marlene played her part and Bertram Herzog his. As incongruous as it may seem, Herzog had an affinity for physical labor. His youth spent in institutional servitude had provided him with a daily outlet for his internal rage. The familiarity of physical labor was somehow tonic to his tortured soul. Herzog actually looked forward to working as a teamster through the fall and spring. He enjoyed it.

This period also gave the duo time to plan their deadly endgame. So far, every step had gone like clockwork. Marlene's marriage to Lamar, her inclusion in the will, the death of Lamar, and winning the trust of the professional and laypeople of Lautenburg all had led to this moment. Patience and finesse, now more than ever, were what the situation called for. Akin to hunters stalking their prey, slow and methodically, Marlene and Herzog inched closer to their ultimate prize.

Herzog's plan, which the pair had mapped out in detail in the hotel in Columbus, was heinously diabolical. Rather than just sell the feed and grain business to the highest bidder and take her half and go, Marlene would propose that the several local farmers, who were the mainstay for the business, form a cooperative and buy and run the company for themselves.

The real payoff for Marlene would come from an addendum to the mortgage arrangements that called for a life insurance policy on each of the co-op members for the full value of the selling price.

Selling the business to the farmers would certainly be seen as magnanimous on her part and would also soften any last bit of criticism of her as an outsider, an opportunist motivated by greed and a desire to fleece Lautenburg of whatever she could get. The tactic of selling the business to the local farmers would put any such whispers to bed once and for all. These doubts would be further assuaged by the fact that Marlene would be willing to carry some of the mortgage debt that the farmers' co-op would assume.

Herzog and Marlene figured, and rightly so, that Marlene's banker would go along with the plan. He expected that most of the money paid to Marlene, either the cash from the sale or the funds realized from the mortgage payments, would ultimately end up right back in his bank. Of course, the Marlene Slottower the banker thought he knew, and secretly lusted after, was not the real Marlene. No one really knew *that* Marlene save Bertram Herzog. The Bertram Herzog who had gone virtually unnoticed since his arrival in Lautenburg, by everyone save a few of his fellow teamsters, men who knew him only as a hard worker, one who was spare with words but had no trouble being understood.

Marlene's announcement to sell the business was to coincide with the completion of planting season in late spring. This would allow the farmers the chance to fully concentrate on the proposal once their seed was in the ground. She planned to discuss the idea with her stepdaughters, but their position, one way or another, was seen as having little bearing on the eventual outcome.

Lamar's daughters, still dealing with the loss of their mother and now the sudden and tragic death of their beloved father, were in a fragile state. How Marlene handled the subject of selling their father's business, which would no doubt seem like a betrayal and abandonment of what was his life's work, would require both tact and finesse.

Marlene, however, was well up to the task. She started very early in her adolescence to perfect the nuanced maneuvers necessary to manipulate men and women alike. She would have no trouble making the girls not only accept the idea but embrace it.

After Lamar's death, the younger daughter, Laurie, had found comfort in the arms of the young man with whom she had secretly been keeping company. He had asked Lamar if he could court his daughter and was politely rebuffed. The boy was the oldest son of Lamar's head foreman and worked at the grist mill as an apprentice miller. He was a decent boy. Lamar, however, had noted that as his own station and standing in the town grew, so did the expectations he had for his daughters. Possibly, this boy would be a suitable husband for his Laurie, but he didn't want to see her future so quickly cast. All that, of course, mattered little now. Laurie and the foreman's son were all but inseparable.

Lydia, the elder daughter, was a completely different case. She was grief-stricken by the loss of her father, but she gained strength from the knowledge that due to her inheritance, she would never have to rely on the support or largesse of a man. Nor would she ever have to be chained to the life of servitude of that of a dutiful wife.

Lydia sought succor in the loving embrace of a childhood girlfriend, who had recently returned to Lautenburg from a year abroad. The two could often be seen riding along the bridle path that ran along the river. And just as the wind blew through the willows hanging over the river, so did the whispers of the townsfolk swirl about. The girls scarcely took notice and, most likely, could hardly have cared.

Marlene knew exactly how to use both situations to her advantage, and at breakfast one morning, she mentioned that she was thinking it might be a good idea to sell the gristmill and the feed and grain business, and she had spoken to the bank manager about the idea.

Marlene knew, and rightly so, that scarcely before breakfast had ceased to be a taste on Laurie's palate, the girl would be telling the foreman and his son about Marlene's intentions to sell the business. So it was that before the courthouse clock had struck twelve that day, word had spread through the mill and made its way into the shops and offices lining Main Street. This was just what Marlene had anticipated, and she had devised the perfect foil for the groundswell that such news would surely have generated.

The day before, she had gone to her friend, the bank manager, and laid out her ideas concerning the sale of the feed and grain business. She had told him that she hoped the prominent farmers would form a cooperative and buy the business and run it themselves. She was sending word requesting they come for lunch the following day. She also suggested that the foreman be guaranteed that his job was secure, and that he be entitled to have an equal share in the ownership and profits of the business.

The bank manager, Simon Graham, had thought that selling the business to a cooperative of farmers was not an entirely sound business decision.

The free states in the North and the slave states in the South had coalesced into two separate and resolute bodies. War between the two had become an all but foregone conclusion. War, however, in spite of all its devastation and destruction, was almost always good for business, especially a business such as Slottower Feed and Grain. Marlene's response to the banker's views on the war issue was that she had no desire or intention of being a war profiteer. (Of course, once war had broken out, Herzog and Marlene became just that, operating in the shadows, wholesaling bogus medical supplies to both the Union and Confederate sides.)

As Marlene had anticipated, the foreman, alerted to her plan by Laurie and his son, was soon striding through the main floor of the bank, making a beeline to the bank manager's desk. The foreman's purple throat was nearly bursting from the effort required to hold back his opinion of the vile and conspiratorial plot to sell the business. A teller informed the foreman that the bank manager was at lunch and added that he had left in the company of Mrs. Slottower.

The foreman, Blaine Hockenberry, normally a levelheaded and polite man, tried as best he could to calm himself as he made his way across the street and into the hotel dining room to confront Mrs. Slottower. As he pushed open the batwing doors, he could see several farmers seated with Marlene and the bank manager at a large round table. This vision stopped him midstride. What was going on? His presence in the dining room was quickly noticed and, for Marlene, not unexpected. Beckoned by a few to join the group, he awkwardly took a seat and looked for somewhere to place his hat.

Quickly realizing that he would have to wash up before joining them, he made his way out to the lobby and down to the washroom at the foot of the basement stairs. Returning, he retook a seat between two of the farmers, Miles Haverstraw and Myron Wingert, two men he knew well and considered friends.

Well, here it seemed that Marlene, rather than having no regard for what the mill and grain business meant to the town, had fully embraced its importance and sought to enhance it. The rage welling up in the foreman's throat had to be gulped down like a piece of unchewed meat.

Opportunity for All

"Gentlemen," Marlene began, "I think by now you have some idea why I've asked you all here today. I want to put to rest any rumors about my intentions well before they get started. As you all surely know, an innocent rumor can do more harm sometimes than a guilty truth. In any event, thank you all for coming. I know you're all very busy, and I had hoped that most of you would have had your planting done by this time and would be able to spare one afternoon to hear what I have to say." Marlene gestured to a waiter and asked him if he could please ask Mr. Zwiedell to come to the table.

Instantly, the hotel manager, Raymond Zwiedell, a man of considerable girth, was standing at Marlene's side. "Raymond, could you please see that these men get whatever they want? I imagine some of them have had nary a morsel since breakfast. I asked these men here. The least I can do is get them something to eat."

"Well, I did come here before I had my dinner," announced one of the men.

"Same here," chimed in another.

"David, get these men some menus, please. And get everyone water and whatever else they care to drink," Zwiedell instructed the headwaiter, his son David. Raymond Zwiedell, as a restauranteur, was always keen on teaching his son the finer points of the trade and added, "We have a very good bratwurst today, and a new keg of the best Bavarian Lager arrived just yesterday."

"What about whiskey?" asked one of the rougher and more unkempt farmers sitting about the table.

Raymond Zwiedell looked down to catch Marlene's eye, and upon receiving a nod from her, he extended his arm across his chest and gave a sweeping gesture, encompassing the whole of the dining room and barroom beyond. A gesture that was universally understood to mean "All you see before you is at your disposal."

"Thank you, Raymond," Marlene said politely as she gently touched his sleeve.

While David and another waiter took the dinner orders from the men, Marlene said to Raymond, "I don't think we'll be here that long, but if we are, I'd like to provide these men with supper as well."

"As you wish, Ma'am," answered Raymond Zwiedell as he nodded and backed away from the table.

"I better wash up," said one man at the table.

"Wait up, Homer. I better wash up too," said another as he got up and looked about before placing his straw hat on the seat of his chair.

As these two men pushed open the batwing doors out to the lobby, the foreman's son and Laurie Slottower breathlessly burst into the dining room.

The other patrons in the room could scarcely conceal their curiosity regarding the goings-on at the big round table and did little to do so. With the arrival of Blaine Jr. and Laurie Slottower, everyone stopped eating and watched intently to see what was going to happen next.

"What's going on here, Father?" blurted Blaine Hockenberry Jr. The young Hockenberry knew everyone at the table and was experiencing the same range of emotions his father had gone through just minutes before.

"It's all right, son. Mrs. Slottower has a proposal she would like us to hear. Who's watching the mill?" asked the elder Hockenberry.

"I guess no one right now. I shut it down before I headed over here," answered the slightly chastened young Hockenberry.

"Everything's all right here, Blaine. I think it would be best if you got back to the mill. I'll talk with you later," directed Hockenberry Sr., privately annoyed that the whole dining room was privy to this exchange.

"What about Laurie?" asked Blaine Jr.

"Laurie is more than welcome to stay. Frankly, I would welcome it," interjected Marlene.

Laurie shook her head sideways. Awkwardly, the pair stood silently, staring at the assemblage, unable to fully grasp what exactly was going on. After what seemed like an eternity, they turned and walked back out of the dining room.

Soon two more farmers joined the group and with the addition of these two all parties necessary for Marlene's presentation were present.

"First of all, I want to thank you all again for being here. But before I begin, I would like to have a moment of silence to reflect on the honor of the man who was Lamar Slottower, to his memory and to his vision. May he be looking down on us now and hopefully be pleased with what may transpire here today."

With that, Marlene bowed her head slightly as did all the men sitting at the table. One man who had yet to remove his hat did so and sheepishly bowed his head along with the others. To a man, they had considered Lamar a close and true friend. Many were still mourning his passing and were somewhat conflicted as to just what to think about the situation in which they found themselves, sitting around a large table in the Hotel Washington's dining room with the bank manager, Simon Graham, and Lamar's widow, Marlene.

"I spoke earlier of Lamar's vision. I knew he had great plans for the mill and equally grand hopes for what the town of Lautenburg could one day become. Frankly, gentlemen, as strong and capable as I consider myself to be, I am not up to the task of shepherding this business forward with the strength and foresight that it so acutely deserves. I know there would be little trouble finding a buyer who would be willing and able to see that the mill, seed, and grain business survives. That alone, and here I believe I speak for Lamar, would not be enough.

"Lamar's business is akin to one of those steam engines that I hear every morning pulling into town. That is why this town is growing and prospering. Every man here has helped fuel that engine of prosperity, and every man here can have a part in keeping that engine running, not only running but gaining steam and momentum. Enough of both to ensure that the mill business and Lautenburg can survive any challenge that may come its way."

Marlene paused here to take a drink of water and saw that the waiters were set to bring the food the men had ordered for their dinner.

"Gentlemen, if you would excuse me for a moment. Please don't get up. If anyone needs anything, don't hesitate to ask one of the waiters," Marlene announced as she rose from her chair, straightened her skirt, and made her way through the dining room doors and into the lobby.

No sooner had the batwing doors settled behind her then the table erupted into a cacophony of questions, some directed to no one in particular but most to the banker, Simon Graham.

"What did she have in mind?"

"Who did she say wanted to buy the mill?'"

"Am I wrong, but does she want us to buy the mill?"

"I don't understand. How can I be involved? I still owe money from last summer when I bought that Moore combine."

"Don't think you're alone, Cyrus. I don't think there's one of us that doesn't owe the mill money."

"Yeah, I owe half on that Moore. Cyrus and I went in on that together," added the man sitting next to Cyrus, his cousin and neighboring farmer, Elroy.

"Men, please, the general idea Mrs. Slottower has in mind is that you gentlemen form some sort of cooperative and buy, own, and operate the mill yourselves."

Simon Graham made this statement as he steepled his hands in front of him, then quickly threw them open, palms pointed upward. "That's basically all I know."

The loud questions had quieted down to murmurs and sidelong glances as the men ate their dinner and contemplated their suddenly unknown futures. These men had generally planned maybe five or six years ahead at best, and all of them had been reaching for those well-planned goals since they forked their first spade of dirt. Now, all of a sudden, those well-thought-out expectations had become blurred. With blurred vision comes a temporary loss of equilibrium.

"Son, could you please bring me a shot of rye and another glass of beer?" asked one of the men of young David.

"I'll have the same, if you don't mind," added another.

These men would normally only have the occasional drink, but as this seemed to qualify as a sort of special occasion, they saw no need not to adhere to that custom.

Marlene had taken her time in the powder room and had stopped at the bar on the way back to the table to give the men more time to talk among themselves. One of the few women bold enough to sit at the bar unaccompanied, she lingered for a moment and slowly sipped a glass of red wine, savoring the moment before she was to give what would be the performance of her lifetime. She smiled to herself, thinking how she had used the phrase "shepherding the business." Now she and Herzog had the sheep right where they wanted them, and ready to be shorn.

As she readied herself to leave the bar and return to the table, she noticed that most of the men were still eating.

"Lawrence," she asked the bartender, "would you please ask a waiter to bring a bowl of that ham and bean soup that smells so good over to my table?"

Although she was as deadly as a viper, Marlene was unfailingly polite and well-mannered. Not wanting to put the men in the position of eating while she sat with an empty plate in front of her, she ordered the soup. Plus, although she wasn't especially hungry, she knew that breaking bread with these men would help put them more at ease.

So far, everything had gone according to plan, and now it was her job to convince these inherently independent farmers that they should unite and work together. She knew they had their differences, old grudges, and latent rivalries. She also knew they shared strong beliefs and common values, plus an unspoken allegiance to one another. They would often help each other at planting or harvest time. But those were limited and sporadic occasions, after which each man returned to his own farm and family, his own hopes and dreams.

The proposal had many common-sense selling points, the least of which was that the farmers could buy their seed, mill their grain, store it, and ship their goods at near or just slightly over cost. The Slottower business also had several non-farm-related sources of income, especially its sales of coal oil and now the more popular fuel and lighting product, kerosene. Lamar had also built an extensive retail hardware and implement outlet that was better by far than any within a day's ride.

Also, something which hadn't been spoken of as yet was the specter of war. A war was definitely brewing, a war that would make commodities like the ones these farmers grew more valuable. Any business with a ready rail siding, warehouses, and a grain elevator would be poised to benefit from the increase in commerce that always accompanied a war. Beyond all this, one fact that could trump all others and carry the day was that there would be income for these hardworking men from something other than the sweat of their brow.

Marlene, as the dinner plates were being cleared from the table, began her careful litany of reasons why it was good business sense for the men to consider her offer. Over the next few hours, many questions were asked and answered. Simon Graham gave the bank's tentative approval to hold the mortgage on the business and properties if certain particulars could be met. Blaine Hockenberry was assured that his position not only would be secure but that, as a partial stake holder, he would be entitled to profit along with everyone else. Lamar's daughters would be afforded every consideration possible. Their wishes would be honored and their futures secure.

Marlene could afford to be generous describing the terms of the contract because, in fact, what she and her invisible partner, Bertram Herzog, were selling was doomed to be a most fleeting grasp of the golden ring for these unsuspecting men.

She was sure to punctuate her sales pitch with fervent references to Lamar and his grand vision. Soon the farmers themselves were invoking Lamar's name and wishes, as if they had spoken with him that very morning. Everything Marlene heard and saw indicated that this deal would go through, and though she hardly felt compelled to state the obvious, she nevertheless did.

The dinner crowd had long since left the dining room, and the waiters were readying for the supper hour when she suggested, "Everyone should, of course, talk all this over with their wives and that we should meet again at everyone's soonest convenience."

With that, she drew the dinner to a close. "Thank you all for coming. It was so nice to get to know all of you better." As the men rose from the table, each gave Marlene a short bow and left the room. One man remained and asked the waiter for another glass of rye. This man, as it turned out, had recently lost his wife and a stillborn baby. Marlene told the waiter to "bring him whatever he wants to drink and if he'd like, supper as well."

She had to admit to herself that she did feel a tinge of sympathy for the man, but her overriding thought was how she longed to be gone from this town and hoped to soon find herself in more cosmopolitan environs.

While the farmers decided whether they were going to take Marlene up on her proposal, there were several more chess moves to be made in the game she and Bertram Herzog were playing. Ideally, a properly executed crime should appear as an accident. If not, suspicions must point to anyone but the criminal. Marlene planned accordingly.

Returning to the house after the meeting at the hotel, Marlene greeted Lydia, who had just returned with her friend from an afternoon of riding. Laurie was readying herself to greet Blaine Jr. after he left work. What Marlene had to announce to her stepdaughters would be of equal interest to Blaine Jr. and most likely to Lydia's friend Marcia, whom everyone called Mercy.

"I should probably wait until Blaine gets here, but let me start anyway. Girls, I've decided to temporarily move into the Washington Hotel until your old house along the river is fixed up. You girls, I should say, ladies, are both full-grown and of legal age. I never really felt it my right to say much about what you did one way or another. However, just my being here, under this roof, I feel it is somehow stifling your freedom to live your lives as you wish. I truly loved your father and bear a genuine fondness for both of you. That being said, I think it would be best at this time that I allowed you to live your lives without my being here."

As Marlene finished, she sighed and heaved her chest as if a sad burden had been lifted from her body. The girls both began talking at once in feigned protest, but very quickly agreed to the idea.

Lydia, the oldest and by far the sharper of the two, broached a subject that even Marlene had been unsure of just how to bring up.

"Marlene, half this house belongs to you. It might be better since you will no longer be living here that my sister and I should have full ownership."

"Well, that certainly makes sense," agreed Marlene. "Possibly we can make an arrangement where I relinquish my partial ownership of this house in exchange for complete ownership of the house along the river, an even swap."

The Slottowers' original residence was a small house situated on four acres along the river. Lamar, once the big house on the hill was built, kept this house and rented it out. However, after several unpleasant experiences with tenants, he decided to keep the house empty and use it as an occasional spot to go fishing and escape the first Mrs. Slottower when her more disagreeable self was holding sway.

Marlene wondered if maybe the house along the river was more important to Laurie and Lydia than she realized. Thankfully, that was not the case, which was proven out when Lydia remarked, "Marlene, that would be more than agreeable. My sister and I never much liked that house. All we ever did there was chores."

"Okay then. Whatever paperwork is necessary, we can have Mr. Graham take care of. Or if not him, maybe that new lawyer in town, that young one, what's his name?" asked Marlene.

"Do you mean Johnny McDowell?" quickly offered Laurie, evidently a girl with a roving eye.

"Yes, that's the one. I think Mr. Graham may be too busy with the sale of the mill, if in fact that happens," Marlene said with an almost uninterested air, ever vigilant to keep her true feelings from being known by anyone but herself, and Bertram Herzog.

She had other plans for how and when the transfer of home ownership would take place, and it did not involve the young lawyer McDowell. Also, Marlene had no real intentions of living in the house next to the Scioto. But she did want the house and its association with Lamar Slottower and the mill to be reinforced.

As recently as early this spring, evidence of the house being used as an overnight refuge for runaway slaves had been noticed. Men tracking the slaves had shown up at the mill demanding the slaves be turned over. No one at the mill knew anything about it and told the men that the house must have been broken into, and after spending a night, the runaways must have moved on.

Kentucky, a slave state, was but fifty miles south of Lautenburg, and the Scioto was a known route on the Underground Railroad. Angry Kentucky slave owners seeking revenge could provide easy suspects, if or when suspects would be needed.

Herzog and Marlene always preferred "accidental" causes for any of their dastardly deeds. But developing readymade scapegoats could always redirect suspicion if in fact anything seemed suspicious to begin with.

One week passed, and then another. Just when Marlene thought that the farmers were going to reject her plan, Blaine Hockenberry Sr. paid her a visit at the Washington Hotel. They met in the lobby.

"Mrs. Slottower, ma'am, the men asked me to come by and tell you that half of them are for your idea and half of them are not. They'd like to have another meeting. The ones that aren't just don't know how everything would work out seeing as they already owe the mill money. Maybe you and Mr. Graham could explain things a little better."

"Why, sure, Blaine. How can anyone agree to something when they don't know what they're agreeing to?"

"Exactly, ma'am."

"Do you know when the men would like to have this meeting?"

"Well, I don't rightly know. What would suit you?"

"Tell the men I would like to have them to lunch again on, say, this coming Wednesday."

"That'll work just fine."

"Blaine, how are Laurie and Blaine Jr. getting on?" Marlene knew this question would make Blaine Sr. a bit uncomfortable but didn't mind keeping him a bit off-balance.

"Well, they seem to be a comfort to one another," answered the mill foreman.

"That's good. And things at the mill?" asked Marlene.

"They're going good. We're as busy as a one-armed paperhanger. Sure selling a lot of kerosene," answered Blaine. "Well, you have a nice evening, ma'am," Blaine Hockenberry said as he looked about the ornate hotel lobby for a moment and then exited out the side door.

Marlene was confident that given the opportunity to remake her case to the farmers, the deal would go through. The next step in the plan was to get the banker Simon Graham's complete and unwavering support for the proposed deal. This, she envisioned, given her diabolical and devious nature, would also be a way of having a bit of fun while at the same time moving the plan onto completion, to wit, the seduction of Simon Graham.

She knew Graham had lust on his mind every time they met, and she made sure they met often, mostly in the bank but sometimes over lunch. She also knew Mrs. Graham, for whatever reason, was an unhappy woman. This, by osmosis, had infected Simon with a general dissatisfaction with his life as well, fertile ground for the seed of infidelity to take root. So the next morning, while in the bank, she set her plan in motion.

"Simon, I saw Lydia yesterday, and she said you had the papers ready to sign for the exchange of ownership on the houses. I'm busy right now, but could you bring them over to the hotel later, say, over lunch?"

"Certainly, Marlene. Is one o'clock okay?"

"One o'clock then."

As one o'clock approached, Marlene went to the clerk at the front desk and told him, "Guy, I'm not feeling well. I'm expecting Mr. Graham for lunch. We have some papers to sign. Could you tell him I can't do that today and to just leave them with you?" Marlene turned away and, almost as an afterthought, said, "Oh, if it's really important, he could bring them up and I could sign them there."

"Yes, Mrs. Slottower. I'll give him the message."

When Simon got this message, it was of course welcome news. He had many times fantasized of being alone with Marlene in her hotel room.

Marlene welcomed Simon into her room. "You'll have to excuse me, Simon. I don't feel very well. Maybe it's the heat? You're so sweet. You've been such a help to me these last several months." Marlene had changed into what could pass for a dress but was more like lingerie. As she drew the curtains, she said, "The light, for some reason, hurts my eyes."

Simon heard very little of what Marlene said, transfixed as he was by the way her dress revealed a good part of her cleavage and how it also clung to her hips and thighs, a picture that surpassed even his most vivid fantasies.

"Simon, maybe I ask too much, but my neck is so tight, I doubt I could even hold a pen to sign those papers. Could you be a dear and see if you could take out some of that tension?"

Simon didn't say a word as Marlene sat down at her writing desk and he began to gently massage her neck. It wasn't long before he was no longer in control of his desires and soon found his hands moving down from Marlene's neck and shoulders to her breasts. Marlene's response, and in no way affected, was to moan softly, letting Simon know that his advances were not unwelcome.

Soon the pair were joined as one, writhing together in unbridled passion, carnal ecstasy.

As Marlene, now carelessly draped in a bedsheet, sat at her desk and signed the papers, she asked, "Simon, unfortunately, you can't spend the afternoon. But I have business in Columbus next week. Do you ever get to Columbus?"

Marlene had to admit to herself, she enjoyed what had just taken place, but as quickly as a person can take off one shirt and put on another, she was back to the business at hand. The tryst that would, without a doubt, take place next week in Columbus was just another part of her master plan.

The Wednesday lunch and meeting with the farmers lasted all afternoon, and thanks to the enthusiastic support of two of them, Miles Haverstraw and his brother-in-law, Myron Wingert, the group was persuaded to accept the plan.

The agreement wasn't all that complicated. Seven farmers and Blaine Hockenberry Sr. would form a co-op and assume ownership of 80 percent of the property and business. Marlene would retain a 10 percent share, and the Slottower girls would each receive a 5 percent share. The First National Bank of Lautenburg, of which Simon Graham was president, would pay Marlene 40 percent of the appraised value in cash. The farmers would pay down the mortgage from the profits of the business. Each of the farmers was expected to provide some measure of labor to keep down operating costs.

An insurance policy held by the bank to cover the full value of the mortgage would be written in case of the untimely event of a fire or flood. Also, a life insurance policy was to be taken out on each member of the co-op for the full amount of the mortgage to be paid to the policy holder. This last part of the deal was written in print so fine, it went unnoticed by all involved save Marlene Slottower. The co-op members' young lawyer, Johnny McDowell, failed to notice the item, possibly due to inexperience or Marlene's ability to charm the young lawyer into assuming everything was above board. Also, to avoid detection, Marlene took responsibility for making the payments on these life insurance policies directly to the carrier herself.

To parlay her stake in Slottower Feed and Grain into a real fortune required someone to underwrite these policies. To this end, Marlene had available to her an old and trusted asset, the top agent at the largest insurance company in Ohio, the man who had handled her two previous policies and claims, the well-respected, and very ambitious Mr. Parquet Dunn.

Mr. Dunn, who had been seduced by Marlene several years earlier, lived in constant fear of being exposed as an adulterer—an event that would ruin his well-manicured reputation and incur the uncontrollable wrath of his shrewish wife, a woman who had married far above her station and to disguise her shortcomings cloaked herself in defiant anger and embraced an especially virulent form of ignorance.

The cost of infidelity ofttimes knows no limit or end, something Parquet Dunn had so quickly and acutely become aware of once the joy of his indiscretion had faded. Marlene, however, was sure to let Parquet taste of the forbidden fruit often enough to ensure the frayed cloth of his moral fiber would go unmended.

Parquet Dunn, the lead agent for the Greater Ohio Casualty and Life Insurance Company, wrote the policies for the co-op members. He was well-rewarded, not only with the full range of Marlene's sexual favors but also with a sizable amount of cash, which ensured there was no doubt as to his culpability.

So the deal was done. Slottower Feed and Grain was now the Lautenburg Co-op Feed and Grain Company.

Only Grief Remained

The first few months of operation were chaotic. Blaine Hockenberry Sr. had gone from having one boss to now having seven. Each one with their own ideas and priorities as to how the co-op should be run. Eventually, though, a workable rhythm was achieved for the day-to-day operations. The financial mechanisms of the arrangement were working well and soon became routine. The mortgage payments to the bank, Marlene, Lydia, and Laurie were being regularly made from the profits of the business.

The bank paid Marlene for her share of the company, a payment that went from one bank ledger page to another, the money never physically leaving the bank, which gave Simon Graham a generous measure of comfort. His misplaced trust in Marlene Slottower would unfortunately lull him into a false sense of security. The total cost of underwriting the mortgage involved a goodly sum, and if Marlene were to close out her account, it could leave the bank vulnerable to being undercapitalized.

Simon Graham hardly gave that eventuality a passing thought. After all, he and Marlene were friends and now lovers. Trust, the mortar that binds any union, when wrongly placed can prove to be more dangerous than overt enmity.

Marlene had done her job. Now it was the job of Bertram Herzog to bring the plan to fruition, a task he was fully capable of doing. In fact, even the idea of it gave him a dark joy only possible for a true psychopath.

The summer of 1859 was an especially good one for the farmers of the Lautenburg Co-Op. Hot sunny days and cool wet nights led to near bumper crops for all. The railroad siding next to the mill could hardly ship the wheat and corn fast enough. The grain elevator was filled and emptied several times.

As an arsonist, Bertram Herzog had an array of tools with which to work: two storage tanks full of kerosene, drums of stored coal oil, a highly combustible grain elevator, kegs of black powder, and buildings made of wood.

At night, Herzog would lie in his room and conjure up one scenario, rework it, reject it, and come up with another. Starting a fire was easy enough. However, this fire had to be deadly and appear to be accidental.

The plan he finally came up with was so diabolical that even he had to wince for a second before smiling to himself, sublimely self-satisfied with his ingenuity.

There was no problem in getting all the co-op members in the same place at the same time. The group met in the new warehouse building the first Monday of every month at 7:00 p.m. sharp. That might do, but Herzog envisioned something historic—a grand conflagration worthy of his unappreciated talents.

As summer turned to fall, that very opportunity presented itself. The members were planning a big potluck at the new warehouse to celebrate their first harvest season of the Lautenburg Co-op. It looked to be as big an affair as Lautenburg's farming community had ever seen.

In the week leading up to the big night, no one took notice when a wagon load of coal oil barrels began to be parked along the rail siding next to the grain elevator, or when an old fire hose lay in among some dunnage underneath the kerosene storage tanks, or the light shining through a knothole in one of the white oak boards on the back side of the grain elevator, the shaft of sunlight glistening off the ever present grain dust.

The arsonist had begun to marshal the main components of his master plan. As the day approached for the big event, Herzog spent an evening weaving together three strands of safety fuse into one, a fuse that he had purloined off a shipment of explosives going to a tunnel project in Pennsylvania.

Also taken off that shipment were two sixty-pound kegs of black powder that Herzog re-stenciled as *NAILS*. These he placed alongside the grain elevator. Herzog wasn't taking any chances. One fuse was to lead to the grain elevator, the other to the two kegs of gunpowder.

Who could understand what was going through the man's mind as he toiled away fabricating these fuses? Fuses that would set into motion a sequence of explosions, each one more destructive than the last—ultimately, culminating in a fire that was guaranteed to leave no evidence of foul play and even very few remains of those who were to perish horribly in the resulting inferno.

This deadly perversion had to be motivated by something more complex than simple greed, a form of avarice very common to man. Was this deadly plan born out of revenge for an unsettled wrong held over from a previous life? Herzog's parents, before the young Bertram incinerated them, were as kind and loving as parents could be.

For some reason, there was a void within him that rendered him alien to all others. Whatever intrinsic good can be called forth from the souls of men, this was absent in Bertram Herzog. But rather than being a stark and lonely place in which to exist, it was for him a sanctuary of solitude, where no human conventions applied save those of his own construct.

Beyond that, whatever the dark need piloting his wretched soul, the path it charted was guaranteed to leave nothing but pain, death, destruction, and sorrow in its wake.

As Herzog made his preparations for the big night, so did the farmers and their families. The women cooked and baked all their favorite dishes. While they happily toiled away, the kids spent their time sprucing up and decorating the new warehouse. The room where the banquet was being held was easily large enough to handle the sixty-some slated to attend.

When the evening finally arrived and the families began to a file into the room, the air all but crackled with a level of excitement and anticipation unknown to young and old alike. The women arrayed their dishes and desserts on long tables set against the back wall. The men carried in one large roasting pan after another. The succulent aromas of baked hams, basted turkeys, and fried chicken filled the air as the men proudly added their contributions to the buffet.

The children had to be cautioned not to run about and try to calm themselves, but the excitement of the moment was so strong that this was something of a losing battle.

Some kind of excitement beat in the heart of Bertram Herzog as well as he lit the thirty-foot safety fuses hidden inside a stack of clay drainage pipe. One fuse led up and into the knothole in the back end of the grain elevator, the other to the kegs of black powder. They were fuses that would take fifteen minutes to burn. More than enough time for Herzog to stop and give the valve on the kerosene tank a quarter turn and watch as the kinks slowly came out of the old fire hose. Shielded from view under the warehouse loading dock, the hose stretched to where its end reached the wagon of coal oil barrels.

As the men complimented one another on their shared achievements and waited for the children and women to serve themselves, Herzog complimented himself on his sinister achievement as well.

Once everyone was served, Blaine Hockenberry Sr. rose and proposed the group say a special prayer of thanks. This announcement was interrupted by Myron Wingert, who said, "Could we wait for Miles and Lorraine? They had to go back to get something. They should be here any minute."

Mrs. Haverstraw, ever the thoughtful and polite lady, said, "Please let's say grace and not let our food get cold. Miles will understand."

At that very moment, as he made his way back to his hotel, Bertram Herzog was saying a prayer of his own. Not really a prayer, but more an incantation to some dark spirit that the two late arrivals he saw on their way to the festivities wouldn't arrive in time to notice anything awry.

Evidently, that devilish supplication was answered, because as he sat in the dingy lobby of his hotel pretending to read a newspaper, an explosion rattled its windows, quickly followed by another and finally a third.

The last explosion illuminated the night sky with a light so bright that for a split second it appeared to be midday.

Everyone in Lautenburg rushed to the scene, only to be held at bay by the heat from the hellish inferno that had engulfed the whole of the mill complex and was spreading to the rest of the town.

Miles Haverstraw and his daughter Lorraine were paralyzed by the horror of what they were seeing. Only when Lorraine fainted did Miles Haverstraw's brain begin to slowly function again.

The water tank next to the rail siding had been blown to bits, as were both kerosene storage tanks. The top of the river next to the mill was ablaze with burning kerosene. The townsfolk were dumbstruck. Those not paralyzed by the sight tried to set up a bucket brigade, but to no avail. Mothers shielded their children from the sight, and men overcome by the horror knelt in the street and prayed.

Thankfully for the town, it was a windless night, and eventually the spread of the fire halted several blocks from the mill. No one who attended the banquet survived. Not only did no one survive, but there was no way to distinguish what had once been human flesh from equine.

News of the Lautenburg fire spread across the nation and the world. Such was the magnitude of the tragedy.

In the aftermath, the governor sent the top fire inspectors in the state to investigate. During the four-month investigation, several theories were put forth, one of which was that the fire was set as retaliation on the part of angry slaveowners who saw the Slottower house on the river as a haven for escaped slaves.

This accusation was vehemently denied by the men who were interviewed, namely the ones that had come to the mill in search of runaways earlier in the year. Of course, the abolitionists were quick to rally behind this reading of the facts. The newspapers on both sides of the Ohio ran the predictable tit-for-tat pieces. Nothing, however, came of the charges. Yet this acrimony was another tremor that worked to upset the delicate balancing act that was trying to keep men from being driven to war.

A leaky valve on either of the kerosene tanks was suggested, but since both had been completely destroyed in the explosions, this theory could go no further than mere speculation. The most logical explanation the inspectors could come up with was that rags used to wipe on linseed oil had spontaneously combusted and sparked the grain-elevator explosion, setting off a chain reaction. The investigation yielded any number of suggested laws to help prevent such a catastrophe from occurring again—specifically, new regulations to better vent grain elevators and safety standards for the disposal of oily rags, but no guilty culprits.

The Greater Ohio Casualty and Life Insurance Company paid all the insurance claims and used this fact as a promotional piece in their advertisements. "Our Policies are Guaranteed, Just Ask the People of Lautenburg." This advertisement only ran in the Ohio newspapers for one week and was quietly removed, deemed to be in bad taste.

Marlene Wolf Scabbe Slottower was now a very rich woman, having collected seven checks from Ohio Casualty, which she quickly converted to cash, all for the full value of the mill. For appearances, she maintained her small suite of rooms in the Washington Hotel and, for the time being, left her original bank accounts undisturbed. However, one year later and one week after Parquet Dunn committed suicide, Marlene closed her accounts in both banks.

She checked out of the Washington Hotel, gave Raymond Zwiedell and his staff generous gratuities, and left Lautenburg for good, all but disappearing into the ether.

Simon Graham was disheartened but not devastated as Marlene's favors had ceased to be something of which he partook.

The mill was never rebuilt and remained a scarred ruin until the Union Army took over the property in 1862.

Marlene Slottower maintained ownership of the house along the Scioto River. Eventually, the property was confiscated by the sheriff and sold for nonpayment of taxes.

Laurie Slottower perished in the explosion, but not so her sister, Lydia, who did not attend the event and now shared the house on the hill with Mercy, her all-but-inseparable companion.

The grim aftermath of what was chronicled above, needless to say, affected all the residence of Lautenburg, as well as the state of Ohio and beyond, but none more than Miles and Lorraine Haverstraw, who lived their lives in a near zombielike state, scarcely having the physical or mental strength to go on. Until they read that item in the local newspaper that an insurance agent in Columbus connected to the Lautenburg fire had committed suicide, which set in motion an eleven-year journey that has led to a high mountain crag and a place called the Crow's Nest. Where the question of whether or not a wounded Bertram Herzog would live through the night or die stretched out on a bloodstained worktable remained unanswered.

27

PRELUDE TO A SIEGE

The night had grown late, and with so many things in flux, Keith figured he could at least quiet one of his concerns—the threat that Herzog presented. Keith told Sarusha, "You and Walt go down and check on Herzog. Sage, you and Johnny go along. Let's move Mr. Herzog into the brig. Why take any chances with this bastard?"

"I'm going with 'em. I've got a few questions for Mr. Herzog." This was from Miles Haverstraw, who put the figure he was whittling down on the table and gave Lorraine a kiss on the top of her head.

Keith picked up a bottle of whiskey, held it to the light, saw it was still about a third full, and handed it to Sarusha. "Here, give this to Flint. I'm sure he'll appreciate it."

The stable was dark save for a single lantern outside the tack room door. Just beyond the reach of its light was the figure of Tubby Flint asleep in a chair. Sarusha gently bonked Flint on the side of the head with the whiskey bottle to wake him and asked, "Any sound out of there? Hell, how would you know?"

Before Sarusha went to unlock the door, Walt Tallhelm drew his revolver and stood ready in case Herzog was awake and looked to make trouble. Herzog was lying on the table, just the way Keith had left him. Miles came into the tack room and stood over him and cursed under his breath, "Murderer."

Then he fairly barked out, "Wake him up. I've got a few questions I've been waiting to ask this bastard." Before what happened twelve years ago, Miles Haverstraw hadn't used any language more profane than maybe "darn it." That was no longer the case.

"Okay, we'll wake him," said Sarusha, who gave Herzog a good shake. "Wake up, you! Wake up!"

Herzog opened his eyes then closed them again. "Water."

Walt turned to Everett, who was standing in the doorway. "Everett, get some water."

"You don't get any water till you tell me where's Marlene," said Miles.

"Who?"

"Who, hell! Marlene Slottower, or whatever the hell she's calling herself now. Marlene!" an all-but-seething Miles shouted.

Herzog closed his eyes and lay still for a minute. "Water," he said.

Walt Tallhelm had heard about enough and pressed the handle of one of his hatchets hard onto the bandage covering one of the bullet holes.

Herzog gave a yelp and growled, "I don't know, I don't know. I ain't seen her since New Orleans."

"When was that?" pressed Miles.

"A few years back. I don't know where she is. Please, some water."

Herzog most likely had never used the word *please* before in his entire life, because he seemed to almost choke on it. Or maybe that was because of his condition. In any event, Sarusha gave him some water. Herzog then closed his eyes and made a gesture of shooing everyone out of the room.

"Not so fast. You're being moved to the hospital wing for the criminally insane," said Walt Tallhelm sarcastically.

Herzog convulsed and screamed as Sage, Johnny, Walt, and Sarusha lifted him off the table and carried him down to the brig. A normal occupant of the brig would be afforded a lantern or at least a whale-oil lamp. But considering the type of person Herzog was, those items were removed. The men laid him on the bunk and closed and locked the door, leaving Herzog in total darkness with only his thoughts to light his world. Given the dark nature of his mind, that world was destined to remain in darkness.

Sarusha gave his report to Keith.

Miles sat down next to Lorraine and told her what Herzog had said about Marlene and New Orleans. The two went over their mental notes about when they were in that city and tried to see if they had maybe missed an opportunity. Nothing concrete came to mind, and the two sat silently, looking into space and thinking.

Nate wanted, more than anything, for Lorraine to have a life where there was hope and joy instead of painful memories and apprehension. But that couldn't happen until this business with Pealeday was over and done with.

Jonathan Keith, like everyone else, had the same thing on his mind. What lay ahead, and when will it be over?

"Let's call it a night, men. Early tomorrow, and I mean early, I want you three to get up into the woods off the cut like we had talked about."

Sarusha, Walt, and Trader nodded their understanding.

"Johnny, I'll have Sage and Bill give you and Fritz a ride out to the rope ladders. I've been thinking Pealeday might figure we'd have someone up in there, so I want you Johnson brothers to join Johnny and Fritz. You two look to cover their backs. You'll have the Spencers, and there's plenty of food and bedding for the four of ya. You boys able to do that?"

"Reckon so. Y'all saved our bacon. We owe ya," said Ray as his brother, Lee, nodded.

"One thing. Me and Lee is gonna need some kinda warm coats. What we had we lost when we hightailed it out that camp," said Ray Johnson.

"We'll take care of that for you boys. You may have to wear some dead men's clothes. They won't need them, that's for sure." Sunny looked the brothers over and said, "Ray, I know Liecaster's coat should fit one of you boys. Aldo Severman's, his might be a bit tight, but hell, forget that. You can have one of mine."

"They can have Conrad's schweren Wintermantel. It's very warm," Fritz Langer said, nodding. The distant gaze on his face made the men think he must have been picturing his dead friend Conrad and the way he would have looked wearing the beautiful black wool

Wintermantel with its mink collar. It would appear Fritz was slowly coming to grips with his friend's death. Being able to part with this coat attested to that.

"Okay, where was I?" said Keith. "Right, you boys can ride out there. Sage and Bill can bring the horses back. Once you're up there, make sure you haul up those ladders and the pull vines.

"Now here's the tricky part. Nate, or should I say Tarlton?" This question put a small smile on Keith's face as it did the others, but not so much as to make Diving Hawk and Drum take umbrage.

"Nate, I'd like for you and your friends here to ride to the far end of the flat and scout that trail. If you see anyone before they see you and it looks like they're going to come out into the open and across the flat, you got a choice. Either hightail it and hope they give chase, letting you lead them right in between the crossfire we got set up. Or you could stay undercover, and once they're far enough down the flat, get in behind them and then we'd be getting at 'em from three sides.

"Or if they stay on that trail and loop around to the cut, get back here and we'll look to greet them with a few pineapples when they come down the cut. Got it?"

"That's a lot of ifs, but I follow what you're saying. I believe we can do that. Doesn't that leave you a little shorthanded in here?" asked Nate.

"Don't worry about us. I got Brow, Bill, Sage, and Lucien. Thaedell will be in the gatehouse, and don't forget Evie, Ronnie, and Lorraine. Also, Lucien's boys can shoot if need be, and what about me and Sunny? We're not too old and blind yet, are we, Sunny?"

Keith interjected this, knowing a bit of levity always went a long way to ease tensions. After all, what Keith was proposing was fraught with danger for all involved. "This ain't going to be no picnic. That's for sure. But we'll be all right. I know Pealeday can be pretty cagey. What we got going for us is he's desperate. Desperate men make mistakes.

"Evie, if you and the ladies could have breakfast ready by six. On second thought, make that five. I want these three in that woods before daybreak. That would be appreciated."

"We can do that, Cap. Don't want these boys heading out with growling bellies."

"Cap, if Diving Hawk and Drum are going to be making a run for it with Nate, maybe they should be riding the Appaloosas," suggested Walt.

"What do you think, Nate?" asked Keith.

Nate told the Indians the idea. They talked between themselves and agreed. Their horses were good enough, but not half as good as the Appaloosas.

Walt said something to the Indians in Nez, and the two of them laughed.

"Okay, what'd he just say?" asked Johnny Dollars.

"Walt told them that the Nez chief gave him those horses, and if anything happened to them, his daughter would have his hide," answered Nate as he gave Sarusha a wink. Walt had really said something much more risqué, but Nate thought to censor that part.

"Oh," said Johnny.

"So there you have it. We don't know when Pealeday is coming, but it's going to be soon. If anyone comes up with any good ideas between now and morning, let me know."

After everyone left the bar, Keith sat down with Sunny, Lucien, and Sarusha and tried to figure out the finer points of their strategy.

Lucien was the first to speak. "Cap, I got an idea. We got all those horses of Chance Parker and them. Why not put them out on the flat around what looks like a camp? Sarusha here and Walt could build a fire, put around some cook stuff. Make it look like Parker's boys are up in the woods or farther down the flat and they's just keeping their horses out of rifle range of the Nest."

No one said anything as they digested this idea.

"This might work. Instead of Sage and Bill taking Fritz, Johnny, and the Johnson brothers out to where they're going, they could ride four of those horses. And you, Walt, and Trader could ride three more. You aren't going to need horses up in those woods. Anyway, you couldn't ride through those woods if you wanted to."

"I see what you're saying. Also, when you think about it, if we got to spend a night or two down in the redoubt, we wouldn't want horses anywhere up top," said Sarusha.

"At some point, we're gonna want to get you and them boys back to the Nest. Just how or when that happens is hard to say. I like this idea, though. Then it's settled. That's our plan. Hell, all this may go right up the flue. But for now, it's what we got."

"Cap, I was talking to Nate and Walt earlier," Sarusha said. "And they were wondering what we should do if we get the drop on 'em. From what Ray and Lee Johnson said, most are ex-soldiers looking for work. Gotta figure the ones riding with Pealeday are the same. Maybe one or two are his diehard Canadians, but most are likely hired guns. What I'm getting at is I don't know about shooting them in cold blood. Should we kill them if we got them dead to rights?" As he spoke, Sarusha rubbed his palms and shook his head slowly side to side.

"I hear what you're saying. If you can get their guns and get 'em good and hogtied, okay. I don't see why we couldn't let 'em live. But no long shots. Some of them may act like they're giving up, but they're just looking for you to drop your guard. Ah, hell, just keep ya wits about ya." It was obvious that Keith was gravely concerned about what was going to take place in the next few days.

Lucien, Sunny, and Sarusha could see this and took the unprecedented move of gathering close to their captain and jostling him.

Then Sunny said, "Hell, don't worry, Cap. We didn't get this far by being careless."

Lucien poured each man a shot of whiskey.

"Men, this is a storm we can't sail around. But one we have to weather. And when we do, may there be a fair wind to see us safely back to port," said Captain Jonathan Keith.

"Aye, aye, Cap. Aye, aye." The men clinked glasses and downed the spirits.

The hour had grown late, but the denizens of the Nest were restless. Keith, on his way up to his quarters, could hear talk coming from Trader and Veronica's room. He saw Walt, Brow, and someone he figured was Bill Diehl out on the back landing having a smoke.

He saw Lorraine sitting on the staircase from the top floor to the third, talking to Nate.

When he got to his quarters, Keith went out back to the top landing and down a flight and joined Walt, Brow, and Bill Diehl. "Looks like you three can't sleep either. What do you say you roll me a smoke, Brow?" Jonathan Keith rarely used tobacco, but he did tonight. "What do you think? We forgetting anything?"

"That's hard to say, Cap. I tell ya one thing. This kind of business was a lot easier to eyeball when we was younger," said Bill Diehl.

"Yeah, when you're young, you think you gonna live forever," mused Brow Herman.

The men stood next to each other, peering into the darkness and thinking about bygone days in their youth. Back then they had wondered as night approached, what unknown adventure awaited them. Maybe it'd be some new gal with fluttering eyelids or some fistfight that could be avoided but wasn't.

Brow Herman started to say something, but Walt stopped him. "Shhhh, put out them smokes. Look at the cut. Is something moving over there?"

Sure enough, there was. A cloud-covered new moon made the night nearly as dark as pitch. But even so, the men could to make out shrouded silhouettes slowly coming down the cut toward the flat.

"Brow, get your rifles, and you and Sage get up to the top parapet. No lights, no lanterns. Walt, go and get your brother and Trader and meet me in the bar. I'll get Sarusha and Lucien. Bill, you go up a flight, and keep watching the cut. See what you can make out. Try to get an idea how many are out there."

It wasn't ten minutes till most everyone was right back in the bar, except for the Brow and Sage up top on the parapet. The bar was cloaked in darkness, as was the whole of the Nest.

Keith had to forget about having Fritz, Johnny, and the Johnson brothers up on the promontory. No way they could get up there now. He shook his head as he begrudgingly scrapped his well-laid plans and instead relied on what he called the "fluid theory"—developed during his seafaring days—to decide how to proceed.

"Lahr, I want you, Johnny, and the Johnson Brothers out in the gatehouse. Those two windows facing the switchback, I want two men in each of those. Take four of the Spencers and a half dozen boxes of shells. Sarusha, you see that happens. Be quiet doin' it. No bells. And tell Ghosty no lights. Then get back here.

"Nate, go down to the stables and get your friends up here. Tell them to be quiet." Keith hardly had to say this. Since Diving Hawk and Drum arrived at the Nest, there had hardly been a word out of them. "Nate, on the way back, you better stop at your room and get some warm clothes and gloves. I'm gonna want you up in that pine tree before first light. Okay, get going."

Keith was giving out these orders like he was standing on the aft deck of the *Celine*, readying for a battle at sea. The natural familiarity of it gave him a certain measure of calm. And that calmness was passed onto those receiving the orders.

"Lucien, you and Sunny get this cannon out here ready to go. Get a blanket from Evie and cover it. I know it's pretty dark, but just the same. No need that barrel catching a glint.

"Evie, make some coffee and we'll see about getting some kind of grub to them up top before first light. Once this starts, I doubt there'll be much time for eating. Another thing, Evie. Have Everett lock the dogs in my room. I don't expect they'll like all the gunfire."

"You got it, Cap."

Twenty minutes later, Nate was back in the bar with Diving Hawk and Drum. They stood quietly next to Sarusha, just back from the gatehouse, awaiting instructions.

"Nate, I know there's already a rifle and some ammo up there, but if you need anything else, get Diving Hawk and Drum to help you get it up there. Before that, you three get all those horses back into the stable downstairs or the stable out back. If you run out of room, tether them up in the woods. No need letting Pealeday know Chance Parker and them aren't going to be joining the party. Get Ev and Ernie to help you with the horses. Then send them back up here.

"Once that's done, show Diving Hawk and Drum where to position themselves at the back stables. Get them each a Spencer and plenty of shells. Make sure they can shoot from cover. Got it?"

"Got it, Captain."

By the time everyone was in place, except Nate and the Indians, it was 4:00 a.m. First light was not quite two hours off. "If anyone can catch forty winks before dawn, I suggest you do it. Once this starts, there'll be no time for sleeping."

"Where ya want me, Cap?" asked Walt Tallhelm.

"Walt, I figure you can be up top with Sage and Brow. You can use my Henry if you want, along with your rifle. Make sure you can sight in where we put those pineapples."

"Sounds good to me. Why don't I grab a pot of coffee and some grub and bring it up to them?"

"No, you just work on getting your guns and ammo together. I'll have Fritz here bring up the coffee and grub. Fritz, you see Evie about that, okay?"

Nate took Lorraine aside and said, "Looks like we got about a half hour before I head out back. Let's sit over here." Lorraine and Nate sat close to each other, not saying a word. They didn't have to. Words would only lessen what was passing between them. The language of love didn't need words. Nate and Lorraine sat silently, savoring each precious second, joined by the absence of all else save the shared truth that little mattered but they be together.

Lorraine couldn't pinpoint the exact moment in the last day when the most important thing in her life went from seeing a dead Bertram Herzog to having an alive and healthy Nathan Tallhelm. Yet there it was. Well, after all, Herzog was now locked up in the brig. And although Marlene Scabbe was still on the loose, a page had been turned. Now Lorraine prayed to God that she and Nate would survive whatever this man Pealeday had in store.

After too short a time Nate said, "It's time I got going." He said this as they slid out of the booth and held one another in an embrace and shared a kiss that plumbed the depth of their souls and extracted every ounce of love that had been lying there, hidden, unsought, waiting for this moment.

Lorraine smiled at the two Indians who had come over and stood next to their friend Tarlton and fighting back tears. She said, "You take care, Nathan Tallhelm."

"Don't you worry. Nothing's gonna happen to me. Look, I got these two watching out for me."

Lorraine gave a small laugh and wiped a tear from her cheek. "Well, just the same. Be careful."

As the minutes ticked away, every pair of eyes on the parapet, in the gatehouse, the deck off the bar, the top balcony out back, and the perch atop the tallest pine strained to see what they were facing as the first gray line of dawn crept over the eastern horizon.

28

Laying Siege

Walt, Sage, and Brow Herman had the best vantage point to see what Pealeday had put in place in the dark of night, and they didn't like what they saw. As the silvery light of the predawn gave definition to what had been just dark shapes, the men began to make out an array of wooden bulwarks.

With every passing minute, these fortifications became more well-defined. They were simple but appeared to be well-constructed. Pealeday had instructed his men to lash together six-foot logs in two- and three-foot sections and moved them to the bare and wide open flat. In the night, these were cobbled together into so many makeshift "forts." Albeit small, these did, however, provide effective protection for Pealeday's men, from rifle fire at least.

Keith had Trader, whom he was using to coordinate the defenses of the Nest, join the men up top on the parapet. Keith told him to have the men, once their eyes adjusted to the dark, pay keen attention, and as soon as it got light enough to see a target, and not a second more, the four should signal one another and take their shot.

Keith doubted Pealeday's men would expect the Nest to be ready so early and may be carelessly exposed. They would wise up soon enough after that first volley, but from here on out, every casualty counted. Although they were in near darkness, it was gray enough in the predawn for Walt, Brow, Trader, and Sage to make out the dark shapes of men milling about.

When Walt gave the signal, they opened fire. Seven men were hit before the others dove for cover.

The Crow's Nest's eight-foot-high parapet ran the length of the western side of the building—here at the top floor, a length of just over a hundred feet. At various heights and spaced at five-foot intervals were T-shaped gun ports. Also, every so often, built into the wall were catwalks allowing the men to stand high enough to shoot over the wall. Walt and the others took their first shots while standing on these catwalks.

While the men on the parapet were fairly well protected from rifle fire, a cannon was a different story, and Pealeday had brought a cannon. Keith had cannon as well and he would need it. He had two of his three cannon up top at either end of the parapet. Keith joined Lucien and Sunny, and the three prepared to sight in on Pealeday's cannon position.

Lucien, thanks to his time aboard the *Celine*, knew what it took to work on a cannon crew. Sunny Martin was an experienced cannoneer, he more so than Lucien or Keith, due to an early stint in the Navy and later his work aboard an escort ship off the Spanish Coast. Sunny had ample experience when it came to coordinating all the steps it took to successfully (and safely) fire a cannon. Keith put him in charge. He was well up to the task. Possessing the uncanny ability to confidently sight in a "felt" aim and regularly hit his target, Sunny Martin was the man for the job.

Keith wanted to knock out Pealeday's cannon and wanted to do it as soon as possible. But it wasn't soon enough, because as Sunny sighted in for his first volley, Pealeday's cannon delivered a ten-pound iron ball dead center into the parapet wall. Luckily for Keith and his men, no one was close to where the ball hit. A flying splinter of wood grazed the side of Sage Heck's face, but no damage done.

Wasting no time, Sunny lit his cannon, and the shell hit the enemy's cannon log surround, but it left Pealeday's cannon itself intact.

"What's that they got out there?" asked Keith.

"Looks to be a Napoleon twelve-pounder, Cap," answered Sunny.

"How the hell did he get that up here? He must have a wagon hidden somewhere," wondered Keith.

"He's damn cocksure of himself, isn't he? He ain't but three hundred yards back off the chasm," Sunny hollered with a note of personal affront.

This last bit of information confirmed what Keith had suspected. Pealeday was taking chances he needn't have. He was desperate to deliver a quick knockout blow and had brought his cannon in too close.

The cannonball from Sunny's next volley must have passed Pealeday's in midflight, because no sooner had it exploded into Pealeday's position than another ball hit the Nest, this time missing the parapet wall but hitting somewhere lower down.

Pealeday had seen enough to let him know he had to move his cannon farther back. He thought, *Whoever is sighting in that cannon has got my range down to the foot.* Sunny's second shot had obliterated the log protection the cannoneers were using, and this gave Walt and the other marksmen open targets, which they took advantage of. Although they received cover fire from Pealeday's other men, it wasn't enough to thwart the rifle fire from Walt, Trader, Brow, and Sage.

Several more of Pealeday's men manning the cannon were fatally hit or, for some a worse fate, a slow and painful death, that was calibrated by the fading screams of their last hours.

This initial exchange of rifle and cannon fire had taken less than twenty minutes as dawn was just now breaking. It was light enough for Keith to finally see just what kind of an assault he was facing. Strung along the flat, from on up the cut to the top of the switchback, were nine small wooden forts, each wide enough to shield a half dozen men.

Evidently, between whatever money Herzog had and Pealeday's financial resources, they were able to hire about sixty men, maybe more. Keith didn't know if there were men being held in reserve in the woods off the cut or not. He figured most likely not, thinking Pealeday would come at him with all he had straight off.

While Pealeday was moving his cannon back, the rest of his men opened fire on the Nest. Keith knew they would be aiming at the T-shaped shooting ports, so Keith's men had strict orders to stay clear of those and well behind cover. The hole Pealeday's cannon had put in the parapet was high enough that the men could safely go back and forth if they just crouched a bit. In any event, no one behind the parapet was going to unnecessarily expose themselves to rifle fire. Their best chance of hitting any of Pealeday's men came in the chaotic aftermath of one of Sunny's cannon blasts. Other than that, Walt and the others stayed safely out of sight.

In the gatehouse, Lahr, Johnny, and the Johnson brothers had yet to throw open the wooden shutters on the windows. Their instructions were to use the peepholes to keep an eye on the switchback and, if someone tried to come down it, open fire. Until then, they were to sit tight.

Keith had to decide just when he wanted Nate to start in on the pineapples. Nate could do some damage by exploding the one at the foot of the cut closest to the flat. There were men in one of the forts right there. But he wasn't quite ready to do that. He was hoping to save them until Pealeday's men were in some sort of retreat mode and would seek "safety" by going back up the cut. He'd hold off on that. Also, he didn't want to alert Pealeday's men to Nate's position. Not just yet, anyway.

Sunny's cannon fire had been effective so far, so why not keep it up? Keith had a mind to drive them back on the flat or force them up into the cut. Either way, he instructed Sunny to use the cannon on the southern end of the parapet to sight in on one of the two forts closest to the switchback.

Once sighted in and before he lit it off, Sunny checked to make sure Walt and the others were ready to pick off any of the sorry bastards once they scattered. Getting the nod from Walt, Sunny lit off the cannon. Boom, direct hit. Just as anticipated, four men ran from the shattered fort, only to be added to the list of casualties quickly depleting Pealeday's forces.

This combination of Sunny's cannon and the rifle fire from the men was replayed several times throughout the morning. With every cannon blast, stifling clouds of smoke enveloped the parapet, swirled about momentarily, and then were blown by cold winter breezes over the top of the Nest and off to the east.

Sunny paid keen attention to this, as it helped him gauge the wind, one more element that allowed for his repeated accuracy.

As Keith refigured his options and strategy, moment by moment, he all of a sudden was struck with something he hadn't thought of—the safety of Lucien's six cows out back. They were out in the open and easy targets. He feared Pealeday may become frustrated and just get spiteful, because nothing else he was doing was working. Keith didn't want to take that chance. He wanted to get the cows into the woods and out of harm's way.

"Lucien, I'm gonna have Sage take over for you on the cannon. I want you to get your cows up and into the woods. Go get Sarusha. He's on the deck off the bar. You and him get ready at the back.

When you hear Sunny's next blast, make for the outdoor stables. The Indians are there. Get them to help ya. Once you're there, we'll do the same thing again with the cannon. I hope you can be quick about getting them up in them woods."

"Don't worry, Cap. I got 'em trained," said Lucien with a smile.

Fortunately, getting the cows safely into the woods went like clockwork.

When Sunny's cannon shot shattered another fort, Walt, Brow, and Trader did their part keeping Pealeday's men pinned down while Lucien, Sarusha, and the Indians herded the cows to the safety of the woods.

It would appear that whatever moral ambiguity Brow Herman had about shooting someone evaporated once those across the chasm opened up on the Nest.

Keith thought, *This is going too easy*. Just then, that changed. The parapet took a direct hit from Pealeday's new cannon position, and both Sage Heck and Brow Herman were hit. Nothing fatal, but Brow was bleeding something fierce from a wound to his head caused by flying timbers. Sage got hit somewhere around his shoulder or arm, because it was hanging limply at his side, covered in blood.

"Trader, you and Walt get 'em down to Evie and the girls. I'll be down as soon as I can," directed Keith. He then went to the rear balcony and hollered down to Lucien and Sarusha, "Get the Injuns, and when I give the signal, you all get back inside and up here."

Keith wasn't thrilled about their having to be out in the open when they made their dash back to the Nest. And he said to himself, "The hell with it." This whole time, Nate had been patiently waiting for the sign from Keith to start in on the pineapples. Keith didn't want Nate to give away his position until it was absolutely necessary. His perch atop that pine was the best vantage point from which to see where all the pineapples were hidden in the bank of the cut.

Well, no sense waiting any longer, Keith thought, giving Nate the signal to shoot the pineapple closest to the flat. It exploded immediately, sending grapeshot and gravel in a deadly spray that took anyone in its path to their grave. The explosion was more effective than Keith had expected. It caught all of Pealeday's men by surprise, and you could only imagine their confusion as they had no idea where it came from or just what exploded. They all knew one thing, though. They didn't want to be anywhere near another one when it went off.

Meanwhile, Lucien, Sarusha, Diving Hawk, and Drum made it safely back to the stables and then up the back stairs.

"Brow and Sage been hit. Lucien, you go back to working with Sunny. Bill, I'm going to have Nate's friends take over for you back here. You go out front on the parapet. Whatever you do, stay clear of that hole, and be quick around those gun ports. Don't bother trying to shoot anyone till Sunny lets go with the cannon.

"Sarusha, before you go out front, tell these two to stay tight to this wall and fire at anyone they see on the cut. Maybe Nate's position is still a secret, maybe not. In any event, this is where I want 'em."

In a flurry of Nez, Sarusha explained to Diving Hark and Drum what they were supposed to do and that Tarlton's life depended on their doing it right. The pair, as solemn as cardinals at a coronation, looked over to Nate hidden on his perch, gripped their Spencer rifles tight, and shook them, defiantly looking toward the cut and then at Sarusha to let him know they knew their job was to give cover for Tarlton and that they would do it unfailingly.

Sarusha got back out to the parapet just as Keith was asking Sunny, "You got that range yet?"

"I think I do. Cap, I gotta tell ya, that barrel of water is good to swab out the cannon, but I could sure use some water I could drink."

"Soon as we get this shot off. I'll get some up here for you, everybody…how far out there is he?"

"Well, it's least twice as far as he was, I know that. I ain't making excuses, but he's got a much bigger target than I do," Sunny said as he wiped gunpowder soot and sweat off his face.

"Just do the best you can," answered Keith, knowing Sunny would always do that, regardless.

His next volley was short of its mark but kicked up enough dirt that Pealeday and his men at least got a face full of dust and gravel. Sunny cursed himself as he and Lucien adjusted the arc for another ten feet of range and methodically went about swapping out the barrel and reloading the cannon. Keith said, "I'll be back with some water."

"A little grub too," hollered Bill Diehl.

Keith didn't realize it, but it was well past two in the afternoon. He thought, *Hell, no wonder they're thirsty.*

Once Keith was back down in the kitchen, his orders came quick and smooth.

"Everett, get these jugs of water up to the back hallway. Ernie, you take these biscuits and that soup. Don't you two go outside. Just leave it all in the hallway. I'll take it from there.

"Evie, you and the gals are godsent."

Keith looked about and was struck by the grit of these women, especially Evie. He wanted to say something, but what could he say? The two looked each other in the eye, and while their deep friendship and allegiance to one another mingled with the moment, they smiled then winked at one another.

Brow Herman was sitting in one of the booths with his head wrapped in a blood-soaked towel. "How you doing?" asked Keith.

"I'll be okay, Cap. Hurts like hell. Looks like Sage got the worst of it," Brow Herman said as Lorraine took off one towel and put on a fresh one. Keith got a look at the wound and saw it was a nasty gash, but coulda been a lot worse.

"Want some whiskey?"

"I don't know. Yeah, I'll have some whiskey." Brow closed his eyes, and Keith thought he was going to pass out. But his head jerked back up and he said, "Yeah, better get me some whiskey."

"I'll get it," said Lorraine, who was making her way back to the kitchen after tossing the bloody towel into a corner on top of a few others.

"Thanks, Lorraine," said Keith. "How bad is it, Evie?"

Evie, who had followed Keith out of the kitchen with her sewing kit, was hard-pressed to answer that question. "I can't rightly say. He'll be all right, but I don't know how good this arm will be. Hard to say."

"Should I stay here and do some stitching?"

"Well, that would help. I got the bleeding under control. Yeah, he could use some stitches."

"Okay, let me clean up and I'll get to it."

"You get back upstairs, Mr. Keith. I've done a fair bit of doctoring myself. It was on animals, but flesh is flesh," Miles Haverstraw said as he rolled up his sleeves and poured some hot water over his hands and into a wash pan.

"You sure?"

"I'm sure," answered Miles, who had been strangely detached ever since his confrontation with Herzog down in the tack room the night before.

"Well, if you're sure, I best get back upstairs." With that, Keith gave Miles Haverstraw a pat on the back, nodded to Evie, grabbed two bottles of whiskey and a jug of water, and headed back upstairs.

When Keith got to the parapet, it was just in time to see Lucien and Sunny congratulating themselves on something. He assumed, and rightly so, that they had disabled Pealeday's cannon.

Sunny handed Keith the binoculars and defiantly crowed, "That should quiet that son of a bitch for a while."

Keith could make out the twelve-pounder, lying on the ground, its mounting carriage in splinters and two dead men lying off to the side. He couldn't tell if one of them was Pealeday or not. "Good work. Why don't you two go down to the kitchen, get some grub, clean up, get a little rest. When you get back, let's have at the rest of these forts."

"How's Brow and Sage?" asked Sunny as he pulled the cannon back and closed the door in the parapet wall.

"That's hard to say just yet. Haverstraw's stitching up Sage's arm, and Brow's head's messed up some. We'll see. Could be worse."

"Always could be worse, Cap." This from Lucien as he and Sunny began to duck and dodge their way back along the parapet to the rear of the building giving Walt Tallhelm, Bill Diehl, Sarusha, and Trader Darcy each a pat on the back as they went.

"I got you boys some hot soup and biscuits in the hallway out back. Water and whiskey too," announced Keith.

"Did I hear whiskey?" Bill Diehl asked.

327

The four men still on the parapet remained poised and ready to shoot anyone who made themselves a target. But none of Pealeday's men were moving out from behind their protection.

"Hey, Walt, looks like they ain't quite as froggy as they was, do they?" said Trader.

"I don't know what Pealeday is paying them boys, but I'd say about now they're thinking it ain't near enough!" Walt hollered back down the line to his cousin Trader.

"Why don't you boys take turns getting some grub? I'll take your spot till you get back," Keith said as he stood in the middle of the parapet next to the hole blown in it by Pealeday's first volley.

The men just looked at each other, but no one moved from their position. Keith saw this and said, "Okay, Walt, you and Trader go first."

"What you gonna do with that?" asked Walt as he passed by Keith, who had stopped and grabbed his Henry rifle from his quarters on the way back out to the parapet.

"I'm gonna see if I can get a bead on Pealeday. When he's done, this whole damn thing will be done."

"Good luck, Cap."

The sun, its path across the sky now favoring the south, began casting slanting shadows across the flat. The flat next to the promontory was already dark and getting darker. Keith figured Pealeday's men, still hunkered down behind their protection, would be thinking about getting back to whatever kind of camp they had for some food and sleep. After all, for them this day began yesterday as they made their way in the middle of the night down the cut and out to their positions on the flat.

Keith cursed himself for not having someone on watch up top here at night. He wondered if maybe he was slipping some. As he had this internal conversation with himself, in his defense he noted that a hell of a lot had gone on in the last two days. Also, really, what could he have done differently? Sarusha and the others weren't ready to take up their positions in the woods or up on the promontory till just this morning. In any event, that was water under the bridge.

He ended these musings as he resolutely stepped up onto one of the catwalks and, with his Henry .44, sighted in on Pealeday's disabled cannon position. At six hundred yards, Pealeday was well within range of the Henry. Keith patiently waited until Pealeday's men began to mill around the disabled cannon. The lull in rifle and cannon fire from the Nest gave those repairing the cannon mount a false sense of safety.

Walt and Trader returned to the wall and, seeing what Keith was up to, said, "Looking to do a little sniping. Wait for us."

Trader sighted in with the Sharp's carbine he had given his father after the war and that Nate had brought along from home. "You say the word, Cap."

"Walt, you take the left side. I'll take the right. Trader, you get ready to brush back anyone who gets a notion to come out from behind their cover. Let's wait till we see more activity."

After waiting not all that long, they could see a half dozen men working around Pealeday's cannon position, coming in and out of cover.

"Hey, don't start without us," said Sarusha as he and Bill Diehl came around from out back, a half-eaten biscuit hanging out of Diehl's mouth.

"Okay, get up here. Walt, me, and Trader are in on the cannon. You two pick a fort. Be ready to duck. After we fire, they'll most likely open up on us. Be ready for that."

Keith didn't have to tell these men that at dusk, a muzzle flash was as good as a beacon.

Walt looked over to Keith and Trader. When Keith nodded, the three opened fire. Quick as you could scratch an itch, four men lay dead either side of the cannon and two wounded. Out from behind two of the forts, three men fired on the parapet. They each got off one round before Sarusha and Bill Diehl shot two dead and wounded another.

Getting down from the catwalks, the men sat down with their backs against the parapet wall. This was a safe place to be as long as that cannon was out of commission.

"Bill, go get that whiskey."

"You got it, Cap," answered Diehl, not having to be asked twice.

For Pealeday's men, the day had not gone the way they'd hoped. Whatever enticement Herzog and Pealeday had used, other than raw cash, it was obvious that that payoff wouldn't come easy. Some took the carnage in stride. For others, it was viewed cynically as just another broken promise to be added to the heap of betrayal they had come to know so well.

At this point, most would just be happy to cut their losses and get back to Lewiston or the Settlement with their hides intact.

Trader Darcy broached a subject that had begun to gnaw at Keith as the bodies of the dead and wounded began to cast flat shadows as the late afternoon sun began to set. "What about their wounded, Cap?"

Trader Darcy was the only one of the men on the parapet who had seen the bloody horror of war firsthand. What conventions of war applied here was an open question, which Keith alone could answer.

"I know, son, I know," answered Keith, who shook his head and grimaced.

"This day is not done yet. Pealeday started this, but by God we're going to finish it," Keith said angrily as his compassion for the dead and wounded lying out on the flat vied with his solemn oath to see that no more of his men got wounded, or worse yet, killed. "We'll have to let Pealeday worry about those men. Right now, I'm figuring on adding a few more to that count. The hell with it.

"I'm wanting Sunny to take out two more of those damn little forts, and God help those bastards who can't find cover." Anger was anathema to Keith's internal makeup, but right now it would appear he was barely able to hold it in check.

When Sunny and Lucien got back up to the parapet, Keith told them to get both cannons zeroed in on two of the remaining forts, and he wanted them to be fired at the same time. While Sunny and Lucien got the cannon primed and sighted, Walt and the others stood ready.

"Don't do anything till I give you the word," Keith said as he made his way out to the back balcony to give Nate the signal to be ready to hit a few pineapples if and when Pealeday's men made a break for the cut.

Keith wasn't overtly Christian but nevertheless made the sign of the cross as he signaled Sunny and Lucien to get ready to light off their cannons.

Right at this very moment, all was quiet, peaceful. For a few fleeting seconds, the soft light from the setting sun bathed the whole of the flat and the Kettle of Tears in an otherworldly amber hue. In normal times, you would pause, stilled by this eerily beautiful light, but now was not that time.

Sunny gave Lucien the nod, and the deafening report from the two cannons quaked through the air, assaulting one granite wall and then the other as the blasts echoed off the deep chasm separating the Nest from the flat.

Again, Sunny's ability to sight in on a target was nearly perfect. Both forts were direct hits, and out of each scattered a half dozen men. The rapid-fire Spencers did their job, and all but two were hit. The others still hidden behind their protection saw this and made a mad dash for the woods up along the cut. Nate waited a minute, then shot out one of the pineapples, waited a minute for the smoke to clear, then shot another. In the aftermath, a dozen men lay dead or dying along the cut and the edge of the woods.

Diving Hawk and Drum took no mercy on those who staggered about. They were sent along with their comrades to wait on the bench for a verdict from Saint Peter.

Keith wondered if Pealeday was even still alive, as he hadn't been able to find him with his binoculars. And if he was alive, would he be calling it quits? One thing Keith was pretty sure of was that there would be no more out of him or his men today.

The sun had set, and the early winter night would only get colder. Pealeday's men could be seen making a few bonfires off in the distance.

"Men, we gotta keep one man up here on watch. Bill, you take the first shift. I'll send your relief up in an hour," Keith instructed as he helped Sunny and Lucien swab out the cannon barrels and retire them for the night.

Before leaving from up top, Keith went around back and signaled Nate to come on down. Keith had learned enough Nez from Sarusha to tell Diving Hawk and Drum, "Good job," and to come with him down to the bar.

Returning downstairs, Keith told Sarusha to go get the men back from the gatehouse. They hadn't been needed, and that was just fine with Keith. He was going to have someone keep an eye on the switchback from the deck off the bar. Plus the trip wires were still in place. Those two precautions should be enough to alert him if Pealeday was going to try something in the night. Keith doubted this, but who the hell knows.

"Walt, I Imagine Nate is pretty cold and stiff by now. Let's hope his legs still work. Don't want him falling out of the tree now, do we?" said Keith.

"Yeah, that'd make a hell of an epitaph: Here lies Nathan Tallhelm. He fell out of a tree."

The men were a bit lightheaded with the combination of no sleep and the relief of how well things had gone—other than what happened to Sage and Brow—on what they hoped was the first and last day of Pealeday's siege.

The first thing the men did who came down from up top was check on Sage and Brow. Sage was asleep thanks to a heavy dose of laudanum. Miles Haverstraw said what he did went well, but the arm wouldn't be the same. He added that before he stitched it up, he washed it good with some pure moonshine so he didn't think it would get infected. Now it was a waiting game to see if gangrene developed.

Brow Herman was awake and more than half drunk what with the combination of laudanum he'd been taking and the whiskey he'd been drinking. His wound wasn't really all that bad; it's just that head wounds bleed so.

Lorraine had gone down to greet Nate as he hobbled into the back of the stables. He was glad to hold onto Lorraine as he climbed the stairs and on up into the bar, but he wasn't joyful. It was going to take some time to get the picture out of his mind of those men being blown to bits. But as he greeted the others, those visions began to fade.

All things considered, the first day of the siege had gone better than could have been expected. One thing, leastwise now, the waiting game was over. Did Pealeday still have any fight left in him? Or maybe, more to the point, could he rally his men to risk their lives in what to any sane man would appear to be a lost cause, snake eyes? These men were mercenaries whose stake in the outcome was different for each one. Did that work to Keith's advantage?

Obviously, for some of those men, at this point, death seemed to be the only option. Not easy to pull back from that comforting netherworld of resignation, where death seems the preordained way. Especially since to turn around and look back at the road traveled, only to see every bridge in flames or sanctuary in ruin. As night approached, these men would have to wrestle with that choice. Not an easy one to make as they listened to the agony of their dying comrades and the tepid bravado of the living to fight on.

The morning light would reveal what path Pealeday and his men had chosen.

29

THE SIEGE, DAY TWO

Thaedell Lahr and Johnny Dollars were nothing but a bunch of questions when they got back to the bar. Their first question was answered before they even asked it. Did anyone get hurt? Seeing the condition Brow Herman and Sage Heck were in took care of that one. "Heard a hell of a lot of cannon fire. Is Pealeday dead?" asked Johnny.

"Not that we know of. We drove them back some and disabled their cannon, leastwise till tomorrow," answered Sunny, who sat in a booth across from Lucien. Both men were opening their jaws and shaking their heads in an attempt to get the ringing in their ears to stop.

"You men hungry? There's soup, biscuits, and stewed apples," said Evie, whose regular serving schedule was put on hold till this thing was over. It was catch-as-catch-can when it came to eating.

"Thanks, Evie, but Perpetua fed us," answered Lahr.

"Who the hell is Perpetua?" asked Brow Herman as he blinked his eyes open and grimaced in pain.

"That's Ghosty's mom," answered Lee Johnson.

"I'll be damned. I've been here how long and never heard her name," said Brow with a strong measure of incredulity.

With real curiosity, Evie Samms asked, "What she feed you?"

"I don't know what you'd call it," said Ray.

"I don't know what to call it either. It was some kind of mish-mash that looked bad but tasted good," said Thaedell Lahr.

"Maybe it was cat stew," said Brow Herman, who started to laugh, but it hurt his head too much and he had to check himself.

"Okay, okay," said Keith. "You men tired?"

"No, Cap. We took turns catching some shuteye. We needed to since Perpetua wouldn't stop reading the Bible and doing it in a whisper, like Pealeday's men could hear us or something. I hate hearing people whisper. On top of that, it was the Bible," Lahr said in a way that left no doubt just how unnerving this experience was for him.

"Don't send me back out there tomorrow, Cap, please," begged Lahr.

Jonathan Keith gave no reply to this entreaty. Instead, he turned to the Johnson brothers and said, "I need someone to go up and relieve Bill on the parapet. Lee, why don't you and Ray go up, the two of ya. Ask Bill what you should do. I don't think there'll be any more shooting tonight, but just in case, stay in behind that wall and away from that big hole and those shooting ports. Someone will be up in an hour. Got it?"

"We got it, sir," answered Ray.

"Christ, I forgot about Herzog. Can someone come down with me while I check on him? Tell ya what, Everett, you and Ernie bring along some of that soup and a couple biscuits. A jug of water too," said Keith.

"Wait, I'll come with ya, Cap. Who knows what that bastard is liable to try. He's got to know Pealeday is here," Walt Tallhelm said as he gulped down his glass of whiskey and adjusted his gun belt.

Turning to Sarusha, Keith said, "I want to keep a lookout here on this deck. Can you take first watch?"

"Sure, Cap. Don't take any chances downstairs."

Keith just nodded and waited to hold the door open for the Samms boys and the two dogs before he and Walt left the bar.

When Bill Diehl came down from up top, he joined the rest of the crew in the booth where Brow had planted himself. Sage didn't have much to say, and the rest of the men tried to show a level of compassion that conveyed their concern without alarming their young friend. Sage's arm was messed up, no doubt about that.

Seeing Brow and Sage in this condition focused their resolve to where nothing mattered in their lives except one thing, seeing Pealeday in shackles or, better yet, dead.

Nate pulled a chair up in front of the stove, opened the door, propped his feet up, and was gazing into the fire when Lorraine brought him some coffee and sat down. "You okay, Nathan?"

"I'm okay. Just trying to warm up. How's Miles doing? I under-stand he's the one what stitched up Sage."

"I think Father is bit lost right now. We've been chasing Herzog so long and now that we got him, he's wondering what do we do now."

"What's Evie got to eat? Are you hungry?" asked Nate as he closed the stove door with his foot.

Nate was glad to have a few questions to ask Lorraine rather than answer hers. Because he really wasn't okay. Far from it. Aside from the fact that tomorrow might end up being worse than today, he was just exhausted. He was exhausted not only from the lack of sleep but also from the cold that had seeped into his body while standing on his perch, plus having listened to Lorraine's soul-drain-ing account of what happened in Lautenburg to all her kin and all their friends. And from the tenterhooks he'd been on until Trader and Veronica got back safely. He wanted it to be over. He wanted to have an unguarded emotion. To close his eyes and know when he opened them that the first thing on his mind would not be killing and death. No, he wasn't okay, but for now, for the sake of all that was dear to him, he had to put that aside and just get this business with Pealeday and Herzog over and done with.

"Soup, biscuits, and stewed apples. Let's go sit with Father." Lorraine could tell, in spite of what he said, that all was not well with Nate. But she was a strong woman, and if she had to lend support when needed, she could. Now seemed to be one of those times.

On his way over to the booth, Nate stopped to tell Diving Hawk and Drum, who were sitting by themselves at the round poker table, to get something to eat and some sleep. The pair nodded to Tarlton, and then both of them began to rattle off a bunch of something too quickly for Nate to follow. What they were saying was very important to them. He could tell that.

Nate went to the doors leading out to the deck and called Sarusha back in.

"I'll stand watch for you. Can you see what they're talking about?" Nate said as he cocked his head toward the two Indians.

Sarusha, Diving Hawk, and Drum had a back-and-forth exchange that went on for several minutes. Afterward, Sarusha stood silently for several moments, staring straight ahead, then went out to join Nate on the deck.

"What's up?"

"They said that before he died, Standing Eagle had told them of a dream he had that there would be another great battle at the Kettle of Tears. That many would die. And that our people again would stand in front of their teepees and watch the sun come up over Laughing God Mountain. They said they hadn't put much stock in the dream, but now they see it is coming true."

"In the dream, did Standing Eagle see death on both sides?" asked Nate.

"I asked them that very question, and they said yes." Sarusha and Nate stood looking off to the flat, wondering to themselves if that part of the dream was in fact true. Needless to say, this information added another element of concern to an already worrisome and dire situation.

"Should we keep this to ourselves?" asked Nate.

"I think so," answered Sarusha. "No need to put everyone more on edge."

"I doubt we could be more careful than we are already," said Nate.

"I am going to tell the Cap, though. Let him decide if he wants to tell anyone else. You go back in. I'll finish my watch, then see the Cap."

As Nate made his way to the booth to join Miles and Lorraine, he paused and nodded to Diving Hawk and Drum and touched the knife of Standing Eagle that Diving Hawk had given him. The two nodded back.

Jonathan Keith and Walt returned from checking on Herzog with little to report. They said he asked for a whale-oil lamp so he didn't have to eat in the dark. Walt said he told him to "pretend he was blind."

Other than that, Herzog hadn't said a word. Keith told him he'd have his bandages changed tomorrow. That was about it. Keith didn't let on, but the whole encounter, brief though it was, had left him with an unsettling feeling.

Keith suggested everyone should get some well-needed sleep. The morning would come sooner than anyone wanted, and everyone had to be ready. After an hour, the Johnson brothers were relieved by Fritz and Johnny. Keith had decided to have two men on watch up top, not trusting that a solitary watchman wouldn't fall asleep.

Before Nate and Walt took their turn on watch, Keith met with them, along with Sunny, Trader, and Lucien.

"Well, what do you think?" Keith asked, having no concrete thoughts other than tomorrow would be a lot like today.

"One thing, Cap," Sunny replied. "That twelve-pounder, if I was him, I'd move it back some. He'd have no trouble reaching us. But those cannon we got up top, I'd have a time getting our loads out to him. Now this Parrott out here, that's a different story. That'll reach, but we ain't got a whole lot of protection out on that deck."

"We could arc the ones up top and reach, I suppose. No one can say for sure. Cap?" ventured Lucien tentatively.

While the men were trying to anticipate what tomorrow would bring, Fritz Langer came down from up top and said, "Johnny and I can see some movement out there. We thought you should know."

"Thank you, Fritz. You go back up top. We'll be right along."

"Thaedell, could you spell Sarusha? Tell him to come up top as soon as he can."

"You got it, Cap."

Once everyone got back onto the parapet, it was clear there was movement on the flat. This wasn't unanticipated, since they figured Pealeday would try to remove the dead and wounded. But even in the dim light of an almost moonless night, it was apparent something else was going on.

It would appear Pealeday was leaving the dead men where they lay and dragging the log sections of the forts back to his new cannon position, maybe eight hundred yards off. There was a large campfire burning, and men could be seen silhouetted against the firelight.

"Here in your country, is there an agreement against shooting your enemy at night?" Fritz asked. Before anyone answered, he went on to say, "With Conrad's Chassepot, I could hit any of those men I see."

Keith and the others just looked at one another and wondered if they did in fact have any qualms about opening fire on Pealeday's men at night.

The rifle Fritz Langer was talking about was one of several the pair had brought with them from Austria. The Chassepot was a long-barreled rifle very popular with soldiers in the French and Prussian armies.

"Hell, if Fritz can hit those bastards out there, I reckon I can too," said Walt Tallhelm.

"I'm as good a shot as you," said Trader.

"What about me?" chimed in Nate.

As the men watched the activity around Pealeday's cannon position and the adjacent bonfire, they were all thinking the same thing. Why not?

"Fritz, you go and get Conrad's rifle. Trader, you go get your Sharps…and stop and get my Henry while you're at it," directed Keith.

Trader was passing by Sarusha as he made his way off the parapet.

"What's up?" he asked Trader.

"The Cap will tell ya."

"What's up, Cap?" asked Sarusha.

"It looks like Pealeday is leaving his dead lay and reinforcing his cannon position. Take a look out there."

Sarusha could clearly see what Keith was talking about.

"Lucien, hand me those binoculars." Keith was still trying to see if he could pick out Pealeday in among the others. No luck.

When Trader and Fritz got back to the parapet, the seven men took positions on the catwalks and let their eyes adjust to the darkness. Keith took the middle position and called out these orders.

"Okay, men, this is what we'll do. Walt, since you're on the far right, you take the man you see to the far right. Lucien you're far left, you take that man. Nate, you pick off the next one in and so on. We want to fire as close to the same time as possible. The bullets will get there before they hear 'em, so we got a little leeway. But once that first man falls, they'll be diving for cover. We get one shot. I'll give the signal."

Keith didn't know about the others, but he was pretty sure they didn't relish doing this, but then again the sooner this was over the better. Every one of Pealeday's men who got killed or wounded was one less man shooting at them.

"Everybody ready? Let's hear it down the line."

One after another, the men hollered, "Ready."

Keith counted off, "Five, four, three, two, one, *fire!*"

Around the bonfire, five men crumpled to the ground. Two more staggered about and then fell.

"Just to keep them on their toes, let's each put a round into that fire. Everyone ready? Let me hear it down the line."

Again each man hollered out, "Ready." Again Keith counted down, and when he shouted "*Fire!*" seven bullets sent chunks of burning wood and embers flying every which way.

"That's enough of that. Walt, Nate, it's your watch. The rest of you get some sleep. We probably stirred up a hornet's nest, but what the hell. It isn't like they were calling it quits. Nice shooting, men. Nice job, Fritz. Too bad Conrad wasn't still around. I imagine he was pretty good with that thing."

"Conrad was excellent at everything he did. He was the All-Regimental Schützenschnur."

Hearing this exchange, Nate thought, *Too bad Conrad was also excellent at shooting off his mouth. Otherwise, he just might be alive.*

"Walt, I'll have Sarusha send two men up in an hour. You and Nate need anything?" asked Keith.

"I reckon we're okay, Cap. Maybe you should get some sleep."

"That's just what I plan on doing." Thankfully, Keith didn't have far to go to his quarters, which were right on the other side of the wall he was using to steady himself. Two days without sleep were taking their toll on the old man. Lucien wasn't jumping around either as the two made their way off the parapet.

"One hell of a day, wasn't it, Cap?" said Lucien.

"I'll say. You get some rest now. Tell Evie thanks for all her help."

"Will do, Cap."

Sarusha coordinated the changing of watches, and the rest of the night passed without incident.

Though no further combat occurred, as the night wore on, the men on watch up top could see movement on the flat but couldn't tell exactly what they were seeing until later on, when the faintest light of the predawn made it shockingly apparent what the movement was. Wolf packs. Not just one pack but several.

The wolves had been gorging themselves on Pealeday's dead mercenaries. This was a particular horror of the confrontation no one had anticipated, leastwise not Keith or his men. Pealeday, however, might have thought this might happen, but likely dismissed it as all part of the bargain when the men hired on.

In any event, when Sarusha and Keith returned to the parapet just before dawn to take over for Thaedell Lahr and Bill Diehl, they cursed Pealeday. They cursed the whole damn mess he had instigated, which he started for no reason other than that he had painted himself into a corner.

With the dawn, the wolves began to leave the flat and return to the woods. Keith had seen wolf packs on the flat before, chasing hares and foxes, but not this many. The wind during the previous day had been out of the west, but in the evening it must have changed and blown from the south, sending the scent of blood into the woods next to the cut. Keith shook his head, wondering if now that the wolves had the taste of man's blood, it had become unsafe for the denizens of the Nest to hunt those woods.

As the sun came up, something else could be seen moving on the flat. Five packhorses in single file were making their way along the southern edge of the flat next to the promontory wall. They were heading for the top of the switchback.

"What do you think?" asked Sarusha.

"I'm not ready to start shooting horses just yet. Get Trader and Walt out to the deck. I want Johnny and the Johnson brothers back in the gatehouse. Lahr too. He'll survive. Get Nate and Lucien up here. Tell Diving Hawk and Drum to go back to their post around the corner here on the back balcony. I don't have to tell you to hurry."

Keith couldn't quite figure what Pealeday had in mind with the horses, but he knew it wasn't benign.

Sunny Martin was the first of Keith's men to get up top. "What do ya see, Cap?"

Keith pointed to the horses about a half mile out and handed Sunny his binoculars. "Well, unless I'm mistaken, those horses each got eight legs."

Sunny handed Keith back the binoculars and Keith looked for himself. "I'll be damned."

"I'll tell you this. I bet those packs are full of dynamite," said Sunny.

Keith had to agree.

"Now what the hell does he expect us to do? Just let him walk five horses loaded with dynamite down the switchback and up to the gatehouse?" asked Keith, mildly bewildered by the affront.

Keith and Sunny stood silently for a minute, trying to figure just how Pealeday figured this gambit was supposed to work. First thing, it was obvious Pealeday didn't know about the trip wires rigged to the two blunderbusses. When it hit one of those wires, the first horse in that line would most likely bolt off the trail, right into the chasm. Who the hell could anticipate what might happen? Maybe all the horses would panic and pull one another off the trail. Anyway you cut it, it spelled doom for the packhorses.

"Cap, I expect those boys hiding behind those horses would peel off somewheres about the top of the switchback, then shoot those packs when the beasts get down to the gatehouse."

"Well, damn, if that's the kind of game he wants to play, the hell with him," Keith cursed. He knew if the gatehouse got breached, it could quickly turn into a bloody melee, and he surely didn't want that. Keith went to the south end of the parapet and hollered down to the deck off the bar. "Hey, Walt, get up here quick and get Bill Diehl. Trader, you stay put and keep your eyes peeled. They're up to something."

"Sunny, me and the others will worry about these packhorses. You and Lucien see how close you can get to taking out his cannon. I know it's a ways, but hell, think of it as a challenge." Keith said this in an attempt to get Sunny to focus on just one thing and not worry about anything else.

When Walt and Bill arrived, Keith explained to them and to Nate just what he wanted to do. "Sunny and I figure those horses out there are loaded with dynamite. Now I'm not nuts about blowing up horses, but we can't have them getting down the switchback. Just like last night, I'll take the horse in front. Nate, you take the second one. Bill, you take one of the ones in the middle. And, Walt, you got the one on the end. Aim for the packs. You got that? Aim for the packs. Count off when ready."

"Ready, Cap. Ready. Ready."

"Five, four, three, two, one, *fire!*"

Sure enough, the horses were carrying dynamite. The one that wasn't hit with a bullet might as well have been, because the concussion from the others caused that horse's dynamite to explode as well.

The sound of the explosion bounced off the forty-foot promontory wall and then reached the eastern wall of the rim and echoed back again. Keith had never heard anything like it. He started to wonder just how many men Pealeday had hired. Because he knew for certain between yesterday, last night, and now, they had killed or wounded at least forty-some, maybe more.

Possibly Pealeday was figuring these men were expendable, because he was expecting to get reinforcements when Herzog and Chance Parker showed up. But that was not going to happen. Maybe if he knew that, he might not be so reckless. Again, this told Keith what he had suspected all along—Pealeday was desperate.

"Walt, you men stay here. Keep an eye on the cut. Make sure you look and remember where those pineapples are. If you're not sure, use the binoculars to find them. I'm going to get some coffee. I'll send some up for you men."

Keith found Lorraine and Veronica sitting with Brow Herman and Sage Heck in one of the booths. The women had taken it on themselves to give them some tender loving care, knowing that sometimes that's the best medicine. In that moment, Keith was doubly proud to know both these women.

He took a seat at the adjacent table, and Evie brought him over a cup of steaming coffee.

"Evie, I wanna send some coffee to the men up top. Can you…"

"Don't worry, Cap. Consider it done. Everett, you and your brother get a jug of coffee up to that top hallway. Don't you two go outside. Be careful."

"What in hell was that explosion?" asked Brow. "We went out, but all we saw was smoke."

"Bunch of horses loaded with dynamite. We blew 'em up. We blew 'em up along with the fools hiding behind 'em. How's *your* morning going?" Keith directed this piece of sardonic humor at himself in some way to acknowledge the level of inhumanity Pealeday had driven him to.

Unfortunately, everything going on was not *in*human but sadly all too human. The very reason he sought out his retreat—this Crow's Nest—in the first place was to escape that insanity, the widely held belief that for you to thrive, you must visit every type of degradation, subtle or overt, upon all others. Even to the point where nothing short of total death and destruction is all that will do.

Yet here it was. The Crow's Nest may very well prove to be unassailable by rifle fire and bomb blast, but his soul had already been vanquished by the battle joined. He sipped his coffee and watched Trader on the deck keeping watch. Trader had been at both Antietam and Gettysburg. What might his thoughts be on the wanton slaughter of men and those who embrace it?

Keith's dark musings were interrupted by a direct hit to the dining room wall, which gave the whole bar and kitchen a shudder. The walls of the Crow's Nest were doubly thick on the western side of the building. But were they thick enough to withstand continued cannon fire? That was the question—an unnerving one to say, the least.

Keith let his coffee sit and went out to the deck. "Trader," he said, "let's get this cannon ready. Maybe we can get lucky and knock out that bastard."

Keith and Trader heard one of Sunny's cannon let go and wondered how accurate it had been. They didn't have to wait for that answer as Lucien yelled down to the deck, "We got the range, just off on the angle!"

This was an encouraging report. But with Pealeday using all the log sections from the forts to reinforce his position, even a direct hit might not be enough to knock out the cannon. Time would tell.

"Cap, we're taking fire from the woods off the cut!" Bill Diehl yelled down to Keith.

"Keep away from that hole. I'll be up in a minute." Keith figured rifle fire from that angle had a good chance of getting through that hole and ricocheting off the wall of the Nest and hitting somebody. "Trader, as soon as I can, I'm gonna send Sunny down to help sight in this cannon. You just sit tight."

When Keith got up to the back balcony, Diving Hawk and Drum were already sending as much lead into the woods off the cut as they could. The parapet wall came all the way to the railing on the back balcony, so the men were using the very last gun port to shoot from. Still, the occasional bullet came whizzing through. Quickness, luck, and maybe the spirits of the ancient ones were keeping these two from being hit.

"Lucien, see if you can get enough angle on that cannon to hit the corner of those woods."

"Nate, how many pineapples we still got out there?"

"I figure we still got four. Two are up the cut a ways. I can get them from the tree. I can see the other two from here."

"Okay, maybe we can flush 'em out with this cannon and one of them pineapples. I want to save the other three. Sunny, let me know when you're ready. The rest of you, let's pepper the hell out of those woods."

Rifle fire from Walt, Nate, Bill Diehl, Sarusha, and Keith had lead whizzing about the woods like corn popping in a skillet. The barrage was so intense you could even see limbs dropping from trees.

"Cap, ready with this cannon!" yelled Lucien over the noise from the rifles.

"Nate, get ready on that pineapple. I'll give you the word. You men hold up, hold up, cease fire!" Keith had to holler this twice. It was so noisy. "Hold up. Now once Sunny…someone go tell the two of them to stop shooting." Diving Hawk and Drum were just out of earshot of Keith and probably couldn't understand what he was saying anyway.

"Okay, now once Sunny and Nate let go, you others be on the lookout for anyone that runs out of those woods. Got it?"

"We got it, Cap," Bill Diehl said, and the others nodded.

Sunny lit off the cannon, and Nate shot the pineapple, which did more damage than the cannonball. The explosion blew off the top edge of the bank, causing a tree to topple, exposing a half dozen men to the rifle fire from Walt and the others. Keith's men continued to send a barrage of bullets into the woods, gradually working their fire westward. It all seemed to work. Any of Pealeday's men still in there had to shoot from deep in the cover of the trees, making their effectiveness marginal at best.

Keith, Sunny, and Lucien sighted in and fired another round out toward Pealeday's cannon emplacement. It hit the log protection he had cobbled together and did some damage, but not enough to silence the gun. "Let's try our luck downstairs with the Parrott," said Keith.

The Parrott ten-pounder, although smaller than its twenty-pounder cousin, was still bigger than the deck cannon Keith had brought along from the *Celine*. The only reason the Parrott was at the Crow's Nest in the first place was to satisfy an old debt another sea captain owed Keith. Although Keith was willing to forget the debt, the captain wouldn't hear of it. So after an arduous trek, the captain and the cannon made their way to the Nest.

The friend, however, engaged in some upfront jiggery-pokery, compelling Keith to buy the shells, balls, and powder loads he would need to use the Parrott, which didn't really bother Keith. The captain ended up staying three months, of which most of that time was spent in friendly wrangling about one thing or another, which Keith enjoyed immensely.

The Parrott could heave a ten-pound ball more than a mile. The problem for Sunny was that down here on the deck, he didn't have a direct vantage point to Pealeday's cannon. Nevertheless, it was what they hoped would finally knock out the Napoleon once and for all.

Over the next four hours, Sunny, Lucien, and Keith alternated between shrapnel shell and round shot. Some were direct hits, which were noted by a lull in the bombardment coming from Pealeday's cannon. Still, by midafternoon, nothing had fundamentally changed. The Nest had been taking a good pummeling all morning and into the afternoon but was holding up well.

Keith knew that couldn't be the case for too much longer. He had Bill Diehl replace him on the cannon crew and went up top to meet with Walt, Trader, Nate, and Sarusha. They had remained on the parapet and were sniping at anyone who came out from the protection surrounding the cannon.

"Men, we can't have this go on too much longer. I've got a plan. I want you men to get to those woods off the cut and get to that damn cannon. It'd be too risky going up the switchback and across the flat. So, Sarusha, if you, Walt, Nate, and his Indian friends are up for it, I want you to climb down the back end of the Nest and back up to the cut, getting yourselves to the redoubt by dark. Tomorrow morning, get in behind their position and end this damn thing. I know it's risky. But I think it could work. From where they are, no one will be able to see you going down and coming back up. What do ya think?"

"What about me?" asked Trader.

"How's that leg of yours?"

"Don't worry about that, Cap. It's all but as good as new." Trader still had some pain in his leg but wanted to show the others and more so himself that he was back to full steam.

The men looked at each other for several moments without saying anything. Walt Tallhelm was the first to speak with a nod toward his brother and cousin. "I'll do it if you can promise me these two won't step on my head when we're climbing back up that wall."

"Step on your head? That'd be finally putting it to good use" was Trader's retort.

"Well, I'll take that as a yes from you two. Nate?"

"I'm in."

Keith knew Sarusha would do it simply because Keith had asked him. Now the question was Diving Hawk and Drum. "Nate, what about your friends?"

"Oh, I imagine they'd do it. I think they'd do almost any damn thing for Tarlton."

This comment elicited smiles all around.

"Okay, it's settled. You men are done up here. Go get some food and something to drink. Sarusha, tell Diving Hawk and Drum what's up. Everything you're gonna need is already in the redoubt. But bring whatever you feel comfortable carrying.

"Getting down won't be hard. There's a rope you can toss over that back end that will reach the bottom. There're ropes already in place that will get you about halfway back up to the cut. Someone's going to have to make that last half on their own and secure a rope for the others. I'll let you men decide who that's to be.

"I don't figure any of Pealeday's men will be anywheres close to that cut after earlier. Anyway, we'll be up here watching out. There are bows and plenty of arrows in the redoubt, so tomorrow morning you might think of getting as many as you can with stealth before any shooting starts."

Walt Tallhelm wasn't wearing his vest with the hatchet lining, but that's what he was thinking about when Keith said about being quiet.

"It's three o'clock now. We got three, maybe four, hours of light. I'd look to be crossing over the cut by six. That'll give you just about enough time to get to the redoubt by dark. Now we got those wolves worrying us. Maybe they ate their fill last night, maybe not. Anyway, if you run into any of them on your way to the redoubt, gotta be quiet. If they'd be coming out again? Most likely it'd be just about the same time when you'll be out there. Be careful, and no noise."

The half hour or so before having to head out, Nate spent in his room with Lorraine helping him put together what he hoped would keep him alive.

Walt spent his time putting on another layer of clothes. He still had a homespun wool sweater his mother had given him before he headed West. She made it for his Pa, but she gave it to Walt. Twenty years later, that sweater, with its tight knit, was still as warm as any coat. Walt, of course, checked his hatchets and the straps they slid into. Didn't want to reach for one and it not be there.

Sarusha took on the responsibility of explaining everything to Diving Hawk and Drum. They understood the plan and embraced it. They knew the cycle of time at the Crow's Nest had reached the top of its arc and was now near to being resolved.

Trader spent his time with Veronica and Jonathan Keith, quietly commenting on different adventures he had had with Nate and Walt when they were kids. How they used to do this or that.

Trader commented, trying unsuccessfully to assuage some of his guilt, that maybe all this was fated to happen, and how Veronica's map was meant to be found, how events were just unfolding as they should, and that all this had started sometime in the distant past. If Trader had known about Standing Eagle's dream, it may have comforted him some that—at least, in the Indian spirit world—this was fated to be.

Sarusha had decided to keep what Diving Hawk had told him about Standing Eagle's dream between himself and Nate. But he thought what another strange ingredient in this centuries-old slurry of conflict and blood that Trader had brought to boil when he deciphered that old saddlebag map.

In all probability, tomorrow morning after the confrontation, this part of the Kettle of Tears saga should come to an end, and another page written in blood would be added to that tragic chronicle. Then, in time, this horrific episode would go the way of all things—lost to time, forgotten.

Late in the afternoon, Keith, Sunny, and Lucien watched from the parapet as Sarusha, Nate, and the others crossed one by one over the cut, up the bank, and into the woods. It was exactly six o'clock.

Still light enough to get to the shed next to the cemetery and down into the redoubt below. Twelve hours till sunrise. Twelve hours till the consequence of Pealeday's contrived vendetta would be adjudicated with hot lead and razor-sharp arrows.

30

THE CONSEQUENCE OF CONCEIT

"God, what will tomorrow bring?" Keith wondered out loud to Sunny and Lucien as they made their way down from the parapet to the kitchen and bar. Whatever it was, it was going to bring an end to this, one way or another. Keith, Sunny, and Lucien weren't religious men, but each in his own way prayed that if there was a God, He would be on their side tomorrow morning and keep their people safe.

Keith was weary and did something that was out of character for him, announcing that fact to everyone gathered in the bar. "I am so damn weary."

Sometimes, what would appear as weakness is in fact mildly heroic. Why hide it? Keith had been staying on top of a very dire situation for weeks, the last two days of which had been heart-stopping in their gravity. He wasn't looking for comfort or sympathy. He knew everyone in the room was weary as well. The commonality he sought was in the shared exhaustion he knew everyone felt.

This evening would no doubt test everyone's emotional mettle. Veronica's concern for Trader, Lorraine's love for Nate, these would twist the sinew of these women's hearts, test the tautness, then twist some more. The dawn could not come soon enough.

Humor was always a welcome tonic in stressful situations, and Keith knew he could draw more than enough of that from the bottomless well of good-natured wit his crew possessed.

"Thaedell, I'm thinking about having you take first watch out in the gatehouse. While you're there, maybe you could help Ghosty's mother read from the Bible." Keith might just as well have tossed a handful of bullets into one of cast-iron stoves. The explosive response from Lahr was so quick.

"Cap, I thought you and me was friends. Oh, Lord, never the day I thought would come that I'd sooner hang myself than help a woman. But that day has arrived." Lahr then placed his head in his hands and, in feigned resignation, pretended to wail and sob.

"Hell, I think I got a hank of rope right here," Bill Diehl offered.

"Wait, if Thae is gonna hang himself, we should first have some scripture read. Who do we know can read scripture? It would be a solemn occasion, so it should be done whispery-like," Brow Herman said, having been waiting for some reason to rally his flagging spirits, and this seemed to be the opportunity.

"Doesn't the gatehouse have those good beams upstairs?" This from Sage Heck, who hadn't said more than two words since yesterday.

"Yeah, they'd do just fine," said Johnny Dollars.

"Then we could have a wake, and Perpetua could serve some of her cat stew," suggested Brow.

"Thaedell, since you won't be needing your stuff anymore, can I have what you got?" asked Bill Diehl.

"Hell, what he got ain't worth having," continued Brow Herman, feeling relief that his head wound was not as bad as he had originally feared.

"Hell, I know that. I just wanted to make Thae feel good about himself at least once before he takes his leave."

"Well, that's big of you, Bill. I didn't know you to have a charitable bend to your nature," said Brow.

"Hell yeah, I do. I've put up with your tired ass all these years," countered Bill.

"Well, you do have a point," Brow answered with a proper level of self-deprecation.

"I think Ghosty's mom is sweet on Thaedell. She may just jump into that grave with him," said Johnny.

"You noticed that too," said Ray Johnson, who had started to feel comfortable enough with the crew that he felt he could join in this banter.

"That Perpetua, she may look like death warmed over, but she ain't ready to meet her Maker just yet, even over losing Thaedell, her true love."

"Okay, that's enough. God, you guys could talk the ears off a brass monkey!" Keith had no idea what a torrent of blather one small suggestion in jest could call forth. This could have gone on for another hour, but Keith had heard enough. "Seriously, I doubt anything is going happen tonight, but I do need a man up top on a two-hour shift."

"I'll take first watch, Cap," offered Sage Heck, his arm in a sling and his spirits on the mend.

"Okay, Sage. I'll have Bill spell you in two hours. You'll most likely see wolves moving about out there. Just keep an eye on the top of the switchback."

"Yeah, I heard about the damn wolves. Bill, see you in a couple of hours," Sage said as he let Johnny help him get his coat draped over his bad arm.

"Cap, I'll go on up with Sage, keep him company."

"Sure, Johnny, you do that," said Keith, more than happy to see these two back to a small level of normalcy.

Keith put Sunny in charge of making the watch schedule and seeing it was kept. Before leaving the bar, he suggested everyone get something to eat and then get some sleep. "We can't ease up now. I want you all to be ready in the morning for whatever's coming our way."

"Aye, aye, Cap," responded Brow Herman, even with his head wound, still the unofficial spokesman for the crew.

Whatever was coming their way in the morning had everything to do with how successful Nate and the others would be on their mission to silence Pealeday's cannon once and for all. So far, that mission was proceeding as planned.

The climb down from the Nest and back up to the cut was not without incident, though. Nate had been elected to climb the last eighty feet to the cut and somehow secure the rope for the others. Twice his handhold broke free, and he slid back down some, luckily catching hold of some scrub juniper, the shrubs themselves clinging to the cliff face.

The men reached the redoubt as the very last slivers of light made their way through the trees. The hidden shelter and cache would do for an overnight stay, but while the underground space itself was dry, the air in there was stale and musty. Cobwebs ringed the room where the walls met the ceiling like sculptured gossamer garlands decorating a marble crypt.

Sarusha left the hatch door open and uncovered the hidden vent behind the cemetery shed. Soon the flow of air breathed life into the small flames of the whale-oil lamps. Sarusha was glad the Captain had Sunny and Lucien clean and restock the redoubt the other week. There was plenty of everything they needed, including a flattop stove vented to the outside. It wasn't long before the heat from a small fire had filled the room. The little bit of smoke coming up the flue and out the vent would never be seen by Pealeday's men. The forest was too thick and the men too far away. The hideaway would do just fine for what these men needed.

Pealeday's cannon emplacement wasn't far off, five hundred yards to the west, six hundred at best. The plan was simple enough. Just before dawn, the men would make their way through the woods and take up positions adjacent to the cannon and Pealeday's camp. As suggested by Keith, they would use arrows and stealth to silently kill or disable as many of Pealeday's men before the shooting started. Sarusha and Walt had decided not to go out of their way to take any prisoners. The others agreed. If his men decided to give up straight away, fine, but otherwise it was strictly shoot first and continue till there was no more need for shooting.

Before the men retired for the night, they went back outside and sat quietly on the bench along the shed wall. Not talking, just listening to the night. They hadn't seen any wolves on their way to the redoubt. Maybe Keith had been right when he said, "They may have eaten their fill."

Diving Hawk and Drum spent some of this time squashing some yew berries they grabbed on the way to the redoubt and daubing the red juice on their foreheads and the bridges of their noses. They offered some to the others. Only Sarusha took them up on the offer and decorated his face the same way.

Around midnight, one by one the men went down into the shelter, each man wondering what lay in store for them in the morning.

Pealeday had originally started out with sixty-eight men. Now he was down to an even dozen. To fire his cannon, he needed four men. That left eight to guard their position and help with staging gunpowder and rounds. Walt and Sarusha correctly surmised that Pealeday's men would have one camp behind the cannon and one up in the woods. They would first target the camp in the woods.

The men didn't know whether it would work in their favor, but as they emerged from the redoubt just before dawn, they were greeted by the sting of a frigid early winter morning. The day was as clear as a day could be but as cold as a hangman's heart. The initial human response to this was to get back down into the redoubt and its cozy warmth.

Sarusha, the Tallhelms, Trader, and the two Indians were all very human, but they were on a mission, and the cold only served to sharpen their resolve. The men drank their coffee and divvied up a loaf of Evie's berry and walnut bread.

"Remember that good nut bread your Ma used to bake? I can almost taste it," said Trader.

Walt and Nate nodded. "Yeah, what Pa used to say? 'Ma, this bread of yours is the very staff of life.' He must have said it a hundred times," Nate said as he, Walt, and Trader stared into the past and pictured the three of them all back home in that big farmhouse in Pennsylvania.

Something about that memory must have struck a nerve in Walt because he abruptly tossed away the last of his coffee and said,

"Damn cold. Let's finish this mess once and for all and get back to the Nest."

"No argument there," said Nate as he and the others downed their coffee, checked their weapons, and headed out the cemetery shed.

Fanning out but staying within sight of one another, the men slowly made their way toward Pealeday's position. Slow going it would be, as the forest here was thick, and the sun had yet to rise. Soon enough, though, they spotted the light from a campfire filtering through the trees and slowly crept close enough to see a half dozen men crouching close in to it.

They were now near enough to hear one man say, "I'll tell ya this. I've about had it!"

Being this close made Walt and them wonder if their freezing breath would give them away. Those who could pulled a muffler or bandana over their mouth and strained to hear what was being said.

"Hell, I thought this Colonel Pealeday was military. But he's a nut. He's as crazy as a red-ass bee. First light, I'm gonna saddle my horse, take one of them extras, and light a shuck. Who's with me?"

At first, this question was met with silence as the men looked at one another and tried to judge if there was general agreement.

"Yeah, Runk and me was talking that very thing last night. After that stunt with the horses and dynamite yesterday, I was ready to go then. I don't care how much money he offered them men. Dead men can't spend money," one man answered as he crouched lower and got closer in to the fire.

"I ain't saying every man for himself, but I'm with ya. I'm gonna take two of them horses myself. Ain't like he ain't got enough," said another.

"Hell, enough for what? What the hell's he gonna do anyway? He's got one more cannonball left and just about enough powder to fire that one off."

"What about the rest of you?" asked the mercenary who had broached the question of leaving. "I don't want to get shot in the back by any of youse as I'm making a break for it."

"Well, it won't be me. I'm going too."

356

One by one, the men nodded yes to the decision to leave, and as soon as they could.

"I'm gonna do it real quiet like, but I'm getting my gear and making my way to them horses. It's almost light. We gotta do this now before them over at the cannon see what's up and get a notion to start shooting at us."

Sarusha and Walt signaled the others to fade back into the woods and forget about this bunch. That left Pealeday and the men manning the cannon. That position was out on the flat about 150 yards from the woods. They had a good-sized fire going, which cast a circle of light out into the darkness.

If Sarusha and the others were going to make their move, they needed to do it soon while the area beyond that circle of light was still cloaked in darkness. The question now was, do they give those men a chance to surrender or just limit their options to whether they die by arrow or bullet?

"I don't think those boys have much fight left in 'em. I say if they want to call it quits, we should let 'em," Trader said as the men waited at the very edge of the woods to decide.

"Okay, then. Let's see about getting the drop on 'em. But I tell ya, one false move and I'll open the ball," a very resolute Walt Tallhelm announced. And right he should. If Pealeday's men decided to fight, any hesitation could cost someone their life.

Staying low, the men left the cover of the forest, and with the animal cunning of panthers stalking their prey, they crept forward, inching their way toward the firelight.

"Don't you men put any more logs on that fire. We need them for our protection," stated Colonel Clayton Pealeday to his less-than-enthusiastic men.

Then Pealeday reached down, grabbed a burning branch from the edge of the fire, and started walking toward his cannon. "What do you say we give that bastard big-time Captain Jonathan Keith a good-morning hello?"

The cannon was primed and ready to go from the night before, only needing a flame to light the fuse, sending a ten-pound ball screaming toward the wall of the Nest.

In an instant, Walt and company sprung to their feet, guns drawn. "Don't do it, Pealeday!" Walt shouted.

"You men drop those guns if you wanna keep livin'!" Nate hollered.

"Pealeday, I'm warning you. Drop the damn torch!" Walt said as he drew back the hammer on his revolver.

Pealeday was experiencing a range of emotions that ran the gamut from surprise to confusion to anger to hopelessness, but none that led to submission.

The others had undone their gun belts and dropped them to the ground.

For Clayton Pealeday, time had become all but frozen, each second drawing itself out, metered by the strange rapid recollection of a lifetime now brought to but one decision.

Resigned to meet his fate, Pealeday lunged toward the cannon, tossing the burning torch onto its fuse. A half dozen bullets spun Pealeday's body around like a corkscrew as he fell onto the back of the cannon, its unchecked recoil catching Pealeday full-square, caving in his chest and cracking several ribs in his soon-to-be lifeless body.

The roar of the cannon echoed off the promontory wall as Sarusha watched closely to ensure that none of Pealeday's men tried anything funny.

Off in the distance, the cannonball slammed into the side of the Nest. Keith's men didn't know where it had hit but hoped it hadn't done any damage.

It looked like the siege of the Crow's Nest was over. Now Sarusha, Walt, and the others had a decision to make. What to do with these men? Nate spoke first and made a decision without first clearing it with the others, but he made it just the same. "We're going to let you men go, but first you have to do something with what remains of your dead."

Walt, Trader, and Sarusha looked at Nate and all nodded in agreement, and Nate turned his gaze intently on Pealeday's former troops.

"It's too damn cold to dig graves, so why don't you boys drag that cannon back from them logs and get to making a funeral pyre?

Don't anyone get any wrong ideas or you'll find yourself burning right along with the others. I'm cold and I'm hungry, and I've about had it. Now what do you say?"

Each of the men nodded in agreement. As they were escorted to the string of horses at the edge of the woods, they could just make out the men who had lit out earlier fading out of view off to the west.

"Sarusha, we'll stay here. Why don't you get back to the Nest?" said Walt.

"You sure?"

"Yeah, I'm sure. Take care to undo them trip wires."

"See you back at the Nest!" a very relieved Sarusha hollered as he swung up on a horse and rode off.

It took all morning and most of the afternoon to gather the dead, or what remained of them, and get them to the pyre. Diving Hawk and Drum lashed together some wishbone sleds and gave them to the men to help transport the grisly aftermath of the wolves' banquet. No one said much of anything. The sooner they got done, the sooner they could get on their way back to Lewiston.

One of the men who was a little older and seemed to come to the fore and coordinate their efforts told Walt, "We didn't bring enough feed for these horses. I'd hate to leave a trail of dead beasts on our way back to Lewiston. You think you could—"

"We'll take 'em back to the Nest. Once we're done here, you pick out the ones you're takin' and we'll deal with the rest," Walt replied. He thought, *I'm glad I never found myself in these boys' situation.* He'd been around long enough to know sometimes things can take a wrong turn, and before you know it, you're in a fix.

When Sarusha got back to the Nest, the news he carried made the women shed tears of joy and the men take it as a good excuse to have an early-morning celebratory drink.

Veronica, Lorraine, and the others wanted to ride out and reunite with the men, but Keith would have none of it. Not until those men were on the trail heading west and back to wherever they came from did he want anyone leaving the Nest.

Sarusha pulled Keith aside and told him about Standing Eagle's dream.

Keith wasn't quite sure what to make of this information but responded by saying, "Well, it looks like we dodged a bullet with that one. I don't think Sage Heck is going to die from that wound to his arm."

With a note of levity, Keith went on, "Although it might just kill me to hear what kind of lies this bunch is going to make up about how heroic they were at the 'Siege of the Crow's Nest.' I can hear it now."

Keith, of course, was talking about the crew, who already seemed to be embellishing one facet or another of the campaign and their part in it.

Although the siege was over and the pressing reality of fighting to stay alive had passed, they still had Herzog to deal with. Just what to do with him remained undecided.

Keith hadn't had time to assess the damage to the Nest, but he knew a lot of work lay in store for the men. The Nest had taken a beating. "Thank God that cannonball this morning was the last one," he said to Sarusha as the two went up top and watched the flames from the funeral pyre in the distance grow higher.

It may have been the last cannonball, but it would prove to be a deadly one. That ball, as fate would have it, had slammed into the Nest right at the back wall of the brig. Through the splintered logs, Herzog saw a bit of daylight coming into his pitch-black cell. He quickly covered over the opening with his bloodstained coat. Later, when Keith and Evie came down—with Lucien standing guard—to finally change his bandages, no one was the wiser. Herzog would bide his time and slowly work at the opening till it was big enough for him to squeeze through.

Pealeday's men left their comrades' bodies to burn on the pyre and hit the trail west with maybe three hours of daylight left. For them, wherever they were at dark would be okay, just as long as it was far away from the Crow's Nest and the Kettle of Tears.

The celebration at the Nest was in full swing by the time Walt, Nate, Trader, Diving Hawk, and Drum made it down to the gatehouse and back up and into the stables. Nate and Trader had no sooner handed the reins of four of Pealeday's horses to Everett and Ernie than their women were squeezing them and holding tight.

Evie had Lucien get one of his cured hams from out back. She then set to raiding her larder to make a feast worthy of Christmas Day. She had already set to baking four berry pies, which she started the moment she heard the good news from Sarusha.

Sunny lit all the lamps in the bar, which had been kept in near darkness for the last three days. They even sent an envoy to invite Ghosty and his mother to the do. The news that they'd taken Captain Keith up on the invite was met with a mixed response.

The drinking and eating went well into the night. What intoxicated the revelers the most was the sense of relief everyone felt, and even more so for Nathan Tallhelm and Lorraine Haverstraw, now able to look to the future unburdened, unbroken, unfettered, to dare to seek all of what Eden had to offer. This was how Nate and Lorraine envisioned their future together.

While all that was going on upstairs, Herzog, using his belt buckle, slowly scraped and worked away at the hole in the wall of the brig, his mind seething with hate as he envisioned what retribution he would exact on those who imprisoned him so. His most cherished inner demon, the arsonist, had teased his mind mercilessly over the last few days, supplying him with vivid visions of what a great sight this building in flames would make.

Along with his fiery visions for the Crow's Nest proper, he also singled out a few for personal treatment. Miles Haverstraw and his daughter were at the top of the list, just above Jonathan Keith and Walt Tallhelm. *Put a hatchet handle on my wound, will ya*, he thought. *We'll see.*

31

MAKING PLANS

As the festivities wound down the previous night, Nate sat down with his Indian friends, and along with Jonathan Keith and Sarusha tried to figure out what to do with the horses. The Crow's Nest now had more than they knew what to do with. They not only had all the horses from Chance Parker and his bunch but also quite a few of the ones from Pealeday's dead mercenaries. Needless to say, more than enough horses to go around. They quickly decided that Diving Hawk and Drum should take as many as they could handle, which turned out to be four each. Although his supply of horse feed was rapidly dwindling and it would tax his reserves, Keith would provide the pair with as much grain as they needed to make it back to their village, a three-day ride.

With Sarusha's help, Keith wrote out a "Transfer of Ownership" document for the men. More and more, with the ever-changing Indian treaties, and what with soldiers and settlers looking for any excuse to cause trouble for the natives, it wouldn't be out of the question that a situation would arise where such a document would answer the question "Where'd you get them horses, redskin?"

Everyone in the Nest had grown very fond of Diving Hawk and Drum. The pair exuded a diplomatic reserve undeniable in its graciousness. Their allegiance to Nate was absolute. That in and of itself would have been enough to cement their bond with the others, but their natural solemnity garnered for them everyone's respect on its own.

This was demonstrated by the fact that one by one, and unbeknownst to one another, Diving Hawk and Drum were given small gifts from almost everyone. Evie gave the men some cooking pots for their women.

Lucien gave each a scrimshaw walrus tooth, a minute likeness of the *Celine* etched into one and a likeness of the Nest into the other. The men proudly wore these around their necks and made a point of showing them off to anyone who was nearby.

Veronica and Lorraine didn't have all that much to give but allowed Evie to give them something to pass along, which took the form of a wool shawl and a quarter bolt of cotton fabric.

Keith was more than happy to give the men the Spencer carbines and several boxes of shells. Nate asked Keith to throw in another Spencer for the absent Owl Eyes, and Keith readily obliged. A smile came onto Nate's face as he pictured Owl Eyes's reaction to getting the gift, and from "Tarlton, the man who shoots once," no less.

Over the years, sentimentality must have leached out of the crew as the only gifts they could come up with to give Diving Hawk and Drum were silver and gold coins from one of their poker pots. Not an insignificant sum, as Keith had divvied up amongst the crew all the double eagles Severman and Dean had in their pokes, resulting in the men not moderating their bets as they usually did.

Walt Tallhelm had a mind to give each of them one of his hatchets but couldn't bring himself to break up the set. Instead, he gave Diving Hawk a pair of bearskin gloves and Drum a bear-claw necklace, mementos from the encounter with that bear back in Quiet Bird's village. One can only imagine the lore, real or embellished, that will follow these gifts through their lifetime.

Trader would have liked to have given the men something special, but almost all his belongings were lost when Herzog and Parker took over his camp. He figured, though, that in the big pile of saddles and saddlebags downstairs—a small room's worth—there must be something he could give them. And indeed, it didn't take long to salvage any number of items Diving Hawk and Drum could make use of. It wasn't swag, and it wasn't ill-gotten pelf. It was the spoils of war. The men who had owned these things had chosen to make war, and they had lost.

The morning after the victory celebration, things got off to a slow start at the Crow's Nest. The leave-taking of Diving Hawk and Drum was supposed to happen first thing. But early morning turned into late morning, and it wasn't until past noon that the two walked their horses down the ramp and through the gatehouse.

Whoever hadn't been down in the stables to see the Indians off watched from the deck. The day was cold, and the string of horses were all but shrouded from view, enveloped in their frozen breaths as they made their way up the switchback and on their way.

Unfortunately, Diving Hawk and Drum had slept soundly the night before. Otherwise, they would have heard Herzog scraping and clawing away at the back wall of the brig. The Indians preferred to sleep in the stables, and they bedded down not but twenty feet from where Herzog's frenzied activity was taking place. Now they were safely away from the Nest and not liable to injury from whatever hell Herzog was planning to visit upon the Nest.

Within the limits of what his patience with the vile Herzog could endure, Keith tried to be a humane jailer.

The prisoner was provided one meal a day, and knowing that he would need to get out of the brig for some fresh air at least once a day, he also made provision for a little outside time. The brig wasn't supposed to be a dungeon, after all. So, under guard, Herzog was tasked with emptying his own chamber pot out in the back. This small concession to humane treatment would prove to be a fatal mistake on Keith's part.

Herzog took this time to make a mental blueprint of the stables and the area out back. With the precision of a master thief, he noted all that he saw. What piqued his interest more than anything, understandably so, were the unused gunpowder loads for the Parrott cannon. These were being stored in an open three-sided shed in back of the stables. As soon as Keith could get to it, once his exhausted crew got some rest, these were to be taken back to the powder magazine located up in the woods, a safe distance from the Nest. Leaving this to later could prove to be a deadly mistake.

So far, the hole in the back of Herzog's cell had gone undetected. That couldn't be the case for too much longer. Already, he told them he wanted his one meal at night, so as not to have any daylight coming in when the food was delivered. One more night might do it. Herzog worked quietly in his cell as he listened to the hubbub out in the stables. He swore, "Try as they may, I will not be thwarted. Never."

Back in the bar, Sunny was busy stoking the stoves and getting the Samms boys to bring in more split logs from the deck and staged them nearby. The Johnson brothers carried in a few armfuls and then stood by the stove near the deck, warming themselves.

"What you boys gonna do now?" asked Sunny as he pumped a small bellows he had rigged up to the bottom of the stove.

"Hell, we ain't rightly sure, are we, Lee?" answered Ray.

"The Cap was mighty appreciative of you boys helping out," said Sunny.

"We didn't do all that much. We owe you all for saving our bacon from Chance Parker, Tice, and them up on the trail. So from where we stand, we're more than even," said Lee.

"We could use a couple extra men around here for a while. If you two got a mind to stick around, the Cap would make it more than worth your while. Think about it." The stove Sunny was stoking glowed red, so he moved on to the other one in the corner of the dining room.

Jonathan Keith came through the curtain and told Sunny to ask the Johnson brothers to come back to his office off the kitchen.

"Sunny said you wanted to see us, Captain," said Lee.

"Sit down, boys. You eat yet?" asked Keith.

"No, we haven't. Not just yet. But whatever I'm smelling sure smells powerful good," said Ray.

The Johnson brothers were tall and lanky. They weren't packing a lot of extra weight and their Ma once said the way they ate, they both must have a "hollow leg." It had been a job for these two not to get kicked out of most every boardinghouse they stayed in for eating too much. In any event, Keith wouldn't torture them by keeping them from their dinner, so he hollered through the side door to the kitchen, "Evie, could you bring in one of those ham-and-bean pies? These boys look like they might just faint from what they're smelling." Keith wanted to make the men feel comfortable and at home before he made his entreaty.

"I want to thank you boys for all the help you've been this last week. I don't know how you got mixed up with Jack Tice, but from what Walt and Sarusha tell me, it wasn't any honeymoon."

"Honeymoon, hell! That son of a bitch hit me up alongside my head and then took my horse. Mister Keith, or I guess Captain Keith, Lee and me was just looking for some women. We wasn't privy to any of this business about Herzog or Pealeday. Damn bastards almost got us kilt!" said Ray Johnson.

Evie brought in the pie she had so skillfully prepared using the leftovers from the evening before. Normally, the two would have lit into the ham-and-bean pie like trencherman after a day's work, but evidently the civility of Keith and the others was rubbing off onto the Johnson brothers. "My, what a delicious smell. After you, Ray.

"We'll most likely be leaving out of here, what with the fighting over now. We got our own horses back, but we'd be much obliged for a couple of them others and a few good saddles," Lee said as he reached over his brother and served himself a slice of pie.

"Well, you boys are more than welcome to a few of those horses. Three each, if you like. You would be doing us a favor. You should end up with a couple good saddles as well. But I got a proposition for ya if you want to hear it."

"Don't cost nothing to listen, does it, Lee?" answered Ray Johnson.

It was difficult for Jonathan Keith to tell which one of these brothers was in charge. In any event, he went on.

"To show my appreciation, I'm writing you each a letter of credit for one thousand dollars. There's a bank in Denver you can take it to and get your money in cash. There's also one in San Francisco." Keith had thought to make the amount larger but settled on the thousand for a reason.

"Damn, you hear that, Ray? One thousand dollars!" said Lee.

"I'm right here, Lee. What's the deal?" This comment from Ray Johnson told Keith that Ray was in charge and obviously the less trusting of the brothers. "This is just a piece of paper. What if we get there and they just laugh in our face?"

"They won't laugh in your face. I guarantee it. Ask Sunny or any of my men. The money is there." Keith had a goodly sum in both of those banks, more than enough to cover those checks a hundred times over.

"If you men would be willing to stay on for a month or so to help repair the Nest, I'd be more than willing to double that amount."

Keith needed the extra help. Sage Heck and Brow Herman were not incapacitated, but their help would be marginal. He could probably get Nate and Trader to stay on a bit, but they would want to be getting on their way sooner than later. Also, who could tell what Miles Haverstraw's plans were with Herzog? Clearly, these two extra men would be a big help.

Keith had set the initial amount of money where he did, figuring the brothers would envision it would be enough money to have all the dance hall girls and boozy nights of gambling they could possibly want, leastwise for a month or so. But two thousand each, that would be a real grubstake. Just maybe they could set themselves up somehow for the long haul.

"What kinda work we be doing?" asked Ray.

"Well, first off, repairing the west wall. That means hauling down some logs from the woods off the cut. Also, getting these cannons back where they belong, and some other odds and ends. Plus, I got to send some men down to the Snake to get the Nest resupplied. Trust me, I got work. In a month or so, you two can leave outa here with some real money. Think about it. If you don't want to stay, no hard feelings." Keith finished his sales pitch by coyly asking, "How's that pie?"

"Can't complain about the vittles here, that's for sure," Lee answered.

"My brother and I, we all appreciate what you done for us. We'll think on it a bit and let you know tonight," said Ray as he and his brother split the last of the dinner pie.

"I gotta get back out front. When you're finished here, go out to the bar and have a drink or two. Too cold to do much else today."

"Captain, when we'd be down getting these supplies, is there time enough to entertain the women thereabouts?" asked Ray Johnson.

"We'd be getting those supplies in Lewiston. Most likely you'd have some spare time."

"Iffen we was to stay and made this resupply trip, you figure you could advance us a little spending money?" asked Lee.

"I wouldn't know why not," Keith said as he was leaving the room, stopping momentarily to coax the terriers to follow and leave the Johnson brothers to finish their dinner in peace.

The Johnson brothers didn't need to wait till evening to make up their minds. The deal was just too sweet to pass up. Also, although they hadn't spoken to one another about it, being around Keith, Sunny, Lucien, and the Tallhelms was starting to change the way the brothers looked at life.

One minute they're riding bareback in little more than their long johns with bloodthirsty gunmen in pursuit and now, less than a week later, they're looking to leave this Crow's Nest in about a month with two thousand dollars each, extra horses, and the good will of some fine men.

Life had taken a turn for the better for the Johnson brothers.

Keith, Sunny, Lucien, and Sarusha didn't have Pealeday to worry about anymore, but there were still several pressing problems, the least of which was feeding all these horses. Lucien had moved his cows out of the woods, and they were now staying warm in the back stables. Most of the extra horses were out back, and some had found their way up into the woods, keeping out of the wind. Lucien had started the fall with a good supply of animal feed, but that was dwindling quickly, and he didn't quite know how to fix the problem. He was already rationing the hay and grain, both of which the cows and horses would want more of, given the cold weather. Resupply couldn't come soon enough.

Evie, too, was running low on some items and had begun to make what she had go a little further. She tried not to bother the

Captain, seeing all that he had on his mind. But she finally couldn't wait any longer since privation loomed. She went straight into his office after the Johnson brothers left and declared, "Cap, we're running low on food."

"Well, we could always eat horsemeat," Keith said this in jest, but Evie Samms let out a shriek before she had time not to.

"Just joshin', Evie. Sorry to give you a caution." Keith meant this. He never wanted to alarm Evie if he could help it. She was not an emotional person and not one to become overwrought. But she did have her tender spots. Keith learned too late that joking about eating horse meat was one of them. "Don't worry, Evie. As soon we get squared away, they'll be heading out for supplies."

"That would be good, Cap. That would be powerful good."

Keith and his men usually had the Crow's Nest well supplied, well heated, and well organized. The business with Herzog and Pealeday wreaked havoc on all of that. Nothing to panic about, but they couldn't wait too much longer to get things back in order. The most immediate issue, however, was what to do with Bertram Herzog.

The closest law was in Lewiston. But considering that had been Pealeday's stronghold, it might prove to be the last place you'd want to bring his partner in crime and expect unbiased help from the law. Just who would be escorting Herzog was still undecided. They could take him over to Missoula or up to Spokane. But their best bet was most likely Fort Boise down to the south.

Keith wanted to have another general meeting after supper to get some of these things nailed down. The sooner the better.

Nate had asked Miles and Lorraine that very question. Answering for the both of them, Miles told him, "We don't know what we're going to do." They had always thought that if and when they captured Herzog, it would be in a city, not on a rocky crag in the middle of the Idaho Territory.

Among other things, there was the issue of the cash reward for the apprehension of Herzog and Marlene Scabbe. Also, the two of them had been tried in absentia for what they did back in Lautenburg. Herzog was just brash enough to want a new full-jury trial. When

Nate heard this, he slid his revolver out of his holster and said, "I got a jury of six right here."

Nate was just about fed up. But as much as he wanted to see Herzog dead, he knew he couldn't be the one to bring that about. Out on the frontier, just how much a man was willing to bend to the so-called will of civilization varied. There is law, and then there is justice. Nate was very close to seeing justice done, the law be damned. The only problem was, it would affect how Lorraine thought of him. No doubt that Bertram Herzog deserved to die, but not at the hands of Nathan Tallhelm.

In any event, Nate and Lorraine spent their time together talking about everything but Bertram Herzog and Marlene Scabbe.

Lorraine had already agreed that the place Nate had been working in the spring would be perfect for raising a family. They hadn't asked him, but they assumed Miles would want to be included. After all, once a farmer, you don't forget that. And Nate expected to have a good-sized vegetable patch going as soon as they could. The future held a few unknowns, but all in all, the light on the horizon had a rosy glow.

The leave-taking of Diving Hawk and Drum provided a perfect punctuation mark for the day. Having survived the siege and the night of celebration with only mild hangovers, the whole of the Nest was still in a celebratory mood, attested to by the lively goings-on in the dining room and bar. This afternoon seemed ready-made for a slow-paced period of recuperation.

Keith and Sunny had some of the crew doing one thing or another, but generally the thing everyone was doing was drinking and telling stories. Harmless embellishments helped disguise the real fear each man had felt at the time. No doubt about it, the Crow's Nest had stood up to everything Pealeday threw at it and prevailed. But the assault did, at times, sorely test the nerves of every man and woman who sheltered within its walls.

But now that was over, and the talk soon changed to what lay ahead. The pair who set the whole thing in motion, Trader Darcy and Veronica, had no intention of looking for the Cave of Stone Eyes anymore. The saddlebag map had been on Veronica's horse when she escaped from Parker and Herzog. Trader and Keith cut it into little pieces and tossed them to the wind.

Although, Trader did have a pretty good idea where the sealed-up cave of was hidden along that rim wall, he also had a better idea of what mattered most in his life. And it wasn't a bucketful of gold. In any event, money was not going to be a problem. Jonathan Keith made good on his promise to pay Trader if he destroyed the map. All Trader had to do now was name an amount.

Keith had always been a generous man, but now as he started to see his horizon narrow rather than widen, he sought to help those he loved plot a course that would be marked by success and good fortune, where want and desperation were mere words and not realities.

"I imagine you'll be heading back to Quiet Bird's," Sarusha said as he sat down in a booth and joined Walt, Trader, and Nate.

"Well, that's one thing I could do," answered Walt with the slightest of grins.

"Don't tell me you're gonna break that woman's heart again. Don't tell me that," said Sarusha, not quite sure if Walt was joking or not.

"Don't worry. I'll be heading that way just as soon as the dust settles around here. We still got that bastard downstairs to deal with."

"By the way, Nate, what do Miles and Lorraine plan to do with Herzog?" asked Trader.

"We're all kinda up in the air about that. Maybe you two would know a better plan. But talking to the Cap, he thinks taking him to Fort Boise would be the best idea."

"Fort Boise, that's what? Three hundred miles? Hell, going full out, that'd still take eight, ten days. Too much time for that man to try something funny. Lewiston be closer," said Sarusha.

"Lewiston might be a problem. Them boys what we sent on their way are all most likely back in Lewiston. That could be a problem. Pealeday's still got people there. I suspect they wouldn't take kindly to us—the ones what did him in—showing up with his partner shackled to one of his horses," said Nate, who had been over all this with Keith and really hoped his brother and cousin could come up with a better idea.

"Nate, when Ronnie and me leave outa here, we're heading back to Pa's. We could all ride together and take him down to Fort Hall," suggested Trader.

"That might just work out. Eventually we'd be stopping at your Pa's on our way to that piece of land I staked out this spring. That's not too far north of him, up in the Yellowstone."

"You men talking about us?" asked Lorraine as she and Veronica pulled a couple of chairs over next to the booth and sat down.

"Well, we was and we wasn't," said Trader.

"What does you mean, Tray?" asked Veronica.

"We were talking about us, Nate and Lorraine and me and you," said Trader with a tone approaching joy in his voice. Here he was sitting with his two favorite cousins, who were really more like brothers to him, alongside his new bride and Nate's soon-to-be bride. From where things were a month ago, sitting here drinking whiskey and speculating on the future, why not be joyful?

"Hey, Brow, where's the closest law around here?" shouted Sunny, who had been eavesdropping on the conversation.

"Why, you thinking about turning yourself in?" answered Brow Herman, who evidently had his sense of humor well intact.

"Very funny, Brow. No, we're trying to figure where we can turn Herzog over to the authorities," said Sunny.

"I tell ya who should turn himself in is Diehl. It ought to be a crime for dealing me the lousy cards I've been getting." Sage Heck said this, clearly marking a foray back into the jocular arena that concern for his wound had kept him from.

The rest of the poker crew were happy to see it.

"Last time I was in Portland, they just finished a brand-new county jail. I wouldn't trust that bunch in Lewiston to keep a dog like Herzog locked up." This from Thaedell Lahr, who had firsthand knowledge of how much trust can be placed in some public officials.

"Maybe you could get Ghosty's mother to read him scripture for a couple days and he'll just up and commit suicide." Lahr added this comment to let everyone know he hadn't yet recovered from that day in the gatehouse.

"I heard someone say Fort Boise. It's far but probably the best place to handle someone like that bastard downstairs." This was Bill Diehl's opinion, and most likely the option that would be chosen.

Miles Haverstraw sat in his spot in the booth closest to the bar and continued whittling small figures. But now he no longer threw them into the stoves and watched them burn. Now he would toss one of these little statuettes to each of the people about, carved with their likeness perfectly reproduced. His gift to Diving Hawk and Drum had been two such tokens.

What was going through Miles Haverstraw's head was anyone's guess. The man said very little. But these little carvings spoke volumes as to how he had finally been able to turn a page and begin the process of living again. Marlene Scabbe was still out there…somewhere…but the search for her now seemed far less pressing than it had been just a few days prior.

Miles knew Lorraine and her man, Nathan Tallhelm, wouldn't be joining him if he chose to continue the hunt. That was all well and good. Lorraine could at last settle down and start a family of her own. Her odyssey was over. His may still go on—a question he would decide in due time.

It was a damn shame Brow and Sage had been injured in the siege. Brow would recover with no lasting damage. Sage Heck's arm was messed up, but he could still use it. Gangrene had not developed, and although a tendon was damaged, in time he might be able to straighten his arm out. For now, he had gone from being right-handed to being a lefty. Needless to say, his injury could have been a lot worse.

As a cold wind blew about a light flurry of snow out on the deck, inside the warm bar, the afternoon was spent with Keith and the others drinking and eating. They also took this time to nail down a schedule of priorities and work assignments and take a concrete inventory of what they had on hand and what they needed. The situation was a concern, but not dire. As everyone retired for the night, the only unanswered question was the big one—when and where to take Herzog to face his reckoning.

Unbeknownst to all of them, Herzog had every intention of being the one to answer that question. And every minute that went by, he got closer and closer to that reality.

32

THE RECKONING

The following morning, the fateful day at the Crow's Nest began in a way that seemed to herald a return to a normal routine. The Samms boys were up early, ready to tend to the horses. Johnny and Sage were making sure the embers in the stoves were brought back to life with some fresh firewood. Although Sunny was in charge of the stoves and fireplaces, he was not an early riser.

Evie Samms was already in the kitchen making coffee and a big pot of oatmeal, a dish that would be showing up on the breakfast menu more often until the kitchen stores were resupplied.

Bertram Herzog was also up early that morning. Actually, he had never slept the night before. Sometime before dawn, he squeezed through the opening in the back wall of his cell. He was lucky that when he came out of that hole, he didn't plunge to his death. The side of the Crow's Nest was but two feet from the edge of the cliff face. Herzog crawled along this narrow ledge to the back end of the Nest.

He then busied himself laying a trail of gunpowder from the outdoor shed into the stables and up to the tack room door, inside of which he found two revolvers and a rifle. Arming himself, he then waited underneath the staircase to greet the Samms boys coming down to begin their chores.

Grabbing hold of Ernie, he put the pistol to his head and said, "One peep out of one of you and you're both dead. Saddle my horse and be quick about it. Hang that lantern over here and get me two more. Where's them dogs I been hearing?"

"They be up in the Captain's. That's where they stay," answered Ernest.

"Mister, your horse ain't inside here," said Everett with a shudder, experiencing fear like never before.

"Then saddle me one of them Appaloosas I seen. Saddle both of them, dammit."

"Them horses ain't be saddle broke," an increasingly fearful Everett informed Herzog.

"Look, you little bastard, saddle me two good horses or I'll slit your brother's throat." A very frustrated Bertram Herzog wanted to scream these words but had to whisper them.

Tubby Flint, up in the rope hotel, the windows of which looked down onto the stables, sensed that something was afoot. He didn't know just what, but the air held a palpable tension that wormed its way through the sodden maze that was his brain and reached his awareness. He carefully and silently rolled out of his hammock and crept over to the window. Only by pure luck was he not spotted by Herzog, who had his back against the opposite wall and appeared to be looking straight at the rope hotel across the stable and above the tack room.

Everett was trying to saddle one of the horses as quickly as he could, but something he had done a thousand times now seemed all but impossible. Finally, he got back to Herzog and his brother.

"Damn it! I said saddles on both horses. While you're at it, fill two saddlebags with some grub and a couple pokes of horse feed."

Everett didn't want to have to tell Herzog that they didn't have any food down here. He saddled the other horse and got the bags of feed, tied them together, and slung them over the saddle of one of the horses.

"Mister, we ain't got no food down here." Everett didn't know what the response to this information was going to be as he and his brother looked to each other, trying to silently draw from and give strength to one another.

Herzog stood there, shaking his head angrily as tried to figure his options. Looking at Everett, he said, "It's early. You go up to that kitchen and get me some damn food. And if I see anyone but you coming back down these stairs, he's dead." With that, Herzog poked Ernest in the side of the head with the barrel of the revolver.

"What I'm gonna tell my Ma?" Everett implored.

"I don't care what you tell her, but whatever it is, it better not get her to thinking. You understand me?" threatened Herzog in a whisper through his clenched jaw.

Meanwhile, Tubby Flint was watching this drama unfold but was at a loss as to just what to do. The stairs up and into the rope hotel were right there at the south end of the tack room, well within Herzog's view. He had to wait for an opening if or when an opening presented itself.

Everett was lucky. His mother was momentarily out of the kitchen, allowing him to grab a loaf of bread, some dried beef, a couple of mason jars of green beans, and a bag of walnuts. He didn't know if it would be enough to satisfy this man, but it was a bag of food. He hurried back down to the stable undetected.

"Put that in that saddlebag and put this rifle in that scabbard. Where's the canteens? Get me some canteens and make sure they got water in 'em."

Thankfully, there was always water in the tack room. Four canteens later, Herzog's horses were finally ready to go.

"Okay, I been hearing that bell now and then. I know it's some kind of signal. What's it for?" asked Herzog. He had an idea but wasn't sure.

"Two rings lets Ghosty know to open the doors to the gatehouse," Everett informed a suddenly very calm Bertram Herzog. His inner arsonist knew its appetite was soon to be appeased. Just as opium going into a pipe gives joy to the addict or watching amber spirits swirl around and fill a glass makes the tippler rub his palms, so, too, the arsonist is intoxicated as combustibles are marshaled awaiting a flame.

"What if that bell don't ring? Can you open those doors?" asked Herzog.

"Them doors is heavy. Two or three men could maybe get 'em open. The Cap got them lashed up to some pulleys or something," answered Ernie, surprised words still came out of his mouth.

"Get up on that horse. Up in front of the saddle." Herzog let go of Ernest and grabbed hold of Everett. "Now tie the reins of that one to the back of this saddle. You know these horses?" Now the boys knew this man was not a horseman.

"They're good horses. They won't throw you, mister." Everett thought, *If my Pa ever got ahold of this man, watch out. Looks like he can't even hardly ride a horse.*

The boys were doing what the man with the gun was telling them, but they couldn't figure how exactly this was going to work.

Meanwhile, Nate and Lorraine, unaware of any of the goings-on down in the stables, had rendezvoused on the short deck off the third floor to watch the sunrise. It was right above the deck off the bar and afforded them an even better view of the Kettle of Tears. They stood leaning against the railing, looking to the east, watching as the sky lightened, anticipating a brilliant sunrise on this clear winter morning. On the deck below, Johnny Dollars was ferrying in armfuls of split logs, staging them for Sunny, who expected a decent stack near each stove and fireplace.

Nate heard the bell at the stable door ring twice. He thought, *Someone heading out early? Who could that be? Is that the Johnson brothers?*

Nate was looking to see the sunrise and half looking to see who was coming out of the stables. Ghosty wasn't usually up this early, so nothing was happening. No one came into view, and the gatehouse doors remained closed. Nate had been around long enough to know not to disregard his instincts, which were telling him something was up.

"Lorraine, get my brother and Trader. Get 'em quick and get 'em out here." With that, Nate climbed over the railing, balanced himself in front, and dropped to the deck below. He skirted around the Parrott cannon and climbed over the deck railing. With both arms behind him, he leaned forward and waited to see just who was coming out of the stable door.

"What you doing, Nate?" asked Johnny, who had come back out to get more firewood.

"Shush, shush" was all Nate replied.

Johnny came over to the railing and looked down to where Nate was looking. Just then, the doors to the gatehouse began to swing open, right at the same time Nate and Johnny heard Tubby Flint holler, "*Fire! Fire!*"

With Ernest in front of him and Everett behind, Herzog had waited at the stable door for the gatehouse doors to open. As soon as he saw them begin to swing open, he heaved three kerosene lanterns back into the stables. Luckily, he had misjudged the distance, and the lanterns didn't reach his trail of gunpowder. But the flames covered a good third of the stable floor and were quickly spreading toward the gunpowder.

Tubby Flint tried as best he could to put out the fire with a blanket, but his efforts were in vain. Worse yet, the fumes and exertion had all but finished the man. As the burning kerosene seeped into the cracks of the floorboards, the fire grew more intense.

The deck off the bar was a good twenty feet above the ramp down from the stables. But as soon as Nate saw Herzog come into view, he jumped.

He landed square on top of Herzog, and everyone went tumbling to the ground. Herzog's gun went off, but thankfully it didn't shoot one of the Samms boys. Herzog had ended up right on top of Nate, both men face up. Nate had the wind knocked out of him and didn't regain his breath until Herzog was up and on his feet.

Johnny Dollars had watched this, and as quick as you can pinch a tick, he leaped through the air and knocked Herzog back to the ground.

Up top, Lorraine returned to the third-floor deck with Walt and Trader, where they heard the faintest of cries from Tubby Flint: "Fire! Fire!"

It couldn't have taken Walt and Trader more than a half a minute before they were bounding down the long staircase to the stables. The smoke now filled the large room as the horses made an ungodly racket, screeching and stomping. The fire was but three feet from reaching the gunpowder.

Walt called out to his cousin, "Trader, the water trough. Trader, help me with the trough!" The trough held about a hundred gallons and weighed over eight hundred pounds, but the men called forth some superhuman strength and, bracing themselves against the wall under the staircase, upended the trough. The tactic worked.

In spots, the floor was still burning, but the lion's share of the fire was out.

Walt and Trader beat out the remaining flames with a couple of horse blankets just as Sunny came flying down the stairs two steps at a time. That's when the men saw Tubby Flint. He had himself propped up against the stairs to the rope hotel.

"He got the boys," wheezed Flint.

"Hang in there, partner," said Sunny.

Outside, Nate and Johnny Dollars were trying to wrestle the gun out of Herzog's hand. It soon went off, and Nate could feel his arm begin to sting. Two more gunshots rang out. Nate grabbed the gun, and as Herzog swung around, he caught Nate in the temple with the barrel of the pistol. Nevertheless, a dazed Nate somehow managed to wrest the gun from Herzog's grip. He staggered about, realizing little more than the fact that he now had the villain's gun.

Herzog looked past Nate and saw the gatehouse door swinging closed. He also saw the horse with the second pistol and rifle on it loping toward the gatehouse, too far away to get to. Momentarily, Herzog stood flatfooted, frozen, desperate to escape but unable. Seeing no real option, he ran to the oil shed. He looked behind it. Nothing but a straight three-hundred-foot drop to the chasm floor. Nate started to regain his senses and drew a bead on Herzog. Herzog swung open the oil-shed door, pulled it shut, and looked to bolt it, but the bolt was on the outside. He could hear it being drawn and locked.

He was trapped.

Walt, Trader, Sunny, and Sage were the first out of the stable and onto the scene. Walt could see Nate had been hit but looked to be okay. Johnny, though, was a different story. His brown wool shirt was covered in blood and getting bloodier. Sage quickly propped his friend's head up and tried as best he could to comfort him.

"Hey, Sage, looks like I caught one. How's the boys?"

"They're okay, Johnny. You saved them." Sage tried with all he had not to let on to just how bad it was.

"I didn't do much. It was mostly Nate," said Johnny. Nate got down on one knee and helped Sage hold Johnny's head up.

"No, it was all you, Johnny. He had the drop on me."

"Nate, you can have my scrip. I know it ain't worth nothing, but just the same."

"That's powerful generous of you. I'd be honored to have it. Knowing it belonged to you, that'll make 'em worth something."

"Sage, turn me around a little. I want to see them mountains again."

Just then, the sun, rising in the east, chased away the last of the stars and bathed the snowcapped peaks to the west in gleaming white light.

"I tell ya, every time I look at them, I get homesick. Damn business is, I ain't never had a home," sighed Johnny. Struck by the irony, he gave the slightest of smiles, and died.

"Ah, damn" was all Nate could say as he watched Sage Heck close the eyes of Jerome Corwell, fondly known as Johnny Dollars.

Sage was silent, as was everyone gathered about.

Nate thought that it looked like Standing Eagle's dream had turned out to be true after all.

Walt took off his bandana and wrapped it around Nate's arm as the two turned toward the oil shed and just looked.

Miles and Lorraine, along with Keith, Lucien, Evie, and the boys, who had hastened to be in the arms of their mother, were up on the deck looking down. Nate signaled to Lorraine to stay put. He was coming up.

"Everett, fetch a bottle of good whiskey down to the stables!" Sunny yelled up to the deck.

Sunny quickly made his way back to Tubby Flint, who was barely clinging to life. Two minutes later, Ernest and Everett both came down and gave Sunny the bottle.

"Here, have some of this. The best we got," Sunny said as he helped Flint hold the bottle. Tubby Flint took one swallow, then two more.

"Did you get that bastard?"

"Yeah, they got him. He's locked in the oil shed," answered Everett.

"Looks like this is the end of the road for me. You'll see I get planted proper, right?

"Don't you worry. We'll do it right," said Sunny.

"I feel kinda funny. Wish I could breathe better. I feel…"

That was it for Tubby Flint. He may have been dead, but Sunny had to peel his fingers off the whiskey bottle one by one. Whatever his faults, and they were legion, Tubby Flint died a hero.

"Let's lay him over here. You boys okay?" asked Sunny, who had known the Samms boys all their lives.

"We're okay, Mister Sunny. I gotta tell ya, I wasn't afraid, but I know Ernie was."

"Hell, I was. Youse were as afraid as me," countered Ernie.

"Well, maybe a little," confessed Everett.

"Me too," agreed Ernest.

"Let's get back upstairs," said Sunny as Walt and Trader carried Johnny's body into the stable and put him on the table in the tack room.

"Boy, look at that!" said Walt as he just noticed the trail of gunpowder leading out the back door of the stable.

"Son of a bitch," said Trader as his body gave a quick shudder.

"Sunny, get Sarusha and the Cap down here!" hollered Walt as Sunny and the boys were reaching the top of the stairs.

It took about an hour to get all the gunpowder safely off the stable floor and off the ground out back.

"Damn, we dodged a bullet there, I'll tell ya," said a more than relieved Jonathan Keith.

"What are we gonna do with this bastard, Cap? I've about had enough," said Sarusha.

"Me too. Me too," answered Keith.

Nate's wound turned out to be not much at all. The bullet tore off a little bit of flesh on the side of his arm, up by his shoulder. Other than that, aside from a pretty good headache, he was okay.

Everyone sat in the bar not saying too much of anything, stung by how fast things could change.

One by one, the men went over to Sage and said a good word about Johnny and gave him a pat on the shoulder.

"You can be really proud of your friend. Johnny was true blue." This meant something coming from Jonathan Keith, who wasn't known to lavish praise on too many people.

After a while, Miles Haverstraw went over to Sage and asked him to come along.

"Meet me out by that oil shed with a feather pillow and a jug of moonshine," Miles directed Sage, who just nodded and went to get what Miles had asked for. He didn't know what Miles Haverstraw had in mind, but he was sure of one thing—the old man wanted Herzog dead as much as he did.

Out in front of the oil shed, Miles took the pillowcase, poured some moonshine into it, and lit it. The feathers didn't catch fire, but they did begin to smolder.

"Get the vent cap off that flue," directed Miles in a voice with such pointed resolve that Sage didn't even question what was going on.

Sage had to go into the stables and get a short ladder to reach the flue vent. By the time he returned, the pillowcase was billowing with smoke, but no flame.

Sage started to wonder if what Miles had in mind might not set the oil shed and its contents on fire. "You can't set that shed on fire," he warned Miles.

Miles just looked at Sage and said, "Don't worry. It isn't going to catch fire."

Climbing up the ladder, Miles began to stuff the smoking feathers into the flue.

Pretty soon, the men could hear Herzog yelling and coughing.

From up top on the deck off the bar, everyone had gathered to see just what Miles and Sage were up to.

"You gonna stop this, Cap?" asked Bill Diehl.

"I'm not gonna stop it. Any of you wanna stop it?" asked Keith.

No one answered. So the group watched with rapt attention as Miles and Sage listened to Herzog's pleas to open the door.

"You want outa there?" asked Miles.

"Let me out!" hollered Herzog between coughs.

"Not yet! Did my wife and kids have a chance to be let out? Did any of them?"

Again, Miles waited then asked again, "You want outa there?" When Herzog didn't answer, he signaled to Sage to slide back the bolt and open the door. Herzog crawled out coughing and retching. His eyes were bulging out of his head, his face purple from the strain of coughing. When the coughing finally stopped, he asked for some water.

"You want some water? Try this instead." With that, Miles grabbed Herzog by the hair, yanked his head back, and emptied the jug of moonshine over his head and chest.

"Sage, hand me one of your smokes. Maybe our friend would like a smoke?"

All the years of festering hate had brought Miles Haverstraw to this point, and even if he tried, he wouldn't be able to stop himself.

Miles lit the smoke and shoved it into Herzog face. "Here, smoke this," said Miles in a very low voice, momentarily thinking of his wife and children.

Herzog tried to bat the burning cigarette away but failed. Soon his face and torso were engulfed in flames. Somehow he got to his feet and stumbled about, flailing his arms and screaming. Miles and Sage backed away and watched as Herzog blindly staggered toward the edge of the chasm, teetering on the precipice, the updraft sending the flames engulfing his body skyward. At that moment, Miles looked up to the deck and caught Lorraine's eye. Turning back, he watched as Herzog fell over the edge, his flaming body leaving a trail of screams that faded as he plunged to his death.

No one said a word.

33

UNIONS AND REUNIONS

Somber and sad—that was the prevailing mood in the Crow's Nest. Not until someone is dead and gone do you realize how much they were a part of the fabric of your life. Johnny Dollars was no exception. Hapless and snake bit as he might have been, Johnny had no real enmity toward anyone. Rather than sow discord, he tried to further harmony. He was missed deeply, already.

The concern now on the crew's mind was the emotional welfare of Sage Heck. First he got wounded, then his best and maybe first true friend was killed. Sage had been quiet, but then again no one was really saying too much of anything. What was said centered around how to curse the existence of Bertram Herzog. The litany of derogatory epithets pointed to the real creativity of some. Thaedell Lahr and Bill Diehl were by far the most proficient at this, none of which can be noted here.

Though spirits were at the lowest ebb of any time at the Nest, Jonathan Keith had learned over the years that the best antidote for doleful stagnation was work. Once Johnny was properly eulogized and laid to rest alongside the hero Winston "Tubby" Flint, Keith made sure few in the Nest had time for an idle moment or thought.

One of the first things attended to was the breach in the wall of the brig. Not that he anticipated there would be an urgent need for it, but Keith didn't want any critters taking up residence either.

The three remaining pineapples were removed from the gravel bank off the cut.

The deck cannons up on the parapet were cleaned, swabbed with oil, and put back in storage in a room off Keith's quarters on the top floor, hopefully in storage for good. Pealeday's cannon was hauled down the switchback and put in storage in a corner of the stables.

The camps up on the promontory were emptied out, and the rope ladders retrieved.

The item that received the most attention and discussion was the resupply trip down to the Snake, principally who would go and how soon would that happen. Sooner than later for sure. Two men who were definitely going were the Johnson brothers. Keith thought, *I hope those boys don't spend all their money in the first brothel they come across.*

Usually it was Brow, Bill Diehl, Sarusha, and Sunny who made the trip. But now Brow was out, and that removed Bill Diehl. Those two only ever operated as a team.

Keith was reluctant to ask Nate and Trader, seeing how they had their women to think about. Walt could go. Quiet Bird had already waited years for Walt to return. A few more weeks or a month would matter little. The important thing was, this time she knew he was coming back.

Keith could hardly wait another day to send the men out for supplies. Late November was no time to be traipsing through these mountains. Usually, Keith had arranged for supplies to be waiting for him farther up the Snake from Lewiston. But now that wasn't the case. He'd have to go all the way to Lewiston to get resupplied. The whole affair would take about ten days. Three, maybe four days out. Two days there getting everything together, four days back.

The sooner the party got going, the sooner they got back. Nate, Walt, and Trader set Keith's mind at ease and volunteered to go. Keith didn't expect any trouble from Pealeday's former men who had returned to Lewiston, but just in case, having Nate and the others along would guarantee no trouble. Nevertheless, they would stay clear of the Settlement Bar so as not to ruffle any feathers. After all, the trip was for supplies, not drinking and carousing.

Lorraine and Veronica understood their men had to go. But any travel in these parts could be risky. One thing Lorraine had to look forward to was that Captain Keith was to perform a wedding ceremony upon Nate's return. After all, he married Lucien and Evie. But that was aboard the *Celine*. Whether or not he had the proper authority to do the same here didn't matter to either Nate or Lorraine.

There would be witnesses, an exchange of vows, rings. To everyone in the Nest, that was a wedding. Nate hadn't told Lorraine, but he figured on coming back with the nicest dress he could find in Lewiston. He also figured he should get two wedding bands. He knew he didn't have one handy and doubted Lorraine did either. This wouldn't be a church wedding, but weather permitting, the deck of the Crow's Nest seemed like a pretty good substitute.

The afternoon before setting out was spent figuring which horses to keep as pack animals and which to barter with. Keith didn't need any extra horses. It was better to trade them away so as not to have to feed them all winter. In the spring, grass to graze on would come back to the flat, but that was in the spring.

Everyone was so busy that they didn't see the five riders come down the switchback and up to the gatehouse. They did hear the bell ring, though. Sunny was the first one out on the deck, and from what he could see, four of the riders were in uniform. Sunny waited for Keith to get to the deck and take a closer look through the spyglass before he gave Ghosty the all clear.

Keith just stepped away from the spyglass and stood for a moment then took another look. Sunny wondered just what was up, because he had never seen a look like this on the Captain's face in all the time he'd known him. Keith gave two slow rings on the bell, turned to Sunny, and said, "That one rider is my son."

Sunny couldn't tell if the Captain was happy about this or not. The gatehouse doors swung open, and the riders slowly made their way up to the stable doors. Keith was down there to greet them.

"Hello, Father." Keith's son was the one who wasn't in uniform and obviously the one in charge. "Lieutenant, see to the horses and bring me that dispatch case," said Jonathan Angelo Keith Jr.

Captain Keith had yet to say a word as he was in a mild state of shock. He hadn't seen his son in twenty-some years but recognized him straight off. He had grown into a tall and handsome man. Taller than his father, but other than, that the spitting image.

"Come in, come in. Sunny, show these men where to take these horses. I couldn't believe my eyes. Is it your mother? Is she okay? Your sister?"

"Mother is quite well. I'm sure had she known our paths would cross, she would want me to give you her regards."

"So what brings you all this way?"

"I have a warrant for the arrest of Clayton Jackknife Pealeday. I can't tell you a lot, but my men and I are on a very unofficially official mission. We understand from what we learned in Lewiston that he was headed this way. London and Ottawa want to see Mr. Pealeday cease and desist with his disruptive efforts to keep this part of Idaho as sovereign Canadian Territory. Beyond that, I can't tell you more. Do you know where he is?" Keith looked at his son and was filled with pride. He had grown up to be more than Keith could have hoped for. His son never had to concern himself with working to keep food on the table or a roof over his head. Keith saw to it that his bankers in England would always provide for his, his mother's, and his sister's well-being. Money was never a concern, but that can be a curse. Many, in such situations, have ended up living dissolute lives that end tragically. Evidently, his son was not among them.

"I do know where he is. But before I tell you, let's sit down and get some food and something to drink." Keith was a little unbalanced and needed to regain his equilibrium. Sitting down and letting the shock of all this settle seemed like the right thing to do.

"Some of your old friends told me about this place. You're quite famous, you know. I started using my middle name years ago. I got tired of answering the question 'Are you *the* Jonathan Keith's son?' So just so you know, my men here call me Angelo."

"Your grandmother would be happy to hear that," said Keith, referencing the Italian heritage on his mother's side of the family.

"Everett, Ernest, this man here is my son."

"Cap, we didn't know you had kin. I'm Everett, and this here is my brother, Ernest. We can look after your horses. Cap, should they pay?"

"No, Everett. I'll take care of you boys on that. You just do your usual good job," answered Keith, mildly amused at the question from the enterprising Everett.

"Food and drink will be nice, but seriously, where is Clayton Pealeday?" asked Angelo Keith.

"He's dead, and his body was cremated along with the bodies of his renegade mercenaries."

"How exactly did that come about?"

"Let's go upstairs. I'll tell you there."

While his detachment of men warmed themselves near the stove in the bar, Angelo sat in a booth with his father, who recounted everything that had taken place in the last two months.

Midway through this account, Evie brought out some food for the men, and Sunny offered them drinks, which they refused until Angelo indicated to go ahead.

"You say Pealeday came at you with sixty some men? I see that Parrott out there. How did that get here?" Angelo Keith was amazed to see not only the Parrott ten-pounder out on the deck but also Pealeday's Napoleon 12 down in the stable.

Without a hint of bravado, Keith answered, "It was at least sixty men, more like seventy, if you count the ones riding with Herzog and Chance Parker. We ended up sending about a dozen back from whence they came. The rest were killed. As for the Parrott, that was payment for a debt. You remember Pap Moran? One of his sea captain friends owed me some money. Anyway, long story short, I've got a Parrott."

"I'm going to have to take a deposition from you for my report. Then I imagine we'll be on our way. I think I can be of some help to the Haverstraws. Herzog and Marlene Scabbe are both wanted for fraud in Montreal. There's an outstanding warrant for their arrest.

They defrauded a lot of people there and in Halifax. I imagine once that's certified and the reward paid, that should suffice as proof in any other jurisdiction where he's wanted. There's a considerable price on those two for what happened in Lautenburg. How exactly did Bertram Herzog die?"

Keith thought for a second then answered, "He was trying to escape and fell into the chasm that lies along that stretch between our stables and that gatehouse you came through. He killed one of the men here. Actually, two. One died trying to put out the fire he set. Damn shame. We just buried them three days ago." Keith chose to omit certain details, and why not? The fact was Herzog did fall to his death while trying to escape.

"Can you and your men spend a couple days before heading back? And where exactly are you heading when you leave here?"

"These men are garrisoned in Vancouver. We'll most likely head to Spokane, then angle up to Vancouver."

"What is your position in the government?"

"There's no real title for it. Basically, I'm an agent for the Queen on special assignment."

"How long do you expect to be in Vancouver?"

"Most likely through the winter. There's some island dispute with the Russians over fishing rights. When that's done, back to London."

Keith then told his son something that had been vaguely on his mind for some time. "Maybe I'll return to England with you. What do you think?"

"Well, I know Mother wouldn't mind seeing you."

"Really?"

"Yes, really. She's kept busy. She's an established champion of the poor—well-respected and not lacking in influence. But she never remarried and has told me that there was something missing in her life. She didn't say that it was you, but if I read between the lines, I think that's what she meant."

Keith didn't know what to say as he poured himself and his son another drink.

Feigning deep thought, Angelo said, "I imagine it might take a few days for me to write my report."

Keith had envisioned his son leaving first thing in the morning. The fact that he was staying a few days set his mind at ease. They had a lot of catching up to do.

The rest of the afternoon was spent with Keith introducing his son to everyone in the Nest. Lucien had met the young Angelo years ago and was glad to see what a fine young man he had grown to be. He was happy for the Captain being reunited with his boy, at least for a bit. Lucien's bond with his family precluded his from being too long away from them. The Captain wasn't that way; that may have changed.

"Captain, could you ask your son if his men know how to play poker?" Brow asked this seemingly innocent question. You can just imagine the quick go-around among the men at the table after the Canadians told them they were untrusting of American card players. Truth be told, sure anyone at the poker table would like to come away with more money than they went in with, but new faces in the game is just what this game needed.

Be it pride or curiosity, it wasn't too long before three of Angelo's men were sitting around the table and looking at the cards that had just been dealt. Thaedell Lahr did not employ any of his card-dealing skills. No need. It was apparent that the men were not very good at cards to begin with.

The talk at the table was about fishing and hunting, what's good for this, where's it good for that. How bad the winter of such-and-so year was, a lot about trails, the Nez, what were they going to do?

But mostly they wanted to hear about the siege. What was Pealeday like? How did Captain Keith ever build the Crow's Nest? Who fired the Parrott? The crew didn't have to embellish very much to gain the men's rapt attention.

"What do you do for women?" That last question kinda put a damper on the flow of the conversation.

"Some women do come through once in a while. Of course, them what's traveling west on that upper trail, they don't quite get this far south," Bill Diehl informed the men.

"We also don't get a lot coming through 'cause we be too far north of the other trail" was Brow Herman's addition to the defense.

"We'd be obliged if you have any extra gals up your way, if you could tell them about us." After Thaedell Lahr made this request, everyone had a laugh, but the conversation moved off the topic of women.

The next day, Sarusha, Walt, and the others left out of the Nest on the supply trip.

Keith and his son spent three days getting caught up, opening old wounds and then stitching them back closed. This time with the balm of mutual understanding.

Angelo Keith was very helpful to the Haverstraws. Turns out that in his dispatch case was a dossier on Bertram Herzog and Marlene Scabbe. Miles and Lorraine were riveted as they read what lay within. Much of it they were aware of. Scams and various frauds the pair had perpetrated. Cities they had been in.

Reading the dossier was not unlike reading a road map of where Lorraine and Miles had been. The last entry speculated that Marlene Wolf Scabbe Slottower might have returned back East to her original home, somewhere near Baltimore, Maryland. She was thought to be currently going by the name Madeline Puree. Why she thought people who knew her as Marlene Wolf wouldn't wonder why she was now Madeline Puree was anybody's guess. In any event, if Miles were to continue his pursuit, he would start there.

The arrival and departure of Jonathan Keith's son and his detachment marked a distinctive turning point in the lives of those who called the Crow's Nest home. Except for maybe the absence of Johnny Dollars, there was no specific reason life in the Crow's Nest could not return to normal. But everyone knew in their quiet thoughts that that was not to be.

Keith had known of ships losing a man overboard and, after a brief period of alarm, simply sailing on. In time, life would return to normal. That wasn't going to be the case here at the Nest. Whatever course the Crow's Nest had been on, that had changed, as did the course of the men's lives living within its walls.

Would the Crow's Nest become a rudderless ship were the Captain to return to England? That remained to be seen.

The supply trip to Lewiston was a success. The men went and returned without incident. One slight wrinkle, however, was that the Johnson brothers had met two sisters who were headed back East, disillusioned with frontier life. The brothers charmed them enough to have them entertain the thought of giving life in the West another try. And of course what better way to do that than in the company of Ray and Lee Johnson?

Keith smiled to himself and laughed when he saw two women in the party returning from Lewiston.

On a bright sunny afternoon in late December, Keith performed the wedding of Nathan Tallhelm and Lorraine Haverstraw. Simply put, the gala that followed was unparalleled in the history of the Crow's Nest.

After the ceremony and when the two sisters saw the matrimonial bliss sparkling in the eyes of Lorraine Tallhelm, it wasn't long before they brought their female wiles to bear upon Ray and Lee. Turns out that after very little coaxing, the Johnson brothers agreed that making these women honest was the right and honorable thing to do. Keith performed two more weddings.

These unions, although made without the benefit of clergy, were in every other way true marriages and would prove to withstand the test of time.

The day after the weddings, a heavy snowstorm hit the Kettle of Tears, and even if they wanted to, no one was going anywhere, leastwise not for a while.

Eventually, though, the snow melted, and soon some of the folks in the Nest started to melt away as well.

Walt gave the one Appaloosa to Sarusha, took two of the packhorses off Keith's hands, and headed out and back to Quiet Bird. Before leaving, however, he and Nate took a few moments to stand on the deck outside the bar. Not given to sentimentality, they quietly drank in the view, remarked on how good it had been to spend time together after so many years, and promised not to let another twenty years go by before they got together again.

Not too long after that, Trader and Veronica together with Nate and Lorraine headed out and back up the cut, retracing the route Nate had taken from Bill Darcy's to the Kettle of Tears some three months before.

Fritz Langer figured it was about time he got back to Austria and traveled with Keith and Miles Haverstraw to Vancouver. Once there, and after he sent word to Conrad Drager's relatives, he decided to stay on this side of the Atlantic. He figured here he had a chance to own land and prosper, unshackled by the constraints of peerage and such that he would find back in Austria. Eventually he returned to the Crow's Nest and struck up some sort of partnership with Thaedell Lahr. He later moved to Portland and opened a small inn with a transplanted Bavarian atmosphere.

Miles Haverstraw was stoically composed when he bid Lorraine and Nate goodbye as they left the Crow's Nest to begin their life together. Of all the people leaving the Crow's Nest, what lay ahead for Miles Haverstraw was the most uncertain. He was quietly glad for the company of Jonathan Keith and Fritz as they traveled to Vancouver. Not having Lorraine at his side was a bittersweet pain he was unfamiliar with. In time, that would pass.

Keith rendezvoused with his son and invited Miles to come along all the way to England and said money would never be a problem. Miles was still undecided on that part of the plan. But he would tag along at least till they reached the East Coast.

Chasing down Marlene Wolf/Madeline Puree and bringing her to justice was still percolating in his brain. He'd see how he felt about pursuing the hunt when he got back East.

Keith, once he was able to make contact, made very generous arrangements with his bank in Denver for Trader, Nate, and Walt. For them, too, whatever problems would come their way, money would not be one of them.

The Johnsons and their new brides were enjoying the Crow's Nest, and with the help of Sarusha and Sunny's direction, they had become part of the day-to-day workings of the place. The pair still had that four thousand dollars waiting for them in Denver. But here at the Nest, they didn't need money. It was just reassuring that it was there, a comfort that had heretofore been unknown to them.

Evie didn't mind having two women around who were very helpful and surely lightened her load.

Sarusha, Sunny, Lucien, Evie, and the crew all missed the Captain. The two dogs, Star and Maggie, who remained behind at the Nest, missed the Captain as well, but the sun still came up over the Kettle of Tears in the morning and set over the snowcapped blue mountains at the end of each day.

Life went on.

CAST OF CHARACTERS

The Tallhelms—Nathan Tallhelm and his brother, Walt
The Haverstraws—Miles Haverstraw and his daughter, Lorraine
The Darcys—Trader Darcy (cousin of Nathan and Walt) and his
    wife, Veronica; Bill and Ruth Darcy, Trader's parents
The Keiths—Captain Jonathan Keith; his wife, Rebecca; and son
    Jonathan Angelo Keith
Keith's right-hand men—Sarusha and Sunny Martin
The Samms—Lucien and Evie Samms and their sons, Everett and
    Ernest
Crow's Nest crew—Brow Herman, Bill Diehl, Thaedell Lahr, Sage
    Heck, Johnny Dollars
Gatehouse attendants—Ghosty and his mother, Perpetua
The villains—Bertram Herzog, Marlene Scabbe, and Parquet Dunn
    Aldo Severman and his partner Dean
    Clayton Pealeday, Chance Parker
    Bill Liecaster and his partner Tubby Flint
    Jack Tice and Marcel Dagget
The trappers in chapter 2—Peepsight Guyer, Carl Bowersox
The trading post owner in Cornertown, chapter 2—Delbert Nelson
The Indians in chapter 3—Snarling Wolf, Diving Hawk, Drum
    Face, and Owl Eyes
The Austrian hunters in chapter 9—Conrad Drager, Fritz Langer
The good guys in chapter 14—Mr. and Mrs. Arthur Howlander
The bad guys in chapter 14—Jedediah Pogue and his son Butch and
    his two brothers; Harold Garbbler
The Nez Perce in chapter 18—Quiet Bird and her father, Chief
    Ironwood; Buffalo Horn
The two brothers in chapter 15—Ray and Lee Johnson

The ship's captain in chapter 5—Patrick "Pap" Moran
People of Lautenburg in chapter 26—Lamar Slottower and his daughters Lydia and Laurie; banker Simon Graham; Blaine Hockenberry Sr., Blaine Hockenberry Jr.; lawyer Johnny McDowell; Washington Hotel owner Raymond Zwiedell and his sons, David and Lawrence; Guy, the desk clerk

About the Author

Robert Boyce was born in Chambersburg, Pennsylvania in 1947, the middle child of seven. After graduating high school in 1965, he knocked around for several years, eventually enrolling at Penn State and graduating with a bachelor of science degree. He moved to New York City in 1975 to pursue a career as a cabinetmaker.

Although custom cabinetmaking requires endless hours of exacting work, his passion for creating kept him in good stead. After thirty years in NYC—punctuated by a three-year stint on Maui building custom houses and reading lots of Louis L'Amour, Zane Gray, and other Western authors—he returned to NYC and eventually moved back to Pennsylvania, where he reunited with an old flame, married, retired from woodwork, and set to finishing a novel that had lain dormant since the late eighties.

Applying the same diligence to writing that he did in his woodwork, he completed *Kettle of Tears*.

Robert resides with his wife, Amy, in Wallingford, Pennsylvania, and, among other pastimes, enjoys golf, gardening, and getting away to the Jersey shore.

CPSIA information can be obtained
at www.ICGtesting.com
Printed in the USA
BVHW031251270421
605954BV00001B/2